SINS OF LIFE

Lynn Santer

© Copyright, Lynn Santer, 2009
All rights reserved

No part of this book may be reproduced in any form, by photocopying or by any electronic or mechanical means, including information storage or retrieval systems, without the permission in writing from the copyright owner of this book.

The author asserts her moral rights.

Lynn Santer: http://www.lynnsanter.com

Sins of Life previously published by
Minerva Press (UK) 1999
And Zeus Publications (Aust.) 2001
This edition published 2009

All characters in this publication are fictitious and any resemblance to real people, living or dead, is purely coincidental. It is not the author's intention to suggest that the life insurance industry today resembles the way it is portrayed in this novel – the Eighties was another era. The author has no claim to authenticate the version of events as they appear in *Sins of Life*.

About the Author

**Keynote speaker ~ Best-selling author ~
Founder of *Passion for Peace* ~ Wildlife Crusader ~
Auntie Lynn with her *Magical Scarecrows***

Beating the odds, challenging the system, finding the common ground among disparate agendas, earning the respect of Hollywood celebrities and senior Government officials, Lynn Santer is one speaker you cannot afford to miss. She's been a keynote speaker in the elevated establishments of 10 Downing Street, the House of Commons and European Union summits in London and Warsaw. She's been a fixed wing light aircraft pilot and a PADI scuba diver who has swum with sharks in Australia and tracked wild predators on foot in Africa. More recently Lynn has been a much sought-after authorized biographer, writing the life stories of such astonishingly diverse personalities as Saddam Hussein's former personal pilot and Australia's original wild man and wildlife warrior Alby Mangels.

Lynn has fought for causes all her life, winning her first award for animal welfare when she was only eleven years old. Among a plethora of awards her most recent honour was a nomination for the 2008 Pride of Australia Medal. She was also responsible for putting two extremely unique teams together. The first was the ***LAND OF THE FREE*** mission, which involved Hollywood legend Tippi Hedren (Alfred Hitchcock's iconic star of ***The Birds*** and Melanie Griffith's mum) with ex Special Forces commandos to plan an undercover mission in Africa to expose ongoing brutal atrocities against endangered big game by some of the wealthiest men on earth. The other team could not have been more opposite. Called **PASSION FOR PEACE** Lynn was responsible for forming and managing an inspirational group comprised of an ultra orthodox Israeli Rabbi, Saddam Hussein's former personal pilot and their Christian friend, a spokesperson from World Vision.

In 2008 Lynn also conceived a never before dreamed of initiative to raise funds for Variety, the children's charity, in the form of **The Magical Scarecrows** International Celebrity T-Shirt Relay. Among those superstars enthusiastically joining Lynn on this journey are Jackie Chan, Hugh Jackman, Priscilla Presley, Jeffrey Archer, and many, many more. Her children's range **The Magical Scarecrows** ™ also runs the multi-honoured **Kids Who Read Succeed** ™ program that provides reading material free of charge to needy children all over the world.

Dedicated to my parents

Acknowledgements

The author would like to gratefully acknowledge the assistance of:

- Liz Jacobsen, Editor
- Ian Bray, Pharmaceutical Chemist
- Senior Detective Constable Darren Bracken, Homicide Squad, Victoria Police
- Kevin Fahey, Life Insurance Federation of Australia
- Karen Eldred, New York State Department of Insurance
- Tony Mooney, past Operations Manager, Capita Financial Group
- Mark Darien-Smith, Mallesons Stephen Jaques
- Colin Richardson, Department of Treasury
- Roselyn Poon, Director, ComputerLink
- Karen Santer
- Gail Blode
- Lisa-Jane Smith (née McInnes)
- Nick Hudson
- Alan Graubard
- And others who would prefer to remain anonymous

Chapter One

Tension washed across his shoulders and down his spine. Standing unnaturally straight, Nick Abbott clenched his fists so hard his knuckles shone white. The rage in his eyes seemed to be burning through his Fifth Avenue office window. He had not slept well the night before – no more than a couple of hours. At each hour he had checked the time, finding, to his surprise, he was willing the night to pass quickly. He checked the time again: three forty-five.

Nick's purpose was clear to him. His image, the myth and the legend that was Nick Abbott, had to be sustained. An image he knew was born out of one fateful bluff. He wondered for a fleeting moment if Ted Upton would surprise him. Perhaps Ted could demonstrate the level of courage Nick had shown when he was in Ted's position. Nick doubted it.

Through his window Nick could see Central Park. A swath of yellow tulips glistened in the sunlight. He observed them jealously, envying the tranquillity of their existence. Suddenly he found himself smiling at the irony of Central Park's timeless beauty; a beauty which survived despite witnessing the countless victims of heinous crimes. What better place, Nick mused, to bear testament to the fact that death is a part of life? What better place to illustrate the need for life insurance?

He cleared his throat; it felt like a well-used grating board: the result of smoking forty cigarettes a day for thirty years.

James will understand what I am doing is right, he convinced himself. I have to bury Ted... to teach the others a lesson. If James wants to follow in my footsteps he'll have to learn that family ties are not more important than correcting professional errors in judgement.

'Tell me when they get here,' Nick ordered over the intercom to his secretary, Shirley.

'Yes sir,' she answered, turning mechanically to type out Nick's reports. The word processor tapped under her swift fingers, sounding like a metronome stuck on fast speed.

Why does it have to be Ted? she asked herself. He's trying so hard. James had such high hopes when he introduced Ted to East West. It's not fair.

Shirley wrinkled her nose, imagining the waft of tobacco which always surrounded Nick by the end of the day, and stared through her bifocal glasses at Nick's reports.

Over her five years' employment with Nick Abbott, Shirley had seen many Ted Uptons come and go. So why am I so worried about one more? she asked herself.

Just five minutes to go. Nick's memorandum had been quite explicit: a meeting for thirty members of his team to share coffee and Danish at four o'clock. To most people who knew him, Nick appeared ruthless; the hardened leader of six hundred agents and twenty-five sales managers; the manager of East West Life's East Coast region. The truth was, however, that Nick felt as professionally vulnerable as any of his rookie agents. Managers, he knew, were only as good as their latest achievements.

The minutes rolled silently past as Nick recalled the time he nearly fired Eddie Schwartz, the agent who became the most successful in all of life insurance history. He knew it would be a long time, if ever, before another recruit like Eddie Schwartz came along. Eddie's achievements had earned him a place in the insurance history books; his piece of immortality. It was a shame, Nick thought, that Eddie had to die so young.

At his post at the window, Nick's thoughts drifted back to the first time he met Ted Upton. It was at James's graduation party. Ted overflowed with enthusiasm for life; a good quality for a sales agent. At six foot one he stood an inch taller than James. His perfectly sculptured face, olive skin, ebony eyes and athletic body attracted many women. He looked like a Latin lover; not the son of a Madison Avenue accountant. It had not been easy recruiting Ted. Nick found he had to wait until Ted became dissatisfied with low wages for long hours in an attempt to prove himself in a junior management role. It was at the moment of maximum discontent that Nick struck. It was at this time, Nick understood, that potential recruits were most vulnerable to the glories Nick could offer them.

James had told his father about Ted's old man being a partner in one of the largest accounting firms in New York – Upton and Jacobs. James understood that if Ted were recruited to the East West team he could open doors to the clients of Upton and Jacobs. Rich prospective clients for life insurance. Once again, James had tried to please and impress his father. Once again, he had failed. Nick buried the disappointment he felt at his son's inadequacy in a labyrinth kept for all unspoken secrets.

A glance at his faint reflection in the window reminded Nick that his hair was turning grey. At the age of fifty-one grey hair was acceptable, he told himself. It looked distinguished. Dangerously dark eyes gazed with determination at the pale-skinned face, which stared back. God, Nick almost prayed, why didn't that stupid bastard take my advice?

*

Ted Upton, dressed in the most expensive suit he could afford, strode confidently to the meeting; on his way he made a point of popping in to Sandra's office to remind her that he was cooking dinner that night.

If Nick has invited me for coffee and Danish, he thought, I might finally be asked to write my testimonial letter. Father will be so proud.

Frank Upton had not wanted his son to sell life insurance but Ted knew he would prove his father wrong. After all, those letters Nick Abbott had shown him spoke for themselves. Letters from agents whose lives had been turned around as a result of joining Nick's team. An open-ended commission-based income made many millionaires in the life insurance business. The letters weren't only from grateful, rich agents either. There were letters from widows thanking Nick Abbott. Thanking him for forcing his agents to make the extra phone call to get the sale. Thanking him, because without the life insurance pay-out they would be destitute today. Nick Abbott was one hell of a guy and Ted was proud to be a member of his team. In time, Frank Upton would understand that too. Ted knew he could never follow the military achievements of his father, a decorated Vietnam veteran, but what he sold saved lives just as certainly as any hero. As Nick told me, he remembered, I can make a fortune by helping others fulfil their financial goals and aspirations. What greater reward for service can there be?

If I can distinguish myself, Ted thought, perhaps Father will accept that I can make the correct choices. Perhaps he will welcome me back to the family and accept Sandra as my wife.

Frank Upton had no more approved of Ted marrying an Aussie than he had approved of Ted selling life insurance. His father had selected a suitably bred female for Ted. It had taken all of Ted's courage to stand up to his father and insist that he would marry the woman he loved. His father, in turn, had refused to accept the marriage.

Being shunned by his father was a bitter experience. East West was the only family he had now.

Ted knew Sandra believed she was marrying wealth when she left Australia to be with him. Although, he remembered, it didn't seem to matter to Sandra when she learned about Frank's attitude towards her. She told Ted she loved him and that he could make his own fortune; he didn't need his father's help.

*

'Mr Abbott, your agents have arrived.' Shirley's voice sounded somewhat distorted over the intercom.

Nick briefly considered the merits of having Shirley talk to the group. There was a woman who understood the value of life insurance. If her husband had owned a decent policy on his life when he died in a car wreck, she wouldn't have to be working for a living today.

As the agents entered the boardroom with seemingly confident expressions, an intense mixture of expensive aftershaves floated through the ducts of the air-conditioning system.

Ted noticed the spring sun glinting off Nick's mahogany display cabinet. The cabinet, filled with crystal and china, stood between lush green rubber plants in huge brown tubs. A mahogany board table was carefully laid with coffee cups, plates, and a creamer – all empty.

Nick waited until they were settled to make his entrance. With an eerie sense of satisfaction, Ted observed the way Nick could light up a boardroom. Nick appeared like the brightest shooting star to Ted. A man he could admire and strive to emulate.

'So you all received my invitation – that's good,' Nick began in a purposeful strong voice which intensified his New York accent. He allowed them to settle into the padded leather chairs. A few moments would be sufficient for them to soak in the opulence of their surroundings: Nick's surroundings.

Nick extinguished yet another cigarette, checking his expression was suitable in the reflection of the highly polished table. With props prepared, his well-rehearsed speech began.

'Do any of you know why there is no coffee in the coffee pot and there are no Danish on the plate?' He paused only long enough to let his agents speculate.

'I'll tell you why. Because I can't afford this stuff! And do you know why I can't afford this stuff? Because you lot aren't out there selling enough life insurance to keep me in bread and water, let alone coffee and Danish.' Nick felt his blood pressure rise with his tone. 'I brought each of you into this business because I thought you had the courage to care for the people of New York. It is your responsibility to ensure that no widow is going to have to move out of her home if her husband dies. It is your responsibility to ensure there will be money to put food on the table, to clothe the children and to keep these people in their own world if a breadwinner prematurely leaves the scene. You carry a responsibility you should treat with pride. Pride in your membership of the East West team of 1984, pride in knowing that you are caring for the well-being of others, and pride in the knowledge that you sell a product which *is* one day going to be needed. Of this there can be no question. And how do you respond to all I have taught you?'

Nick turned to light up a huge chart on the front wall of the boardroom. All of the agents' names and sales figures were illuminated in a glowing bar graph.

James watched Ted's reaction, feeling a pang of fear as he noticed his name was once again at the top and Ted's, once again, was at the bottom. Nick had drawn an ominous thick black line through the chart. James knew immediately what that meant.

'Ted, my man,' Nick began. 'You appear to be on the wrong side of the line. Would you care to explain that?'

Ted stood to answer, straightening his jacket. Nick could tell his palms were sweating from six seats away.

'I am selling above the average number of polices per month,' Ted announced, sounding proud of his achievement. 'But I am selling to working-class families who just can't afford to take out all the insurance they need straight away.'

Nick looked coldly into Ted's eyes. It was a strong stare which made Ted wither in this man's presence.

'No family can afford *not* to take out all the insurance they need,' Nick explained. 'Or are you able to tell them exactly when they are going to die?' Nick asked forcefully. 'What's wrong with you? I brought you into this industry. I gave you the benefit of my knowledge and experience, and after six months this is the best result you can give me. You work for the Nick Abbott region of East West Life: the largest regional office, in the largest life insurance company, in the world. We have standards to maintain here.'

Ted was stunned into a nervous silence.

'You've just returned from your honeymoon, right?'

A personal question, thank God, Ted thought. This must just be a warning, not a dismissal. Surely Nick would not be asking such a personal question otherwise.

'Yes, that's right,' Ted responded, running his fingers through his thick black hair.

'Well, Ted, my man, you know what I always say,' Nick answered.

The other agents glanced toward Ted. Instinctively knowing what was coming they tried to cushion the blow with consoling expressions.

'When my faith in you turns to hope, I'm giving you

charity, and Ted, I'm not in the charity business. Your new Aussie wife has just become the breadwinner in your family.' Nick turned to the board, flicking off the switch that had illuminated Ted's name.

Ted opened his mouth to speak but couldn't find the words to explain how worthless Nick had just made him feel.

'This isn't right.' James suddenly sprang to Ted's defence. 'Ted has followed all your training to the letter. Perhaps he has just been a little distracted with the wedding. At least give him a chance to prove what he can do.'

James's presence easily equalled that of his father's. From his diction the agents guessed James was the product of an expensive private education which Nick had not benefited from, but he was unmistakably his father's son.

James understood his father's impressive status. Nick Abbott is the king, no question about it; but it was Nick who taught me nothing is as constant as change, James remembered.

Ted's dismissal weighed heavily upon James's conscience. James had treated Ted like a brother when Frank disowned him for marrying Sandra. It was hard for James to admit that Ted just wasn't a good soldier. He should never have got into the business in the first place, James told himself. It's all my fault.

Even as he fought with his father, the other agents noticed James looked immaculate, as usual. With six foot of lean masculine form, perfect features engraved into ivory skin, jet-black hair and soulful brown eyes, James looked like a contemporary, high-rolling Jesus Christ.

Nick hid the anger and surprise he felt at his son's outburst with masterful ease.

'Son, this is a business. If you can't take the pressure of making tough decisions, perhaps you shouldn't be here either.'

Ted meekly turned to leave. He didn't want James's career on his conscience as well as his own. He laid a heavy hand on James's shoulder as he left, trying to say that James shouldn't worry about him. The burning sensation of tears welled up in his eyes as he gazed across the office of East West Life for the last time. He fought them back valiantly. His father would be so ashamed of him. He must not add to his father's shame with effeminate tears. God Almighty, what am I going to do? he asked himself. He questioned his very existence. How could I have let this happen? Nick gave me the chance of a lifetime and I blew it. Damn, he thought, the elevator is taking forever.

Descending in the elevator, Ted thought of his new wife, Sandra. Oh God, he thought, why did I go into so much debt to get married? What am I going to tell her? What a mess. What a disaster. Nick gave me the chance of having it all and now I have nothing.

By the time he reached Fifth Avenue, he had to admit he was a failure. There was no one to blame but himself. That was the truth of it. He had tried to be strong like his father; tried to make everyone proud. He felt a repulsive churning in his stomach as he bowed his head and stared down at the sidewalk.

*

'I've done the kid a favour, you know,' Nick continued. 'If he can't earn a decent living in this game, it's better to know now than to wait till he's got the missus pregnant and then finds he can't feed the family.'

'You disgust me,' James spat. 'You talk about our responsibility to the people of New York yet you cut down people in the prime of life as though they mean nothing. I can't just stand by and see this happen again.'

James stormed out of the office, leaving the door open.

As James left, the vision of having once been in Ted Upton's position flashed through Nick's mind. Instead of meekly turning to leave, Nick had stood up to his manager. After all, what did he have to lose? His manager had been an idiot, and the rest of the team knew it. It had taken Nick Abbott to stand up and speak his mind. A bluff, a gamble, but one that had paid off. Nick's peers had admired him for it. Before long the manager had been dismissed with Nick Abbott his replacement by popular request. Nick might not have been the greatest sales person but he knew how to command a group of people. It was this unteachable charisma, Nick understood, that was the foundation of his power.

'Does anyone else feel this way?' Nick asked quietly.

There was a deathly silence from the remaining agents.

'Good,' Nick answered, 'because as I have just lost my highest producer, the rest of you are going to have to make up for it. We are going to have a little competition. It's called "Save my Skin". Whoever is bottom of the list at our next meeting, follows Ted.' With that, Nick turned out the light behind James's name and left.

The silence gradually became a low hum as each agent in the room realised he had just become a deadly enemy of his colleagues.

*

James rushed to catch up with Ted. By the time he reached him, Ted had entered the bowels of the subway. Ted looked completely isolated in the midst of a hundred people. James could see Ted had turned a frightening shade of white. His eyes were wide and vacant.

'Don't worry about it,' James urged. 'You can always

get another job. You have your health, a beautiful wife. Things are going to be fine.'

'You're right,' Ted answered. 'Things are going to be fine.' Ted removed his wedding ring and gave it to James. 'Take care of her for me.'

For a moment James looked confused.

'Ted, no. For God's sake...'

James closed his eyes tightly to escape the vision before him. Ted's blood splattered across the rails and on to James's suit as his bones snapped like twigs under the oncoming train.

*

Nick's head felt as precariously balanced as a rain-burdened flower, too heavy for the delicate stem that held it up. The murderous rage which so often engulfed him, was rapidly taking over his consciousness.

'Get me some coffee and my messages,' he said quietly to Shirley as he headed towards his office, trying to retain control.

Sinking into his high-backed leather chair, Nick considered what James's next move might be. He couldn't have his star agent going to work for the competition. He looked around his office, smiling at his Salvation Army jacket. Nick had never been a member of this organisation, this was one of his many props. When sales were down he would put on the jacket and rattle the poor box. His team knew that meant someone was heading for the axe. Casually he reached for the phone.

A deep-throated, sexy female voice answered the phone: 'Joe Austin's office.'

'Joe Austin, please.'

'Who shall I say is calling?'

'Nick Abbott.'

'Just one moment, Mr Abbott.'

Some inoffensive music played as Nick swivelled in his chair. In every part of his office Nick could see a symbol of his success. Potted palms from Jamaica were positioned at each corner. A solid gold business card holder sat at the rear of his desk behind a burgundy leather blotting pad. To the left was a photo frame housing a picture of Nick receiving his 'Manager of the Year' award.

'Nick.' A low gutsy New York accent spoke over the phone. 'How are you doing, you son of a gun?'

'Fine, Joe. I'm just fine. How are the kids?'

'Young Davie turns twenty-one this weekend. Hard to believe, isn't it?'

'Is that so? Congratulations.'

'Thanks. So, to what do I owe the honour of this call?'

'Joe, I need a favour.'

'Well, I didn't think you'd be calling your major competitor to wish him luck.'

'I've had an argument with James,' Nick explained. 'I think he may come to you for a job. You know what families can be like, Joe. Whatever we would steal from one another, I know we both feel families are sacred.'

'You want me to send the boy home?'

'As a favour to an old colleague, Joe.'

'You owe me one, Abbott.'

'Thanks, Joe. I knew I could count on you.'

Nick breathed a sigh of relief and commenced calling every other manager in the business whom James might approach.

'Your messages, sir.' Shirley carefully placed the black coffee and messages on the rear of Nick's desk, and left quietly.

Nick shuffled through the little yellow slips of paper, bored with the usual requests for commission advances, until one caught his eye.

Gus Fletcher, CEO, East West, would like you to call as soon as possible.

Nick dialled Gus's direct line immediately.

'Gus Fletcher,' a well-educated voice answered. It seemed, to Nick, like an older version of James's speaking voice.

'Gus, Nick Abbott, returning your call.'

'Nick, thanks for calling back. I have a little project for you. When can we meet for lunch?'

Without looking at his diary, Nick answered eagerly, 'How about Wednesday at twelve thirty?'

'That sounds fine. Shall we say at the club?'

'Perfect. See you Wednesday, Gus.'

Trying to narrow down Gus's reasons for the meeting, Nick wrote a note for Shirley to cancel all appointments for Wednesday afternoon and then left his office. For a moment the chaos in the office seemed normal; the buzz and hubbub of agents trying to get appointments and make a sale. It took several seconds for the sight of his son covered in blood to register with Nick.

'Son…'

James glared venomously at his father before turning to the policeman he had arrived with.

'I would like to break the news to her personally,' James said to the policeman.

'Sure,' the policeman answered mechanically.

James could see that Sandra in her glass-walled office already looked distressed. There were three agents with her; James guessed they had broken the news about Ted's dismissal. Her office was wall-to-wall computer manuals and printouts. The Aussie girl had done well, James realised, to learn the American insurance rules and adapt new presentations for Nick's team.

James walked slowly towards her office. Curious faces

fell silent as they watched the bloodstained son of their leader ask the agents to leave her office. Softly he shut her door behind them.

'What's going on?' Nick asked the policeman.

As the situation was explained to Nick he could see Sandra's huge blue eyes become clouded with tears. James was obviously trying to console her as best he could. Recognising this as a potentially volatile situation, Nick joined his son after knocking gently on the door.

'Sandra, I've just heard. I am so sorry,' Nick said with deep sincerity in his voice. 'If there is anything at all I can do, you must tell me. I am here not just as a representative of the company but as a friend.'

Her face was ashen. Her long blonde hair seemed to have become limp and lifeless. As her head rested on James's shoulder, Nick gently stroked her delicate, pale skin.

'I am here for you,' he insisted.

Sandra felt cold and numb. Nick's words weren't registering. Nothing was registering except the fact that the man she loved was dead. It was inconceivable, impossible, but it was true. She looked into James's eyes for some sort of explanation as Nick left them alone.

'I'll be back in a minute,' James said, putting her gently into her padded chair.

As he left the office, James could hear the agents muttering in hushed voices.

'You just never know when the pressure of this business is going to get to you,' one said.

'Yes,' agreed another. 'Whether you're the best or the worst, the pressure is the same.'

'And what violent deaths,' the first said again.

'Deaths?' the second enquired.

'Yes, remember? Eddie committed suicide too. Cocaine cut with rat poison, what a way to go.'

James froze in horror. He had known Eddie committed suicide with drugs, but he'd never heard the details before. Rat poison! Oh God, James shuddered. 'Mother,' he murmured, trying to fight back the tears. His fists clenched in convulsive rage. The truth finally registered with the force of a thunderbolt. His father was a murderer. There was so much James suddenly realised he had to do.

'Father,' James called after Nick in a bitter but resolute voice, storming into Nick's office. 'Did you mean what you said about helping Sandra?'

'Of course,' Nick answered calmly, aware he was being watched by at least two dozen people.

'Then I assume,' James continued, 'that Ted's life policy will be honoured?'

'You mean the half a million dollars' term cover I give all my agents when they join my team?'

'I do.'

'But son, Ted was not a member of my team when he met his untimely demise.' Nick smiled mockingly at James. He would not have his son and Ted's widow joining forces against him. That would be intolerable. No, Sandra would have to stay exactly where she was. Ultimately James would realise he must stay too.

'You son of a bitch,' James growled. He opened his mouth to hurl further abuse at the man he had come to despise as deeply as he had once admired him. In doing so, he realised the futility of words.

'You are no longer my father,' James said in a low, cold voice. 'I divest myself of any association with you. You have now driven away your son as well as your wife. Don't bother trying to find me. James Abbott no longer exists.'

Nick didn't fully understand his son's tongue-lashing. James had been making childish threats to leave his father ever since the death of his mother. This, Nick was sure, was just another one. He would get over it.

James returned to Sandra who was staring at Ted's wedding ring.

Without urgency, without hope, she numbly turned the shiny ring in her pale slender fingers. Time and place ceased to have meaning for her. The world seemed very far away from the silent void which surrounded her. She did not see James return, but suddenly became aware of his presence. She did not look up; she feared the sorrow she sensed, feared meeting his eyes.

'Tell me I'm dreaming,' she begged James, in a mixed Australian-American accent.

James embraced her firmly. 'I told Ted I'd look after you, and I will. Where do you want to go?'

'Home,' she answered simply.

'Sure, I'll take you home.'

'No, James. I mean home to Australia.'

'Australia?'

'I never liked New York much anyway,' she explained. 'I'll pick things up where I left off, before Ted came and swept me off my feet. He spoke about you often. He worshipped you – and your father.'

'Australia,' James said reflectively. 'Perhaps that will be a good place for me to start again as well. But first there is something I must do...'

Sandra had built such big plans for her life. Her family had been simple farmers without any ambition but Sandra had been blessed (or cursed) with natural entrepreneurial flair. She had recognised that there was a future in computers long before it became fashionable. She taught herself the intricacies of computer language and how to programme the fearsome machines. Once her skill was mastered she went about researching the larger corporations, finding out what they wanted from their support systems and designing her packages to solve their problems. It was during this research phase that she came across Brett McLeod. Brett had been the chief executive of a large computer company and immediately saw the value in a liaison with Sandra.

It had been a hard road – often she had to work eighteen hours a day – to get her career off the ground. There had been times when she wondered how much of her efforts were meaningless, a meagre attempt to prove to some non-existent person that she was better than them.

Perhaps, she often thought, I would have been better being born a bimbo. They marry wealthy husbands and never have to worry about anything. They have time to play tennis and get their nails manicured. Sandra felt she might go grey before her time. Then Ted walked into her life. A dear sweet man whom she met by chance when he visited Australia. He swept her off her feet completely, telling her she could have a great career working in the software design section of East West Life. Ted was sweet and kind and gentle... and now he was dead. She felt a darkness descend and, at last, began to weep freely.

*

Driving to his Park Avenue apartment, Nick reflected over just how far he had come. Nick's father, a poor German migrant, had been a clerk at East West Life until the day he died, unrecognised and unremembered. Nick himself had been a scrawny child and the memory of it sickened him. His mother had told him he was special, his warm and loving mother who was taken from him when Nick was only five years old. Nick had quickly learned to fend for himself, to live off his wits. Kids taunted him like some animal because he had nothing to offer. He was poor, unathletic and had a foreign accent. Why couldn't his father have seen that the money, and therefore power, was in sales? No kid would have dared to make fun of him if he had been wealthy.

Nick had learned that physical appearances weren't important when you were rich. Determined to make amends for his torturous childhood through his adult years, Nick knew now he had reached the number one position it was a title he must guard jealously. He had discovered his strength and knew how to use it. He might not have looks but he had charisma – and now he had money too. A bitterness festered beneath the surface, always there to remind him that he must never slip back, never allow anyone to drag him down. His resolve brought with it an air of strength which demanded control from his disciples: his agents. With every new success Nick lusted for more. When Nick Abbott died he knew people would say, 'There lived a great man, one who will be remembered and admired.'

Why can't James appreciate the bigger picture? Nick reflected sadly. He wrapped himself in a cloak of silence and once again recoiled into a world of poisonous anger. All the ugly emotions which had festered within him since childhood erupted leaving a corrosive stain in his mind.

*

To gain membership to the New York Athletic Club, one of the oldest clubs in New York, you must be rich, Christian, white and have at least two generations at an Ivy League college. Nick qualified on three counts but Ivy League colleges had been out of his reach. Gus Fletcher, on the other hand, had been a member there as long as Nick could remember.

Through a long corridor of trophies and photographs of sporting stars on the second floor, Nick found the entrance to the bar. Just one drink, he decided, to carefully plan answers to all the questions Gus might ask. The old-world dark wood and lines of still more trophies gave a comfortable presence to the stylish club. It was sufficient to relax Nick for his meeting.

Already seated at his regular table in the dining room on level three, Gus flicked through a large file of correspondence, his glasses perched perfectly at the end of his pointy nose. Despite his sixty years, there was barely a wrinkle etched into his distinguished face. His thick silver hair reflected the restaurant's light, almost giving him a halo.

Nick arrived looking crisp and confident. His mind focused clearly on the man who could make or break careers. He spotted Gus sitting between two tables of dark-suited businessmen. It was with some satisfaction that Nick observed Gus to be the most distinguished of those around him.

'Gus, my man. How are you?' Nick shook his hand vigorously.

'Fine, Nick. Can I buy you a drink?' Gus answered, his Life Managers Association tie clip shining from a royal blue Yves Saint Laurent tie.

'Thanks. The usual.'

'Two manhattans, thank you, Ernie,' Gus ordered, keeping vigil over Nick's expression and straightening his customary red lapel carnation.

'I was very sorry to hear about Ted,' Gus said solemnly. 'People like Ted should never be recruited into this game.'

'He could have been a star if he'd listened to me. You know his father is one of the most respected men in the finance industry and Ted wouldn't go to him for help. I had to let him go for his own good; he was going to starve. There are no salaries to keep the likes of Ted and me fed if we don't sell.' Nick felt that was sufficient justification. Gus was a master of the business. He knew how tough it was to make a living in life insurance.

'Couldn't tap into the old man's contacts, eh? How is

James taking it?'

Gus hid the significance of the first question behind one which illustrated his well-known concern for family harmony. Despite being one of the most powerful men in the business, Gus was a devoted husband and father.

'He's angry and hurt, but he'll get over it. He's still the heir apparent when I retire.'

'That may be sooner than you think,' Gus said, bringing out his Ventolin spray to ease his familiar wheezing.

'Are you all right?' Nick asked, noticing Gus's distress.

'I'm fine. I visited my daughter this morning. Her darn cats always bring on my asthma attacks.'

'Oh.' Nick acknowledged the comment with little interest. Gus's comments about retirement had disturbed Nick. *Did* he know the truth? Nick glanced across the restaurant as though Gus's words meant nothing. He noticed two men deep in conversation; one was pulling on his ear in a gesture that all sales people recognise as an admission of guilt. Gus, Nick resolved, will see no such gesture from me.

'Nick,' Gus continued, 'we both know that the success rate of agents in our industry sucks. Eighty-four per cent fail in the first four years. It's just not good enough. The Life Managers Association has been trying to find new ways to lift the standards of people entering our industry. I don't just mean the agents either, I mean the managers too.'

'What's your point?' Nick asked as nonchalantly as he could manage.

'Are you still using that phoney file to recruit?'

Was that what this was all about? Nick wondered. It was a common ploy to write letters from agents and widows expounding upon the virtues of life insurance. They may have been written by Nick, but the signatures were authentic. Of course, what grieving widow wouldn't sign a letter when her mind was still ablaze with the injustice of just having lost her husband? And what agent would ever dare say no to Nick Abbott? Surely this couldn't be upsetting Gus.

'I use it sometimes. It depends on the situation. Sometimes people need to be *shown* that life insurance is a worthwhile product rather than just told.'

'Agreed. But we believe there is a better way. The image of this industry is in the toilet. People think of us as used car salesmen, not to be trusted. And what are we doing about it? We are perpetuating it by using techniques like the phoney file.'

'What do you suggest?'

'The Life Managers Association wants me to choose a sales manager, one with a proven track record, to act as its international consultant. It'll mean six months of travelling – a temporary retirement from his position. He'll go to London, Johannesburg, Sydney, Auckland and around the States. We want to pick the eyes out of what is right in a selection process of sales agents from companies around the world. In return we can offer advice, where it is appropriate. It's a bitch of a job, Nick, but someone's got to do it.'

Gus smiled. He could see Nick was trying to remain composed while visualising all the rewards a tour like this could bring. The contacts, the ideas, the recognition: the potential was limitless.

'Are you saying you want me to be your consultant?' Nick asked as though he didn't already know the answer.

'Well, can you think of anyone more qualified? You were the manager of Eddie Schwartz. He's a legend all over the world. And besides, you know what they say... if you can make it in New York, you can make it anywhere. Well, Nick, you made it here and you made it big. You are the one we want to conduct this project.'

There was a long silence before Nick answered. Gus hated himself for massaging Nick's ego this way, but he had to get Nick out of New York for as long as possible if he was to check out the allegations James had made. Besides, this could finally break up an affair Gus knew had to end.

'I'll do it,' Nick conceded.

Nick's shaded understatement nearly caused Gus to say, 'Of course you will; who wouldn't?' but he kept silent for a moment longer, taking another puff of his Ventolin.

Nick observed his discomfort curiously.

'Good,' Gus said, getting his breath back. 'I need you to get organised as soon as possible. Lloyd Sutcliff, the general manager of Winston Life, will be your host in London. I imagine you'll spend about one month there before flying to Johannesburg. Now that's going to be a real treat. We've got Tom Weinstein lined up for you there—'

'Weinstein.' The name escaped from Nick's lips with thinly disguised jealousy. 'Isn't that the man who took a brokerage house to the number one life office in South Africa?'

'That's the man. And his right-hand man, Phil Langdon-Smythe, achieved a fifty-four per cent survival rate over four years. Beats the hell out of an eighty-four per cent failure rate, wouldn't you say?'

Nick nodded in reluctant agreement.

'I expect you to come back with some red-hot recommendations from that stop.'

Gus contemplated for a moment the wisdom of selecting Nick Abbott for this tour of duty. Nick was undoubtedly the most recognised of all agency managers. Despite this fact, however, Gus considered him to be the most cunning and lecherous bastard that God had put on this earth. At least he would know once and for all if the suspicions he had harboured for years were true. If for no other reason, the tour would be worthwhile.

For nearly five hours Gus and Nick planned itineraries, agendas, contact points and objectives. The sense of vulnerability Nick felt at the beginning of their meal had long since been forgotten. He was being handed the opportunity of a lifetime: not only a chance to make a difference to the industry as a whole, but the chance to tap into some of the best minds in the world. It was a breeding ground for new concepts and he knew it. To hell with East West Life! To hell with Ted Upton! To hell with meagre responsibilities! Thirty years of playing out a charade was coming to an end. Nick Abbott would be seen as the master of the world industry.

In a state of excitement Nick caught a cab outside the club. He had to get back to his apartment quickly.

His plush Park Avenue apartment seemed somehow hollow to Nick. It echoed with memories of happier times when Norma was alive and nurturing their beloved baby son. Nick married Norma Hudsen when they were both the tender of age of eighteen. She was the first woman to ever take an interest in the scrawny kid with no money. Norma could understand Nick's dream and gave him encouragement. He loved her for it. He loved her even now.

In return, Norma had loved her family dearly. Having grown up as an orphan, her sense of belonging had been more important to her than anything she could imagine. All the love in the world, however, could not hide the lines of torment which became etched into her once pure complexion during her final months. Nick knew that as he rose to fame and fortune in the industry Norma became aware of the other women chasing after him, not for sexual reasons, but because they were interested in using Nick as a stepping stone for their careers, or as a sugar daddy. They were leeches trying to suck him dry. Despite her understanding, the burning love Norma once harboured for Nick cooled with each new infidelity. She gradually came to loathe Nick with the same passion with which she had once loved him, turning to cocaine to numb the pain.

Cocaine, Nick thought, the socially acceptable escape of the obscenely rich. Nick remembered how she threatened to leave him, attempting to bury his career in the process. Norma knew his career was his one true love. The only way to avenge her pain was to strike out at the one thing that meant anything to her husband. Nick felt a cavity growing in his conscience as he remembered the pain and suffering of her final moments.

The memory swirled in Nick's mind, sickening him. Perhaps I should have spent more time with James when it happened, he thought. Perhaps James would have understood me better.

'Oh, why did you ever start to use cocaine, Norma?' Nick asked aloud. 'I do miss you. I miss you both.'

Nick poured himself a drink as waves of conflicting emotions washed over him: regret, anger, love, hatred and an overriding ambition to conquer – no matter what the cost. As he sat down with his drink, he wondered how long it would be before his son came home.

*

'No word from James?' Nick asked Shirley as he entered his office. His eyes reflected the emotions which swamped him. Anger, conflict and concern.

'I'm afraid not,' Shirley answered.

He glared at Shirley which forced her to sit upright, feeling an overwhelming sense of being controlled.

'How did your lunch go with Mr Fletcher?' she asked in an attempt to avert an outburst by Nick.

'Shirley, it went very well. Why don't you get us some coffee, come into my office, and I'll tell you all about it.

Have all my calls held.'

Shirley rushed off to get the coffees. By the time she reappeared a spider's scrawl was flowing from Nick Abbott's Mont Blanc pen as he made lists of all the things that had to be done before he left.

'Come in, Shirl. Put it down over there.' He waved without looking to the meeting area in his office.

Shirley placed a tray on the table between two leather couches. Silently she poured the coffees; one just the way Nick liked it, straight black, and a white one with two sugars for herself. She drank hers slowly while Nick continued to scrawl, letting his coffee get quite cold.

'Tell me,' he finally said, bringing his notes over to the coffee table. 'How do you think Algy would cope running this show for six months?'

Curiosity and anxiety flashed through Shirley's consciousness. Is Nick leaving? she wondered. Do I still have a job? She looked at Nick's face for some measure of reassurance and in doing so relaxed into a contented smile. She was about to be the first to hear Nick Abbott's big news and she felt privileged.

'Algy would be fine, Mr Abbott. He's been your operations manager for ten years; no one knows the way things run better than Algy—'

'Except you.'

'Thank you, Mr Abbott, but running this motley crew isn't my scene.' A faint embarrassed laugh escaped from her lips. 'Algy will never take your place, but he'll do a reasonable job in your absence.'

'Shirley, I've been invited to become the LMA international consultant. Gus Fletcher wants to send me on a six-month consulting tour.'

'Mr Abbott, what an honour.' Her eyes shone with excitement and a touch of relief.

'Well, I am the best of the best, you know. I'll be

leaving in four weeks so we have a lot to do. The first thing I want to do is have a meeting with Algy – this will probably make his whole year. Make sure there are no takeover bids while I'm away, won't you, Shirl?' He didn't wait for an answer. 'Next, I must meet with my top guys. I think a staff cocktail party is in order to announce the move. And I want no leaks before the event.'

Shirley's pencil moved efficiently across her notepad taking down all the demands.

'Okay, that's all for now. Better get cracking.'

Nick was breathing deeply as he paced the thick oriental rug in his office. He hadn't touched his coffee, he was too busy thinking. He tried to calm himself. It wasn't working. Whenever Nick became agitated, which was quite often, he would try to calm himself by looking at the plaques of his achievements. This always had a calming effect.

Algy passed Nick's open office door, keen to ask about Nick's meeting with Gus Fletcher. Seeing the state of concentration his boss was in, Algy decided not to disturb him.

Neither acknowledged the other.

Nick unlocked and opened a small safe on the far wall of his office. It revealed a number of files, a few floppy disks and an old German Luger pistol. The pistol was the one memento Nick kept of his father – he was never quite sure why. He packed a few files and the disks in his briefcase. Glancing back towards the safe the pistol caught his attention. He packed one last item before leaving.

*

Nick took a slow walk to the Plaza Hotel. The hubbub of New York was pumping in his veins. The grime penetrated every pore of Nick's face and he loved it. New York made him feel alive. Dirty yellow cabs whirled down Fifth

Avenue and around the horse-drawn carriages at the Plaza. A faint waft of manure spun around the plush hotel.

Nick sauntered into the Plaza lobby, gazing around to get a feel for who was there. A woman, about twenty-five and curved in all the right places, smiled seductively when he finally made eye contact. Long soft swirls of fiery auburn hair danced around enchanting catlike green eyes as she ambled towards him.

'Here on business or pleasure?' she asked in a sultry tone which told Nick she didn't give a damn why he was there.

'Business,' Nick replied, smiling. 'Personal business.'

'Miss me?' she asked.

He was overcome with a wave of passion for his lover. He grabbed her, pulling her quickly towards him.

'What do you think, Samantha?' he answered.

Her mouth opened beneath Nick's, full, confident, welcoming. Her gorgeous eyes closed as their lips met.

'I trust you enjoyed your little break in the Bahamas?' He grinned.

'I would have enjoyed it more if you had been with me. What happened?'

'A few things came up I had to deal with. I'll make it up to you, I promise.'

'Seems to me something's come up which you have to deal with right now,' she answered, moving close enough to feel the growing bulge in his trousers.

'Why don't we skip dinner?' he asked rhetorically.

As he led her towards the lobby elevator, Samantha thought about her disloyalty. She had tried to be faithful to her lover, finding, to her disappointment, that her passionate nature overcame her intention of fidelity. As each day passed in the Bahamas and Nick had not appeared, she let her resentment at his absence blossom. She had slept with many men, hoping that she would find one who could satisfy her the way Nick did. Despite her experimentation there had been none. The young bucks with their healthy bodies were all very well to look at, but they couldn't compare with a man of experience and skill. Finally she had determined that she would give up her fruitless search. She amused herself with occasional bursts of cocaine use; something she knew Nick would have been furious about.

She remembered using the substance once before, in Nick's presence. He had scolded her mercilessly for it. 'I've seen it all before,' Nick had reprimanded her. He had gone on to explain he had seen people die of treated drugs. 'Give it up, Samantha,' Nick had warned her. 'Give it up or pay the price.'

She had pouted like a child but was secretly glad Nick cared enough to warn her. She cared for him too. It wasn't love, but a deep understanding affection for the type of man he was: powerful and strong.

Nick unlocked the door to a suite he had reserved, a small token to apologise for missing the trip. Scrutinising Samantha's luscious form, he couldn't help feeling she was not going to react well to the news of a six-month separation.

'The bedroom's that way,' he directed Sam, collecting a bottle of port and two glasses before joining her.

'Oh, Nick,' she breathed, as he lowered her on to the bed, ripping off her clothes with a savage urgency.

'You set me on fire, Sam.' Nick looked at her as if she were the only woman he had ever seen.

Samantha ran her fingers over his firm bones. 'Only you,' she whispered. 'It's only like this with you.'

Nick dipped his finger in a glass of port he had poured. It felt cold and sticky. He rubbed a generous amount over her nipples, noticing how Samantha's body heat caused the port's aroma to fill his senses. It somehow made both the alcohol and the moment more intoxicating. Slowly he cleaned the port away with circular movements of his tongue. The sensation felt so erotic it was all Nick could do to keep himself from biting right through her flesh.

A warm tingling excitement in her breasts forced Samantha to wriggle within Nick's grasp as a river began to stir inside her. She surrendered completely to his fantasy, responding instantly to his word and touch.

She altered the angle of her pelvis, spreading her legs and striving to engulf him. She could no longer bear the dry friction against the inside of her upper thigh. She wanted him to feel the warm welcome she sent down for him and glide deep inside her. At that moment she felt such a sense of joy she could have wept out loud.

Nick held her still upon his heaving chest. Little beads of sweat formed and trickled from her body like drops of nectar. She clung to him with both arms wrapped around him tightly.

'I'm going to miss you, Samantha,' he whispered at last.

'I don't understand,' she murmured. 'What do you mean?'

Nick had to tell her sooner or later. 'I'm going to have to go away for a while,' he confessed, and commenced to tell her the whole story.

'Isn't there someone else who can go?' she protested violently and sat up, feeling invaded and used.

'It's too good an offer to turn down,' he said simply.

Samantha pouted while she considered the ramifications of what Nick had told her.

'I bet you won't even miss me,' he laughed, trying to defuse her possible anger. 'You'll take up with some stud and won't even notice I've gone.'

'You know that's not true,' she lied.

'Samantha, come here.' Nick tried to pull her towards him but she moved away.

'He's done this on purpose,' she complained.

'What are you talking about?'

'My father. I'm sick of him trying to run my life. He introduced me to his latest choice for my future husband last week. Yuk.' She shuddered at the memory. 'He's sending you away to keep us apart,' Samantha exploded.

Nick's solemn expression caught Samantha Fletcher off guard.

'That's impossible,' Nick responded in a tone which told her it wasn't impossible at all. 'He can't know about us.'

'Really? First an impromptu LMA meeting which stopped you going to the Bahamas and now this.'

'It's just business. Perfectly normal. I *am* the logical choice for this assignment. Besides, I'll be back for you,' he promised with hollow insincerity.

Shadows danced across the ceiling as Nick rose to get dressed. Another bleak and meaningless ending, he thought. At first it had been satisfying having an affair with Gus Fletcher's daughter. Gus was the one man who held more power in the industry than Nick. Screwing his daughter, even covertly, allowed Nick to feel he had the edge. An edge was no longer necessary, however. Gus had given him the opening he needed to become master of the industry – globally. Samantha had just become a liability he would do well to dispose of as quietly and quickly as possible. Nick wondered for a fleeting moment if there was any virtue left in his soul.

Chapter Two

In the wake of the dying operational freedom life insurance companies once enjoyed, many things began to happen exceedingly fast and at a rising tempo. The news of Nick Abbott's imminent arrival was received with some relief by Lloyd Sutcliff. Lloyd had been in touch with the LMA on several occasions, asking for guidance. Governed more by legislation than management, results were more important than ever. His sales force was not up to scratch, and he knew it. It was unfortunate the assistance of an American was required, he mused, but changing times and all that.

In Heathrow's buzzing terminal, Lloyd waited patiently, along with others clad in all manner of attire from scruffy jeans to Savile Row suits. The wait was taking longer than he had anticipated, but Lloyd had learned in his early years at the City of London boys' school, and later at Oxford, that an Englishman must remain patient and in control at all times. Standing a touch under six foot, Lloyd's dark hair was beginning to grey, which added a refined air to his already stately poise. A neatly trimmed grey moustache just tipped the edges of his upper lip which never twitched with a sign of emotion, unless it was considered appropriate. In a dark pinstriped suit and a Burberry cashmere overcoat, Lloyd looked every inch the traditional affluent Englishman. In his left hand he held a board with Nick Abbott's name – deliberately in the left hand – leaving his right hand free to offer in greeting when the American expert arrived.

I do hope he won't be wearing a loud chequered sports jacket, Lloyd thought. He imagined most Americans considered such clothing compulsory.

Nick saw his name on the board before noticing the Englishman behind it. He was relieved to be out of the madness of customs, being concerned only with escaping from the throngs of 'little' people surrounding him.

'Nick Abbott, East West Life. Pleased to meet you.' Nick used his most formal speaking voice to introduce himself.

'Lloyd Sutcliff. Delighted to meet you, old boy. Almost thought you'd missed the plane. What's going on back there?'

'Your Limey system of making us Americans go through the alien channel. Didn't anyone tell your customs guys that we won the war for you?'

'Oh, yes. Quite.'

The brief encounter planted a seed of aversion in both men for the other.

So, Mr Abbott, you are one of those Americans who like to try to make the English feel inferior. Lloyd looked over his colleague with a degree of contempt, considering the tired cliché of 'We won the war'. Lloyd recognised this for the hidden jealousy it was. A typical example of those who have no breeding trying to disguise their deficiencies with crass, overbearing arrogance, he decided.

Nick had quickly placed Lloyd too. He's a product of a bygone era, trying to hold on to the pomp and circumstance that has no place in a fast-moving, remorseless business world, Nick concluded. He understood, however, that the old school tie network did have some worth. Lloyd would be valuable for introductions so he would be discreet about his feelings; for now.

Up ahead the grey sky was dotted with black umbrellas. The cold damp smell in the air reminded Nick of the damp odour in his childhood apartment. A memory he quickly shook from his mind.

'Well, this way, old boy; the chariot awaits.'

'Not so much of the "old boy", if you don't mind.'

'Sorry, ol'… It's just an expression; we don't mean anything by it. Here we are.' Arriving at his brand new 1984 model navy blue Daimler, Lloyd loaded Nick's cases into the boot. 'I take it this is your first time in England?'

'That's right.'

'Well, you'll love it here. The weather's so predictable.'

'You mean it's always like this?'

'Oh, this is just April showers bringing May flowers. We have splendid summers. Last year it fell on a Tuesday.' Lloyd brushed the beads of rain from his overcoat as though they were pollen falling from a shaken flower.

'That's very funny,' Nick growled.

'Here, if you look in this envelope you will see a list of the formal arrangements I have organised. You might care to glance over it on the way to the hotel.' Lloyd handed Nick a large yellow envelope with the words 'Winston Life' written on it.

The Daimler smelled of a mixture of pipe tobacco and dog hairs. Nick observed a few brown hairs on the back seat and, judging by Lloyd's appearance, assumed that they belonged to a breed of hunting dog.

'Mind if I smoke?' Nick asked, already reaching for his Chesterfields.

'Not at all, old boy. I rather fancy some of the old Gold Block myself.' Lloyd retrieved a dark pipe from the car's ashtray, carefully setting fire to the bowl while paused at traffic lights.

The first highlight Nick spotted on his itinerary was the LMA formal dinner to be held the following evening at the Guildhall. The month was dotted with meetings, seminars, lunches and dinners. The English clearly intend to get their money's worth out of me, he smirked.

'You've arrived just in time, you know. The whole industry is rife with confusion.' Lloyd glanced sideways at his colleague to gauge a reaction.

'Really,' Nick quipped, 'what are they confused about?'

'We're still trying to come to terms with the impact of Aids. You know, do we increase the premiums, make medical screening tougher? We have to protect ourselves. The repercussions could be devastating. Then there's this blasted legislation regarding commission disclosure. Why should we have to tell people what commission we earn from selling life insurance? I don't know another business in the world that has to tell their clients what they're making out of them. It's outrageous. What's your view on this?'

'I think that if the government is going to legislate to enforce commission disclosure, we'd better spend our time learning how to deal with it rather than whining about it.'

'Quite.' Lloyd knew he had been put in his place. His resentment of this American colleague grew.

Big gold letters spelled out the name Hilton on an imposing building at the end of Park Lane. Lloyd had booked the Presidential Suite. He knew a VIP of Nick's reputation would have expected nothing less.

Looking around the suite, Nick realised it was elegant, although not as lavish as its American counterparts. He noticed that a reproduction Queen Anne period coffee table graced the centre of the lounge, complemented by two velvet-covered settees and an armchair. To the left was the dining room filled with polished oak furniture. A king-size bed faced velvet drapes which were neatly gathered by heavy golden cord tie-backs.

Quite nice, Nick thought without commenting. He didn't want the Englishman to think he had been unduly impressed. The best is what I should expect, Nick told himself, only anything less could provoke a reaction. Nick harboured a deep-rooted jealousy for Lloyd's type. Lloyd had been born into a position of money and the privileges that went with it. He could never appreciate them, Nick decided, because he didn't earn them. Yet he could make Nick feel as though he was being patronised with a single glance. I can ignore the pomposity for a month, he thought. If Lloyd pursues me for knowledge, as I know he will, I will continue to hold the upper hand.

Nick Abbott wondered at his own cynicism as Lloyd watched him unpack. There was no question about it. The fastest way to get into the pulse of London's life insurance industry was through Lloyd Sutcliff. He would be the pawn. The pawn who trapped himself.

Having formed an indelible first impression of his American colleague, Lloyd considered the chasms between both their professional and personal upbringings. The man is dangerous, Lloyd thought, he could strip us naked as easily as show us the way. He remembered someone once said, 'All men dream, but they are most dangerous who dream with their eyes open.' Nick Abbott, Lloyd concluded, was such a man.

*

The office of Winston Life glowed with both history and tradition. Standing under an oil painting of the original office of Winston Life in a wide entrance foyer, Nick absorbed the essence of his surroundings. The dark oak panels showed their age with dignity. If only the walls could talk. Nick grinned at his own cliché as he noticed Lloyd approaching from the corridor.

'There's a call for you in my office,' Lloyd announced. 'From Tom Weinstein.'

Lloyd ushered Nick in the direction of an overcrowded office, saying he would wait outside while Nick took the call.

'Good afternoon, or is it morning there?' Nick asked, realising Lloyd had left the door ajar.

'No, it's afternoon here too.' A hard South African accent spoke over the phone. 'It's good to talk with you, at last. I've heard a great deal about you.' The voice was firm and self-confident. 'I thought I should call to ask if there are any special arrangements you would like me to make for your visit here?'

'As long as you have the sun turned on, I'll be happy.'

'Ya, England's not the warmest country in the world.' A faint laugh touched his voice. 'I will send one of my drivers to collect you at Jo'burg. Is that all right with you?'

'Sure. That's fine.'

'Well, Nick, I look forward to meeting you next month.'

'Me too. Thanks for the call.'

Replacing the receiver Nick looked around Lloyd's office. It had some of the trappings of success; leather chairs, an oak partner's desk, and a view of Hyde Park, but it was all so small.

'I'm sure I would die of claustrophobia if I lived here,' Nick muttered under his breath.

A few Napoleonic prints graced the walls. For a moment they caught Nick's attention. Battles were something he could understand. Through the window Nick noticed a busker; a victim of thalidomide. He played the violin passionately as if oblivious to the rain. I suppose, Nick thought, when you have such a disability to contend with, a drop of rain isn't going to bother you very much. He admired the victim's spirit. Such courage in the face of adversity would have made him a good salesman if Nick had had the time to cultivate him.

Casting his eyes back inside, Nick noticed a tall blonde woman pass by Lloyd's door. Her clothes were businesslike but her walk, expression and posture suggested to Nick she was the kind of woman who didn't fit into this austere English environment. He had to meet her. Nick was about to leave the office when he heard the voice of Lloyd Sutcliff. He was very close but speaking in an undertone, making it impossible for Nick to clearly make out the words. Before Nick had a chance to follow the sound, Lloyd re-entered the office, this time with the tall blonde by his side.

'Nick, I would like you to meet Cathy Williams. Cathy is the manager of public relations for Winston Life London. Cathy, this is Nick Abbott, from New York.'

'How do you do, Mr Abbott.' Her eyes sparkled mischievously, immediately arousing Nick.

'Please, call me Nick,' he said, offering his hand in greeting.

Cathy managed to look correctly interested. She had waited a long time for an opportunity like this.

I have to impress this man, she thought.

She hadn't believed the rumours about Nick Abbott, but even as she looked at him a chill shuddered down her spine. There was something intriguingly ruthless about this man.

'Nick is here to observe our methods of recruitment... and recommend changes where it is necessary,' Lloyd explained.

'That's right,' Nick began with a smile as though he wasn't taking the conversation too seriously, 'but after lunch with some of your managers today it seems it is not only the sales side that needs advice.'

'Oh?' enquired Cathy, taking a seat in one of Lloyd's visitors' chairs. She considered that to sit without being asked gave the impression of appropriate confidence, not impudence as some might think.

'That's right. Tell me, Cathy, how much profit did your public relations activity directly bring into the firm last year?' There was a light mocking smile on his lips.

'Well, I don't know exactly. I would have to examine all

the campaigns we launched; see how many were image building, how many were direct marketing, and—'

'I see.' Nick's well-timed interruption threw Cathy off guard. As always, Nick's timing was perfect. 'You know, if my public relations manager said that to me, I'd fire him.'

Nick directed a cold, firm stare openly at Cathy. Her huge brown eyes flashed angrily at his comment.

She was furious. Blast, I should have known better than to answer him that way. Now he'll never take me seriously. If you're trying to make a good first impression, she said angrily to herself, you're off to a flying start. Frustrated by her uncharacteristic emotionalism, she assured herself she would not allow Nick Abbott to get to her.

'Steady on, old boy.' Lloyd jumped in, trying to defuse the situation.

Nick continued, ignoring the fact that Lloyd had spoken. 'That's right. You have to be able to measure your success or you don't know if you're wasting your money on ineffective methods. Don't you agree?'

'They say a picture paints a thousand words, Mr Abbott, I mean Nick. Perhaps you would like to see some of my work.' Cathy was certain that if Nick saw her work his attitude would change.

Nick could sense her concern; he smelled the fear. She made it too easy, he thought, and smiled. He greeted Cathy's suggestion with a distinct lack of enthusiasm by shrugging his shoulders, hiding the automatic sexual response her appearance had created.

'That's a splendid idea, Cathy,' Lloyd chirped. He was smugly satisfied that his public relations manager had stood up to the American. Encouraging the meeting would show this Yank what his girl was made of. 'Nick, you do have some time up your sleeve. I didn't want to rush you off your feet on your first day here. If it suits you, Miss Williams can give you the tour of the office, while I deal with this pile of messages. I've arranged dinner for seven at the Café Royal.'

'Fine.' Nick was fond of one-word answers. They were short, sharp and could throw people off guard if delivered properly.

Okay, Mr Abbott, I'll show you, Cathy thought, getting her emotions in check.

She directed Nick through a maze of dark wooden corridors before reaching her office. It was even smaller than Lloyd's, but much neater. There were enough piles of paper, all stacked neatly, to make her look busy without being disorganised. She considered she'd done well for herself so far. Lloyd had introduced Cathy to the company as an overconfident twenty-three year old; four years ago. She had idolised Lloyd then. The kind and distinguished older gentleman who first interviewed her appreciated her talents and gave her a break. Lloyd's assistance in promoting her career, however, had plateaued since his own responsibilities had become so onerous. She knew she needed high-level recognition if she was to get ahead.

'Here we are, Mr Abbott, I mean Nick. This is the dossier on corporate profile. It shows the methods I've adopted to increase public awareness of Winston Life. We don't just want to get people thinking about buying life insurance, but about buying it from us.'

'Good,' Nick said, taking the file. He thumbed through it, sceptically at first, barely looking at the contents. It wasn't until he was halfway through that a couple of things caught his eye; there were a few noteworthy ideas.

'This works every time, doesn't it?' Nick was pointing to a picture of a newborn baby in its mother's arms. The caption under it read: 'You insure your car, your home, your contents, but if you didn't come home last night, which would they miss more?'

'Powerful, emotional advertising, but unfortunately the

sort of advertising necessary to wake people up to their responsibilities. I believe in my product, Nick, and I want that to show in my campaigns. What do you think of this one?'

Cathy showed Nick a flyer depicting a woman in mourning with the caption: 'If every wife knew what every widow knows, no home would be without adequate life insurance.'

It's working, she thought excitedly. I can see it in his eyes; he likes my work.

'That's good, but how does it make the public want to buy from this company rather than another?'

'Simple. We follow up those themes with this.' She showed Nick a photo of Nelson's Column with a caption saying: 'Winston Life, as noble as the man, as successful as his endeavours and as established as his column. Winston Life, we're here for life.'

'Strength, stability and patriotism,' she spouted, as though the words had been planted in her mind by a third party. She hoped her belief in herself would make Nick seem less forbidding, but as she watched a scowl carve its way across his granite-like features, she realised this man was every bit as cold and disagreeable as she had been told.

'Not bad,' Nick admitted, taking the file and sitting in Cathy's chair, aware that this gesture accentuated his position of power. Cathy, forced to sit in one of her own visitors' chairs, seethed at his arrogance.

'Do you have anything on agent support?' Nick asked, closing the file in front of him.

'Right here. I'd like to take this opportunity to thank you for the time you are spending with Winston Life, Nick. If there's anything at all I can do to assist you while you are in London, please just ask.' Blast, she thought. I've just moved straight from confidence to grovelling. Blast my own stupidity.

Nick could sense her frustration.

'Thank you. I will. I understand that you haven't been public relations manager very long?' he commented, taking the new file.

'A year. But I've been with Winston Life for four years.'

Nick opened the agent support file and started scanning the top pages. They seemed to be moderately intelligent.

'Tell me about Lloyd. How long have you known him?'

'Lloyd gave me my first job at Winston Life. He was my mentor but now we hardly see one another, except at meetings.' *Now why would he want to know that?* she wondered.

'I see. Tell me a bit more about this.'

Nick picked up the file and moved around to the vacant chair next to Cathy. In asking the question he put the file on her lap, brushing her arm as he did so.

Cathy had never dealt with Americans and, while she found the intrusion of her personal space disturbing, she dismissed it as part of the American way and explained her ideas.

Nick knew that a person in Cathy's position, with the right ambitions, could be quite useful, not to mention downright enjoyable, if used properly.

'What's your point to all of this, Cathy Williams? What is it you want out of your efforts?' His gaze was inscrutable.

'What I want, Nick, is to be the first female international public relations manager for Winston Life. Do you think I'm on track?'

'I don't know. Your campaigns are quite good, but what are you doing to get noticed?' He leaned back in his chair, waiting for her answer.

'Doing the best job I know how. Listening to all the suggestions the agents give me. Representing their interests at meetings.' She turned to look unashamedly in Nick's eyes. Was that what I was supposed to say? she mused to herself.

'That's good,' he said. 'But there are many factors that go into making success. What are you prepared to give up to achieve your goal?'

'I don't understand.'

'Success isn't built by winning easy battles. It's built by losing the hard ones and coming back to fight again. Have you got what it takes?'

'I've fought my share of battles to get where I am today,' she said confidently. 'Don't worry about me.'

'I wasn't. But an attractive girl like you; what about your husband? Maybe he'd prefer it if you were raising a family rather than raising a corporate profile.'

'I'm not married, Nick. I haven't found the time.'

'It can get awfully lonely at night with just your campaigns to keep you warm.'

That annoyingly mocking smile returned to Nick's lips. She could have hit him if he wasn't so very important.

'I have a marvellous central heating system, thank you – that's when I make it home. Between my business and social life I'm hardly ever there.'

'Good girl,' he said, patronisingly patting her thigh as he stood to leave.

Oooooh, he was an infuriating man. He commanded attention and at the same time patronised her in her own environment. How dare he? She wished she could find the words for her fury.

'I have to get back to Lloyd now. Why don't you join us for dinner tonight? We can continue our discussions then.' He smiled charmingly.

She considered saying something clever like, 'In your dreams, buster.' The urge to put Nick Abbott down was overwhelming, although to do so, Cathy understood, would have been a monumental folly. Instead, Cathy chose to be alluring and feminine in her response.

'Thank you. I'd love to.'

Both thought that they had already won.

*

Moulding themselves into red velvet armchairs at the Café Royal, the three life insurance executives began to talk about the market share potential for Winston Life over the next five years.

'Would anyone care for pre-dinner drinks?' asked the wine waiter.

'Yes, I'll have a Manhattan,' Nick replied to the tall, thin, pale-faced man.

'What on earth's a Manhattan?' Cathy asked. With each passing moment she felt herself becoming more intrigued with Nick Abbott.

'Whisky, vermouth and a dash of bitters.'

'How unusual. I'll have one of those too, thank you.'

'That's a bit daring for you, isn't it, Cathy?' Lloyd's tone was paternalistic.

It annoyed Nick as much as Cathy.

'You only live once, Mr Sutcliff,' she answered as a titter wriggled free from her rosebud-shaped lips.

'The things you've been telling me are hard to believe,' Nick said, directing his remarks towards Lloyd, 'not so much about the sales figures as about your company's structure. Has anyone ever suggested any change?'

'There have been murmurs from time to time, but everyone seems relatively content with things as they are.'

'Content doesn't make greatness. Do you want to achieve greatness or do you want to be content?' Nick was remembering Lloyd's earlier comments about his sales managers feeling secure with their salaries, company cars and bonuses.

'Well, obviously we want to achieve greatness or you wouldn't be here.'

'Good. Do you know what I earned last year? I mean net earnings after I paid my staff and office expenses? Six hundred thousand dollars.'

Both Lloyd and Cathy's eyes widened.

'And that's without any salary or company car. I simply live off a cut of what my sales people make. The way I figure it, I can't recruit people into a commission-only job if I'm not prepared to take the same risks as they are. Higher risks equal higher returns; if you're any good, that is. How do you think your people would feel about that?'

Lloyd threw his head back and laughed. 'If we make comments about taking away our managers' salaries and replacing them with overriding commission and then tell them that they have to pay all their own expenses, I think they'd all quit.'

'Not if it's packaged and sold properly. They will have to convince themselves, as well as you, that they are actually worth what they are being paid.'

Cathy was hungry for information. Her warm brown eyes gleamed with enthusiasm for Nick's idea. 'It's inspired. Nick's quite right. Why should the sales managers be on salaries when their agents aren't?'

Lloyd frowned at her impulsive acceptance of Nick's suggestion.

Nick's attention darted discreetly back and forth. He registered Lloyd's frown but also noticed Cathy's hair catch the light as she tossed it away from her desirable breast and behind her ear. The urge to ravish her hit him hard. He forced it down with a scowl.

'I'm sure many of the managers you have right now would give knee-jerk reaction to this idea,' Nick admitted. 'So, get rid of them. This is one tough, son-of-a-bitch industry. We can't afford to give charity to those who aren't recruiting, or to those who aren't making recruited agents sell like there's no tomorrow.' Nick reached for one of his cigarettes and lit it, allowing his English colleagues' time to consider an answer.

'If you don't mind my saying so, I feel it would be a bit foolhardy to just try to push such a radical change on the organisation.'

'I agree,' Nick conceded. 'We can't change things overnight, I'm just giving you some food for thought. I'll be gone in a month, so I suggest you listen to as many ideas as you can in that time. I'd like to be gone but not forgotten – I want to leave you with something that will help change Winston Life for the better.'

'I see your point.' Lloyd rubbed his chin reflectively. 'We both know that Winston Life needs a lift. Let's talk about this in more detail in my office tomorrow.'

'Excellent,' Nick answered, cheerfully.

'Nick,' Cathy said, her speech becoming thicker with each glass of wine. 'They call you the manager's manager. How do you do it? How do you manage so many people and have them all producing so far above the average?'

'Damn hard work, my dear.'

She hated the patronising way he said, 'my dear', but decided it was wise to let it go.

'I have to constantly keep my eyes out for new recruits, new ideas, new products, system changes, and wean out those who are becoming ineffectual. It's a jungle out there. Survival of the fittest; no compassion.' He looked in her eyes for a reaction.

'But aren't we in the business of selling compassion?' she asked as Lloyd nodded in agreement with her.

'Exactly!' Nick pounded his fist on the table, causing several of the other diners to turn their heads in astonishment at such an outburst. 'We sell compassion. If we care at all about the people we are selling to, it is our duty to make sure that those selling it don't ever give up. People don't like to buy life insurance; they don't even like to talk about it. It is our duty to make them, and it's a goddam unpleasant duty. But if we don't, then we are personally responsible for all the wives and children who are left in financial hardship when it could have been avoided. No family ever went bankrupt because they paid for life insurance, but plenty went bankrupt because they didn't.'

Nick had his audience in the palm of his hand. The trouble with the young and the rich, he decided, was not that they took their position and their living standards for granted but that they couldn't comprehend that money was a true catalyst to power and because of this, a frightening thing.

Nick leaned over the table to give emphasis to his next statement, without embarrassingly pounding the table again. Lloyd and Cathy watched his movements with as much curiosity as concern.

'We have to succeed if we are to get what we want. It is our moral obligation to the community, as well as to ourselves.'

Lloyd's voice was in low-gear alarm as he spoke. 'Just what is it you want?'

'Immortality,' Nick answered simply.

'I beg your pardon?'

'The LMA and I; we want the same thing. Immortality, by changing the industry to become one that people will speak of with pride.'

'You've got a long way to go,' Cathy said, noticing her glass was once again empty.

'I think that's enough business for one night.' Lloyd folded his napkin and placed it neatly on the table indicating that the topic of conversation was closed.

'But Mr Sutcliff, Nick's only here for a short while and

I, for one, want to hear everything he's got to say.'

Nick smiled, displaying his nicotine-stained teeth in a wide, triumphant manner.

'Tomorrow, Cathy,' said Lloyd. 'I have a long drive home to Surrey and I'm sure Nick will want to get some rest before his interrogation continues. I'll drop you both at the Hilton. You should be able to get a taxi home from there without any difficulty.'

*

Cathy pulled her coat tightly around herself to ward off the chill in the night air. Glancing at her watch, she realised it was only eleven o'clock. She wished Lloyd had not decided to go home so early. For all Cathy knew she would never get another opportunity to talk to Nick Abbott. There was no particular reason for her to think that, but instinct told her that she must make the very most of this man while she had the chance. She had spent several weeks familiarising herself with Nick's work before he arrived, so as to be able to make the appropriate intelligent comments. She let her imagination run riot as she pictured the rewards an upwardly mobile career would bring. A fast red sports car, an apartment in Mayfair, maybe even membership at Annabel's. Cathy knew that tomorrow Nick would be in meetings and then at the annual dinner. She had to arrange an invitation for herself to that dinner.

Nick watched the young woman in silence from his position at the Hilton's entrance. If she intended to stay and talk to him, it certainly wasn't evident.

What was it she had said over dinner? 'Nick's only here for a short while and I, for one, want to hear everything he has to say.' Damn English, he thought, she must be waiting for a proper invitation.

Just as a cab arrived, and Cathy stepped towards it, Nick

asked her if she'd like to come in for a nightcap.

'You can continue your interrogation if you wish.' He smiled disarmingly.

She turned to the porter who had hailed the cab. 'I won't be needing this just yet, thank you.'

'Very good, madam,' he answered mechanically.

Nick tipped him for his efforts and directed Cathy to the rooftop bar. He chose a corner table with a breathtaking view of London's shimmering lights.

'Would you like another Manhattan?' he asked.

'No, thank you. A G&T will do nicely.'

Placing her handbag by the side of her chair, Cathy tried to remember all the questions she had so carefully planned.

'So are you going to tell me the secret?' she asked, trying to probe as subtly as she could.

'What secret?'

'Everyone has their own little success secret. What's yours?'

'Ah, well. If I told you that, it wouldn't be a secret any more, would it?'

'You're teasing me.'

'There is no secret, Cathy. Just a balance. Hard work, tough decisions and taking some time out to smell the roses along the way. What does Cathy Williams do when she takes time out?'

'Apart from smelling roses?' She repeated his words to give her time to think of something suitable in response. She was unprepared for the conversation to change from business to personal matters. She wanted only to pick the American's brains and impress him with hers, but if he wanted to know about her personal life to set the scene, she supposed she could oblige.

'I go to Stringers sometimes, and I quite like the restaurants around Covent Garden. TGI Friday is always good for some casual fun.'

'Stringers? TGI Friday? What language are you speaking?'

'I'm sorry,' she laughed, with a coquettish tilt of her head. 'Stringfellows nightclub and the restaurant called Thank God It's Friday.'

'Oh.' He paused longer than necessary before speaking again.

Cathy looked around the room at the other people all deep in conversation and wished desperately she could think of something to say to break the silence.

Why did he look at her that way? Although, Cathy told herself, a man who had helped so many succeed couldn't be all bad, she couldn't quite relax in his company.

'My man,' Nick called to a plump, Spanish-looking waiter across the crowded room. 'Do you have any Chesterfield cigarettes?'

'No sir, that's not a brand we carry.'

'I see. Thank you.' Turning to Cathy, Nick sighed. 'I'm sorry, I'm out of cigarettes. I have some of my brand in my room. If you don't mind waiting for me, I'll go and get them.'

'Not at all.'

'Or,' he added, as he stood to leave, 'we could finish our drinks in the Presidential Suite if you prefer?'

Her guard was down. The late hour, the wine and the intoxicating company combined to confuse her. Was that a pass? No. It was quite normal for VIPs to have their business conversations in their suites, everyone knew that. Anyway, she'd always wondered what the Presidential Suite looked like.

'That's sounds fine.' The words escaped from her lips before she had decided on the prudence of such a move.

Nick moved nonchalantly, knowing Cathy had passed the point of no return.

Still concerned about her possible indiscretion, Cathy

headed for the sole armchair in his suite. Nick could not allow this. Walking sufficiently faster than her to get to the chair first, he stood in front of it unwrapping his new packet of cigarettes; just until Cathy was comfortable on the settee.

'What would you like to drink?' he asked, moving towards his minibar.

'Just a mineral water, thank you.'

Handing Cathy the drink, Nick joined her on the settee leaving enough space between them for her to be at ease.

Quietly Nick lit his cigarette, leaving Cathy, once again, to wrestle with topics of conversation. Nick listened patiently to an assortment of subjects from advertising to company structure, until the arousal he'd been feeling since his first glimpse of Cathy Williams overpowered him. He had to satisfy it. His eyes didn't waver from hers as he slowly traced the shape of her mouth with his thumb. When her lips trembled apart he lowered his head, his intent exposed. Cathy couldn't think, much less move or speak. Before she could dredge up a single word of protest his lips covered hers in slow, drugged kisses, sending her head into a spin. Her fingers tightened on her glass. The breath she had been unaware of holding shuddered out as his clever tongue teased its way between her lips. As Nick found his way around her, she felt a charge of adrenaline, then numbness. She tried to pull away, at least she thought she did. Nick's hold was firm. Not harsh, but firm, and for eternal moments unrelenting.

As he loosened his grip to allow Cathy a few seconds to consider what had happened, Nick saw the shock but also the satisfaction. He knew what Cathy wanted and what she would do to get it.

'This is too fast,' she said unsteadily.

'We don't have a lot of time. You said so yourself.'

With that, he pulled Cathy towards him again. This time

she didn't try to pull away. Her strong will had fallen limp. Her intent to reject this man withered with the wonderful tingling sensation pulsing through her. Was it the thrill of having a powerful man want her? she wondered. Or was it the immoral thought that an affair might assist her upwardly mobile career?

Slowly Nick eased his hand down the left side of her body, lingering to squeeze her delightfully soft breast. Feathering his hand towards her thigh he unfastened her suspenders while kissing her lily-white neck. Her head was thrown back, revealing her throat in the way so many animals do in surrender. Her eyes were closed, her breathing rapid and she smelled like a ripe blossom about to fall.

Nick didn't take long to expertly remove both sets of clothing and roll their naked bodies on to the floor. He took a long look at her firm, pale body and felt the strength of absolute control. Pert little breasts faced him, provoking in him an instinctive reaction to lick one nipple then the other. Her body rhythmically followed his every movement. Rolling on to his back, Nick pulled Cathy on top of him.

'I want *you* to do it to *me*, Cathy Williams.'

She felt overwhelmed by a strange wildness of mind and body. Awaking from her trance-like state long enough to register the meaning of Nick's words, she softly directed him inside. Nick grasped her breasts as she gyrated. She wanted to please him more than be pleased. Angling herself into the proper position, she strove to engulf her new lover.

Suddenly Nick pushed her away and on to her belly, thrusting himself back inside. His actions shocked her. For a moment Cathy longed to be back in the security of her flat.

'Do you want it, Cathy Williams? Tell me when you want it.' His tone was deliberately forceful, almost threatening. Sliding his hands underneath her, he clutched both nipples, causing her to scream. He felt the primitive side of his nature take over any conscious thought. The primeval power swelled inside him, his heart racing with a hungry desire for the kill. Something dangerous flickered in his darkened eyes; his all-seeing eyes which Nick knew inspired both fear and fascination in his prey. Outside the wind howled as if some lost spirit cried a warning. He dug his fingers deep in her hips to keep her moving with him before the power took them both. In that instant Nick became Cathy's new master.

*

Nick held back a corner of the dining-room curtains to reveal a jet-black sky, last night's memories of Cathy Williams still vivid in his mind. Warm air rushed from a vent filling the room with a dry heat, yet the window was cold to the touch. Outside Nick could see tiny beads of rain clinging to the glass and brightly coloured vehicle lights scurrying around Park Lane. He hadn't adjusted to the new time zone and was finding sleep difficult.

Over a cup of black coffee he formulated his strategy for the day ahead. Lloyd had a meeting booked with his number one sales manager at ten o'clock. Nick tried to imagine what this new Englishman would be like. Perhaps he would be like Lloyd, conservative and resistant to change despite the fact that he knew it was necessary. Or perhaps he would be more of a streetwise cockney. That type of person Nick knew he could identify with. They were used to taking risks to survive and would be easily convinced that the Nick Abbott way was right.

All of these diversions, however, could not cloud the nagging concern for his son. James had simply disappeared and despite using every contact at his disposal, Nick had been unable to locate him. He found himself wondering about James's safety. If he was all right, surely he would have tried to make contact, even if only to get revenge for his friend's death. Nick almost welcomed the idea of an attack from his son, at least then he would know James was alive.

'Here you are, old boy. I brought you your very own umbrella.' Lloyd, looking dapper despite being moderately moist, handed Nick a black rolled-up umbrella.

'Thanks. This could well be the most useful gift anyone has ever given me. Next you'll have me wearing a bowler hat.'

Lloyd smiled quietly to himself at the idea.

'So tell me about this Arthur Webb we are about to visit.'

'Arthur's a good man. He's been with us four years and comes from a background in wine sales. He manages the north London team and, although the industry was totally foreign to him, he seems to have taken to it like a duck to water.'

Nick absorbed some of Lloyd's commentary but discarded most of it as superfluous. Nick realised Arthur's background in a totally different industry could have been a worthwhile fact, had it been more recent. After four years under Lloyd's guidance, however, and producing well by their standards, Nick felt he might as well be starting from square one.

The entrance to Winston Life's north London office was about what Nick had imagined. The ceilings were high, the main doors thick and the walls covered with posters of Cathy's PR campaigns. There were blue fabric chairs for visitors to sit in either side of a table strewn with financial magazines. Behind the reception desk Nick could see a corridor with many doors leading to offices. All were closed. He presumed they housed sales agents hard at work on their phone calls. This was all as it should be.

The girl at reception had a sweet, fresh face and neatly

tied back blonde hair.

'Hello, Joanne. Will you kindly tell Mr Webb that we are here,' Lloyd ordered.

'Certainly, Mr Sutcliff.'

Nick couldn't quite place her accent. It wasn't like Lloyd's, a product of the public school system, but it wasn't cockney either. Despite this, it was unmistakably English. Nick observed that Lloyd always used their Christian names when talking to subordinates, yet they called him Mr Sutcliff. It was a good measure of respect. Nick approved.

'Ah, Arthur. Good to see you. I would like to introduce you to Nick Abbott, from New York.'

A man, shorter and stockier than Lloyd, with a handlebar moustache of brown matted hair, gave a broad smile. It was the well-practised smile of a salesman with a solid handshake to match.

'Delighted to meet you. I've heard so much about you. Come into the boardroom. We can talk in there. Would you like some tea?'

'Coffee would be nice,' Nick answered.

'Yes, coffee; of course. Joanne, would you arrange some tea and coffee, please?'

The boardroom's white walls reflected the bright fluorescent lighting, giving it an almost sterile atmosphere. In the corner of the room stood a whiteboard with details of the targets for Webb's sales team and comments by the side showing where each agent stood in relation to target.

Making a mental note of the data unwittingly handed to him by Webb, Nick started doing some calculations for the meeting.

'Lloyd tells me you're the number one sales manager of Winston Life. You must be very proud of your achievements here,' Nick began.

'Yes, I am. Lloyd gave me a team of half a dozen

average agents and we've grown to a team of twenty, with two in the top ten for the UK.'

'Not bad.' Nick paused. 'But not good enough.'

'I beg your pardon.' Indignity washed across Webb's face. He couldn't allow himself to be undermined in front of Lloyd Sutcliff. Perhaps the unfamiliar American style was not supposed to be as harsh as it sounded. That was not unreasonable, but although he tried, Webb couldn't believe that.

Is Nick Abbott here to give advice or to cut me to ribbons? Arthur wondered. At the thought Webb felt a flutter against his ribcage like a trapped bird trying to escape.

'I manage twenty-five sales managers and under them six hundred agents,' Nick announced. 'Our annual recruiting average is seven agents per manager, to allow for natural attrition. This is a minimum standard. Any less than that and we're going backwards. For example, just how many of your twenty agents are producing above average standards right now?'

Arrogant Yank, Lloyd thought, without a trace of emotion on his face.

Webb had a lump in his throat. In his confusion he tried to recall whether it was nine or ten agents. Ten. Yes, it was definitely ten.

'Fifty per cent of the team are above average, and of the other half, five are rookies,' Webb answered, realising he should have taken the reports of the American's tactics seriously.

'My man, if you have agents who aren't producing satisfactory results within six months, you get rid of them. Have you worked out what your time is worth per hour?' Nick asked.

'Well, er.'

'You must know this stuff. How much does each agent earn you per hour versus how many hours do you have to put into that agent to develop him? Are these figures up to date?' Nick moved towards the whiteboard pointing to the lower end of the agents' earnings.

'Yes,' Webb answered quietly.

'Well, I suggest you do two things. Step up your recruiting programme and call a team meeting.'

Webb tried to think. What did one order have to do with the other?

Nick wandered back to his chair, lit a cigarette and looked in Webb's eyes. Seeing the pensive consideration Webb was giving to Nick's words, Nick knew he would soon be hooked.

Damn, Webb thought, I deliberately placed the damn whiteboard in the boardroom to show off the figures of higher producing agents. Now my own ammunition has been turned against me.

'You know what sort of whiteboard I have in my boardroom?' Nick asked, in a mockingly compassionate voice. 'One with little red dots. Each red dot represents an agent. There is a line through the middle of the board. Agents above the line are producing well and no one, but no one, fucks with my little red dots. Agents who go below the line... *die.*' He emphasised the last word. Only after the word had left his lips did Nick remember the death of Ted Upton. Sometimes, he realised, his metaphors were so real. 'I don't care if he comes bleeding to me about an invalid mother who needs hospital treatment or he's going through a divorce. It's not my concern. My concern, and yours too, is making this business great.' Nick paused, looking away from the two men as he finished his cigarette. 'You know what I do?' He didn't wait for an answer. 'I get a pop gun from my desk' – he demonstrated the actions with the forefinger and thumb of his right hand – 'and *bang bang*, he's fired.'

Both Webb and Sutcliff were silent in disbelief.

'How long has this Freddie been with you?' Nick waved towards the lowest producing agent on Webb's board.

'Nearly a year.'

'Well, do you want some advice?'

Webb had to say yes, but he hated himself for it.

'I'm going to get you to fire him at the team meeting.'

Webb suddenly became hot and flustered. He felt quite sick at the thought of dismissing young Freddie in this way. Freddie had been a slow starter, but Webb knew not all good agents got off to a quick start. Although, Webb admitted to himself, he had harboured doubts about Freddie's future. He should have fired him before Nick Abbott came along. Too late for that now.

'The problem with most managers I meet,' Nick explained, 'is that they are too soft. They prefer to be seen as a pal rather than a leader. Which is it you want to be, Arthur, a pal or a leader?'

'You're right,' Webb reluctantly admitted, without answering the question. 'I can see now why you get paid the big bucks.'

'Yeah, well that's another thing we should look at. If I don't recruit, and my recruits don't sell, I don't eat. There's no salary and company car where I come from.'

The blood drained from Webb's face.

'Does that frighten you?'

'Well, er. No,' Webb pronounced the word 'no' firmly as if he just realised there was value in what Nick Abbott said.

After all, Webb thought, he is Nick Abbott. He is rich, successful and obviously the man to listen to. Damn being a pal, Nick is right.

'Just how does that work?' Webb enquired with a new-found strength.

Lloyd Sutcliff watched the verbal contest with growing concern. He doubted that Webb could ever adopt the harsh tactics of the American, but he could see now how Nick won all his battles.

The meeting of agents was called for four o'clock.

At four o'clock precisely Webb's team assembled. It reminded Nick of his own last team meeting which had been an absolute triumph. The pawn, Ted Upton, had reached an unfortunate end, but the sales had skyrocketed as a result.

Webb introduced Nick Abbott with the familiar build-up, to which Nick feigned embarrassment by looking first to the floor, then the ceiling and finally around the faces of anticipation in the gathering.

'Thank you, Arthur. I am very happy and honoured to be a guest in your fine country. I have only been here for two days and already I have learned many things. I have learned that Americans have to go through the aliens' channel at Heathrow. I didn't know that we'd turned green and grown antennae.'

The group laughed on cue.

'I have learned that to dine at Simpsons, one needs to give the impression that you have been freshly starched.' Nick shrugged and grinned at the memory of yesterday's lunch with Lloyd's managers, prompting further laughter. 'And I have learned that there are apparently some among us who do not take the business of selling life insurance seriously.' Nick leaned over the table, piercing each agent in turn with a challenging glare as the silence became suffocating.

'Let's take you as an example.' Nick pointed to an agent at random. 'What's the biggest policy you sold this week?'

A man around thirty years of age rose from his chair and stood a full six foot off the ground. He pulled at his right ear, tilting his head sideways, before answering. His greased-back black hair and brown eyes shone under the fluorescent lights.

'Fifty thousand pounds of life cover,' he answered with

a hint of an Indian accent.

'Not bad.' Nick's eyebrows rose. That was definitely a decent-sized policy, but he knew how to cut down its impressiveness. 'What was the mortgage of that family?'

'Ninety thousand,' the agent answered.

'So you sold an amount of insurance that wouldn't even cover the family home, never mind produce an income for the widow. Is that right?'

The agent's face reddened as Nick asked his next question.

'Why so little?'

'It was all the cover they wanted right now. They said they would build it up over time.'

'I see. If he died tomorrow would he need a will?'

'Of course.'

'Then he also needs adequate life insurance. You failed in your duty to sell the clients what they need. Instead you sold them what they wanted. There can be no justifiable reason on earth why your prospect doesn't buy the cover that he needs from you, unless' – Nick wrote the reasons on the whiteboard as he explained – 'a) you haven't explained to them properly what happens to a family when the breadwinner is prematurely removed from the scene; b) the breadwinner doesn't really love his dependants; c) you haven't explained properly just how much money is needed to keep dependants in their own financial world; or d) the breadwinner is lying to you about something. Arthur, would you take over?'

Webb went unhappily about the task that had been set to him, Lloyd carefully watching his manager act out the American's training.

'It appears some of you may need a refresher course in the basics...'

Webb discussed all the things he knew his agents already understood. He would have said anything to delay the inevitable moment.

Nick had discovered, through discussions with Webb, that young Freddie had sold a policy to a man with Aids without the due caution that had been taught in his rookie school. This fact, combined with Freddie's poor results, made him the perfect choice.

'When you are signing a client that you think is suspect, it is your duty to warn the underwriters if you believe there has not been full disclosure,' Webb reminded his team. 'Let them decide if further investigations are required. You have to know if your client is a man living with another man. If you push the policy through without comment, just to get your commission, I'm afraid you will find that you will pay the price. Freddie, would you please stand up.'

A young man, about twenty-two, stood up. He looked awkward. His manly spread had not yet caught up with his burst of height, making him appear gangly. His cropped blond hair was gelled in a modern style Nick didn't approve of for a sales agent. He looked more like a rock and roll star than a person selling financial futures.

'We all know Freddie.' Webb took a deep breath. 'Well, Freddie made the mistake of selling a policy like this. The person insured died of Aids eight months after taking out the policy. As a result, Winston Life is not honouring the contract. Legally speaking, the client did not fully disclose all relevant information and we are within our rights to refuse payment. However, the beneficiary, a dependent mother, is suing. We will win, of course, but this is going to cost us in legal fees, time for witnesses and, most of all, media coverage. This situation never should have happened and we cannot allow it ever to happen again. Freddie, I'm sorry, but this, combined with your level of production, is just not good enough. I'm afraid I am going to have to let you go.'

Meek words, Nick thought. He could have done better.

Nick looked around the table. Everyone seemed dumbfounded, glancing at one another in a state of shock, but none were courageous enough to look at Webb or Freddie.

'Just like that?' the cockney-accented Freddie blurted out in anger. 'I didn't know what I was doing back then. It's not fair. Christ, I'm allowed one mistake, aren't I?'

'One mistake, yes. But this is a whopper and your sales haven't convinced me that I should invest any more of my valuable time in putting you straight. It's over, Freddie. Your things have been put in a box by the front door. You can collect them on the way out.'

'Well, fuck you,' Freddie yelled. Before he left, Freddie took a long look at Nick Abbott. He realised the American had more to do with his dismissal than was immediately apparent. 'And fuck you too, Mr High-and-Bloody-Mighty Yank!'

Webb watched Freddie leave, surprised at his own sense of power. He hadn't liked the idea of a public dismissal, but now he had been blooded Webb felt almost ashamed at how good it made him feel. He was the one in control, not these nancy boys. He would show them how the Nick Abbott way was going to work in London. Now Webb too had a new master.

*

Nick draped a towel over his body and walked out of the shower. He had been very drunk the night before. Actually he had started drinking early in the afternoon at the Sutcliff's country residence and by midnight was so far gone that the inane ramblings of Lloyd Sutcliff didn't matter any more. It had been difficult to bounce back with a commanding air at the seminar that day, but somehow he had managed it. From his initial triumphs in England he spent most of the weekend analysing, to the best of his ability, the affairs of Winston Life. Now he was prepared to walk among his colleagues. It was clear to Nick there was little to learn from his London colleagues. The best way to take advantage of this stop was to convince them to try out a system he had long been convinced would work, but Gus would never allow implemented. Living off a cut of his agents' commissions was all very well if the commissions were realistic, he considered. Gus, however, refused to recognise what 'realistic' was. He branded Nick's ideas reckless, saying they would bankrupt the company. Nick was sure he was wrong, and Winston Life was just the place to prove it.

His ultimate goal never left his mind: to leave his mark wherever he went and find a product to revolutionise the industry. He kept notes of ideas that seemed plausible in his briefcase. He kept sensing the formula was nearly there, but always just out of reach. He'd be a legend in his own lifetime, and beyond. He could hear people talking about it; he could hear them now. He, Nick Abbott, would be the toast of the international insurance industry. These Limey bastards, with their highfalutin, condescending ways, would have old Nick to reckon with. He laughed out loud, feeling the full measure of his power.

'What's so funny?' Cathy asked, still wrapped in the sheets of Nick's bed.

'Nothing. Just an idea running through my mind.'

'A wicked one, I'll bet.'

'Not at all. If you must know, I'm putting a revolutionary new product together.'

'Really. Can you tell me about it?'

'Not yet, it's still under wraps.'

'I've had an idea for a new product for some time, but nobody seems to want to listen to me.'

'Really? I'll listen to you. But please, not like that. Put some clothes on first.' He theatrically covered his eyes.

'What's the matter? Do you find me too distracting?'
'Definitely.'

Cathy pulled on Nick's smoking jacket and jauntily took her place on the settee where their affair had begun.

Cathy was thrilled. At last someone was listening to her ideas, and what a person to have chosen to listen. She had it made, she knew it. It was only a matter of time now.

Nick needed to enlist Cathy's help before he left. What he had to ask of her would be difficult. For once he wished he had some old sage to turn to for advice. The words of Eddie Schwartz drifted through his mind. Eddie had been a scoundrel who had invented some of the most outrageous stories and techniques to get his sales. He remembered something Eddie had once said to an agent who had tried to mimic him and who'd been exposed unmercifully. 'Use part of the truth. See if it helps. Find some reason for what you're doing. Just enough to throw them off the scent.'

Nick had made lengthy oral and written recommendations to Lloyd. Unfortunately for Lloyd, he was not entirely convinced. Arthur Webb, on the other hand, was performing like a man possessed. He liked his new-found power and had his agents standing to attention like little soldiers. Lloyd had expressed his concern to Nick about the transformation but Nick explained to Lloyd that his concern would go away when production began to double.

It was so wonderfully self-indulgent to stand back and watch a master plan coming together. Nick couldn't afford to leave the impending restructure in the hands of one, less than committed, individual. Cathy was going to have to be put to work.

Cathy wallowed in the attention lavished on her by Nick. She knew she shouldn't become emotionally involved, and had tried desperately not to, but he was so fascinating, so enlightened. He was just plain inspirational and, she reasoned, why shouldn't she take advantage of the situation?

'There's something I must discuss with you,' Nick began. 'I want to talk to you about the recommendations I've made to Lloyd.'

'Oh.'

Cathy was flattered to be treated with such confidence. He must be impressed with my ideas to treat me with such privileged information, she decided. She considered her sentiments and questioned how much of her reasoning was purely justification for her somewhat dubious moral behaviour with this man. If he left her in a position of power, what did it matter?

'This has been a very memorable month for me – in many ways,' Nick said, as if making a confession to Cathy. 'I want to make sure when I leave here that everybody is better off than they were a month ago. In helping me achieve that goal, you, Cathy Williams, will be ensuring that you are one of those who will be better off. Much better off.'

'I'm listening.'

'I want you to start conducting a survey of all the sales teams. Ask them what useful information they received from my visit, what changes they would like to see as a result, who they are comfortable dealing with at Winston Life, and who they are not. And the reasons why. When you've completed the survey, I want you to prepare a report and present it to the board, quite independently of what Lloyd is preparing.

'I've been talking to the agents. They like you and they respect you. What's more important is that the board knows that the agents like and respect you. Your survey findings will cement this, believe me. If the board members see the same recommendations coming in from every angle, they will have to adopt them. Not only that, but they will have to recognise you for acting on your own initiative, for being intelligent and observant enough to have grasped the importance of what these changes will mean and for having the courage to stand up and say so. How do you feel about that?'

'I'm honoured that you have thought of me for this. I'll be more than happy to do it, but it's a stuffy old board. Lloyd holds the most sway. I'm not sure how seriously the members are going to take me.'

'But this is my whole point, love. You're not going to be on your own. There'll be Webb, and others. United you'll stand. It's the only way to be sure. You know how I feel about you. I respect you, I like you, and I want to see you get ahead. Winston Life is going nowhere at the moment. This could be your big chance to take the company to the top, with you as one of the pilots. How does that make you feel?'

'Powerful.'

'Good, isn't it?' He didn't wait for an answer. 'Tell me how you feel about Lloyd; I mean really feel.'

'I told you, he was my mentor.'

'Yes, I know that. But that was four years ago. What about now?'

'He's a nice man...'

There was that word 'nice'. God how Nick hated it.

'We don't have enough to do with one another any more for me to really think about it.'

'Well, you may have to think about it and you may have to have something to do with him. You want to be international public relations manager, right?'

'I'd love it.'

'Who or what stands in your way right now?'

'Neville Farnsworth, for a start.'

'And how long has Neville been international public relations manager for?'

'Five years.'

'So don't you think he might be looking for greener pastures by now too?'

'I suppose. But where can he go?'

'How about international operations manager?'

'But we don't have an international operations manager.'

'Not yet, you don't. My recommendations take some of the power away from the current general manager of operations. I believe there should be an operations manager in each country, not just one, and that each operations manager should report to an international operations manager, instead of Lloyd alone reporting direct to the board. It will give a broader and more accurate perspective of what the organisation really needs. It also makes the operations managers more effective because they are more accountable. There will be fewer places to hide.'

'Lloyd's not going to like that.'

'I'm not here to be popular. I'm here to do a job.'

'I see. Of course, you're right. Poor Lloyd.'

'Not poor Lloyd,' Nick said, pounding his fist on the table.

The shock caused Cathy's spine to straighten and her lips to part.

'If Lloyd can do a good enough job in his new role, he'll be earning more money than he is now. All my recommendations carry a strong incentive-based salary package for the non-sales staff.'

'But how do you imagine you'll get Lloyd to present the same proposal as me? He's not going to recommend a change that downgrades his own responsibilities.'

'He has to submit something. It's expected of him. He may try to water it down but he's not going to be able to sufficiently disguise it as to take away from the power of the true recommendations – the ones you are going to put forward. Do you think you can handle it?'

'You'd better explain to me exactly how this is going to work.'

Nick smiled to himself, thinking how perfect she was. Cathy was quite astute. It didn't take Nick long to explain the intricacies of the ploys she needed to use. He felt confident that she would be able to pull it off.

*

'Would you like to order something from room service?' Nick asked.

'Um, no, later.'

Cathy was reading through her notes while Nick poured a couple of cognacs. He stretched his back to relieve the stiffness of a two-hour tutorial.

Without a warning Norma slipped into Nick's mind. He remembered her saying that all men had a spark of goodness in them. He found himself fantasising about what his life would have been like if Norma was still alive. Why did she have to change so dramatically from the wide-eyed teenager who loved him so? Why did she have to make stupid threats against his business? He had loved her, he was convinced of that, and yet she had threatened to tell influential people terrible things about his past; to petition for fifty per cent of his empire. It had been too horrible to contemplate.

Power was undoubtedly the ultimate aphrodisiac, Nick decided. As tired as he was from giving lessons in corporate manipulation, the arousal Cathy created in him still stirred. Returning to the dining area, Nick placed Cathy's cognac in the middle of her notes. Business was terminated.

Despite Cathy's enthusiasm and desire to please, Nick felt less than satisfied with their lovemaking for the first time. He decided to take another shower to clear his head.

He let the harsh spray beat down on his face until the tiny blasts of water hurt his skin. He adjusted the faucets so that the water became more gentle, like a woman's caress. He turned to let the water run down his back. His eyes were closed, but he instinctively knew he was no longer alone.

Nick felt a surge of strength as he pulled Cathy towards him. The process had become automatic but nonetheless still pleasurable. He lowered his fingers inside her womanly warmth as beads of tepid water trickled down them. Both bodies gleamed as though they were sprinkled with morning dew. At that moment Nick knew what he wanted.

Lifting both hands on to Cathy's shoulders, he exerted just enough pressure to give her the message. Slowly she lowered herself to her knees, relaxed her throat muscles and swallowed.

He held Cathy's head gently, throbbing with delight at her every move. The scene perversely reminded him of a game of Roman gladiators. The controlling Romans enjoyed the kill with complacency for the foreplay. The gladiators themselves weren't important. They weren't even considered humans, just well-trained amusements for the rich and powerful to enjoy. Two men, who trained side by side for months, never daring to befriend one another, knowing that one day they would meet in the arena and have to fight. To kill or be killed. These well-trained amusements of the rich.

Just like you, Cathy, my little gladiator, Nick said to himself as he lowered her to the floor, parted her legs and went in for the kill.

Chapter Three

Tom Weinstein sat in his Johannesburg office looking at the corporate jungle around him. The only thing Tom could see through his window was towering office block after towering office block.

For a continent covered with some of the most spectacular scenery on earth, he mused, it is not much of a view. Tom smiled to himself as he considered the brutality of both jungles. Whether it was the jungle of the animals or the jungle of the corporate giants, the same basic rule still applied: survival of the fittest. He considered this very philosophical observation as he thought about Nick Abbott's forthcoming meeting with Phil Langdon-Smythe.

Tom remembered the day he first met Phil Langdon-Smythe. It had been at a recruiting seminar Tom had organised; a rusty effort back in the early days when Tom was still experimenting with his own techniques. Phil had attended the full day's programme, his eyes wide and bloodshot. Tom had arrived that morning, after a day of recruiting in Pretoria. From the moment they met the chemistry was there. Phil's enthusiasm was unparalleled but it hid a deep pragmatism which became evident as he grew in years and accomplishment. They fought side by side for six years until the little brokerage house known as Sovereign Finance had challenged and beaten every rival in its path. In the dusk, when the war was won, those rivals still active had either joined ranks with the new Sovereign Life or quit the business to start a career in something less aggressive. Tom and Phil had helped each other out of the woods of anonymity and into the history books.

'Blood brothers, whether you like it or not,' Tom had proclaimed, grinning at Phil.

They had been occupying the number one position for two years now but both men knew their time in South Africa was running out. From his file, Tom had noted that Phil had relatives in Australia. From this single piece of information, Tom had formed a plan to take their expertise and leave this place of racial hatred to build again in a fertile, naive economy which was ripe for the picking.

As the descendant of a Jewish family, Tom understood only too well what racial hatred could develop into. He had no intention of following the fate of his forefathers. The only difference in South Africa was that this hatred had nothing to do with Jews. This time it was simply blacks against whites. It will be a bloody battle, Tom thought, and no mistake. Already there were tales of servants turning on white boss men. Rapes and robberies; the blacks were getting braver by the day. The time was drawing near when he knew they must leave.

So Phil and Tom hunted together as they had fought: side by side. They referred to their quiet evenings of planning, and drinking cognac, as directors' meetings. It used to amuse Phil to adopt various roles for different circumstances. In front of the financial giants they needed to impress for loans, Phil would slip into the 'Persuader mode' calling Tom names like international financial expert and the company crusher and acting out a charade of some bygone colonial era.

'Don't be a fool. You demean yourself,' Tom protested at first.

'It's what these idiots expect,' Phil had reasoned. 'We are selling them an illusion. They are lending us money to build a vision, your vision. You have to be seen as the all-powerful master with his intelligent, but nonetheless obedient and hero-worshipping men behind him.'

Tom had reluctantly gone along with the act.

When they were alone, Phil changed into '*Homo sapiens* mode' and became the thoughtful, intelligent educated man he truly was; each of them perfectly at ease in the company of the other.

'Look Tom, don't worry too much about losing that opportunity with Mutual Life of Australia. We'll find another way in,' Phil assured him.

'Give me some idea, some measure of comfort. I could do with it,' Tom answered pensively.

'We could try for the second largest company in Australia, instead.'

'No good.' Tom shook his head. 'After this fiasco, I'll have the mark of the beast on me.'

'We'll apply again, in my name,' Phil suggested, and smiled mischievously. 'I'd make you one of my directors and you can call me boss.'

They laughed together, the mood lightening, and when Tom left Phil that night he felt cheerful and optimistic for the first time in days. Phil had the power to effect that transformation in him. Tom had gone home and thought about the problem over and over until a flash of lightning hit him and he knew he had the answer.

*

The dry heat of South Africa was a welcome change from the cold, wet London weather for Nick. Checking into the Carlton Centre, he was impressed by the massive entrance.

The receptionist, a blonde girl with skinny hips and a short pointed nose, processed Nick's paperwork while he flicked through the hotel brochure. Nick noticed the hotel had a gym, a spa, a health club, many shops, restaurants and other facilities. The Carlton was known as the finest in Johannesburg. Every facility the weary traveller could conceivably desire.

Moses, Tom's driver, helped Nick get settled. Nick looked at the shorter-than-average black man, who grinned at him incessantly with a row of Cheshire cat teeth, and for a few moments his thoughts wavered. He allowed himself to drift back in time to when slaves were the expected accessories in a civilised American's household. He fixed his stare on Moses. His gaze was long, steady and very much alert. To the observer, the two appeared to be nothing more than a boss and his staff member, pausing before the next orders were given. Secretly, however, Nick yearned for the days when a man was master of all he surveyed, only having to raise his hand and know that his every order would be obeyed.

'Is there any thing else you require?' Moses asked.

'No. That will be all,' Nick answered thoughtfully. He added curiously, 'Does Weinstein look after you properly?'

'Oh, yes. He's a good man. Tough but fair. You'll see when you meet him. It's something you can feel in his presence.'

Nick thought he might be sick. The interminable list of Tom Weinstein's qualities now had 'compassionate' added to it. It was infuriating. He wondered why people were so impressed with this man. It disturbed Nick deeply to think that there might be another who possessed the same charismatic leadership qualities that he did. He had been looking forward to meeting this Tom Weinstein to pick his brains, but seeing Moses' reaction actually made Nick feel jealous. He had to admit it; that was the word, jealous. How could one man have it all? Compassion, charisma, wealth, success. There had to be a weak link. I have to find out the useful qualities of this man, Nick discerned, also what is weak and exploitable. Nick knew he must acquire this knowledge quickly.

Nick dismissed Moses with an acceptable tip and fell on

to his bed. Gratefully he realised that sleep was coming on. It had been days and weeks filled with never-ending pressure. He slowly removed his tie and unfastened his buttons. Nick knew he had to gather his senses as best he could. Weinstein would have to be handled with both respect and caution.

It was a couple of hours later when Nick awoke. He noticed the ambience of his suite for the first time. There were arrangements of proteas in several strategic locations. To Nick the protea, the national flower of South Africa, had an appearance as harsh as the accent of the land. The protea had none of the delicacy of a carnation or a rose; it looked more masculine than feminine. With dark brown flanks and deep pink internal flesh, they looked imposing, stern and somehow forceful.

Reading the day's headlines in the *Star* newspaper, Nick could see hints of the racial trouble Tom had briefly spoken of during their telephone conversation.

If Tom wants to leave South Africa, perhaps I can help him, Nick thought. Perhaps this can be the leverage point to bargain from if, indeed, any bargaining is to be necessary.

The paper was filled with stories of coups in neighbouring black nations and diabolical atrocities being inflicted on one tribe by another. Aids was rife in Africa; famine raged in Ethiopia, Angola and Mozambique; the governments of Uganda and Zambia were a farce; and the corruption across the entire continent was staggering. Nick had quite an unpleasant picture of this land by the time Tom arrived for drinks at three o'clock.

A burst of sunlight caught the dial of Nick's Rolex, shooting bursts of brightly coloured lights around the room, as probing conversation began from both sides.

'There are many things we must discuss while you are in Jo'burg,' Tom began. 'It will be a busy working schedule but I have allowed you some time to see the sights. We can't let you leave Africa without visiting a safari park, now can we? From LMA's viewpoint, however, you are going to be most interested in Phil Langdon-Smythe. I have arranged a meeting for you tomorrow. He can explain to you why his recruits' survival rate is so high.'

'And what is it you attribute *your* success to, Tom?' Nick asked.

'Me? I'm an actuary by training and a salesman by nature.'

'What a combination,' Nick announced with raised eyebrows.

'Ya. A winning combination.'

It was hard for Nick to imagine the two qualities in the one man. An actuary was often described as an accountant without personality. Algy was the actuarial type, not Tom. But if it was possible to combine that skill with a salesman's personality, Nick could understand why Tom reached the top so quickly. He also understood how Tom could be useful, although he realised he would have to disguise his questions well. A new product, perhaps even Cathy's, could be part formulated before he returned to New York. He'd pick Tom's actuarial brains and make notes to give the product a kick-start when he returned. What a bonus. Nick smiled.

*

Work began at eight thirty on Friday morning. Phil Langdon-Smythe was not at all what Nick had pictured. He was a tall skinny man with an absurd grin. His skin was pitted and dull but his bespectacled dark brown eyes shone with bright enthusiasm; the sort of enthusiasm one might have expected in a man many years Phil's junior. His office was neat and precise. All his furnishings were of a light colour and easily cleanable texture: grey Formica and dusky pink fabrics.

Phil had barely said hello when he charged headlong into business conversation. Tom stood by like the proud father, watching the conversation as Nick tried to throw in a question here and there. It was quite a different situation for Nick from the one in Arthur Webb's boardroom a month ago.

'You see, it's not in the recruiting,' Phil began. 'Of course, that's important. But it's the way you select an agent from your batch of recruits that is vital. This is where people fall down. They put all recruits on, to give them a chance, and simply hope that some of them stick. This is how I do it.'

Phil grabbed some scrap paper and a pen and drew pictures of his sentences as they were formed. This was the only way Phil had of slowing his speech: pictorial aids to assist the comprehension of the student.

Nick listened intently. He couldn't remember when he had last been so stimulated by the intelligence of another man. He could see why Sovereign Life's position was secure with men like Phil and Tom at the helm: highly motivated, quick-witted, sales-orientated and financially aware. Nick wasn't going to be able to tell these two very much. He decided to treat the visit as pure observation. It would be futile to try to advise such experts by talking about company structure or product development.

Nick let Phil finish his story, taking appropriate notes where he saw it was possible to refine his own recruitment and selection programme. The building blocks of Nick's master plan were slotting, one by one, neatly into place.

Nick had an adaptation of East West's agency system, altered to pay higher commission than that currently offered and increasing the responsibility of sales managers to pay all their running costs to compensate. This was the Nick Abbott system, the one he had so confidently recommended for Winston Life. One that rewarded those who dared to be different and, if necessary, ruthless.

It is the only business in the world, Nick told himself, where you need no capital and no expertise to start out. The life insurance company will give a low interest loan to buy a car, a computer and the other equipment necessary to start a business. The life insurance company will train you in the products and their sales techniques. And the life insurance company will pay a percentage of what agents earn in commission. East West had adopted this system some years ago, but Nick had noted it could be improved upon. Why pay fifty per cent commission when the profits showed that they could clearly afford seventy-five? Winston Life would be a good testing ground to see if his theories would work. On top of this, Phil had handed him the finishing touches to a selection programme which would wean out the Ted Uptons of this world before they became a liability. Excellent. Nick just needed to refine his revolutionary product and the package would be complete.

'Tell me about your retirement planning product. What commission does it pay?' Nick asked casually.

'Fifty per cent in year one, dropping to ten per cent in years two and three, and five per cent every year thereafter,' Phil explained.

'I see. And what if somebody wants to stop paying for a while?'

'We cancel their policy. Why, what would you do?'

'I was just wondering about your flexible payment programme.'

'What flexible payment programme?'

Good, Nick smiled, Phil has taken the bait. Nick knew that if he made it sound as though such a product already existed, Phil would quickly strive to find a way to make it work within his products, without realising it was a revolutionary new idea.

'Back in the States we have a product where a client can stop payments for up to two years and, if the payments are to cease permanently thereafter, we can change the type of contract without letting it lapse. It was originally conceived because we recognised the female market's needs to keep a policy going during maternity leave, and thereafter if they decide not to return to work. Why should we forfeit a policy just because a woman decides to have a child and can no longer afford to pay premiums? How do you think that could work with your products?'

Tom Weinstein observed both the question and Phil's response with an uneasy quiet. You're a clever man, Nick Abbott, Tom thought. And Phil, you are just that little bit too keen.

Tom seated himself across the table in a position to watch the body language of both men. He drank a cup of coffee in silence and watched Nick's face as Phil floundered with the concept this American had thrown him. Tom suspected Nick was hoping he would throw in a few comments of his own. Instead Tom listened attentively as he rolled the bitter taste of coffee over his tongue.

'Phil, could I have a word with you?' Tom said quietly, when he'd heard enough.

This Nick Abbott is trying to pick our brains for his own gain, not that of LMA. Tom was quite sure. He took Phil outside, excusing himself by explaining there was an earlier message he should have given to Phil and it had slipped his mind until that moment. Shutting Phil's office door, he spoke in hushed tones.

'Phil, I want you to play with this idea for a while, but don't give anything away. Not yet, anyway.'

'What have you got on your mind?'

'It occurs to me that we have more professional knowledge to offer Nick Abbott than he has to offer us. But he could be useful in other ways. Find out what it is he needs to know and don't tell him, not yet. Give him an idea that you could help, but say that you need more time to think things through. It will give me a chance to find out what really makes him tick.'

'Do you think he can help us with Australia?' Phil spoke softly, his enthusiasm nonetheless evident.

'I don't know. It's possible. Why don't we find out?'

'As you wish. You're the boss.'

*

Nick had sat without speaking for the entire flight. Every muscle in his body itched with the anticipation of seeing Kruger, the most famous safari park in all the world.

Tom had hired a four-seater Cessna and pilot, preferring to show the game park to his visitor in private, but wanting the assistance of an expert game ranger. Helen Van Der Spec, the twenty-five-year-old daughter of Robert Van Der Spec, an expert ranger in his own right, seemed the perfect choice. She had grown up on the park and knew every inch of its harsh territory. She would be able to guide them without the cumbersome intrusion of tourists, Tom decided. Tom had frequently used Helen as a guide in the past. Her alert spirit sensed game long before the city dwellers were aware of its presence.

'You must realise that this is not a zoo,' Helen explained to Nick. 'Animals in the Kruger are here at their choosing, not ours, and may decide not to show themselves today. We must be quiet and we must be patient. The best time for game viewing is dawn and dusk and mainly around the waterholes.'

Nick could appreciate that this statement was accurate. The heat was rising rapidly, even in winter.

Up ahead there were kudu antelope, standing out with their curved horns which looked like heat-twisted rods.

Wildebeest grazed aimlessly. Nick judged their appearance, likening them to the homeless in New York; scruffy and only interested in filling their bellies.

'When the lion isn't hunting,' Helen explained, 'the animals will sense his contentment. They will not run. They may even stare at him, in the same way they will stare at us as we approach.' She pointed toward the antelope by way of explanation.

'We will stop here for a while.' Helen halted the party near Crocodile River.

Anticipation sharpened their senses. A cracked twig sounded as excruciating as a snapped human bone; a wisp of wind like a hurricane.

Without a warning, Helen froze. She slowly lifted her right hand in a motion both Tom and Nick understood to mean, 'Stay still and don't say a word.'

'Look,' she whispered.

Nick grappled to focus on he knew not what. A small triangular ripple slithered across the dark surface towards an unsuspecting impala. At the end of the ripple were two black bumps, no bigger than a couple of plums but moving with incredible speed. No one breathed. Nick's lungs swelled, his heart raced; he could now see the impending doom that faced the defenceless impala.

A crocodile, which Nick estimated to be fifteen feet from snout to tail, reared out of the water.

Despite an excruciating desire to yell, 'Get away, get away', Helen was muted by the grandeur of the spectacle. The impala had no chance, its efforts to wriggle and kick free only deepening its wounds.

'The crocodile's jaws,' Helen whispered, her heart pounding from both anguish and excitement, 'are not designed for a quick kill. They draw the victim under the water, rolling it in a frenzy until drowned. It is then left to mature for the feast.'

The law of the jungle at its devastating best, Nick thought. He hadn't imagined the impala stood even the smallest chance of survival until an unexplainable, unnatural intervention stunned the three who witnessed it.

As the crocodile wrestled with its prey, two flickering fanlike images approached the barbarous hunter. The ears of a hippo. Despite its slow, lumbering appearance, the hippo, one of the most deadly and feared animals in Africa, is capable of moving at frightening speeds if it chooses.

Only God will know the reason why, but that day the hippo's sights were set on a rescue. Jolting the crocodile until its powerful jaws freed the impala, the hippo followed the blood-soaked beast back on to dry land, licking its wounds. The dark red ooze clung readily to the huge rubbery tongue of the hippo. The impala turned thankfully and curiously towards the hippo, as confused as the observers were as to the motives of this would-be saviour. The impala gazed with huge heavy eyes into the face of the hippo – the brightness of those eyes flickering like a dying flame in a wind.

As valiantly as the hippo tried, the blood loss had already been too great. After some thirty minutes the last breath of life left that special impala. Still the hippo persisted nudging, as its mother might have done, trying to encourage the impala to struggle to its feet for those first uncertain steps. The limp body quickly cooled and stiffened. When at last the hippo realised its efforts had been in vain, it turned its head and let out a noise which annihilated the deceptive peace of a savage land: a deafening, defeated cry that thundered in the highly charged breasts of the onlookers like an earthquake. Birds raced into the sky, zebras turned to run and the vultures welcomed the sound that told them a meal had been prepared. All the time, the crocodile patiently lurked in observation. Its keen lifeless eye recognised that the prey would once again be his.

For the first moment since the episode began, Nick turned away. He looked at the reaction of those in his company. Helen's eyes were red, their stare transfixed on the inexplicable display of heroism. Tom's gaze, however, was stern and planted forcefully in the direction of Nick.

Nick felt an involuntary shudder visibly leave his body. He felt suddenly aware of his own mortality and the law of the jungle that ruled him. What he had just witnessed cemented Nick's view about the survival of the fittest. Here was a lumbering beast, a do-gooder, one who risked his own life to save another, and for what? The impala, the weakest of the creatures, died. The hippo, an animal who offered a futile gesture of goodwill, was grief-stricken. The crocodile, the cunning and ruthless hunter, was ultimately rewarded with his prize. What is the point of trying to do anything for anyone else in this world? Nick asked himself. It is all such a waste of time.

He looked back towards Tom. It disturbed him to notice Tom scrutinising him as though he could understand Nick's every thought.

That night Nick went back to the Weinsteins' house. Angela Weinstein was what Nick might have called a typical Jewish mother. She had solid child-bearing hips, a slightly larger than average nose, and an artillery of photographs of the children. Every exposed part of her olive-skinned body was draped in diamonds. The pear shape around her neck must have been at least five carats, Nick judged. A rock on her finger was not much smaller, all together a dazzling array that would have put Tiffany's to shame. Despite the obvious wealth, however, her cow-like brown eyes held a reflective quality. Angela and Tom both seemed burdened with a worry that Nick didn't understand.

Angela chattered like an excited child about the events

Tom and Nick had witnessed that day. 'This has given you an experience you will remember for the rest of your life,' she told him in a motherly tone.

Nick stretched out in a high-backed wicker chair, with only a standing lamp illuminating his face. Tom rested on his settee looking like the supreme commander. Nick gestured towards Angela and smiled knowingly at Tom. Tom acknowledged him with a wry grin.

Nick let his eyes gaze around the room until they settled on a painting on the far wall. The painting was of a ruined structure surrounded by bearded men in black hats, who were praying before it. It was drab in its colouring – beiges and dusty reddish browns – but somehow it radiated significance.

Angela noticed Nick's interest. 'Beautiful, isn't it?' she commented.

Beautiful was about the last word Nick would have used to describe it, but he nodded to encourage further explanation.

'It's the Wailing Wall in Jerusalem. The painting really captures the beauty of its spirit, don't you think?'

'What's the Wailing Wall?' Nick asked, scrutinising the painting more carefully.

'It's the last remaining wall of the Temple of Solomon.' Tom took over the conversation. 'It's the holiest of all symbols to our people. The men you see are rabbis and other religious Jews praying for anything from the coming of the Messiah to, well, to winning a football match.'

'Tom, don't mock,' Angela scolded him. She knew her husband didn't share her deep-seated belief in their religion but was furious when he shamed it in this way. She took it upon herself to finish the explanation.

'People will actually write their prayers down and stick them into crevices in the wall to remain there until the prayer comes true. I have one there myself.'

'Really? What does it say?' asked Nick, alive with curiosity.

'That one day all my family will be living in the promised land.'

'I thought you wanted to get away from the threat of racial violence,' Nick answered, and immediately wished he hadn't.

'Israel is the holy Mecca for three main religions, not just Judaism.' Tom took control again, ignoring Nick's comment. 'The Christians, the Muslims and the Jews all see it as the birthplace of their religions. At the Passover ceremony Jews hold every year, the words repeated by each of us are "next year in Jerusalem".'

'So are you planning to leave South Africa soon?' Nick asked.

Tom sighed deeply, considering his readiness to confide in Nick Abbott. 'We will leave as soon as we can get residency elsewhere,' he admitted.

'Israel?' Nick asked.

'No.'

'Then where?'

'Where do you think you might go if you were a white South African who loves his lifestyle but wants to escape the political situation and still maintain his professional future?'

Nick thought of New York, but that certainly didn't fit. Too much snow and, despite his achievements, Tom would still be a small cog in a big wheel. London was out of the question, far too cold and dismal. Before Nick could finish thinking, Tom answered.

'Australia.'

'Australia? Why Australia?' Nick moved forward in his chair. This news was intriguing.

'You think about it,' Tom said. 'The weather, the seasons, the population, all similar to South Africa. It is a young and naive country, the economy is booming, and within two years there will be deregulation of the finance industry. It's perfect. Absolutely perfect.'

'So why bother to build Sovereign Life into the number one company if you intend to leave it?'

'I would have thought that was simple. Marketing. I have achieved what I was told was impossible, and in a far more uncharitable environment than Australia could ever be. Just think what I will be able to achieve over there. This is how I will market myself to the largest institutions.'

The man was inspiring, but more inspiring was Nick's sudden realisation of Tom's weakness. Nick knew exactly how he would be able to help.

'Do you have any particular company in mind?' Nick asked, pretending to be only moderately interested.

'We spoke to Mutual Life Australia, that is to say, Phil and I. That was a big mistake. They are already so large and powerful that they don't think they need anyone. But once I started thinking about deregulation, I realised it wasn't the life insurance companies that interested me at all... it was the banks. Just think of it; an entire industry suddenly able to sell life insurance and not a life insurance brain in sight. It's too bloody wonderful. Can you think of a better man for the job than a man who turned a brokerage house into the number one life insurance company in South Africa?'

Nick found himself unintentionally swallowing, partly from admiration and partly from resentment of that admiration. This man's vision was huge. He was undoubtedly worth cultivating for the future.

Chapter Four

Brett McLeod, the new chief executive of Australian Life, had been waiting a long time to meet Nick Abbott. He knew Nick was the only man to help him achieve his goals in Australia and somehow he had to find a way to enlist his help. At last the day arrived when he was able to collect Nick from Sydney's Regent Hotel, just as Gus Fletcher had arranged. Brett, a shiny-headed, short man with big glasses which accentuated his small brown eyes, appeared comfortable with himself.

He spoke in a relaxed voice, not a bit like the brash sounding Australian accent Nick had expected to hear. The day was humid but a comfortable twenty-two degrees. Looking at the cloudless sky, Nick found it hard to believe it could have ever been any other way.

'How much do you know about our company, Australian Life?' Brett asked.

'Not a great deal.'

'Let me fill you in. I think you may find it quite interesting. Australian Life is known as the sleeping giant. It's a big safe company that just lumbers along. As a close friend of one of the board members, I was asked to find a person with the knowledge and management skills to wake up the giant. They want Australian Life moved from fifteenth position to, well, to as high as it can go. The board told me Australian Life had huge cash reserves, so money wasn't a problem. I had a good look around, considered what was needed and decided, without a doubt, I was the best man for the job.'

'I like your attitude.' Nick grinned. He considered he would have done the same thing in Brett's position.

'Thank you. At the time I was chief executive for DJF...'

'The computer company?'

'That's right. So although I had management experience, I didn't have a great deal of knowledge about the life insurance industry. I am now in the process of scanning the world to buy in the best brains in the business to take this company where it belongs. To the top. Here we are.'

Brett parked his silver-grey Mercedes in the underground car park. He took Nick up in the elevator without saying a word. Brett felt it wouldn't do to have staff hear of his plans before he had announced them officially.

The building was old and badly in need of renovation. Even the colourings were horribly out of date: cheap dark wood and mustard-coloured Formica. Brett explained to Nick that renovations were under way. They would be finished to coincide with a change of name to Prime Financial Group. An entirely new corporate image for the company. It was all part of his overall strategy for quality development, he explained.

Brett's office had some air of majesty about it, despite its need for a facelift. A large desk, which swamped Brett's slight stature, was the focal point. Around the desk the expected palms, chairs and coffee table were all suitably appointed. An old company picture hung on the rear wall: *The Flight from Pompeii*. It was chosen, Brett explained, to symbolise the fact that Australian Life would protect its clients from any peril.

'I have managed to buy in the man who knows more than anyone about superannuation, that's pension planning funds, in Australia.' Brett continued his explanation, which sounded more like a series of boasts to Nick. 'He actually wrote the act which governs superannuation investments, so no one can beat us on that score. I plan to break away the superannuation division into a wholly owned subsidiary company specialising in superannuation law and marketing. We will have many specialist companies under the main company: a high-powered sales group that will just sell savings plans; a training company that will concentrate on moving our agents into the higher net-worth markets; an investment company that will look at special investment programmes for the group such as retirement villages; a finance brokerage, and so on. No other life insurance company will also be a group of specialist companies as we will be.'

'And you need to find people to run each of these companies?' Nick asked.

'Yes. And the main life insurance company as well, of course.'

'That's quite a plan. How long do you give yourself to pull it all together?'

'Five years all up.'

'And then?'

'I retire a very wealthy man.'

There was that word, 'retire'. Nick realised with that one word Brett was not the sort of person he could work with. The plan, however, aroused Nick's curiosity.

'What about the number one life company in Australia, Mutual Life Australia, how far ahead in the race are they?'

'About ten laps, I have to admit. But their time will come. I have just signed their two top sales guys to come and work for me: George Hamilton and Ralph Black. No one in this country has ever bought out alliances before. George and Ralph are the first to change companies for a large sum of money.' He smiled. 'But I dare say they will not be the last. This will really set the cat among the pigeons.'

Brett looked satisfied with his achievement. His eyes

enlarged and his smile spread, making him appear supremely confident. Brett knew, without a doubt, that if he could find the right brains for his new child he would take it to the number one position in the country. Nick Abbott had to be one of those brains.

'You see,' Brett continued, 'George and Ralph are not only the top two producing salesmen for MLA but they have formed a company that trains top sales agents. These agents are handpicked by MLA and Hamilton Black together. They have to be in the top twenty per cent or George and Ralph won't take them. Their training programme shows the agents how to start treating their selling career as a business, not just a job. As a result of this change in attitude they can prospect more confidently in the higher net-worth markets. Instead of selling fifty thousand dollars' worth of life insurance to mister and missus average, George and Ralph get them to sell policies worth five hundred thousand dollars to the key people of businesses. That's what I want my boys selling. The big stuff.'

'What are your plans for Hamilton and Black? Sell a heap of big policies?'

'Certainly not. Why should I have two men selling when I can have two hundred men selling? I want George and Ralph to take two hundred of our best agents and show them how to penetrate the high net-worth markets. Hamilton Black will be a wholly owned subsidiary company of Australian Life, employed purely for the purpose of training my agents.'

'Don't you think it's a waste buying the best two sales people in the country and not allowing them to sell?'

'Not at all. Not if we can get them to train the others.'

Nick wasn't convinced. Oh, salesmen needed training all right, but there was only so far you could go in training. No one could ever be trained to be an Eddie Schwartz, not with the sort of methods Brett had in mind at any rate.

'I'd be very interested to meet these two men,' Nick commented.

'They have an end of financial year party with their staff, agents and major clients,' Brett explained. 'As this will be the last one they ever have at Mutual Life Australia, I dare say it will be a big one. They don't officially start with Australian Life until later in the year. The whole deal is still a big secret right now. As a visiting VIP, it will be no trouble at all to get you a spot as a guest speaker in their training session, and an invitation to the party afterwards.'

'Sounds fine.' Nick sensed Brett was up to something, but he hadn't quite managed to pinpoint it. I am a representative of the Life Managers Association and nothing else matters, he kept telling himself until he believed it was true.

'If you will excuse me, I have to make an important phone call. Can I use the meeting room outside?' Nick asked.

'Under one condition.' The bald-headed man raised his voice sufficiently to stop him.

'What's that?'

'That you give due consideration to a proposition I have to offer you.'

Nick Abbott turned and faced him quizzically. 'What kind of proposition?'

'You will see in due course.'

'I'll be back soon,' Nick responded as he walked thoughtfully through the door.

Excellent, Brett thought. If I can get Abbott to work with Hamilton Black, I'll have the final piece of my jigsaw puzzle in place. Abbott can recruit and train the sales managers to manage the salesmen in Hamilton Black's training programme. Even if I can only prise him away from East West Life for a year or two it will be enough.

Blazing exchanges flew across the Hamilton Black boardroom as Brett McLeod and Nick Abbott entered silently from a rear door. It was rare, but not unheard of, to have two visitors to their sessions and several MLA agents eyed the strangers carefully.

Two towering Australians paced the platform at the end of the room. The polished pine tables, which formed a U shape, had the occasional ring mark on them where agents had forgotten to put their coffee mugs down on mats. There must have been forty agents in that boardroom, Nick observed, and these only represented the cream of Sydney.

A podium had been placed on the stage, although Nick really didn't know why since neither man was using it. Behind the podium were crazed scrawlings on a huge whiteboard. Opposite the whiteboard, on the back wall near Nick, was a full bar. It looked to Nick like these two Australians were used to entertaining as well as teaching.

'You're telling us to lift our sights and sell million-dollar policies,' yelled an overweight agent, rising from his seat, red and sweating with anger, 'but you don't tell those idiots in the ivory tower to accept them. What's the matter with these people? Almost every time I sell a big case, my client just about has to be bloody Superman for MLA to grant the cover.'

The clean-shaven, grey-haired agent had a solid, slab-like head. He wore a jumper over his Mutual Life Australia tie and black slacks. After his outburst he returned to his seat, looking as though he was relieved his complaint had been voiced. Patiently he awaited words of explanation from George Hamilton.

George Hamilton, a man whose demeanour demanded obedience from all in his vicinity, stood three inches over six foot, with a slightly rounded belly and incongruously skinny legs. His eyes were almost unnaturally large. His blond hair was cut close to his head; so close he could have been in the Marines, Nick thought. It was all together a terrifying appearance even when George was silent, but when he spoke he became ogre-like. His voice was loud, gruff and unashamedly uneducated; he had one of the broadest Australian accents Nick had ever heard. He had to listen very carefully to understand all the words. The 'fucks' and 'shits' came through loud and clear, but he had to concentrate to hear the words in between. Typical rednecks, Nick concluded. The type of down-home Alabama boys who'd sit down and have a cup of coffee over the stove with Uncle Hester and ask how Aunt Mable is doing. They'd always walk out with the sales all right, but these guys weren't the type of people Nick Abbott could respect. Brett must have been thinking of something else when he bought them out to train the higher end of the market. It was surely the lower end of the market that these men belonged in.

George muttered an obscenity loudly under his breath in recognition of the point the agent had just made. 'Well, I am aware of the problem and Ralph and I do have a meeting with David Anderson next week. We will try to explain to him that life on the streets is not always as simple as the instructions in his underwriting manual...'

'You see,' Brett whispered to Nick, 'this is one of the reasons I have been able to pull them away from MLA. George and Ralph are ten years ahead of their time in Australia, and even a company as large as MLA can't keep up with them. It has caused them infinite frustration and me infinite delight.'

Jesus, Nick thought, if these two are that far advanced by Australian standards, I'm going to be like the spaceman who landed in ancient Egypt when I speak. Furthermore, Nick observed, if Eddie Schwartz had wanted something changed at East West Life he would have had it changed.

When you are the number one salesman you hold power, a fact these two clearly don't appreciate.

Ralph interrupted George's talk. Ralph was just as imposing as George, but an inch taller. His hair was not quite as fair, or as short, as George's, and his fearsome qualities waxed and waned, whereas George's were permanently fixed. Ralph had piercing passionate blue eyes, which flashed when he emphasised a point, and eyebrows that raised every time he was excited. His grimace could switch to a glowing smile and back again in an instant. He was not the type of man an agent would choose to cross swords with, even to Nick that was obvious.

'When you send your case up to the puzzle palace for assessment,' Ralph explained, 'you must send a letter to show the underwriter the presentation you gave the client. You have to explain to these boffins why a man earning fifty thousand needs five hundred thousand dollars' worth of life insurance. You've got to hold their hands. Explain, if your client is in partnership, what happens if one partner dies. The surviving partner suddenly has to find an amount of cash, equal to half the business, to buy out the deceased partner's spouse; or face the prospect of going into business with her. And ask him how he would fancy going into business with his dead partner's wife. He'll pass the medical quickly enough then, let me tell you.' Ralph was criss-crossing the floor, pounding a fist into his open palm. 'You must realise that the underwriters just don't understand what it's like out there for you guys.'

'On the other hand,' he continued, 'let's not forget how much commission we're earning on these cases. For twenty grand a case, you must be prepared to put in a little hard work. You're still acting like you're selling thousand-dollar policies and you're not. There's a big difference, let me tell you.' Ralph had made it back to the podium, raising his voice to a deafening yell, humbling the agents in his presence.

George cut in again.

Brett and Nick watched the performance for half an hour. It could not be called anything less than a performance, especially George's introduction for the visiting American VIP. It was an introduction that would not have been out of place at the Stardust Hotel in Las Vegas, Nick considered.

Nick gave his standard speech of the agent in the eighties. The speech in itself was well received, but the agents generally were far more interested in learning about Eddie Schwartz.

'What was he like?'

'How did you meet him?'

'How long was it before you realised he was going to be a million-dollar producer?'

'What was Eddie's best answer to the "I'll buy later" objection?'

As George observed the American, he remembered the last time he met Eddie. All the top sales agents from around the world were gathered at the Million Dollar Achievers Group in New York. As the number one in the States, and the number one in Australia, George and Eddie found they had an immediate rapport. Eddie took George out to his favourite haunt one night, Club Fifty-Seven. He became quite drunk and told George that he was troubled by how easy it was to sell policies which could be horribly abused. George hadn't fully understood the implications of Eddie's ramblings, but there was one thing Eddie said which deeply disturbed him. 'I'm going to set the record straight; there have been too many pay-outs from my sales and it's time the company knew the truth behind my success.'

The next morning, Eddie was found dead in his hotel room. It had rocked the entire insurance community, particularly as his death had been linked with illegal drugs.

Thinking of Eddie's rise to success brought back visions to George of his own past. He was just a child when his father died leaving him as the man of the family. It was a special aura of dread that surrounded his new responsibilities. His mother was weak and sickly. George was the one who had to make a living if they were going to eat.

It hadn't taken George long to realise the ways of the world. He had lost his older brother to a hit-and-run driver the year before and now his father was gone too. He died of a worn-out, overworked heart and no bastard gave a damn about George. No one but his mother, who loved him dearly. She told him that one day he would be a man respected by many men. It was a mother's intuition, she told George. Innocently he had believed her.

He took every job he could get; paper rounds, delivery boy. It didn't matter as long as he earned some money. He was ten years old when he had his first memorable encounter with the kids in the country neighbourhood. One night, while he was following his regular path home, they stopped abruptly in front of him. There were eight or nine of them; George couldn't remember exactly. They tried to cajole George into stealing with them. George was fast on his feet and spun a good yarn. He would be a good patsy if they could convince him to join their gang.

He admitted to himself that he had considered the option briefly. The money would certainly be better than that he earned doing paper rounds. But even at the tender age of ten he couldn't bring himself to do what he knew was wrong. George's nature was rowdy, but noble. They had beaten him up mercilessly when he refused.

'Cowards,' he yelled, 'let me take you one at a time.'

They just laughed at him as they left him bleeding in the dirt. He had gone to the local lake to try to clean himself as best he could before he went home. The last thing he wanted to do was cause his mother any additional grief.

He had learned to drink and smoke and fight by the age of twelve. After his encounter with the local kids, he was determined to look tough and know how to back up the image in the future. He was always larger than boys of his age and when his voice broke early, he discovered a prize-winning deep-throated sound that could strike fear into the heart of any man if it was used properly.

His teenage years were half spent when he left his home town to find fortune in the city. He had done pretty well for himself in the country but the opportunities there were limited and he wanted greater things for his mother and himself. He remembered his mother's words; that he would be a great man respected by many men.

The first office he came upon was Mutual Life Australia who offered him a job as the lowest of lowly clerks. He worked hard and studied every brochure and form he could find. Life insurance seemed a good thing. If his father had been covered by a life insurance policy, his mother's life, and his own, would have been so different. He read the rate books. He analysed the sales pitches and by the time he was nineteen George decided he was ready to start selling life insurance on his own. His superiors had laughed at him at first. His speech was so rough; no one in their right mind was going to buy from this funny-looking, loud-mouthed kid. But they were wrong. People bought insurance from George Hamilton like it was going out of fashion, and they bought for one reason. They could see in his eyes that he believed – believed deeply – that what he was selling them was going to make somebody's life better one day. It wasn't a luxury; it wasn't even an option. Life insurance was simply something that everybody who loved anybody had to have.

He went home to his mother often, promising that one day he would return to take her away from the country for good.

George wasn't afraid to try to sell big policies. Some of his peers preferred selling small policies, believing that they were easier. As a result they had to sell twice as many to earn the same living. George decided they must lack a belief in their product. By the time he reached twenty-one he was breaking records set by agents far more experienced than himself and he was very proud. This was a noble industry indeed.

Many agents still tried to make fun of him saying he wouldn't last. 'There are only so many people in Melbourne,' they would say, 'who will buy from a loud-mouthed bullfrog like you.' God, they made him mad. They reminded him of the kids back home who tried to cajole him into doing things he didn't believe in; things below his standards. Just because he'd been poor did not mean he had to be dishonourable, and he'd be damned if he'd let tyrannical misfits bring him down. In fact, he would be the most honourable man that those moronic, short-sighted pricks had ever seen. He'd forget the nickel and dime market he was working in and develop concepts that would sell in the big business market.

Inspired by his idea he sat in his office day after day putting a business plan together. Grasping at straws in a clumsy effort to get his master plan together, George lost sight of everything around him. As he struggled, the weeks became months until he realised that he had used up every penny he had earned and was broke. He returned home once more to find his mother had grown seriously ill. She could barely move and there had been no one around to care for her. She had refused to call George because she knew that if he hadn't come home it was because there must be something very important happening in the city.

George rushed to the edge of town to bring the doctor back but there was little he was able to say to comfort George. All George could do was make her final hours as comfortable as possible. As much as she tried to cling to life, her efforts became weaker and weaker, until finally she was still and silent except for the faint hiss of her breathing.

It took two more days, through which George sat steadfastly by her side. She gave no outward sign of passing from life to death other than the cessation of her harsh breathing, but George knew it in an instant. He lowered his head and howled out his grief until the tears ran dry.

A week later she was buried next to his father and George left her, and their grief-stricken past, for ever.

It was two years before he went back into life insurance. He just couldn't adjust his mind to the rights and wrongs of what had transpired.

Mutual Life Australia had often asked him to return but, wrestling with his guilt, he kept turning the offer down. He agreed to share one Christmas with his old colleagues and it was there, at the MLA Christmas function, that he first met Ralph Black. A man as large and loud as George, the two immediately became good friends. George shared his old dreams with Ralph. The large man listened carefully and then disappeared for a full week. When he returned he had pads and pads of notes full of concepts, ideas, and plans to make George's dream a reality. Together they formed the Hamilton Black organisation and concentrated on selling insurance only to cover the key people in businesses and partnerships. They became the first salesmen in Australia to sell a million-dollar policy; the first to sell ten million dollars' worth of business in a year and earned the recognition of being the pioneers of business insurance in Australia. When the international sales organisation, the Million Dollar Achievers Group, heard of these two they were immediately made life members and invited to attend every meeting; an honour which saw George and Ralph mix with other legends, such as Eddie Schwartz. They could have wielded great power in the insurance industry, but their only dreams were to care for themselves and their families, and be the most ethical salesmen the business had ever known.

Many agents aspired to be like George and Ralph. They became the gurus of life insurance in Australia. It had been Ralph's idea to form the training group. 'As so many agents come to us for advice, we should start our own training programme and charge the bastards for it.'

Mutual Life Australia had readily agreed and set Hamilton Black up in offices, just outside town, to run these sessions. 'They may be loud country boys at heart,' said their manager, 'but they have earned the respect of the entire industry for their outstanding achievements.'

'What did you think of them?' Brett finally asked, when he and Nick got back to Australian Life's office.

'A lot of talent and no class.'

'Would you say Eddie Schwartz had class?' Brett laughed.

'Eddie was a scoundrel, but he had class. He knew how to be successful by using the system; nothing wrong with that. These two don't have that type of skill.'

'Maybe that's why they're still with us. From what I hear, the pressure of using the system became too much for Eddie.'

Nick looked into Brett's eyes to gauge the depth of his statement.

'Eddie fell victim to a syndrome many successful people suffer from,' Nick explained. 'He became too rich too quickly and kept experimenting with new ways to indulge himself with his new-found wealth. We should include a section on dealing with success as part of our training programmes.'

Brett nodded in agreement. He understood only too well about the rich not coping with the pressure of their responsibilities.

'He used drugs to get his highs, poor, stupid son of a gun. I hate drugs. They've killed too many people close to me.'

'Drugs are like success,' Brett said quickly. 'As long as you know when enough is enough, there's no harm in the occasional social snort.'

Nick grunted in disapproval. 'The socially acceptable escape of the obscenely rich, that's what my wife used to say.'

Brett nodded.

'So what type of sales managers do I need to keep the agents that they train in order?' Brett asked, changing the subject.

'Damn tough sons of bitches if you ask me.'

'I agree. How do you suppose I go about finding them?'

Nick looked at Brett, choosing his next words carefully. Before he could speak, Brett answered his own question.

'You know you're the best man for the job, don't you, Nick?'

'I'm sorry, Brett. I'm not your man. For one thing, I couldn't work with those two rednecks. For another, I have no intention of leaving New York.'

'You're away now for six months. Perhaps I could entice you to come back as a consultant for, say, another six or twelve months. What do you think of that?'

'I don't know,' Nick rubbed his chin, thoughtfully mulling over the suggestion.

'Name your price, Nick. You're the final link I need to make my plan work. Think of what it will mean if we can do to Australian Life what Weinstein did to Sovereign Life. Just think of it, Nick. It's within your gasp.'

*

The last months of Nick Abbott's consulting tour were gruelling but uneventful. His agency at East West Life was buzzing with the news of Nick's imminent return. He marched into the office like a triumphant knight returning from the battlefield, bloodied and heroic.

'Still no word from James?' he asked his secretary, almost rhetorically.

'I'm afraid not, sir,' she replied despondently.

Nick went to his safe to file the reports from the trip. As the heavy door flew open the hair on the back of Nick's neck prickled with insects of horror. The files on Eddie Schwartz were missing. Nick's brow wrinkled with anger. How could anyone have gained access to his safe? James was the only other person alive who knew the combination and no one had seen him in months.

'Shirley,' he growled at his secretary. 'Who has been tampering with my safe?'

'No one, Mr Abbott,' she stammered, scurrying into his office. 'The only people who have been in here are myself and the cleaners. Oh,' she added, 'Gus Fletcher did come to talk to the group shortly after you left. He came in here to make a couple of calls after the meeting.'

Nick gave Shirley a murderous glare. 'Thank you,' he said with a forced calm. 'You can go. Shut the door.'

As Shirley left, Nick threw his coffee cup across the room. How in God's name had Gus managed to get the combination? Why had he even tried to get the combination? There were too many dangerously unanswered questions.

'Brett McLeod on the phone for you, sir,' Shirley stammered through the intercom.

'Thank you, Shirley.'

Brett had persisted in his pursuit of Nick Abbott throughout Nick's consulting tour. With Christmas around the corner, Nick was not surprised to receive Brett's last call for the year. He looked at the flashing light on his console, lifted the receiver and pressed button number one.

'Brett, my man. How's life down under?'

'Hot. Forty degrees today.'

Nick looked out over the blanket of snow that had settled on Fifth Avenue and wondered if now could be a good time to go to Australia after all.

'I hear one of your agents won 'Rookie of the Year, USA'. Congratulations.'

'Thank you.'

'Nick, I need your expertise,' Brett almost pleaded. 'You're the only one who can pull this project together. I can pay you whatever you ask. There's a fabulous apartment I'm going to buy, just overlooking Hyde Park in Sydney. You could walk to work. It's yours if you want it.'

Nick remembered Hyde Park vividly. The giant chess game on the sidewalk that took a grown man to move each piece, the huge leafy trees and the bustling streets nearby. The view wasn't dissimilar to the one he faced right now, except that he doubted Hyde Park in Sydney had ever seen snow.

'What about your two rednecks?' Nick quipped. 'Can't they find anyone for you?'

Brett ignored the sarcasm. 'There's only one Nick Abbott, we both know that.'

'All right, all right. I'll put a proposition together for you.'

'Wonderful!' The news lifted Brett's spirits. 'I'll look forward to receiving it as soon as possible. It looks like we are going to have some competition on our hands. Champion Life have just appointed a new national agency manager. A compatriot of yours.'

'Really, what's his name?'

'James Cartwright. He seems to be shaking them up well and truly. It's going to be a race to see who reaches number one first.'

'I've never heard of a James Cartwright. He can't be such hot stuff, or I would know him. Don't worry, Brett McLeod. I'll show you how to take your company to the top.'

All right, Nick thought, I'll give him a proposal. It will be so outrageous McLeod will never accept it. If he does, I can cope with living in Australia for a year. If he doesn't, it's of little consequence.

Nick started drafting.

Nicholas Abbott will contract to a one-year consulting term with Australian Life whereby Nicholas Abbott will:

1. *Train Australian Life sales managers in the finer points of recruitment, selection and training of sales agents.*
2. *Recruit, select and train new sales managers.*
3. *Review the performance of existing sales managers and suggest replacements where appropriate.*
4. *Review remuneration structure of sales managers.*

Nicholas Abbott will receive as follows:

a) *US$500,000 per annum consulting fees, paid monthly.*
b) *A fully maintained Mercedes.*
c) *First-class return air travel.*
d) *One trip back to New York during the twelve-month period.*
e) *All travel around Australia to be first class.*
f) *An additional death and disability policy for US$2,000,000.*
g) *Commission of thirty per cent on the increased sales revenue during the year.*
h) *Phone, apartment and office, to be paid for by Australian Life.*
i) *Pension planning investment premiums, invested in Australian Life at the maximum allowable under the*

insurance and superannuation commissioner's guidelines.

Nicholas Abbott will also be supplied with:
i. The unlimited use of the apartment in Hyde Park.
ii. The necessary visas.
iii. Top-level executive offices.
iv. A fully trained secretary with 60 wpm typing skills and 120 wpm shorthand.

That ought to do for starters, Nick thought. He decided to have his lawyers draft the agreement and send it by air courier straight away.

A neat pile of messages and mail lay in Nick's in-tray. He shuffled through them nonchalantly to determine if there was anything that needed attention. Only one caught Nick's eye. On the top left-hand corner it said 'Private and Confidential' just underneath an airmail stamp. He slit the white envelope open with the edge of his finger. A thin scarlet line appeared as the paper tore at Nick's flesh.

Winston Life
95 Park Lane
London W1

25th March, 1986

Mr Nicholas Abbott
Regional Manager – New York
East West Life
Fifth Avenue over Central Park
New York, New York, 10019

Dear Mr Abbott,
I don't know what kind of perverted trick you were trying to

play on our company, but clearly the guidelines which you set out would have bankrupted us had they been implemented. Whatever your scheme was, it failed. Despite your efforts to turn Arthur Webb, Cathy Williams and others against me, I have finally managed to make them see sense. Unfortunately it was too late for Webb; he started firing everyone who wasn't a star and depleted the north London sales team to virtually nothing. I had to let him go to save the area. I analysed your proposal in great detail with Cathy and the board members, and your figures simply didn't add up. The last time we checked there were only one hundred pence in the pound, not two hundred as you seemed to try and squeeze out. I simply fail to understand how you expected to pay seventy-five per cent commission to the agent, forty per cent to his manager, twenty per cent to the regional manager and still have money left over to pay for running costs at Winston Life.

    This letter is for the sole purpose of telling you that at no time will you be welcome back at Winston Life. We are seriously considering terminating our relationship with the Life Managers Association International if you are an example of what they represent.

Yours sincerely,
Lloyd Sutcliff
Operations Manager, Winston Life

Nick read the letter three times. It was possible, he considered, that he had been a little careless with the figures, but not to the extent that Lloyd raved about. Lloyd wasn't taking into consideration the income that Winston Life would earn. Firstly they were skimming two per cent off investment returns, and secondly management charges would cover a good deal of the budget. Of course, the company could have afforded to pay higher commissions.

Anyway, what about the money the company would have been saving by getting the sales managers to pay their own rent, power and light? It proved one point conclusively: Sutcliff was a small-minded fool. Nick would get the system to work in Australia instead.

He lit a cigarette and with the same flame burned Lloyd's letter, watching it transform into wafer-thin ash in his trash can.

The only other item of interest was a message from Gus Fletcher, summoning Nick to a meeting to discuss the tour the following day.

*

Gus's office was situated one block away from Nick's and, despite the fact that it was a miserable day, Nick decided to walk.

'Have a seat, Mr Abbott. Mr Fletcher won't be long,' Gus Fletcher's secretary said automatically. She was a prudish-looking woman of about forty, with her brown hair pulled back into a bun and her mousy eyes peering through John Lennon glasses.

Nick hated sitting still; it was unproductive. He looked at the many certificates around Gus Fletcher's entrance hall. There was a business degree from Harvard, as well as numerous recognition certificates for work in the industry and for charity. It was an impressive collection.

Nick sensed that the prude with the John Lennon glasses knew that something was going on. With her head down and her mouth shut, she went silently about her business.

Why was it the area around his collar was moist and hot, he wondered, and why was there a burning dry sensation in his mouth?

'Tell Mr Abbott I will see him now.' It was a serious, refined accent that spoke through the prude's intercom.

Nick knew for certain this was trouble; big trouble. Gus Fletcher never called him 'Mr Abbott'.

It was a deeply distressed face that greeted Nick; the face of a man who had some terrible decisions to make. Gus Fletcher's eyes were inflamed with rage, a rage directed firmly at Nick. Instinctively Nick went to shake his hand, but halted the motion before it was obvious. He struggled to finds words which were useful; there were none.

Gus directed Nick towards the oak meeting table which was near the window. It was empty except for one file. No ashtrays, Nick noticed.

'Have a seat,' Gus urged.

He waited for Nick to sit before joining him. Slowly Gus began to tap the file with his fingertips, as if searching for the right words.

'I have called you here on a very serious matter. Do you know what this file contains, Nick?'

'No,' he answered honestly.

'I thought for many years that Eddie's rapid rise to success was a little suspicious. I can't believe you encouraged him to do this.'

'Do what?' Nick asked, knowing that the records Gus had acquired gave no *evidence* of foul play.

'So many deaths. It's horrendous. This could ruin us if it got out. Hell, it could ruin the entire industry. Do you have any concept of what you have done?'

'All I did was show Eddie how to illustrate a need for life insurance and sell record numbers of policies. There's no shame in that.' Nick smiled. Gus might think he had some damning evidence but Nick suddenly realised it was in Gus's interests, as much as Nick's, to keep the file quiet.

'Illustrate a need. My God, man. You are responsible for these deaths. Fifty million dollars' worth of pay-outs over ten years. I cannot find the words to express my disgust.'

'You've taken leave of your senses. How can I be responsible for the deaths of policyholders? What possible advantage could that have for me?'

'You know perfectly well what I am talking about. Jesus Christ, what makes a man like you?'

'Men like you, I guess. I never heard you complaining about the sales when Eddie was alive and breaking records for your company.'

'I can't believe Eddie was a party to this,' Gus said blankly.

'Eddie was a starving kid from the Bronx when I found him. He'd have done anything to make a buck, and so would those people he sold to.'

'I do not want this matter ever discussed again.'

Gus took the file to his shredding machine and began feeding the records in one by one.

Nick sat back, supremely satisfied that Gus had obviously made the right decision.

'I don't know what you're making such a fuss about. It's all ancient history anyway.'

'Because Eddie's dead?' Gus asked accusingly. 'Did he have a change of heart? Is that it? I never believed he was the suicidal type. You've got away with murder, Nick Abbott, and I won't have you in my company for another second. You are fired. And I will personally see to it that no company in this country will ever employ you again.'

Gus removed his handkerchief to mop his brow. The allegations he made sounded like fiction in its most unbelievable form. The unholy truth was he knew that they were true. Even now he could not bring himself to vocalise the details of this fraud. The implications were too enormous for his mind to cope with.

'Gus, settle down. I'm your best manager. You can't fire me. What reason would you give?'

'You think you're so smart, don't you? Well, your meddling has created your own noose.' Gus handed Nick another letter, this time from Lloyd Sutcliff.

Nick felt a solid lump of phlegm lodge in his throat. Lloyd was threatening to expose East West Life as a company setting out to destroy all the competition through sabotaging other companies' systems.

'You're right,' Gus said, as Nick finished the letter. 'I'm not going to fire you because of some non-existent records which would ruin us as well as you. This is quite sufficient justification for dismissal, and quite sufficient justification to make other companies wary of employing you. It's over, Abbott. Now get out of my sight before I feel tempted to throw you out of that window myself.'

A cold chill swept through Nick's body. He had never suspected anything like this, not in his wildest nightmares. Jesus, Nick thought, it must have been James. He's the only one who knew the combination. He must have planted these fears in Gus's mind before he disappeared.

Nick turned towards Gus. He sat in silence, except for the hiss of his Ventolin.

Nick became red and flustered. How could this be happening to him? It was impossible; it was a nightmare. Cold sweat ran down Nick's back. He'd been played for a damn fool, and by his own son. His gut lurched. Pounding thuds resounded in his brain. He was dizzy, hot and incredulous. A core of violent outrage burst from his eyes.

'Nick, these are the facts,' Gus said, pointing to Lloyd's letter. 'They are irrefutable and they are damning. As a man of such a long-standing reputation with our firm, and more to protect our name than yours, we will not press charges. We will, however, recoup some of the losses from those pay-outs by impounding your office equipment and freezing any assets that you have in East West Life. A statement will be issued that after thirty years of service you have decided to take a sabbatical. Now get out of my office before I decide not to be so lenient.'

Gus watched Nick Abbott leave a shattered, broken man who had lost everything. Gus had triumphed over the disgrace that Nick had nearly caused his company. Eddie had been led astray by the high-rolling, fast-talking magic that Nick Abbott wove so well. Now it was Nick's turn to pay. Nick had experienced the full wrath of the most powerful man in life insurance today; more powerful than Nick Abbott could ever aspire to be. His reign was over. Gus decided that James, if he ever reappeared, should take over Nick's realm. It would be an appropriate reward for uncovering the truth. Gus felt sure that would please him. He obviously harboured no affection for his father, Gus assured himself. Nick Abbott, the vile, filthy piece of worm-ridden slime that he was, would be grovelling with the peasants from whence he came. How dare he defile the industry – and Gus's daughter – in such a way? Gus knew Nick had no second chances. Gus would dance on Nick Abbott's professional grave. He wondered how long it would be for James to re-emerge and claim his rightful place as his father's heir.

*

A heat swelled inside Nick Abbott. A large creature awoke from the blackness. It was a swift reptilian creature that lurked in the part of Nick's brain reserved strictly for revenge. It hissed violently, spitting and lunging at a vision of its prey, Gus Fletcher – and his own son. Nick couldn't remember ever feeling such deep-seated indignation; such injustice. Nothing in his past came close to this. This new feeling was so violent, so basic that he thought it would surely engulf his soul. He reached for a cigarette outside Gus Fletcher's door.

The prude with the John Lennon glasses thought for a

moment she might tell Mr Abbott that smoking wasn't allowed. Nick's glare, however, was sufficient to turn her head away from him in silence.

I have never accepted defeat. Never, Nick thought. He raced back to his office, planning a little farewell gift for Gus Fletcher. A pure-bred Siamese cat seems appropriate, he thought. All I have to do is make sure he can't get to his damn Ventolin spray and it's all over.

A burst of satisfaction spread over Nick at the simplicity of his plan. This would be a new and exciting type of death to witness.

*

'Mr Abbott,' Shirley called over his intercom, 'there's a man here to see you.'

'Tell him I'm busy,' Nick hissed, the whites of his eyes flashing madly with murderous intent.

'I'm afraid this can't wait,' the man said, entering his office. 'Lieutenant Harper,' he said, showing Nick his badge from the Homicide Department.

'What's this all about?' Nick demanded.

'I just have a few questions for you, sir.'

The lieutenant's tie was loosened, his top button open. His eyes hid the revelation which James had revealed to him six months ago. No one in the New York Police Department had wanted Lieutenant Harper to reopen the files on the deaths. 'There are plenty of new cases to keep us busy without digging into the past,' his boss had told him. But the lieutenant was a stickler for details. Two deaths, three years apart, both classified as suicide... both with the same MO. At first there had been no obvious motive to link one death with the other but James had managed to clear up that mystery. All the lieutenant needed to do was ruffle this bird of prey's feathers just enough for him to go to his superiors with something on which to get the files reopened.

Nick swallowed his rage and handled Lieutenant Harper with cool indifference. No dishevelled cop was going to get in his way. All right, he admitted, Gus's fate would have to be put off for a while. It didn't matter. What neither Gus nor the police were aware of was Nick's impending Australian visit. The entire fiasco suddenly took on a new perspective. Brett McLeod wanted Nick Abbott to run the life insurance company of his group of companies; wanted Nick Abbott to take it to number one in Australia. But why stop at Australia? I could take Australian Life to a position where it could rival the best in the world, Nick thought smugly. It would take time, sure, but Nick had plenty of time on his hands now. It was beautiful. The gods, if they existed, were looking after Nick Abbott well.

'Let's see how you feel about this when you find out, you scheming bastards,' Nick seethed. 'I'll turn the tables on you no matter how long it takes,' he growled under his breath. 'You'll come crawling back to me begging for help, for mercy, for resurrection. And I promise you, there will be no such resurrection. When I destroy a man, I do it properly.'

'Never leave an enemy behind': that was a line Nick remembered from studying one of the few men in history he admired, the Zulu leader Shaka. Fletcher had left his enemy alive and kicking; for that he would pay dearly.

Chapter Five

Sandra stood for well over two minutes without moving, although the need to do so was almost unbearable. Every muscle in her body seemed to quiver with anticipation for the moment when she would take up her new position. Standing at the base of two towering pillars, she felt overshadowed by the new masculine colleagues she was about to join. She regretted her feelings of inferiority.

Without moving her head, Sandra swivelled her eyes towards the entrance of the tower, noticing dozens of people. She knew they didn't see her nervousness. Even in her discomfort the confidence of others made her angry. This whole ironic situation filled her with violent, conflicting emotions. Nothing that would be said or done that day would leave her untouched. Her new ambition dominated her life. She hated it and loved it with equal passion. She would eventually have a chance to face Nick Abbott again, to see for herself if he was the monster James accused him of being, or simply a tough businessman. Either way she had to deal with Nick if Ted's spectre was to be finally laid to rest. Despite her resolve she waited submissively, as if she expected someone to take her hand and lead her in the right direction. Her own duplicity sickened her.

Taking a deep breath, and filled with questions, she marched inside the silent cube of motion that would deliver her to her new environment. On the forty-third level she noticed an expanse of workstations. It was a cool, austere environment she tentatively walked through to reach Brett McLeod's office.

'Good morning, Sandra. Looking forward to your first day at Australian Life?' Brett asked cheerily as she peered around his open office door.

'Yes, Brett,' she answered correctly.

She hadn't been in Brett McLeod's new office before and was very impressed. With the renovation nearly complete, Brett's office was a shining example of the comforts of senior management. She looked past him to the spectacular view of Sydney Harbour and a nervous smile crept across her face.

Brett had taken a special interest in Sandra as soon as he found out she was back in Australia and had worked for Nick Abbott while she lived in New York. He had concluded, when he first met her as an ambitious twenty-two-year-old, that she had great potential. Having now had the experience of working for Nick Abbott, she was without question the best person for this new role.

After being back in Australia for only six months, Sandra didn't like the idea of changing positions again so soon. She had to admit, however, that taking the role of product development manager at Australian Life was going to give her some unequalled opportunities. She remembered the farewell party at her last company. Even though she'd only been there six months, she had made some close friends and they threw her a party to end all parties when she left.

Sandra had blossomed under the influence of her new colleagues. They had updated her on the changes which had occurred in Australian law while she was living in New York and had explained the general direction the industry was now taking. Nothing this company could offer her, however, matched the opportunity she was accepting from Australian Life. When she left DJF to go and live in New York, she remembered, Brett had not taken the news too well. Yet just as she was becoming comfortable in a new company, Brett called her out of the blue to offer her this exciting new role.

Sandra, her new agency manager had observed, was strangely reticent about working with her ex-boss again.

Sandra and her agency manager were the last to leave the office on her last day of her old post. They both knew she was taking a big step.

'This has been some day,' Sandra murmured in pointless rhetoric.

'I think every agent in the company rang me today to say how sorry they are that you are leaving.'

'Well, I never could have made it so quickly without your help.'

He winked at her.

'I loved working here. You're very special to me. I just hope I'm doing the right thing.'

'You'll be fine,' he said, trying to sound tough.

Sandra realised he was going to be as sorry to see her go as she was in making the decision to leave.

'How about one for the road?' he asked.

'You're a *real* friend,' she said sincerely, without answering his question.

'And I always will be. Come here.' He placed his hands firmly on her shoulders. 'If there is ever anything I can do for you, I'll do it. If you want to talk, I'll always be here for you.'

'I know,' she said feebly.

'I knew Brett would come running after you as soon as I mentioned your name at the last LMA meeting. We just can't offer you anything like Brett is.'

The urge to embrace him was overpowering, but he held her at arm's length.

'Come on,' he said, 'I'll take you home.'

*

That night her recurring nightmare came again. She saw Ted, still in his business suit, splattered across the front of a New York subway train, but this time it was different. In a subway of crowded people she spotted Nick Abbott. She yelled at the top of her lungs but no one heard. Her screams fell silent, as if controlled by some diabolic force. She sprinted across an endless sea of people without realising how much the gap between herself and Nick Abbott had closed. Suddenly she felt a cold hard bulge inside the waist of her skirt. Reaching down, Sandra retrieved a loaded revolver. Fear left her. She stood for a second then rotated on the spot to face the torment of her night-time hours. She was facing Nick Abbott; he had the face of a distorted monster.

She grabbed him by his throat, forcing his head down to the level of her knees, a force born from a new strength she had discovered within herself. Slowly, deliberately, she raised the revolver to his temple when suddenly she realised it was James's face, not Nick's. She dropped the gun in horror and woke in a cold sweat, cursing the visions of her nightmares.

Charged with uncertainty, Sandra realised for the first time she was beyond the boundaries of the security alcoves she had created for herself. There was nothing to protect her here, she was on her own. She felt vulnerable yet strangely alive, more aware of herself than she had ever been. It was a new and exhilarating sensation.

Brett's eyebrows rose frequently as he discussed Sandra's potential at Australian Life with her. He had been valiantly searching for the token woman to join his management team. Sandra represented everything he had been looking for.

'You know,' Brett said, 'I wanted you working here as soon as I heard you were back. I was very sorry to hear about Ted,' he added. 'You understand that Australian Life is going through massive changes right now, don't you?' he asked.

'Yes, I've read the papers.'

'We are headed for immense changes, and very soon. It's only six months till our annual conference. There will be some far-reaching announcements made at that time. That gives you six months to carve out a niche for yourself in this firm: do you think you can pull it off?'

'To tell you the truth, I've got no idea,' she admitted. 'But I'll give it a damn good try.'

'Good,' he answered, relaxing slightly as though he had needed to hear confirmation from her lips. 'I'm going to introduce you to three people who will help you learn everything you need to know. We need something really sensational to pull this company up. I hope my faith in you is going to be justified. Product development has not been your area of expertise, I know that. But with your background, understanding of systems and capacity to learn, I am confident you will come up with a product which will justify my faith.'

'What about the three who are going to teach me? They have to be pretty good, don't they?'

'Ah, well, that's the trick. They are all experts in their own fields but our agents are becoming very disillusioned. There are no new ideas being developed. These people seem to think that Australian Life owes them a living just because they have the knowledge, even though they are not capable of structuring it into something new. I don't need to tell you how important it is that the sales agents and the product development people can communicate with one another. We need someone who not only has the knowledge, but who understands the needs of sales agents.'

'Well, I think I can confidently say that I have worked for the most demanding agents in the business.'

'Exactly. If you can survive at East West, dealing with

the agents here is going to be a cinch. You will be meeting Mark Fitzgerald and two of his senior consultants. Mark is the operations manager.'

'And how does Mark feel about me taking on this role?'

'Let's just say that when you come as highly recommended as you are, the issue of staffing is not a matter Mark has to concern himself with. As long as you prove yourself, Mark will be happy.'

'So you're throwing me into the lion's den?'

'Don't worry. You'll blitz them; take my word for it.' He smiled confidently.

A cold sweat formed on Sandra's body. Brett was placing her in a foreign environment, among unfriendly colleagues, to invent a new product in a company she knew little about. If I wanted a challenge, she thought, I certainly have one.

Brett took her around to a glass-walled room with dusty pink blinds pulled across the walls. It had a stark feel about it. A grey Formica table stood in the centre of the room surrounded on three sides by dusty pink chairs. At the foot of the table there was a whiteboard. The three men, already seated when Sandra arrived, stood for the introductions. Mark Fitzgerald was the tallest, around six foot two. He had a baby face and wide blue eyes. His fluffy brown hair was beginning to show signs of balding despite the fact that he could not have been more than thirty-five years old. Alan Carmichael was a short man, with jet-black curly hair and ebony eyes. He had grown a full beard and moustache which made him look quite sinister to Sandra. He was in charge of all the life insurance products, Brett explained. It was Alan's job to explain the products to the agents and invent new ways in which to market them.

'Alan will be able to give you all the details of our product range,' Brett said confidently.

Vince Caleo, the third man, was in charge of superannuation products. He was the quietest of the three. He stood stiffly upright, looking down his long pointed nose, scanning his new adversary with steely blue eyes. His limp brown hair had been skilfully blow-dried into a flamboyant, but nonetheless masculine, style.

'Between these three you will be able to learn all there is to know about Australian Life. It should be more than sufficient for you to get a handle on what is required to build a new product here.' Brett looked sternly into the eyes of the three men and left.

Mark instantly took charge of the meeting, drawing diagrams on the whiteboard and saying 'but the reality is' at least twenty-five times that Sandra counted. It was an information explosion. She tried desperately to figure out how she was supposed to absorb the knowledge of a hundred years in six months. Alan and Vince remained silent for most of the meeting. She could sense their resentment. Not only had she been thrust upon them by their CEO, but she had no product development experience and, worst of all, was a woman. It was obvious that none of these men wanted Sandra in the company. Each of them clearly considered they could come up with a new product without the assistance of some outsider.

Just because she worked for that damn Yank, Mark thought, Brett reckons she'll be able to come up with something that we can't. Well, we'll see about that.

Mark had made a point of learning all he could about this Nick Abbott. Leaning forward in his office chair, Mark had read through all the clippings of articles and accolades he could find on Nick Abbott, studying them several times, wanting to make sure he had the facts correct.

Mark considered all the possibilities the Nick Abbott visit could mean for Australian Life. Mark was a company man to the core. He loved his work. He loved his company and he knew that his future was assured now that Brett

McLeod had taken over. Mark remembered the day he had started at Australian Life. They still had their juniors wearing shorts in those days. He had worked his way through the ranks, step by step, diligently fulfilling every role given to him in the most efficient manner he knew how. His diligence had paid off. At thirty-five years of age, he was one of the youngest operations managers ever appointed and, he felt sure, in line for Brett's job when he finally retired. It was just as well that Nick Abbott would only be in Australia temporarily or otherwise Brett might be looking for a new heir apparent.

For three months Sandra struggled to cement her role at Australian Life. She needed to know exactly what made the company tick if she was to achieve at her task. She understood a whimpering novice would stand no chance of gaining ground. To find out what the agents needed in a new product, she had to know the driving force behind them, she conjectured. In this case that meant Australian Life. Despite her best efforts to acquire knowledge, however, she found that every time she went to Vince or Alan or Mark, they would have to rush off to a meeting, or take a phone call. She felt like yelling, 'If you don't want me here, why don't you just bloody say so?' But corporate politicians were far to slick too be caught out by such outbursts, she realised, trying to calm herself.

In an attempt to acquire the knowledge she needed she read books, company reports, asked questions of the agents. The agents seemed to like her at least. She had always managed to have a rapport with the sales people; that fact alone would impress those who mattered. She had learned from her time with Nick that without the respect of the agents, a person's tenure in the life industry is likely to be very limited.

Slowly she began to understand Australian Life and what was required of her. Agents were ringing Sandra, in favour of the other consultants, to ask questions about existing products and underwriting requirements. They had even begun to request her presence on sales appointments. Although this wasn't her responsibility, she felt it would be useful to acquire information directly from the market place about what clients wanted to see in insurance industry products.

Greg Prattler, a boyish-looking agent, had been trying to sign up a small engineering company's entire staff in the Australian Life's company superannuation plan. He had been trying for six months. They had finally agreed in principle, Greg told Sandra, but had requested some technical information before they finally agreed to proceed. That was where Sandra came in.

Gathering her courage, Sandra escorted Greg Prattler to his appointment. They arrived at a scruffy-looking office on the edge of town around two o'clock one afternoon. Greg darted out of his car, almost tripping over himself, while Sandra tried ardently to appear cool, calm, and in control. Getting slightly red in the face, Greg pushed open the glass door by its wooden handle for Sandra to enter first. She looked up the flight of black-tipped, white laminate-covered stairs, and wondered what type of business could possibly operate from such dowdy premises. Her shining, new, black Italian briefcase was cutting into the centre pad of her left hand. She was right-handed by nature, but wanted to leave that hand free to drive into the prospective client's palm, without having to shuffle her briefcase awkwardly from one position to another. She checked inside her jacket pocket to make sure that her business cards were within easy reach.

'Sandra,' Greg said, reaching the office door of the managing director, 'I'd like you to meet Bill Barclay. Bill, this is our national superannuation expert, Sandra Upton.'

She held back the urge to yell, 'What the hell are you

talking about?' to Greg's face. Greg had been practising a variety of titles to use on the way to the meeting. He had started out at 'product consultant' and was liable to end up at 'chairperson of the board'. Sandra decided her business card was best left in her pocket. Her phone number, she realised, was on the presentation anyway.

Sandra felt relieved when Bill Barclay assumed a casual posture for the meeting. He wore a plain dark suit and red tie, but looked as though he would be more comfortable in a pair of well-worn overalls.

'Have a seat,' said the tall Aussie with a gruff voice, ushering her into a chair. 'So you know all about superannuation?'

'Well, that's what they tell me,' she answered, trying not to lie.

'Good.'

He spent an hour asking Sandra questions that she was able to answer with astonishing ease. It hadn't occurred to her, until that moment, that the little she knew about the subject of 'super' was ten volumes more than anybody else knew. It was easy to sound like an expert.

'Okay, where's the paperwork?' Bill's question had a note of finality to it.

'I just so happen to have it with me,' Sandra said with a smile.

'Hey, Greg. I like her. You can bring her here again.'

Greg had been silent throughout. Sandra had tried valiantly not to smirk at Greg's ridiculous grin as he listened to the conversation with profound interest. It wasn't until the forms were safely signed that he finally spoke. It was as though the floodgates had opened and Sandra could not get one word in edgeways.

He raved unrelentingly about the fantastic job she had done and proceeded to tell everyone he came in contact with at Australian Life the same thing.

'Congratulations, I'm proud of you,' beamed Mark Fitzgerald when Sandra returned with the signed documents.

She felt a charge of satisfaction. This was high praise indeed coming from Mark Fitzgerald.

'I always knew you'd be the star on the team,' he smugly announced.

Bullshit artist, she thought. There was about as much sincerity in Mark's praise as there would have been if he was congratulating a rival football team for just defeating the team he followed. Within moments she overhead Mark on the phone to Brett, telling him about the deal that had been closed as a result of Mark giving Sandra the information to use. Her fury raced through her. How was she supposed to achieve anything against these odds?

She took piles of documents home, analysed all the existing products and their cost structures and tried to narrow down the best area for a breakthrough product development. She began to look drained each morning when she entered the office. She caught Mark and the others smiling at one another, as though they realised they were winning the war in wearing her down. But the war's not over yet, she told herself confidently.

For five months Sandra had wanted to face Nick, to put the spectres of the past to rest. James had whisked her away from Nick straight after Ted's death but somehow she needed to see him again if she was finally to come to terms with her situation. With the conference only a few weeks away, she knew she would soon have her chance. Perhaps then, she thought, I'll be able to work with a clear mind. Maybe Nick will even be able to help me.

*

A large board in the foyer of the Regent Hotel directed delegates to the ballroom where tea and coffee were being served before the conference began.

'Congratulations.'

Sandra turned around to see Nick Abbott. It was the first time she had laid eyes on him since she left New York. The sight of him made her feel weak. The vision of Ted's crushed body superimposed itself on the vision of the man before her. It was all she could do to remain composed.

I chose to face him, she told herself, so here's my chance.

'Congratulations on landing such a great job,' Nick continued. 'It's good to see you again.'

'Thank you,' she said politely. 'It's a small world, isn't it?'

'Yes, you could say that. I am glad to see things are working out for you. At least your time with me set you up for this position. I'm pleased something good came out of it,' he said charmingly.

'Oh, yes. Things are working out fine. I must admit, I'm curious about something though.'

'What's that?'

'What is a die-hard New Yorker doing working in Australia?' Even as the question left her lips, she realised she was being daring beyond reason, given what James had told her about Nick.

'Well, it took a lot of convincing to get me here, I can tell you. But I'm only here as a consultant, to help this company get where it wants to go.'

'I see. So you will be going back to New York?'

'You sound particularly keen to get rid of me.' Nick looked at her questioningly.

'I'm sorry,' Sandra stammered, feeling overpowered in Nick's presence. 'I didn't mean it to sound like that, it's just…'

'Sandra, you don't have to explain. I understand the way you must feel about me and I'm truly sorry. Please believe me when I say I had no idea Ted would – I mean, I had to…'

'I know. Business is business and Ted had plenty of other options. I'm slowly coming to accept that. But I don't need to tell you how hard it is to cope with the death of a loved one, do I?'

Once again she felt her boldness had overstepped the mark, until Nick's expression softened.

'No,' he said quietly. 'I know exactly what you're going through and I meant what I said in New York about being here to help you.'

The softness in his voice and eyes took Sandra by surprise. She had expected to loathe this man, instead she felt empathy with his pain.

'Well, we may be able to help each other,' she laughed.

'Oh, how is that?'

'Perhaps we can talk about it at the annual dinner tonight?'

'Of course, I'll arrange for us to be on the same table.'

'Perfect. I'll look forward to it,' she said uncertainly.

Nick wondered if Sandra knew anything about James's disappearance. If he managed to get her trust back, perhaps she would have a vital clue as to his whereabouts. It was a possibility he couldn't leave to chance. In any event, she was far more useful as an ally than an enemy. An enemy who could ask a lot of embarrassing questions.

'I suppose I should congratulate you too,' she said in a friendly manner. 'There can't be many agency managers asked to consult in such a major capacity to an overseas company.'

'Well, I am the best of the best, you know,' he said, smiling at her disarmingly.

'Yes,' she said, and smiled back. 'I have heard that rumour.'

'You look fabulous. You've shed that "little girl lost"

look. It never suited you,' Nick commented.

'Nick,' Sandra laughed, flushing at his insolence. 'Little girl lost? Is that the way I appeared to you?'

'Ah huh. I still know how to make you blush,' he said, without answering her question. 'How is the new revolutionary product coming along, anyway?'

'Well, that's one of the things I'd like to discuss with you over dinner.'

'Hello, you two,' Brett said, approaching the two colleagues. 'I'm glad to see you are getting reacquainted.'

The bell had sounded to signify the start of the conference.

'Come on,' Brett blustered. 'We don't want to be late for my opening comments.'

'That man's enthusiasm never ceases to amaze me,' muttered Nick.

Brett's small shiny head appeared over the podium at the front of the hall, illuminated by spotlights. His glasses, Sandra noticed, had been replaced with contact lenses. Obviously all part of the new image he was bringing together on that day, she concluded.

'Greetings and welcome to what is undoubtedly the most important annual conference in our history. Today we don't only change a name, we change a culture. It is not my intention to be the biggest, it is my intention to be the best.'

'Like hell,' Sandra heard Nick say under his breath.

'We at Australian Life are about to enter a new age. An age which will see our share markets earning fantastically high returns. An age which will see deregulation bring with it the spectre of new competition from the banking industry, and an age which will shed the old sleeping giant image of Australian Life for ever. Today we become Prime Financial Group; a force to be reckoned with in the financial world.'

Spontaneous applause filled the room as the first slide shone across a screen behind Brett. It was the word and the logo of Prime. The logo was designed around the word itself and gave the impression that the letter 'r' was a person with its arm outstretched around a smaller person to its right, the letter 'i'.

'Today,' Brett continued, 'our superannuation department becomes an entity in its own right: Prime Benefits Consulting. Today you will hear about many changes but the most exciting is that we have new blood injected into this company in the form of Nick Abbott. Nick was the manager of Eddie Schwartz, a man whose achievements I know each of you aspire to. Nick was not easily prised away from his healthy agency in New York to take this position, but after much persuasion on my part, I have convinced him to stay on for a second consulting year. That means we have eighteen months left to pick the brains of the expert. I hope this time will be as rewarding and enjoyable for you, Nick, as I am sure it will be for all of us. Without further ado, would you make welcome to the podium, Mr Nick Abbott.'

Every person in the ballroom applauded earnestly.

'Thank you.' Nick removed the microphone from its stand to allow himself freer movement around the stage.

'During the last six months I have travelled over every state in your beautiful country. I have been examining your recruitment methods, your training programmes and your retention records. And now I can tell you something. It sucks.'

A deathly silence fell over the hall.

'We've got a long way to go before we realise Brett's visions. We are going to have to make some tough decisions, maybe unpopular ones. But the decisions we make today are going to shape the future for all of us.'

Sandra noticed George Hamilton as Nick continued his opening address. There was a coldness to George's eyes that Sandra couldn't place. Looking around the room, she could see expressions of fear, curiosity and admiration in the eyes of her colleagues, but George's eyes were cold. Why did George's expression trouble her so? Perhaps, she told herself, it was some form of jealousy. After all, there had been no one in Australia who came near to having the reputation and recognition of George and Ralph, until now.

'It means,' Nick continued, 'that there will be some fundamental changes made.'

A diagram of Australia was flashed on the screen with little 'p's representing Prime's main sales offices.

'As you can see, I will be regionalising the sales teams. The main states, Victoria and New South Wales, will have three regions. The others will have one or two regions depending on size. Each of these regions will be headed by a regional manager who reports to one person, and one person only – me. Your existing state sales manager will cease to exist on 1st January next year. The new regional managers will be powerful men in this organisation. In future no decision, at any level, will be made until the question has been asked: how does this affect the sales agent and his regional manager? I am looking for twelve regional managers in total. I already have my eye on a couple of men within Prime's existing resources, others will have to be recruited in.

'The sales manager's role of managing small groups of agents within regions will remain, although perhaps in a slightly restructured format. So the new look will go something like this.' Another slide flashed up on the screen.

Nick Abbott			
Regional Manager East Victoria	Regional Manager Central Victoria		Regional Manager Western Victoria
Agency Manager	Agency Manager	Agency Manager	Agency Manager
Agency Manager	Agency Manager	Agency Manager	Agency Manager
Sales Agents	Sales Agents	Sales Agents	Sales Agents

'I expect the twelve regional managers to recruit, train and guide the sales managers. This will be done under my strict supervision to start with. I will expect the regional managers to appoint assistants; people who can help them recruit. The assistants will be trained over a period of time to become sales managers in their own right. This will enable Prime's agent numbers to grow three times faster than is currently possible under the one state sales manager per state system.

'All you state sales managers out there who are worried about your positions, don't be. If you're any good, you'll be a regional manager with more money and power than you'll ever earn being a state sales manager. If you're not any good, then we don't want you anyway.

'To the administrative people out there, and to people in subsidiary companies of Prime, obviously this structure will have minimal effect on you. This is purely a change for the sales side of the life insurance company. I shall be looking at new computer systems to back up the changes, which you will obviously have to learn, but other than that your jobs will remain the same.'

Nick's mind was racing. This is what he had dreamed of all his life. The chance to take a shell of a company and turn it into something great. First the biggest in Australia, then the world. The excitement of seeing his plans graphically designed in lights before him gave him a charge no drug could ever match.

There were times Nick wished Brett McLeod was not the man heading Prime. Brett didn't understand the insurance business. He would ask Nick innumerable questions each time Nick put a suggestion forward. Brett had dismissed Cathy's product idea as an impractical concept. He told Nick that because of the high upfront commission, based on a concept which had long-term administrative problems, he could not condone it. It was likely to put too much strain on Prime's reserve levels, he explained. Now Nick had to rely on Sandra's computer literacy and creative mind to come up with the product he needed to blitz the market and fulfil his plans.

Trying to explain the complexities of restructuring the responsibilities and remunerations of all sales people had also resulted in countless futile and exhaustive meetings with his new superior. Despite giving Nick the green light, Brett branded some of Nick's plans as reckless. He was not happy with the higher commission levels, even taking into account the reduced running costs. Brett told Nick to be wary of getting trapped by his own genius. Nick dismissed his warning as witless.

In the audience, listening with both concern and interest, was Mark Fitzgerald. He could feel the increased money and power of a regional manager itching at his fingertips. It was just inches away, but inches that could turn to miles if he wasn't chosen. The anticipation grew in Mark's huge eyes as he hungrily listened for more. He had to be one of the regional managers, that was beyond question. Mark had worked in the insurance industry for ten of his fifteen working years, and had to admit that he had some pretty impressive records behind him. He had started out by selling insurance door to door, the hardest, most unrewarding bitch of a job that anyone could ever want.

'If you can survive this stage,' his manager had told him, 'you'll be set.' A lesser man than Mark may not have taken kindly to such words, but Mark was streetwise and entered the insurance business to make his fortune, and by God that was what he was going to do. Over the last four years as operations manager, however, he had stagnated. Now this snippet of a girl challenged all he had been working for. Nick Abbott represented everything that he aspired to. He was going to get to know this Nick Abbott very well, learn his every move, his every mannerism; Mark planned to master them all.

Sandra entered the Regent's ballroom that evening in an elegant strapless gown of black and emerald taffeta. The bodice fitted snugly, pointing into a V waistline which opened into a full, gliding skirt. A double rope of pearls with an emerald clasp graced her delicate neck. With her hair in a French roll, earrings of teardrop pearls could be seen swaying slightly as she walked. Sandra noticed that the younger members of staff, and rookie agents, didn't look quite comfortable in the hired tuxedos. She smiled to herself, thinking the boys had a few years to go before they could look natural with a stiff neck. Checking the table plans, Sandra was delighted to see Nick had been true to his word and placed her on the top table with Brett, Mark, George, Ralph and himself.

The ballroom shimmered with statements of Prime's ambition. Sprays of white orchids and gardenias adorned each table. The new Prime logo was suspended above the head table and was festooned in gold and white streamers. Each chair had a white helium balloon tied to it with

'Prime' proudly printed on it in gold.

Nick immediately singled out Sandra as a dance partner. Sandra reluctantly had to admit to a pang of satisfaction at being the chosen one.

'Huh,' Mark grunted with envy, as he settled at his table, 'looks like the Yank prick's got her marked.'

Nick returned Sandra to the table, gallantly pulling out her chair while scanning the table for faces he did not know.

Sandra observed him in silence, thinking how charming he could be.

'Our girl's carved out quite a niche for herself over the last six months,' Brett said to Nick.

'Yes, thanks to my guidance,' Mark added quickly.

'I see,' Nick answered, looking towards Sandra to see how she would react to such obvious provocation.

She simply smiled sweetly at Nick, cool and composed.

'It would be fair to say that Sandra wouldn't be where she is today if it wasn't for my influence. Isn't that right?' Mark asked her forcefully.

'I would say that's a fair estimate of the situation,' Sandra responded sarcastically.

'Tell me, Nick,' George Hamilton asked, changing the direction of the conversation. 'What happens to your whizbang system when you go back to New York?' George tried to dismiss his feeling for Nick as bias against Americans. Instincts, however, told him that it was something far more serious.

'I'll groom a successor from one of the twelve regional managers,' Nick explained.

'Jesus, you're going to have a job finding twelve people of the calibre you're looking for among this lot,' George laughed.

'Who says they have to come from within the company? Maybe we'll poach some more people from Mutual Life

Australia. There must be twelve men in the whole of Australia who are capable of following me for half a million bucks a year.'

'I'd follow you for that,' Mark piped up.

'Do you think you could run a region?' Nick asked patronisingly.

'Why not? I've run the operations of this entire company for four years.'

'Maybe that's why they needed to bring me in,' Nick quipped.

Mark seethed at his arrogance, but quickly realised he must curb his anger in public.

'And why did you decide to stay in Australia for another year?' George asked.

'Brett convinced me that I couldn't leave the job half done and that one year wasn't long enough,' Nick explained.

'You'll be applying for permanent residency soon,' Mark Fitzgerald joked.

'You just never know,' Nick answered charmingly.

The band started playing 'Chattanooga Choo Choo'.

'Care to dance again?' Nick asked Sandra.

'Thank you. I'd love to.'

'You're a very talented dancer,' Nick spoke softly, gliding his way around the floor trying to determine where Sandra needed to fit into the scheme of things.

'Thank you.'

'So what do you think of my plans for the company?' he asked casually.

'Well, I'm hardly going to say they stink now, am I?'

'Smart girl. Do you have any ideas about who should be the regional managers?'

'I guess Mark *is* a likely candidate for one of them.'

'He doesn't have to be. Would you appoint him if you had the choice?'

'Surely you're not going to appoint someone on the strength of my opinion.'

'Of course not. But I'm interested in your opinion.'

His gaze was cold and penetrating. Sandra found it partly threatening and partly fascinating.

'To tell you the truth, Nick, I have had a few problems with Mark.'

'Would you care to tell me about them?'

'Yes, I would…' Sandra proceeded to recount all the difficulties she was facing trying to get new products and concepts developed.

'Basically,' she explained, 'they resent me because I was pushed on them by Brett, and they are threatened by me because I am achieving what is expected of me, despite them trying to block me.'

'So what's the problem? It sounds like normal company politics to me.'

'I'm sure you're right. But if you want to help Brett lift this company to number one, I'm sure you would rather see it achieved efficiently and quickly without the interference of a threatened bureaucrat.'

'You're a smart girl. I always knew you were. But why haven't you spoken to Brett about this?'

'Partly, I guess, because he kept saying he had so much faith in me I didn't want to make him think I was weak, and partly because he's been far too busy to reach anyway.'

'I see your point. Well, don't worry. I'm in charge now. Anything you need to get done, you tell me and I'll look after it for you.'

'I don't know what to say,' she answered, feeling a charge of relief in her breast.

'Say thank you.'

'Thank you,' she said delicately.

Sandra could feel the eyes of her bosses upon her as Nick gracefully danced with her. She could feel their envy and found a strength of determination born from it.

'I have to ask you something,' Nick began cautiously.

'What's that?'

'I know James helped you when you moved back to Australia. I've lost touch with him. Do you have any ideas as to his whereabouts?'

Sandra felt chilled at the mention of James's name. She remembered how he longed to leave his father's past behind him.

'He came out to Australia for a while,' Sandra began. 'He said... he said...'

'Yes, what did he say?'

'I don't know how to tell you.'

'Just say it,' Nick urged.

'When Ted died, James blamed you more than I did. James and Ted were almost like brothers.'

'I understand that, but what did he say?'

'He said he wanted to make a completely fresh start and remove himself from anything that reminded him of you. I'm afraid that included me. I really don't know what happened to him after we went our separate ways.'

'I see. Do you think there's a chance he's still here in Australia?'

'I suppose so, but I wouldn't know where to start looking.'

Nick sighed. It was a dead end after all.

'Although,' Sandra added, 'I do have friends who could do some checking through visas and things. Perhaps they'll be able to locate a James Abbott.'

'Would you do that?' Nick asked, genuinely surprised.

'You help me, and I'll help you. Isn't that how it works?'

Nick looked searchingly into Sandra's expression and was satisfied that she was his.

'Despite the pain I endured after Ted's death, I always

felt James's reaction was a little melodramatic,' she said tentatively.

'He has his father's hot blood.'

'I suppose so,' she answered.

'Thank you, ladies and gentlemen,' said the band leader, 'we will now take a brief break for you to enjoy your entrées.'

'I think we're finally going to start separating the men from the boys, and a bloody good thing too,' announced Mark to Brett, as Nick and Sandra returned.

'That's my man,' Nick said, apparently pleased at Mark's positive reaction. 'What do you plan to do to make me choose you as one of my twelve apostles?'

'Lift the sales figures to highest in the country, recruit new agents and shape up my existing management.'

'Oh?'

'Yes. It's about time I got back to the real action, I realise that now. Working in the ivory tower has made me lose touch with the market place, but I'll soon have that problem fixed.'

'Good. Tell me, how many of your agents do you intend to have in the Hamilton Black training programme by the end of the year?' Nick asked, ignoring the presence of George and Ralph completely.

'About thirty-five per cent,' Mark answered.

'That's not very many,' Nick commented.

'I know. But they teach the high end of the market. Agents with only one or two years' experience in the industry will get confused if I put them in Hamilton Black straight away.'

'Perhaps Hamilton Black are a waste of money. Is that what you're saying?'

Nick was acutely aware of George's growing tension. He knew George and Ralph had not been impressed with his credentials. While they posed no threat to him that he could think of, they annoyed him intensely and he'd prefer it if they were pushed into the background. Mark was liable to give him the initial ammunition to recommend this.

Nick appreciated the fact that the Hamilton Black training programme was the brainchild of Brett McLeod and that, as yet, Nick was not in a position to overrule his decisions. But collecting a group of regional managers together who were not in favour of the Hamilton Black programme would be a big step in the right direction of getting rid of them.

Mark felt awkward and a little unsure how to answer. 'I'm not saying they're a waste of money. They have a damn good programme and the marks on the board. I'm just saying that you have to be very selective about who you put in their programme, that's all. I'll tell you about something that Sandra and I are working on together,' he added quickly by way of a diversion. 'We're pooling our resources to form a cross-selling concept across both life insurance and company superannuation. It should help boost both companies' sales.'

'Are you now?' Nick asked, watching Ralph holding George back.

'Yes,' Sandra explained. 'My idea is to teach the agents to get their foot into the door of large companies using company superannuation and then cross-sell to all the staff members, using individual counselling sessions to explain the benefits of their company super plan. What do you think?'

'Excellent,' Nick said. 'You must tell me all about it.'

'I'd love to,' Mark answered, trying to race Sandra for the attention.

'Good. I'll get Sandra to brief me on it tomorrow. There's nothing like teamwork to get a company moving, now is there?'

Mark and George both felt like digging the knives into

Nick's back, but both knew Brett was supremely satisfied with his new lieutenant and an outburst in front of the CEO would not enhance their career prospects.

'I feel like dancing again,' Nick announced.

As he left with Sandra, George turned towards Brett. 'Are you sure you know what you're doing with this man?'

Brett's eyes widened. 'Are you drunk, man? How can you ask such a question?'

'I don't mean to speak out of turn, but how well did you check his credentials?'

'Credentials?' Brett shouted. 'He was the manager of Eddie Schwartz, for Christ's sake. His own company selected him for a world consulting tour. What better credentials do you want? Besides, Sandra worked with Nick for a year in New York. Don't you think she would have said something if there were any buried secrets?'

'I don't know. They look pretty chummy to me. Doesn't it strike you as a bit strange that the best in the world would come to Australia for two years?'

'Not if you knew what I was paying him,' Brett laughed. 'You're just jealous. You were king pin until Nick Abbott arrived with a reputation bigger than Texas.'

'I'm not jealous, I'm concerned. Concerned for all of us. I knew Eddie and there's something that troubles me about this Nick Abbott.'

'Look,' Brett said in a fatherly manner, putting his hand on George's shoulder, 'I'm going to the international LMA meeting in a couple of weeks. I'll be personally meeting Gus Fletcher. I'm sure if there is anything I should know about Nick Abbott, he'll be the man to tell me. Stop worrying. You're beginning to make me think I shouldn't have taken on a petulant child to run my training programmes.'

'Just don't say I didn't warn you, that's all.'

'Don't worry, George. I'll never say that.'

'You're quite a girl, Sandra Upton,' Nick whispered as he pulled her close. 'I'll be watching your progress with interest over the next twelve months.'

'Thank you. I'm very honoured.'

He brushed her cheek with his.

A little charge surged through Sandra's conscience. The intrusion of her private space was uncomfortable but, she decided, it was a harmless enough gesture.

*

'Mark, great news,' Sandra chirped like a bird, fluttering into Mark's office.

'What's that?' he asked disinterestedly.

'It looks like we're finally going to get some help with our cross-selling concept. Apparently Nick Abbott spoke to Brett, who in turn spoke to George, and they have agreed to put some time and money into preparing visual aids for us and include the concept at the Hamilton Black training sessions.'

'Great. Have a seat.' Mark realised he had better cultivate his relationship with Sandra Upton or she might turn the boss man against him permanently.

'Thanks. I thought we should put our heads together and send up a couple of designs, the way we like them, just as suggestions of course, before they put something totally boring together up there. What do you think?'

'Great idea.'

He shoved the pile of papers he was working on out of the way and started scribbling on a notepad.

At last he was starting to treat her with some respect. Even if it had taken the fear of his own position to get things moving, at least now she could work without blocks.

As Mark explained his ideas, Sandra's eyes darted from one side of the paper to the other, her lips pressed firmly together.

'What do you think?' Mark asked.

'That's very good. If we combine these with some of my drafts, I think we've got the makings of something very solid to start training with.'

'Great, I knew we could do it,' he said rigidly.

'Mark,' his secretary called from the open office door, 'Mr Abbott is here to see you.'

Mark jumped to attention. 'We'll finish this later. Keep it under your hat for now, if you don't mind, Sandra.'

'Sure.'

Sandra passed Nick waiting impatiently at Mark's secretary's desk as she left.

'Sandra, it's good to see you again,' he said almost in an undertone as though they were secret lovers.

'Hi, Nick,' she tried to sound casual, despite concerns that Mark was about to try to pass their joint plans off as his own.

'Wait a minute,' he called after her. 'I have to go into a meeting now but Mark is meeting me for cocktails later. Would you like to join us?'

'That's sounds fine. Thank you. What time?'

'Shall we say six thirty?'

'I'll look forward to it.'

She headed back to her office feeling mildly honoured that Nick had invited her to join him.

*

She met Mark and Nick, intentionally a few minutes late, at The Rocks, a place named after the rocky harbourside on which it was built. With Sydney Harbour glistening in the background, Sandra noticed an array of small boats which seemed to dance upon the water. She spotted Nick Abbott straight away.

'I'm glad you could make it.' Nick smiled charmingly.

Mark looked up as though Nick had now given his approval to concede the girl's existence. Nick pulled a third chair towards the vacant side of their table.

'So,' Nick continued the conversation. He judged Sandra with the fine instinct of a gifted philanderer, for it was, of course, a gift. He had read with great attention Casanova's memoirs and there the old rogue had been described precisely. When she is receptive, every woman gives out subtle little signs, breathing, flushing, change of poise, tiny body movements, even an odour that very few men can recognise, let alone interpret. It was a gift that only the great lovers possessed. Knowing when to act, how far to push each stage, that was the trick, he told himself.

It sounded to Sandra like Mark was trying to impress the big chief, which was not at all surprising.

'Thank you for the opportunity,' Mark said, getting out of his seat. 'I'll leave you two now.' He winked at Nick, with his face turned away from Sandra as if to say, 'There's only one thing she's good for, we both know that.'

Nick studied Sandra. It was almost fully dark outside. He pulled his chair around as close as possible to hers and sat forward, resting his arm on the side of her chair.

'The guys are very impressed with you.'

'Really?'

'Yes. And so am I. I've been talking to a lot of people and they all say the same thing.'

'Which is?'

'That you've got a talent far beyond your role. What are you planning to do with it?'

She hadn't thought about it precisely until that moment. Just progressing stage by stage would have suited her. But this was indisputably a chance at more.

'I guess I should reserve comment until I see what the new opportunities are in your structure, wouldn't you say?'

'I would say. That will give us a chance to understand one another a little better in the process.'

Nick rubbed his eyes with a serious, almost mournful expression on his face.

'It can be a very lonely place at the top, you know. Are you sure you want to climb the corporate ladder?'

'I don't plan to take over the company just yet, if that's what you mean.'

'It's not what I mean.' He sat back in his chair and sighed. 'Everybody wants a piece of you. There's nothing left for you at the end of the day. It can be a hollow victory. I go home to my apartment, alone.' He emphasised the last word.

'I go out for meals, alone,' Nick continued. 'It's the only chance I get to stop and think about myself. Even someone like me needs a friend sometimes, you know.'

A transformation took place before Sandra's eyes. He was no longer the ferocious leader of a thousand men. The cold ruthless ruler who people spoke of in hushed tones became a meek, nearly pathetic figure with a melancholy sadness to her. She felt her heart go out to him. She couldn't share his feelings but she could imagine what it must be like. She knew it was not a feeling she wanted to experience. She wanted to console him but all the words she thought of seemed to be the wrong ones. She considered for a moment taking his hand but quickly dismissed the idea as an embarrassing indiscretion.

He was silent, sensing every thought running through her mind. There was a gritty determination about her, yet she seemed every inch a vulnerable woman. The thought of developing her slowly was tantalising.

'What's that?' she asked, pointing at his stickpin in an effort to break the mood.

He looked down to the lapel of his pink sports jacket.

'That represents a charity organisation I work for in the

States. A group of us formed together and said that it was great that we give to Ethiopia and Bangladesh, but what about the people at home in America who need our help? The homeless, the street kids. The pin represents three people reaching out and holding hands.'

'That's beautiful. But when do you find the time?' Emotions were tumbling round inside her. Confusion. Awe. Excitement.

'If it's important enough, you can make time.'

The piano player started playing 'New York, New York'.

'Hey, they're playing my song,' Nick said.

'Do you miss New York?'

'Sometimes. But Sydney's a good place. I like it here. Do you know what my secretary calls me?'

'No.'

'Dundee. She says I'm Crocodile Dundee in reverse.'

'It suits you. That's what I shall call you from now on.'

The use of the nickname removed another layer of mystique from Nick Abbott. He was becoming a warm, charming, interesting man to Sandra Upton. She knew Nick was trying to cultivate her trust.

'So what do you do when you're not making up nicknames for your senior executives?'

'A variety of things. I like to go horse riding, water-skiing, skin diving.'

'An outdoor girl. I realise how little I knew you, back in New York. We really should get to know one another better.'

'I'm flattered that you feel that way.'

'Don't be flattered, you deserve it.'

'What do you really think of Mark?' Sandra asked, casually changing the subject. She smoothed her skirt to avoid looking at Nick. She still found being this close to Nick somewhat disturbing.

'I don't know what to think yet.'

'He's come up with some ideas for the cross-selling concept,' Sandra announced, as though she didn't know that is what they had been discussing.

Nick looked up. 'He's trying something out, yes.'

Nick motioned to the waiter to bring another round of drinks, temporarily avoiding Sandra's gaze.

'Then you've discussed them with him?' she urged.

'We were just finishing off our discussions on it when you arrived tonight.' Nick passed Sandra another Scotch and soda, aware that she had raised the matter only because it concerned her. 'It sounds very solid to me. Why do you ask?'

She pulled out her draft designs. 'Did he show you these?'

'Yes, and he did tell me they were your ideas. I don't think you have to worry about him any more. He may still resent you, but he knows he can't touch you. Not while I'm around.'

'Well, that's a relief.'

'Your concept is a good one, but I hope you're not going to rest on your laurels. We still need a new product.'

'I know. I'm working on it. Sometimes I don't sleep all night, trying to wrestle with the options we have available.'

'You're very diligent,' he smiled. 'I know I can count on you. But for now, relax. It's a beautiful evening, the stars are out. Let's not talk business for a while. You have to stop to smell the roses, Sandra.'

'I suppose so,' she agreed.

With one sentence Nick had managed to relax her completely. From that moment Sandra chatted incessantly, asking Nick about his consulting tour and the exciting spots of the world he had visited. She became so involved in this man's company, it was several hours later before she realised that they were the last people in the place.

'I really should be leaving. It's quite late.' The words toppled feebly off her tongue.

'Are you sure?'

'Quite sure.'

'Well, I'll walk you to the door then.'

Nick handed a taxi driver fifty dollars. 'Take the lady wherever she wants to go.'

'We must do this again some time,' he said quietly.

*

With the weekend only hours away, Sandra decided she could finally take a few days off for herself.

'A delivery for you,' Sandra's secretary said, arriving in her office with a huge bunch of red roses. The note read: 'Let's have dinner – Dundee.'

'Nice flowers,' Mark commented, entering her office.

'Thank you. They're from Nick,' she said proudly.

Mark dropped a shade in colour and became quite fidgety.

'He's quite a character, isn't he?' Mark asked rhetorically.

'Yes, he is,' she answered, smelling her flowers.

Mark watched her carefully. He had decided to discuss some new ideas with her, having realised he needed to get Sandra on his side. After months of blocking her progress it was going to be a tough road to get her confidence, and seeing those flowers simply enraged him further. He could not have some lustful American destroying his chance at success.

'It's good work if you can get it,' Mark said sarcastically, immediately wishing he hadn't.

Damn, she thought, he thinks the only reason I'm getting ahead is because I'm sleeping with the boss. Damn him for not recognising potential when he sees it. Damn him for thinking that's the only way a woman can make it. Damn them all to hell. The images of chauvinism spun around her mind in blurred and blazing circles. That conniving little weasel, she seethed quietly to herself. It is not my problem if he forced this situation of conflict on our work. She was furious at his attitude.

'Goodnight, Mark,' she said, trying to adopt a tone that said his words had meant nothing to her. 'Have a good weekend.'

She thought about Nick's conversation the other night a dozen times. Sitting in her Celica and toying with the ignition key, she took a deep breath while rationalising the situation. So Nick treated her like a lady; paid for her taxi and brought her flowers. Was that a crime? He was charming and witty and good company and she was pleased that he chose to befriend her above the others. You take everything too seriously, she told herself. Once the facts were neatly compartmentalised in her brain, Sandra felt satisfied. It's about time you let your hair down, she told herself.

With a torrent of new-found freedom running through her mind, Sandra decided it was time for a night out. Centrepoint Tower seemed as good a place as any to start. In the heart of the city the high-rise construction was crowned with a revolving restaurant with shimmering lights which glowed like jewels against the skyline. Sandra chose to start with a few drinks at the piano bar, situated underneath the shopping area on the ground floor. It was a small but comfortable atmosphere with the resident Indian pianist already entrenched in a medley of jazz numbers. Sandra sat on one of the stools around the piano, rather than sitting alone at a table. The Indian sang with an accent which indicated he had had a very expensive English education. He obviously loved his work and Sandra quickly became swamped by the emotion in his music.

'I thought I'd find you here.'

Sandra heard a familiar voice utter those words. She spun around to see an intensely sensual face. His deep brown smouldering eyes examined Sandra's form with curiosity. She admired his thick black hair and dazzling smile as his full lips parted to speak.

'Good evening,' he said slowly.

Even his voice made Sandra tremble with desire.

'How are things going with the new job?'

'Fine,' she squeaked, and on hearing how ridiculous she sounded immediately cleared her throat.

'The old man isn't giving you any trouble?' he asked.

'None at all. It's going like clockwork.'

'I told you it would.'

'Yes, as usual you were right.'

'So, you have managed to make yourself a permanent fixture?'

'Definitely.'

'Well, I guess my company better watch out for the competition, eh?'

'I hardly think you can consider me much of a threat,' she laughed.

'I don't know about that. I've seen the old man turn adversity to advantage too many times in my life.' He sat down on the stool beside her and sighed deeply.

'I can't help worrying about you,' he said. 'I feel as though I've thrown you into the lion's den.'

'I don't remember needing a lot of persuasion to take this role.'

'That's what worries me. Sometimes I see traits of my father in myself and it scares the hell out of me.'

'Oh, James. I'm a big girl. I can take care of myself.'

'I don't want you taking care of yourself. That's my job, remember?'

He moved towards her and embraced her firmly. The warmth of his body stirred a tingling desire through every fibre of Sandra's being. She could never remember being so stimulated by a man, not even by Ted.

'I'm very pleased I met you, James Cartwright. And pleased you vowed to look after me, too.'

'Let's go to one of the tables. I think it's time we reviewed this situation.'

She followed him silently, thinking how like his father James was in many ways, but how different too. He had all of Nick's charismatic charm, and had learned many of Nick's manipulative skills, but James maintained an air of goodness about him which was totally devoid in Nick. But damn that charisma – in both of them.

'He's still searching for you, you know,' she said, taking her seat.

'Good. Let him look. It obviously hasn't occurred to the old bastard that I could have changed his family name. Jesus, what an irony. I come to Australia to get away from him, and here he is, restructuring a company I am challenging for number one position in Australia.' James shook his head in disbelief. 'You are sure he has no idea James Cartwright and James Abbott are the same person?'

Changing his surname had seemed a little theatrical to Sandra but if he wanted nothing to do with his father that was his business and nobody else's.

'Absolutely. He doesn't consider James Cartwright or Champion Life a threat whatsoever. All Nick is concerned with is getting his new system up and running, finding a revolutionary product and overtaking Mutual Life as number one in Australia—'

'And then the world, no doubt,' James added.

'Well, if you're right about the reason he was dismissed from East West, I'm sure he'll be planning revenge. If he is what you say he is, he won't be taking defeat lying down.'

'If he is!' James exclaimed. 'Why is everyone so blind?' he cried in exasperation. 'I tried to tell Brett at the last

LMA meeting to check him out with Gus Fletcher and he told me I was jealous because Australian Life picked him up before Champion Life could. At least it gave me the perfect opportunity to drop your name. I'm sure it won't take you long to find some reason to discredit him before he can do any harm in Australia.'

'That's *if* you're right, James. I still can't believe what you say about him.'

'How can you doubt it? He killed your husband.'

'Ted committed suicide, James. He was a dear, sweet man but he couldn't sell and he couldn't take rejection. That is not Nick's fault.'

'Am I really hearing this from you? He's getting to you, isn't he? I knew it. The old bastard is getting to you. Maybe we should call this off and bring you back into Champion Life. This is too dangerous.'

'It was your idea, remember? And I intend to see it through now. We both must find out the truth or neither of us will be able to live our lives in peace.'

'I suppose you're right. But I already know the truth, I just can't prove it. If I know my father it will only be a matter of time before someone provokes him to strike again. I just pray to God he doesn't find out about us, or that person is likely to be you.'

Sandra felt a chill slither down her spine as the reality of James's suggestion took full impact. He actually believed his father was a murderer and that she could be his next victim.

'Is he happy with your progress as product development manager?' James asked cautiously.

'So far, so good. He likes my cross-selling concept; that should keep him happy for a while.'

'But sooner or later he's going to want a real product and I can't let you give that to him,' James insisted.

'James,' Sandra said, taking his hand and looking into

his eyes with a motherly expression. 'I miss Ted too. I agree that your father is a tough businessman, but that is not a crime. I cannot believe he is a murderer. He's doing fantastic things for Prime. Let go of your hate. He's your father and he loves you. Go back to him, James. Talk this out, please.'

Her eyes opened wide, their moist softness touching his heart. He had to make her realise the truth.

'Don't you find it in the least bit suspicious that two people committed suicide in the same way?'

'A coincidence, yes.'

'I don't believe in coincidences. He killed Eddie because Eddie couldn't stomach the web of death my father led him into. I was too young at the time to understand, but now that I think about it, I realise that my mother's delirious ravings, as my father called them, were right.'

'James, you were only a child when all this happened. Surely the police investigated. He couldn't have got away with murder.'

'I told you, Sandra, he's a very clever man. I'm bloody sure the police suspect him, but they can't prove anything apart from knowing that the cocaine supply was laced with rat poison. Even knowing Nick had a motive doesn't prove he committed the act.'

'Dear James, how do you live with so much bitterness?' she asked sadly.

'I guess I just don't have your gentle, understanding and forgiving nature. There's too much of my father in me, and to tell you the truth, it scares me.'

Sandra felt a giddy sensation as though her logic and responsibilities had been stripped from within her. What James suggested was too fantastic to believe. It seemed there was no past, no future, only now. She found herself gazing deeper and deeper into James's hypnotic eyes. She wanted to run her fingers through his thick black hair; to press herself against the small wiry curls on his strong chest. She craved to know intimately every part of James Cartwright.

'When I was growing up I worshipped my father,' James said reflectively. 'He was a self-made millionaire who gave me everything a child could want. The best clothes, the best education. I wanted for nothing, he was my hero.' He paused for a moment. 'I went to the police before I left New York. They told me I didn't have enough for them to reopen the files. So I went to Gus. I thought at least if I could discredit him with East West he'd be out of a position of power, unable to hurt anyone again. As usual when it comes to my father, he found another way.'

She sighed deeply at the tortured face of the man before her. She couldn't imagine what it must feel like to harbour such deep hatred for a man you once loved and admired as a hero.

'James, this bitterness will destroy you.'

'No. I know I can count on you as a guiding light in this world of darkness.'

Sandra found herself responding to the warmth of his smile.

'When I grew up I discovered many things weren't exactly as they were portrayed to be too,' she commented, thinking how her own father had flown into a rage when she had moved to the city to pursue a career.

'You are very beautiful, Sandra Upton. You have a beauty within beauty, and I won't let my hatred, or Nick's ambitions, spoil that in you.'

'That is very kind of you, but I'm not anything special.' She blushed.

'You obviously haven't taken a look at yourself lately.' He cupped her face in his hands and kissed her softly on the forehead.

He was so warm yet so wounded; she felt herself becoming totally absorbed in his presence. In a swirl of events that never cleared in Sandra's memory she was transported from the piano bar to the bedroom of James's Vaucluse apartment.

'You are the most desirable and exciting woman I have ever met,' he breathed softly in her ear. 'So beautiful and vibrant.'

He lowered his head over hers with a gentle kiss. Slowly he pulled away to look for acceptance in her eyes.

He kissed her again, a different kind of kiss, hard where the first had been soft. She opened her mouth below his, instinctively exploring his body with a savage urgency. She could feel her nipples harden against him and the friction of flesh meeting flesh.

Fighting for patience, James forced himself to go slowly. His mouth drank from hers with a gentleness he hadn't known he possessed; his hands moved up and down her back, his fingers dancing along the delicate bones of her spine in gestures meant to soothe even as they sought to arouse.

Kissing James was like falling into a dream. Sandra wanted to think, to analyse every dazzling sensation, to ensure that later she'd remember everything about this moment. She felt the floor tilt beneath her. She swayed, her fingers tightening on his shoulders, her body curved against his, her soft sigh muffled by his mouth.

They drew apart in unspoken agreement. He cupped her chin, his fingers strong and possessive, but heartbreakingly tender.

'I've never wanted a woman like I want you,' he said.

As they knelt upon his bed, their thighs almost touching, his fingers explored her face.

'You are gorgeous.'

This glorious, reckless moment was one she would remember all her life. She wanted it to be perfect. She wanted to be perfect. She wanted to be the most beautiful woman that James had ever made love to.

'I haven't been with a man for a long time...'

He ran his hand down her hair. 'I won't hurt you.'

'I know.' Her eyes glistened with tears she had never allowed herself to shed.

In the muffled glow of the bedside light, she looked so fragile and so beautiful.

His skin shone irresistibly; she reached out to touch him. His flesh beneath her stroking fingers was soft but the muscle underneath was hard. She pressed her lips against the warm, moist flesh, drinking its texture, its taste and its earthy male scent.

When her tongue trailed wetly down his chest, something in James snapped. Patience was forgotten. He pulled her against him, his hands greedy, his mouth hungry.

He was warm and heavy on her body. It seemed only a few sweet moments before her legs closed around him. The feeling of euphoria that swept back and forth through her body was unlike any sensation she had a memory of. Making love to James was like partaking of a feast after a long fast.

He was wild and demanding, driving her towards delirium, making her feel alive for the first time in a year. Sandra did not want gentleness. She clung to him, her nails clawing at his flesh, her mind cleared of everything but swirling sensations and a blinding pleasure just this side of pain.

Chapter Six

Constant changes in legislation over the next six months brought with them new marketing opportunities for Sandra's sales concepts. She worked tirelessly to unravel the mysteries of the Labor Party's latest ingenious methods that claimed everyone would be tax advantaged. She was delighted with the relative ease with which she was able to unravel the complexities of this new minefield of legislation. The agents were equally delighted with the simple way in which Sandra was able to explain her appreciation of the situation to them.

Mark Fitzgerald, concerned by her growing rapport with the sales force, decided, as a 'gesture of apology for his earlier behaviour', to invite her to a dinner with the insurance and superannuation commissioner.

'When I started out,' he would say, 'I knew as little as you did. A few meals with the ISC helped me more than months of study. I think it will be very helpful to you to hear what he has to say.'

Besides, if Sandra became more involved with the complexities of the fine print, it would distract her from the agents for a while. He could not have her overpowering him in a race to win credibility with Nick.

Sandra's capacity to absorb and understand the complicated formulas and explain them in simple language to the sales agents was a gift Mark had never envisaged when Brett McLeod first forced the young woman upon him. He instructed Sandra to meet Edward Townsend, the ISC, and himself at the Rock Pool for dinner at seven o'clock. He deliberately chose that restaurant not only because it was located in the trendy area of The Rocks, but because of its reputation for serving the finest meals in Sydney.

The atmosphere was casual but elegant. The restaurant buzzed with all the socialites of Sydney. It was the place to be seen if you were anyone of note in this town. It seemed to Mark to be a suitable location for their meeting.

Edward had a distinguished air about him. His grey hair and glasses added to the poise of a firm and resolute leader. He had readily accepted Mark's invitation as he too had a few questions to ask.

'If you could see the piles of complaints we get every day from people who bought policies they didn't really want, and never understood, you would understand why I have grey hair,' Edward explained.

Sandra laughed at his comment, not designed to be a joke.

'The government is going to have to get harsher with its penalties for people who don't comply with the rules of your business,' he continued. 'It is only a matter of time now before I get the power to impose severe penalties and restrictions; some of your sales agents may be getting quite a shock.'

'But how do you know when the agent is in the wrong?' Sandra asked, wildly curious.

'It isn't always straightforward, I grant you. But we are going to be closely scrutinising every new product which comes out of the industry from now on. So you'd better make sure the 'i's are dotted and the 't's crossed before it hits the market place.'

Sandra sat upright in her chair. A lightning bolt hit her. She felt an overwhelming urge to rush to the ladies and write it down before she forgot but instead managed to remain calm and say nothing.

'I'm very glad to hear it,' said Mark. 'It's about time the industry was forced into lifting its act. There have been too many scam merchants ruining the reputation of the industry for all of us.'

'That's right,' Edward agreed. 'Conmen who keep finding new ways to prey on people's greed and ruin them financially in the process.'

'That's horrifying,' gasped Mark in mock abhorrence.

'At least it's good to know we have someone to turn to from now on if something unethical looks like hitting the market,' Sandra said resolutely.

*

Sandra went straight to James after dinner to discuss her idea.

'It's inspired!' he shrieked over the din of his hi-fi.

'Don't get too carried away and rush it through recklessly now.'

James hugged the girl-woman next to him and felt a surge of joy. There was no other word but joy. She was a delight that filled him with pleasure and warmth. Her eyes reflected the intimacy between them. James tried hard at that moment to disassociate her from her undercover work, finding to his disappointment that he could not do it. He wanted to make her his woman, his alone. But that was not possible while his father was still at large.

'I love you very much,' he said.

'I know.' She looked at him and her eyes had a hint of tears. 'We love each other, isn't it extraordinary?'

'Are we going to relax tonight?' he asked in a chirpier tone of voice.

She turned her head sideways, ever so slightly, and clasped his hands.

'Oh James. My dear, sweet James. What would I do without you?'

He held her tightly and made his mind up that he would

have this woman for the rest of his life.

'I'd say it's time we took a break. What about a midnight walk?' he asked.

James had a way of making Sandra want things she had no idea she wanted, and he made her feel things that she vowed she would never feel again for any man.

The night was cool but cloudless, the pale moon shining brightly above the city's skyscrapers.

'Cold?' he asked, noticing a shiver.

'Yes.' She looked up at him. 'But I like it. It's stimulating.'

'Cold air and business, are they the only things that stimulate you these days?'

Sandra was disturbed by his tone.

'Of course not.'

'I'm glad to hear it.'

'I just want this moment to last forever. I feel so free out here in the open.'

'I suppose I can understand that,' James said. He realised how obsessed he had become. Seeing Sandra glistening under the stars suddenly put a new perspective on his feelings. 'I have a proposition for you,' he said thoughtfully.

Sandra's smile was warm. 'You know I can never resist one of your propositions.'

'Why don't we steal a few days to get away together. Indulge ourselves in each other's company and forget the world.'

'But—'

'Sweetheart, it's called relaxing. Being a workaholic myself, I can understand if you've never heard of the concept, but from what I've been told the experience can be quite pleasurable.'

'I can't think of anything I'd rather do, but...'

James tried to distract her by sliding his fingers across

her skin.

'We can't go away now, not at such a crucial time.' She looked puzzled at this sudden change in attitude.

He could feel her pulling away from him, withdrawing into herself. Frustrated he gripped her shoulders tightly and glared in slanting, silent scrutiny.

The gesture was frightening. Sandra stiffened in his arms and pulled away.

Damn, he cursed himself, what was I thinking of?

'Sandra,' he said, running his hand gently over her hair. 'I'm sorry. I just can't bear the thought of sharing you with anyone, especially that man.'

'I know,' she sighed and rested her cheek on his chest.

He sighed deeply with her, sensing her painful unspoken memories.

'Ghosts.' She lifted her head to look at him. 'We all have them.'

*

Sandra took a copy of her findings and theories home in a desperate effort to figure it all out. She had changed into a tracksuit and was almost asleep over her work when James arrived.

'Hello, James. Late hours tonight, I see.'

'I'm afraid so. Did you miss me?'

'Miserably.'

'What have you got there?'

'Copies of the annuity laws,' she said, unfolding some of the papers so he could read them.

'More work,' he murmured, sounding exhausted.

He took the forms and sat on the settee, removing his jacket and tie. There were sweat marks in the sleeves of his shirt that told Sandra he'd had a rough day.

'I know we have to talk about it,' he said with a sigh.

'So you better tell me what's going on.'

'I think I have the basis of a new product you can use. I need somehow to get legal opinion from a section of the insurance law act. Do you think you can arrange that quietly for me?'

She explained the ramifications of her find in minute detail.

'You're quite the super sleuth, aren't you?'

'I learned from the masters,' she said, smiling.

'Very funny,' he scowled, not entirely approving of her innuendo.

'Anyway, sleuthing has nothing to do with it. These interpretations are beautifully vague at best, so I believe they will give you the new product, I'm certain of it.'

She had moved to the front of the settee, kneeling by James's side with her arms resting on his lap.

'You're quite comfortable with developing this for me, even though the old man's breathing down your neck?' James asked, aware of the danger he was putting her in.

'Of course. No one tampers with my programmes, and I have all the development plans locked behind a password. Everyone thinks I'm working as normal,' she said confidently.

'Nick's bound to find out sooner or later.'

'I can handle Nick. If he discovers the project prematurely, I'll just tell him it still needs some fine tuning.'

'It's a dangerous game you're playing, my love.'

'Nick takes me seriously: he won't be a problem,' she assured him.

James was tired of hearing Nick's name. At first getting Sandra to act as an infiltrator had seemed a brilliant idea. But now he saw a different Sandra. The woman he loved did not view his father as a serious threat and admired Nick almost as strongly as James once did. At times he felt that Nick was a rival for Sandra's affections. As much as he tried to dismiss the thought as ridiculous, he couldn't completely eradicate it from his mind. James had never loved anyone the way he loved Sandra. She was everything a man could ever want. Why couldn't they both forget this silly crusade he had started and fall lovingly into one another's arms? He wanted her exclusively, but for now, he realised, he would have to be content to have her share his home. At least it was one area he had managed to reach a compromise on. It was a most unacceptable set of circumstances, but if he wanted her, he knew he must be patient.

*

The intercom on Sandra's desk seemed to buzz harshly, disturbing her from her daily analysis of the market figures.

'It's Nick,' the voice said. 'I have some news. Can you come up here right away?'

'I'll be right there.'

She ran up the fire escape stairs, knowing that would be quicker than waiting for the elevators.

'What is it?' Sandra gasped. 'What's happening?'

'Good news. I've spoken with the ISC and I think I've found the breakthrough we've been looking for. If you can package this properly I think we've got a real winner on our hands.'

Sandra looked intently at the report Nick handed her, recognising the data immediately.

'Well,' he urged. 'What do you think?'

'I think I can do something with this,' she said confidently, wondering how on earth she was going to manage this juggling act.

'Good. Well, what are you wasting time talking to me for?'

'Okay, chief, I'll get right on it.'

'Sandra,' he called after her as she was leaving, 'there's a big bonus in this for you if we can get there first.'

'Message received and understood.'

'Let's have dinner tonight. I'd like to discuss the best way to attack this thing.'

'Sure,' she said casually, thinking about a justifiable reason to give to James for breaking their own dinner date. What had started out as a ploy to get James and his father back together was fast becoming a precarious balance of loyalties. A dangerous game indeed, she realised.

'Excellent,' Nick muttered. 'I'll be back in New York before Gus knows what's hit him, if this goes according to plan.'

James often has to work late, she told herself, this time it's my turn. He'll just have to understand. Jesus, Sandra, she thought angrily to herself, how did you ever manage to let yourself get trapped between these two? James wasn't joking when he said it was going to be a dangerous game.

*

'Centrepoint Tower. You won't get a better view of Sydney from any other restaurant,' Sandra explained with a feline smile to Nick.

'Very nice. You've got class, Sandra Upton. How did you come to fit into this whole insurance scene?'

'By accident, the same as most of us in this business.'

'I'd like to know more about you. Brett has told me about your work for him before you went to New York. You had great vision to realise the opportunity in software design so early. Where did you get the idea?'

'It's a long story.'

'We've got all night.'

From their table, Sandra and Nick had a view of the city lights. It was a heady atmosphere and Nick, as usual, was charming. Once again Sandra felt herself becoming enveloped in Nick's company. He told Sandra new stories about his trips around the world. He was so different in person from the image that people created about him. 'The Slayer of Sydney' they called him, the pitiless butcher of countless jobs. Yet in person he could be soft, sincere and even tender.

'It's been a tough year in Australia. Just a few months now and it will all be worthwhile,' Nick said reflectively.

'And then do you go back home?'

'I don't know yet. Are you in a hurry to get rid of me?'

'Don't be silly,' she laughed.

'That's not an answer,' he insisted.

'I think this interpretation you found gives us plenty of scope,' she said, changing the subject. 'But we need to tread carefully. The computer illustrations alone could take months to prepare, and we can't get final authorisation before Brett comes back from his trip to the international LMA meeting.'

'Don't worry about Brett and fine details... will the product work?'

'I believe it will,' she answered reluctantly. 'But it is not a cut and dried matter.'

'Don't bother me with the "what ifs". The interpretation seems clear enough to me.'

'I'm sure of that,' she said nervously. 'But with all due respect, you are not a lawyer or an actuary and these things must be treated with extreme caution unless you don't care about it backfiring on you.'

'Boffins, bloody boffins,' he scoffed. 'Why is there always someone trying to make my life difficult?'

'I'm sorry, Nick. But I was employed to get a new product which will increase our profile, not bury us.'

'Yes, you're right,' he admitted. 'I don't want to talk about work any more. It's like I told you, you've got to stop and smell the roses.'

He looked at her questioningly. Just how much did she know, he wondered, about everything?

'I'll take that drink now,' Nick said, turning to the waiter.

'Can I trust you?' he asked Sandra.

'Would you be asking me if you doubted it?'

'You're very astute. I want to ask you a very special favour. You're destined for better things than product development, we both know that. I want to entrust you with a special task and, if you can do it well, we can talk about a future direction for you. Do you understand?'

'I understand.'

'Good.' He folded his napkin to signify that what he was about to say was more important than eating. 'I'd like you to be my eyes and ears. There are many rumours about dissenters in the ranks. The stories all filter back to me but it's so hard to know if a complaint is genuine and needs action. I think I can trust you.'

'I'm flattered, but if I understand you correctly, you're asking me to be a Judas?'

She took another sip of claret, thinking that it was not an entirely savoury proposal.

'All I am asking is for you to be aware. Listen to what is being said and by whom. I want to know who believes in my system and who doesn't. The disbelievers aren't likely to say so to my face but they can spread their doubts in other people's minds. I can't afford to let that happen.'

'I see. I wasn't aware that concerns about your new system were surfacing though. From what I have gathered, everyone's fighting to be chosen as a regional manager.'

'That's true. But those who fear they will not be chosen are trying to say the numbers don't stack up.'

'I see,' she said thoughtfully. 'But does it really make any difference? Surely Brett is going to listen to you, that's what you're paid for. You're the expert on the system.'

'I just don't want to leave any stone unturned. I know the agents see you as a mate, so it shouldn't be hard for you to check out the situation.'

'Fair enough,' she agreed. 'I'll see what I can find out,' she said, wondering if that sounded genuine. Somehow she managed to look Nick straight in the eye as she spoke.

Nick could feel his project coming together; it was so close he could smell the victory. Nothing could be left to chance at this crucial time. As for McLeod, he had become an enormous thorn in Nick's side. He had tried to force Nick to keep the commission levels down. Nick had explained that to achieve the volumes of sales necessary to take the company to number one, he had to increase not only agent numbers but agents' incentives. McLeod, however, told him that, with Nick's reputation, he should be able to achieve the volumes he wanted without having to offer the agents more commission for it.

McLeod was a moron not to concede to Nick's vast wealth of knowledge and experience. If he tried to get in the way of this new product, Nick decided he would have to take some drastic action.

*

'Oh no you don't. You've had quite enough for a naughty girl who stayed out half the night.'

Sandra pushed herself up on to one shoulder and watched her lover's chest heave in exhausted pleasure.

'I'll have you know,' he continued, 'I ate a McDonald's last night. It wasn't much of a meal when I think about what I was promised just yesterday.'

'I'm sorry. It was business. You have been kept late on business, as well you know. I'll cook you breakfast instead.'

'Some consolation,' he muttered, pulling on his black and red silk oriental robe.

Sandra rose from the bed with difficulty. She was slightly hung-over from the night before and still trying to remember all the things Nick Abbott had told her.

'Here's the morning paper.' James handed Sandra a copy of the *Australian* and took a seat at the breakfast table.

The smell of eggs and bacon was less than enthralling to Sandra, but she couldn't disappoint her lover again. Serving him breakfast, she sat down with a cup of black coffee and proceeded to read the paper.

ISC CHECK INTO COMPANY RESERVES

English-born Edward Townsend, the driving force behind Australia's newest life insurance watchdog, the ISC, today revealed that many companies are engaging in new methods of remuneration in an attempt to steal market share. As agents become aware of the choices opening up to them in the market place, interest-free loans and huge upfront commissions are being used to attract the cream in the business from one company to another. Whilst it is not in the ISC's interest to question the remuneration structures of life insurance companies, it is of some concern that these excessive incentives may be stretching the companies' reserves to a dangerous level. While the markets continue to run at an exponential bull rate, the risk is minimal, but should the market take a downturn, a company's investments in stocks would be wiped out overnight, leaving no capital to pay for these new structures. Critics of this new system claim these new structures are not sustainable and agents who are allowing their allegiances to be bought out should be wary of having no place to go if circumstances change.

Sandra thought back to her conversation with Nick. She

remembered the comments Nick had made about Brett McLeod. He had grumbled about having a man in charge who had no life insurance experience.

'James!' She looked up to observe James intently studying the *Financial Review* as he devoured his eggs and bacon.

'Um,' he mumbled, still reading, and still angry that he had missed his special meal.

'The remuneration system Nick has copied from New York. It never occurred to me, until last night, that there could be a risk involved in increasing the commission base as high as he has.'

'That's very interesting,' he mused. 'But business is all about the survival of the fittest. There's nothing sinister about that.'

He thought no more about it, hurriedly finishing his breakfast.

Sandra threw the paper on her chair as she left to get dressed. For some reason it caught James's eye.

'What do you suspect, Sandra?' James asked as he followed her to the bathroom, holding the folded copy of the *Australian*. 'What does this article have to do with it?'

'What difference does it make? You said it's all part of business.'

'Don't be cocky.' He gave her a friendly tap on the backside as she walked into the shower. 'What's the connection?'

'It's just that Nick asked me to keep an ear open for critics of his system. He made it sound very casual, but now I'm not so sure.'

'I see.' James rubbed his chin thoughtfully just as his father might have done.

'Nick also made a couple of comments about thinking it was inappropriate for someone from the computer industry to be running a group of insurance and finance companies.'

'Do you think he has something planned for Brett?'

'I'm not sure, but it's you who said you don't believe in coincidences.'

She suddenly felt chilled. What if James was right?

*

Toxic effects: petechiae, ecchymoses, frank haemorrhages into joints and from nasal mucosa. Possible liver degeneration. Haematuria. Toxic dose can be as little as 100mg daily for two to three days.

Perfect, Nick Abbott said to himself, returning the little yellow book of toxicology to the appropriate shelf in the City Library. Nick had everything he needed for his week in Melbourne. It was convenient that no one in Australia knew of his history, he considered. And even more fortunate that McLeod had the same weaknesses of his previous victims but then this was a common denominator among many of the wealthy, and even the not so wealthy.

Brett had returned from the LMA conference with all the concerns that Nick had feared.

'Abbott,' he had yelled, 'you've conned me. Gus told me the whole story and I can't believe I've been so foolish as to let you run amok in my company.'

'What are you talking about?' Nick had asked innocently.

'Winston Life, that's what I'm talking about. I knew the commission rates were too high. Now I know why you took a job in Australia: no one in New York would employ you when they found out what you nearly got away with. Jesus, I damn near let you bankrupt my company.'

'Calm down. You've seen the sales figures. We're ranked at number three in Australia. Our reserves are fine. Lloyd Sutcliff is a man without vision and Gus totally overreacted to the situation. Look at the reports for yourself. We've never been stronger. Nobody every *proved* my system didn't work, they were just too frightened to try it. Well, now we have tried it, and it does work. Fletcher's got you all fired up over nothing.'

Brett had sat down on Nick's visitors' chair to consider the situation. Prime was performing extraordinarily well, recruiting agents from all the other companies and rising up the industry rankings faster than Brett had believed possible. Perhaps Gus and Lloyd had been overcautious.

'Perhaps you're right, but I still want to see a detailed analysis of our current situation as soon as possible. And no new product launches until this matter is cleared up.'

'Whatever you say,' Nick had answered calmly. 'Why don't we go away for the weekend to discuss these matters in peace and quiet, away from the chaos of the office?'

'You know,' Brett had said, relaxing somewhat, 'I think that sounds like a bloody good idea.'

*

Brett had arranged tickets for all of the events offered during Melbourne's spring racing carnival. They would start with the Derby Eve Ball at the Hilton, then go to the races on Saturday, Derby Day. Monday evening, Beverley Brask, the socialite, was holding her annual Cup Eve party at her husband's restaurant. Tuesday was Melbourne Cup day; the horse race that stops a national and is likened to the Kentucky Derby in the States.

Brett and his wife, Pamela, entered with Nick through a flowered archway which led to the Hilton's ballroom for the social event of the year.

'Daaarling, you look beautiful,' cheered Beverley Brask to a lady dripping in diamonds and taffeta.

The media were clicking their cameras and flashing their flash bulbs as though they'd suffered a year-long drought of celebrities. If that had been the case, they were in for a real flooding tonight. Nick recognised film stars, TV announcers, film reviewers and many other famous faces among a crowd of well-heeled social climbers who had all fought to get tickets to this prestigious evening.

The ballroom was a celebration of affluence. The array of decorations, flowers and dazzling dresses was a feast for the eye to behold.

Nick and Brett's table was on the edge of the dance floor. Reading his menu, Nick noticed on the left-hand side the events for the evening. Brett, he decided, had good taste in choosing this particular event to show Melbourne off at its best. Firstly, the cabaret act was Jackie Love. Nick hadn't seen her in cabaret before but had heard she was one of the best entertainers in the business. She was to be followed by the crowning of Miss Melbourne Cup.

A small bottle of Aramis aftershave was on the table for each gentleman, with Armani for the ladies. The entire hall smelled of spring flowers; it was as though every flower in Melbourne had been used to create not only the massive archway entrance but also the showering displays on the tables.

Nick overheard a man on the table next to him saying that he came every year. The man explained to one of his guests that he was the ambassador to Norway based in Hong Kong.

'Of course,' he boasted, 'I only leave Hong Kong twice a year, once for Ascot and once for the Melbourne Cup.'

He wore a white evening jacket which gave the appearance of being ex-military. Nick couldn't place his age, he could have been anywhere between seventy and ninety. Whatever his age, Nick smiled, he was obviously many years senior to the voluptuous young blonde who sat beside him. The blonde wore a dress which, Nick guessed, he must have bought for her. She looked totally out of place, uncomfortable in the elegance; even bored. Just waiting around for the old man to die to collect the loot, I'll bet, Nick judged.

Entrées of smoked salmon and capons were hurriedly served to enable the evening's festivities to start. They attended the ball every year, Brett told Nick. Pamela loved the races and Brett loved the business contacts.

'Oh, look,' Pamela said. 'They have given us little race books and pens for tomorrow.' She picked up the white plastic-covered racing guide with 'Victorian Racing Club Derby Eve Ball' and the VRC symbol embossed in gold on it.

'Have you picked your horses yet?' Pamela asked Brett, thumbing through the pages.

'No, not yet, shall we have a look? Um, At talaq, that's the horse owned by a sheikh. As the sheikh isn't even attending, the horse can't be much cop. My bet is for Empire Rose, the big red lady,' said Brett confidentially.

'What about Derby Day?' Pam asked excitedly. 'Let's see, Priceless Prince, in the Derby, I fancy him.'

'You fancy his name, woman.' Brett rolled his eyes in a theatrical motion to the ceiling. 'Drought, that's the horse to back each way in the Derby.'

'Do you have a hot tip or is that just a guess?' Nick asked, curious to know how much of his hard-earned money he should place on this horse.

'It's a tip,' Brett said with wry smile. 'Trust me.'

'And now ladies and gentlemen,' announced the master of ceremonies, 'the moment you have all been waiting for – Miss Jackie Love.'

Nick's eyes widened to absorb the vision of loveliness before him. With impish blonde hair and watery-blue eyes, this girl's appearance created a ravenous hunger in Nick. Clad in a figure-hugging leotard with white feather ruffles around her arms, she performed a dance routine with two male back-up dancers which brought the house down.

The Miss Melbourne Cup Pageant paled in comparison to Jackie Love. Six fresh, pretty little girls all stood up to say they enjoyed racing and wanted to help the community. Why couldn't one of them be original for a change? Nick wondered.

At the racetrack it amused Nick to listen to so many people trying to sound like they'd attended private schools in England. The ladies stepped around the members' enclosure, pulling spiked heels out of muddy grass, while the men dazzled their preening ladies in full morning suit regalia. Champagne flowed as if it were water in the members' car park. Nick doubted if any of the people were aware there was a horse race at all. The women were all trying so desperately to throw themselves in front of a journalist's camera; the race was definitely rated as second billing to these fancy fillies.

'Shall we go and watch the first race?' asked Brett, handing Nick a pair of binoculars.

'Sure,' Nick answered. 'I hope your tips are as good today as that each-way bet on Drought for the Derby.'

'It only came second,' Brett reminded Nick.

'But on an each-way bet, that's good enough. So what do you fancy in this one?'

'I think you'd be well advised to put a bet on Colonial King and a few shillings on Midnight Fever for the Myer fashion stakes.'

'Do you still favour Empire Rose for the Cup?'

'Definitely.'

'Okay,' Nick said, heading for a bookie.

'Here Nick, put a bet on Empire Rose for me too.'

Pamela thrust a few dollars in his hand.

The fever piqued, the crowd gathered. Nick remembered a scene from the movie *My Fair Lady* where Audrey Hepburn, dressed for the part but having not quite mastered her studies in the finer points of public behaviour, had yelled at the top of her lungs: 'Move your bloomin' arse.'

Brett, Pamela and Nick secured a spot at the front railing of the members' enclosure. They could see Beverley Brask to their right in a red suit with a large red hat adorned with as many flowers as were in the whole of the Hilton for the Derby Eve Ball.

'And they're off in the 1986 Melbourne Cup. And it's...'

A collective breath was taken by the crowd as the barriers went up, then frenzied screaming came from within the members' enclosure, as well as outside. Facades of elegance were quickly stripped away as the crowd watched eagerly, hoping to make a fortune.

'Come on, Empire Rose,' Pamela yelled.

The dust flew as if a sandstorm had been aroused by the forces of nature to blind their vision and twenty-four horses raced past.

'Who won? Who was it?' Pamela asked to anyone who'd listen; but all eyes were fixed firmly on the notice board.

'And the winner of the 1986 Melbourne Cup,' the voice boomed over the loudspeaker, 'is At talaq.'

A huge cheer rose from the crowd.

'And what about Empire Rose?' Pamela asked.

As if answering her question, the speaker announced: 'Second place goes to Rising Fear and third place to Sea Legend. Kiwi ran fourth and Empire Rose fifth.'

Pamela tore her ticket up and threw it on the ground in disgust along with hundreds of others.

'Maybe next year will be Empire Rose's year,' said Brett casually. 'So much for the sheikh not showing up, it must have brought him good luck.'

'At least you'll have another chance on Oaks Day,' Nick said to Pamela, 'while Brett and I go fishing.'

'Try not to match the national deficit when we're away, will you, dear?' Brett implored her.

Pamela just smiled sweetly.

*

'Have you enjoyed your week?' Brett asked, driving to the isolated log cabin in a hired four-wheel drive.

'It's been great,' Nick responded automatically.

'The best is yet to come,' cheered Brett.

'I know,' Nick said in an undertone, looking at the expanse of near barren country fields.

'It was very decent of Denis Granger to lend us his log cabin at Enoch's Point,' Brett commented.

'Well, he hardly gets time to use it now we've got him recruiting like crazy.' Nick smiled. He could sense Brett was relaxing slowly.

'He's turning out to be a good sales manager, isn't he?'

'For an ex-vice squad cop who dropped out to live in the backwoods of Mildura, he's bloody amazing. I think he stands a chance at being number one sales manager this year.'

'Really?'

'Yes. He says he's found his true vocation. He keeps telling me how grateful he is to have been recruited.'

'Huh. It's incredible. You just never know where the talent is going to spring from do you? I never would have picked someone like Denis to build up our business to such a level.'

'That's why you put me in the job, remember?'

'And remember I told you only Nick Abbott could pull this project together?'

Nick shrugged and grinned. 'Mind if I get some shut-eye?' he asked. 'Those sleeping pills of yours are still making me drowsy.'

'I told you it was too late in the evening to take anything,' Brett scolded him. 'I had no idea you would get so hyped up at the races that you'd need a sleeping aid.'

'I should have taken your advice, as usual.'

'That's what happens when you're not used to taking drugs.'

'I suppose you're right,' Nick conceded.

'Go ahead. I'll wake you when we get there.'

Nick slept while Brett drove for a couple of hours, waking for the last part of the journey through winding roads and natural bush lands. All around Nick could see eucalyptus and breathtaking mountain landscapes.

By the time they reached Enoch's Point, the faint coolness of the evening breeze seemed to awaken wild birds from their heat-drunken stupor. In the undergrowth on the banks of Big River a lyre-bird imitated the sound of the kookaburra's laugh. The lyre-bird could imitate any sound, Brett told Nick. It was the bird's method of natural protection, and the origin of its name. A bellbird, rarely seen, was visible at the base of a white gum, calling with an eerie echoing chime that sounded nothing like the chirp of a regular city bird. Raucous rosella parrots glistened with metallic red and blue feathers in the branches directly overhead. Brett slowly lifted his head to watch them with intense pleasure. Though he was close enough to see their fluffy down, the rosellas continued to flit and preen as though he was a part of the tree.

Still watching the tree, Brett became aware of a sudden tension. Nick had stiffened, his fingers on the handle of his fishing rod clenching slightly, his sense of excitement clearly discernible. Brett could see Nick staring at Big River, but though Brett stared hard, he could not see what had excited Nick.

'Look,' Nick whispered, 'the biggest rainbow trout I've ever seen. You're going to learn what life is all about this weekend, my friend.' Even as he spoke, Nick considered the deceptive double meaning in his words.

'Not a bad little shack, is it?' Nick commented as they headed inside the cabin.

'It's lovely,' Brett agreed. 'It seems a shame to spoil it with talk of business.'

Nick had been to Denis Granger's cabin just once before. Denis had taken Nick there when he was still deciding whether or not to appoint Denis as the sales manager for Mildura. The cabin was several hours' drive from the town of Mildura but when Nick had mentioned that fishing was his favourite hobby, and one he rarely enjoyed these days, Denis had insisted that they take the weekend to finish their discussions. It had been a move which assured Denis of the position he had been pursuing.

Being built of part log and part bluestone, the cabin looked as if the first bush rangers in Australia might have hidden there when the nearest town still thrived on mining gold. A stone chimney was blackened from previous visits. It was evident, however, that it had not been used for some time. The air inside was musty compared with the sweet unpolluted aroma outside.

There were just five rooms: two bedrooms, a kitchen, a bathroom and a large rambling living area. The open fire had the mandatory kangaroo skin rug in front of it and an incongruous moose's head above it. There was a dining table with matching chairs in weather-beaten dark old wood, and a settee with two armchairs either side, all covered with squelchy-soft chequered cushions. A small square table with a chess set stood near the fire. A second larger table stood just in front of the settee.

'We better get unpacked then,' Brett said, slapping his thighs and filling his lungs with a long, deep breath of the pure country air. 'Now this I've been looking forward to.'

Brett threw a small plastic vial of white powder on the

lounge table. He had transferred the white dust from its original packaging of folded foil to a small vial purchased from a chemist store, knowing he was less likely to lose any in spillage that way. He grappled in his pockets to find two snort straws which he added to the table.

'Perhaps I'll convince you to share in my indulgence this weekend?' Brett slapped Nick in a friendly gesture on the back.

Nick felt sickened at the thought.

'Perhaps I will,' Nick said, taking one of the snort straws and putting it in his pocket to block at the earliest opportunity. 'Where's the bourbon?'

'In the blue Esky with the other food and essential substances, in the kitchen.'

Nick went to retrieve the bottle and two slightly discoloured glasses, using the time to block his snort straw with cotton wool from their supplies.

'Here's to a great weekend.' Nick offered Brett a glass.

'*Skol.*'

They both finished their glasses in one gulp. The first and last for Nick as he knew he needed to keep his wits about him from here on in.

Before his next drink, Brett carefully sprinkled his cocaine on a small board in front of him. He played with it using a small metal spatula for a moment as if he were mixing icing for a chocolate cake. He had waited long enough. Hungrily he took his straw and sniffed up two little trails along the snowy white surface.

'Here,' he said, pushing the board in Nick's direction. Brett closed his eyes waiting for the satisfaction to settle in.

Nick went through the motions of holding and sniffing the straw. He prayed to himself that the cotton wool had wedged the opening completely. He managed to create identical tracks to McLeod's by pushing the substance with the end of his straw. In McLeod's state he would never know the difference.

The combination of bourbon and cocaine transported Brett into a state of total euphoria. He stood up and wandered aimlessly around the lounge. He noticed the moose and, patting it gently on the head, began talking to it as though it understood.

'I think I'll go for a walk,' McLeod slurred. He meandered out waving his arms and smiling a wide vacant smile.

The time was right. Nick collected the vial and the small board and hurried them into the kitchen. There he produced a small plastic vial of his own, one filled with the rat poison, warfarin. He tipped the contents of both vials into a third larger vial and stirred the contents together with the spatula, returning just enough of the mixture back into McLeod's vial to make it look as full as it had been. Nick wiped his fingerprints off the spatula with a tissue. He returned the vial and the board to the small square table, pouring a little back on to the board and drawing tracks where they had been before. Nick's two vials were put back in his jacket pocket, to dispose of later. The entire operation had taken no more than a minute. Just sixty tiny seconds to ensure that the man who stood in Nick's way would soon be facing oblivion. Nick marvelled at the simplicity of his plan and the stupidity of McLeod to have allowed himself to be trapped so easily.

Trying to reproduce McLeod's actions of euphoria, Nick followed him out into the bush where they rambled together for half an hour.

It was late in the night before Brett decided he needed another fix. The pair of would-be fishermen had been playing cards on the smaller table by the open fire. It had surprised Nick how cold it could get at night when the day had been so tepid. It was the type of place that he could count on for no interruptions. It was perfect.

Brett walked over to the larger table to collect his

powder and accessories.

'Who gives a damn about business anyway?' Brett asked rhetorically, taking a deeper snort than before.

Nick watched anxiously as the poison entered McLeod's nostrils. He visualised it dancing freely, penetrating the membranes in his epidermis before whisking its way down, with diabolical speed, to the pockets of his lungs where it would cause devastating, terminal damage. McLeod hadn't felt a thing. His wide vacant smile appeared again.

You absurd-looking, wretched creature, thought Nick. It won't be long now.

Nick was aware that it would take three or four doses to do the job properly, but that was going to present no problem. Nick had first learned how easy it was to lace drugs when a kid at his senior school had bullied him mercilessly. It had been the first time Nick had used this technique and he had found it to be foolproof on many occasions since.

He became like a wild animal on a feeding frenzy. Whenever a person pushed him too far, it started the same way. His fists clenched in convulsive rage; his eyes flashed with murderous intent. The intoxication of power gave Nick a high no drug could emulate. The power to take the life of an inadequate individual, and one who stood in Nick's way, was the peak of satisfaction. Drugs had always proved the simplest of the methods he had experimented with. Nick understood that, without evidence of the act of administering those drugs, no policeman was able to get a conviction; not just based on motive, opportunity and guesswork. A hideous physical change swept over Nick. He held the power of life and death in his hands. It was a mysterious strength which the normal mortals around him lacked.

Brett fell asleep in his chair while Nick went to bed to sleep a peaceful sleep. He dreamed of James that night, and wondered, when he awoke, what he might be doing these days.

'Morning,' Nick said cheerfully. 'Ready for a good day's fishing?'

'What? Oh, yes,' Brett yawned, wiping the sleep from his eyes.

'Fancy some breakfast?'

'You know I never eat breakfast. I'll have some coffee though.'

'Right. Two coffees coming up.'

Nick was ravenous. The country air had given him a healthy appetite and he chose to cook a meal of eggs and sausages before returning with the coffees. Nick guessed McLeod must have caught a whiff of the meal as he ran past the kitchen door, a pale shade of green, with his mouth firmly shut, heading towards the bathroom. The sounds of heaving, coughing and spluttering were audible all over the cabin.

'What's wrong?' Nick tried to sound caring as McLeod reappeared, no longer green but a deathly white colour.

'I think I must have had too much to drink last night.'

'Well, we did polish off the bottle.' Nick held up an empty bourbon bottle as evidence.

'Oh, that explains it.'

It was an obscene sense of uncontrollable, self-gratification that spread through Nick's being. It exhibited itself in his thinly curled lips that had not a trace of guilt about them. His master plan was everything. No ineffectual, exasperating individual was going to stand in Nick Abbott's way. McLeod was a boil to be lanced. Nick had nearly lost control altogether at the Cup Eve party when McLeod had insisted all product development be halted indefinitely. Christ, if there had been one sentence which sealed McLeod's fate, that had been it.

'Drink this.' Nick offered McLeod a glass of water.

'What you need is some fresh air, you'll be fine when you get outside.'

'I guess you're right. Come on then, let's get out there.'

They marched through large rocks and tall eucalypti before they found a suitable spot. Nick saw his first native koala in a tree above their position, hanging sleepily from the nearly nude branch. Nick turned his head and looked straight into McLeod's eyes. He was smiling. Absurd bloody arsehole, Nick thought.

'Hey, look. I think you've caught one,' Nick reeled in a huge trout from Brett's line. 'This will make a magnificent dinner, my friend.'

He held the wriggling, slimy creature down, giving it one swift blow with a mallet, instantly ending its struggle to cling to life.

It was after one o'clock, when a rain cloud passed over, that the pair decided to make their way back to the cabin.

'Victorian weather,' Brett complained. 'If you don't like it, wait a minute and it's bound to change. Coffee?'

'Yes. Thank you.'

Nick moved Brett's cocaine into a position that he imagined might catch his eye and encourage him to sniff again. He felt like a lion crouching in ambush. Tawny and gold in the early sunlight, looking warm and furry and friendly with an unseen seer of cold death at his wily fingertips. Nick knew that death was near. He could sense its vast mysterious presence in the darkened room; detected its breath, warm and spicy over clammy cold exhalations. Death had been Nick's closest ally in life. Without death, Nick had no living. It was the ultimate irony.

Brett took his straw and snorted again. The euphoria hit at first. It lasted a full fifteen minutes before the pain started; sudden sharp pain in the depths of his chest. He heaved as a thudding ache hit his ribs. His hands shook and his body became moist with unwelcome sweat. He tried to find a position which offered some relief from the pain which was growing inside him.

'Are you all right?' Nick asked in the most caring voice he could engineer.

'I think I'm having a heart attack,' he croaked. 'My lungs feel like they're going to explode. Help me.'

'Sure. Sure. I'll help you. Come and lie down on the couch. Take these.'

'What are they?'

'Painkillers.' Nick handed him the two sleeping pills he had supposedly taken before driving to Enoch's Point. 'If these don't help, I'll rush you to the nearest doctor.'

'Thanks.' Brett swallowed the pills gratefully and quickly fell into a deep sleep, snoring from the blocked mucus in his breathing passages.

The nearest medical attention was in Eildon, sixty kilometres away. Nick had researched this carefully before leaving Melbourne. There might have been a phone or a house of some type between the two locations, but that was of little consequence.

Nick had forgotten how repulsive this part of the process was. For a moment he reflected on his actions, wondering if he could see it through. The power to take another human life was thrilling but at that moment it was also disgusting. He watched the wretched creature sleep, aware that he was taking his last breaths of life and wondered how he might feel if the situation was reversed. He considered briefly the existence of heaven and hell and divine intervention. Was there a life after death? Would McLeod come back as some twisted evil spirit to torment Nick's existence? It didn't matter. Nick was past the point of no return now. Committed. He reminded himself of the reason for this euthanasia, of his ultimate goal to avenge himself upon Gus Fletcher. To build Prime into a position where it could overpower East West. It was not impossible, it was a reality close at hand.

He went over his story to pass the time. The clever story he had devised for the police questions he knew would be inevitable. He hoped they didn't send some super-slick youth who was trying to earn his first points. That would be a nuisance. He considered all the possible loose ends and convinced himself that they'd been tied. Now all that was left to do was cook dinner.

'Good evening, sleepyhead. How do you feel?' Nick asked casually.

'Much better, thank you. Except for this awful pain in my back.' Nick remembered the words in the little yellow book as Brett rubbed his lower back: 'possible liver degeneration'.

'You must have slept at a bad angle,' Nick assured him. 'Tonight you are going to experience a rare delight – Abbott cuisine.' Nick raised the country saucepan theatrically in one hand, waving a spatula around in the other. 'I'll have you know that you are very honoured. There aren't many people I would cook for.'

'Sir, I am indeed flattered.' McLeod stood and bowed, looking fully recovered from his earlier interlude of suffering.

Brett enjoyed his meal, eating like a man who hadn't dined in weeks. It was not surprising, he considered, when he had eaten nothing all day and emptied what there had been in his stomach before they left to go fishing. His healthy glow returned. He looked as though he could live a hundred years.

The doubts began to creep back into Nick's mind. He thought about the little yellow book again: 'toxic dose is indeterminate; fatalities have followed 100mg daily.' Perhaps McLeod was not going to be so easy to dispose of.

'Do you feel ready for some hair of the dog?' Nick offered him a glass of brandy.

'Absolutely. *Skol.*' Brett happily drank and rubbed his belly with a fulfilled, contented expression on his face. 'That was a fine fish, superbly cooked. Why don't I relight the fire?'

'Don't trouble yourself. I'll do that in a moment. Fancy some more of your friend here?' Nick held up the small board of white powder.

'No thanks. I think I've had enough today.'

'What? One snort at lunchtime? I thought you intended to make the most of this little retreat.'

'You're right. I did. Hand it over here if you don't mind.'

'Certainly.'

'Visitors first though,' Brett said, pushing the coke back in Nick's direction.

Nick took his snort straw from his pocket and turned towards the fireplace, taking an obvious breath while shuffling the straw down the powder to make tracks. McLeod was just sufficiently relaxed and intoxicated not to notice the deception.

Nick sat down and smiled, feigning the euphoria he had closely observed before. Brett looked for a moment at the powder and back to Nick's contented state and convinced himself to sniff again.

That's three doses, thought Nick. No man can take more than that.

Brett inhaled badly. He started to cough. Nick could see he was experiencing extreme pain. His face distorted, he thumped his chest and rolled on the floor as if trying to exorcise a demon within him. The coughing intensified; he regurgitated phlegm and blood. Nick folded his arms and tried not to watch the death dance before him.

Brett didn't make it to the bathroom this time. Bile, blood and trout came up in a kaleidoscope of colours that discharged a repugnant scent. A scent which leaped with remarkable precision into Nick's senses; first smell then fear. The smell turned Nick's stomach, causing violent motions to twist and turn within him. It was as though, in his death role, Brett had managed to direct some of his pain and suffering back towards the perpetrator of this evil.

Brett crawled on to one of the armchairs. A dribble of saliva, spotted with remnants of vomit, ran down his chin to his chest and his nose started to bleed. The deep red substance just peeped through at first before falling freely over his upper lip and into his open mouth. With his eyes half shut and a disgraceful odour clinging to him, his life's essence could now be counted in minutes.

His skin was neither green nor white; it had turned a shade of grey. The final colour in the rainbow of death, Nick thought poetically. The brightness had gone from his eyes: Nick's closest ally was at hand.

Nick left the pathetic figure to take his last breath alone. To lift his spirits, Nick thought through the words he would be using tomorrow. 'We had been laughing and drinking, Officer, I had no idea Brett used drugs. He knew my opinion on that subject so I guess he waited till I went to bed to use them.'

Were there plenty of empty bottles around the place? Yes; bourbon, beer, port, brandy, that was adequate. 'He seemed fine yesterday morning, in fact we caught a huge trout and ate it for dinner.'

Nick took the excess mixture from his vial and filled Brett's, carefully wiping his prints off Brett's vial. It would be easier to dispose of his vials and straw if they were clean.

Jesus, Nick thought, I have just pulled off the biggest deal in my life and no one can ever know.

Under the morning sun Nick took a detour via the next town's local tip to dispose of his vials and straw, before heading into Eildon to alert the police of his grisly find.

The extra mileage on his speedo could be easily explained by his getting lost in his state of extreme distress.

The local police only took a brief account of the events before following Nick back to the cabin.

'Coke,' one officer said simply on seeing the white powder.

The officer wiped his hands clean and straightened his trousers legs. 'Were you aware he was taking drugs?' he asked Nick.

Nick looked into the small brown eyes of the officer and saw no sign of emotion.

'No. He knew my view on drugs. I hate them.'

'I see. So I don't suppose you have any idea where he may have purchased the stuff from?'

'None,' Nick answered, frowning in contemplation.

He watched the two officers examine the scene, deciding it was safest to say nothing unless asked. They didn't look very sharp but any word could be misconstrued. The two officers were careful not to disturb anything as they looked around.

'Is this how you found him?'

'Yes. I touched his wrist and couldn't feel a pulse so I raced straight into town.'

'Have you any idea why his nose may have been bleeding?'

'No. Maybe he tripped over in his drunken or drugged state.'

'I don't think so. There's no bruising, you see.' The officer called on his portable radio to alert the local station. 'Better call in the local CIB,' he said, avoiding eye contact with Nick Abbott as he did so. 'The scene is preserved. Signs of drug abuse and bleeding with no signs of physical violence.'

'Was anyone else here with you last night?' the officer asked, putting his radio down.

'No.'

'I'd better get a few details.'

The officer ushered Nick towards the dining table, while the second officer went outside to examine the surroundings.

Within four hours the whole area was crawling with police. The local CIB had called in the crew from Melbourne. There was one officer dusting for fingerprints, someone taking photos, another putting white tape around the cabin and two police on permanent duty; one logging everyone in and out and another monitoring the activity inside. Nick had hoped that the local police wouldn't bother calling homicide, they could waste too much of his valuable time.

There were absolutely no tracks linking the murder to Nick Abbott, even if they suspected him.

Ray Cooper, the detective heading the investigation, looked around the scene to check for what the locals may have missed. Ray Cooper had little respect for the country cops; they had no ambition and therefore no reason to conduct a thorough investigation. Ray, on the other hand, was very ambitious. He would work around the clock if it was necessary to get a conviction. He always got his man, well, nearly always, and the ones that got away were not forgotten. Ray would pursue them in between his other cases. He would befriend their rivals, their enemies, anyone that may have that one elusive piece of evidence that would bring the case together. If it took twenty years, it didn't matter. It was seeing the bastards were put behind bars that counted.

Despite his youthful appearance, Ray had eleven years' experience in homicide and was well trained in the finer points of making his suspects feel at ease one moment, on the edge the next. He had a gut feeling about Nick Abbott. Everything about the scene was suspicious. Obviously the drugs had been laced, which could have been done before they came to the cabin, but Nick looked too controlled. Ray knew that salesmen and policemen were better trained actors than anyone in Hollywood and in this they would have to respect each other's talents.

'Ray Cooper,' he said, offering Nick his hand with a congenial smile.

'Nick Abbott.'

Nick tried to assess Ray's level of intelligence by searching the window to his soul, his eyes. There was nothing. Not a glimmer of the thoughts that formed in his investigative brain. No way of judging him.

'Were you staying here with Brett McLeod?' Ray asked calmly.

'Yes. We were on a fishing trip.'

Ray looked through some of the notes the local police had taken.

'It's a long way to go fishing when you live in Sydney, isn't it?'

'We came down to Melbourne for the Melbourne Cup and decided to go fishing afterwards.'

'Ah huh.'

Ray's utterance reminded Nick of his local doctor back in New York. He used to make that same sound when he hadn't reached a prognosis.

'Does this cabin belong to you?' Ray asked as a matter of routine.

'No,' Nick answered. 'As a matter of fact it belongs to an ex-colleague of yours.'

'Really?' Ray seemed genuinely interested.

'Yes, an ex-vice squad cop who decided he couldn't earn enough money on the force and joined us. Maybe we should talk about that.' Nick smiled.

The arrogance and confidence of this man was far in advance of anything Ray had encountered before. He annoyed Ray intensely, although experience had trained him not to show it.

'And could I have the owner's name, please?' Ray asked politely.

'Certainly. Denis Granger.'

'Oh, Denis. Yes, I worked with Denis on a couple of cases.' Ray smiled casually. I know how to play you at your own game, Ray thought contentedly.

'How did you know Brett McLeod?'

Nick explained the nature of his work and reason for being in Australia. His nerves suddenly jangled as he realised that Ray Cooper might check him out with the States. Even if Gus Fletcher told Ray he had fired Nick because of Winston Life, even if he told him about Eddie's sales, or even Eddie's death, it still wasn't evidence that could convict him. Slowly Nick managed to calm himself. All the suspicion in the world couldn't convict a man without evidence.

Ray was sure he had his man. He had a promotion in his sights and this conviction could be just the thing to set it in concrete.

'I'm going to take you down to the local station now, and notify Brett's next of kin, while we try to straighten out what actually happened here.'

Inside the local police station Nick could hear muttered profanities about the city cops and how they thought they owned the place. Ray directed Nick to a small interview room, telling him that Nick's testimony would be useful because he knew Brett so well and was the last person to see him alive. Ray patiently explained that he needed Nick's help to untangle the circumstances that led to Brett's death and that he would make the process as quick and comfortable as possible for Nick.

A coroner and pathologist were on the scene by this time; there were a dozen ways they knew to look for the cause of death. It was clear to them that this was not a death by misadventure. They immediately suspected that blood thinners had been mixed with the coke as soon as they saw the trickles of blood from nearly every orifice. No dealer would lace his own coke with blood thinners unless he had a pretty good reason for wanting to reduce his clientele. This was a murder of the first degree, no question.

Ray sat opposite Nick in the interview room, not allowing one flicker of the theories that were formulating in his mind to show through his cool blue eyes. A battle of wills and wits was developing even at that early stage of investigation. Ray was young for a detective of his seniority, just thirty-two. He had kept himself physically fit and mentally alert exercising regularly; playing squash, skiing. The sport wasn't important, it was a means of keeping up the strength to sustain a long and intricate challenge with controlled precision.

If the situation had been different, Nick conjectured, Ray would probably have made a damn fine recruit.

'So you sell life insurance?' the detective asked.

'Not me personally. I haven't sold for years. I recruit others to sell and to manage those who sell.'

'What was it like, selling life insurance, I mean?'

'It's a bitch of a job, but the rewards are worthwhile.'

'What rewards are they?'

'The rewards of knowing that you can never sell the wrong product to a person. Everyone in this world needs life insurance of some sort.'

'Is that the only reward?'

'Of course not. There's damn good money in it. We get paid well for what we do. Hour for hour we get paid higher than any other professional who works as hard.'

'Are you telling me I'm underpaid?'

'Well...'

'I suppose you could say I'm a salesman too.' Ray considered that point for a moment. 'You sell life insurance and I sell jail terms.'

He smiled at Nick. If Nick was guilty, and every instinct told Ray that he was, it was a very clever ploy to pick a location owned by an ex-copper. Nick would have assumed the police would assume no one would dare commit premeditated murder in such a place. A clever double bluff, Ray mused. But not clever enough.

Nick managed to contain his anger before it could visibly escape and attempted to return Ray's smile.

Ray spent the next hour asking Nick if Brett had been acting strangely, if he could think of anyone who may want to get rid of Brett, if Brett may have wanted to commit suicide. To all of this Nick managed to give acceptable, but nonetheless unhelpful, answers. The detective finally left him on his own.

Straining his ears, Nick could just make out the conversation outside the door.

'Do you know,' one cop was saying to another, 'most criminals who report the crimes that they commit believe that this immediately exonerates them. And what's more, they all think that they are the first ones to think of it.'

Bastards, Nick thought. He could tell they were using well-practised techniques on him. They were going to keep a subtle pressure on him, to try to get him to slip up, to contradict himself. These boys just didn't know who they were dealing with, Nick convinced himself, and was pacified.

'You'll be pleased to hear we're taking you back to Melbourne,' Ray announced, returning to the claustrophobic room.

'To the Regent?'

'Not immediately. We'll have to take a recorded statement at headquarters, but it won't take long.'

Ray had ordered a search of Nick's apartment in

Sydney, Brett's home, the suite they had occupied at the Regent and their hire car. He was leaving no stone unturned. He put Nick in the back of an unmarked Ford Falcon, having a second detective do the driving back to Melbourne, while Ray covertly recorded the entire conversation on the way back to headquarters.

Ray completed a few basic formalities on entering the St Kilda Road headquarters of homicide. Nick had to be signed in and given a badge before being led to the elevators and taken to the ninth floor.

Through a maze of untidy desks, Nick was directed into a second interview room, much larger than the first. Inside there were cheap plastic-covered chairs and one cloth-padded chair with a small section missing from one of the arms. Instinctively, Nick headed for what appeared to be the most comfortable chair.

'Sorry, that's my chair,' Ray said in a friendly voice.

'My mistake,' Nick growled.

As Nick took his place opposite a face that was becoming much too familiar, he realised why he had been ushered to the plastic chair. He faced a piece of glass on the rear wall that he immediately realised was a two-way mirror. There was almost certainly a video camera behind it, Nick thought. Although the room was clean and bright it had an austere feel about it. Nick found himself fantasising about the scum who had sat in this chair before him, and felt it beneath contempt that he now shared the same space when all he was guilty of was exterminating vermin.

He could hear air-conditioning working in the room but found the air uncomfortably hot. Nick determined the heat must have been the result of having so many bright lights blazing down on him at once. It was curious that the same heat didn't appear to affect Ray Cooper. He kept his sleeves rolled down and his tie fastened neatly around his neck, looking cool and controlled. Damn, Nick thought, he'd make a good recruit.

Ray asked the same questions he had already asked and a host of new ones, writing down every word that Nick uttered. When he was finally satisfied there was nothing left to ask, he gave Nick the transcript to read into a tape recorder before signing. Despite his best efforts, Ray had found nothing to hold Nick on.

'Thank you very much for your co-operation, Nick. You've been very helpful.'

'You mean I can go home?'

'Yes,' Ray said, reluctantly.

Nick left the police station in a taxi, a much more dignified mode of transport to the one that had taken him there, and believed that was the last he would ever see of Ray Cooper.

Chapter Seven

Nick read with immense joy Prime's Christmas newsletter.

Welcome to Our New Chief Executive.
On behalf of everyone in Prime and the Prime Group of companies, I extend a most warm and sincere welcome to our new chief executive, Nick Abbott.

Elsewhere on these pages you will read of his outstanding achievements, overseas as well as in Australia, and you may judge for yourself how singularly fortunate we have been to attract a man of such high calibre to our company. There is no question in my mind, nor in that of the chairman and members of the board, that he is going to make a vital contribution to our future. We relish the prospect of working with him.

You will be interested to learn the reasons for his permanent position at Prime Financial Group.

Nick Abbott was held in high esteem at East West. The announcement that he would join Prime permanently was greeted with great surprise by his former colleagues.

I must stress that Nick Abbott is now the managing director of the Prime Group of companies. His responsibilities cover Prime Life Insurance, Prime Benefits Consulting, Prime Retirement Villages, Prime Managed Funds and the boutique subsidiary companies such as Hamilton Black.

As a director of the Life Insurance League, after establishing his Australian name here during the early months of his consultancy, he gladly accepted the invitation to run the Prime Financial Group after the sad and sudden death of our late chief executive, Brett McLeod.

I trust you will join with me to wish Nick Abbott a long and prosperous future with Prime.

Mark Fitzgerald
Manager Operations

'Not a bad wrap, eh?' Nick asked rhetorically, showing the article to Sandra.

Brett's office had taken on a new shine in Nick's eyes now that he occupied it.

'How do you like your new office?' she asked, trying not to choke on the fear which had lodged in her throat.

'It's not bad. How do you like your new title, Ms Director of Sales and Marketing?'

'I like it very much,' she said. 'And how does it feel to be a permanent resident of Australia?'

'It's given my new shadow, Ray Cooper, a few more questions to ask.'

'He's trying to flush out the dealer who sold Brett the stuff. Have you seen the newspaper reports?'

'I've seen them.'

A small seed of doubt was germinating in Nick's mind. Ray Cooper had not given up as easily as he had hoped. He was now the one person who stood between him and the master plan. Nick had entertained ideas of disposing of this obnoxious little ferret. He had invented any manner of slow and painful ways to eliminate him, it had been a very enjoyable vision. He would poison his coffee, or have him run over by a bus or driven off a cliff. It had been a disappointment when he had to wake from his fantasy and realise that the ferret was still on his tail.

'Have you told Mark he's got the regional manager's job

yet?' Sandra asked, returning Nick's mind to the present.

'No. I'll tell him this week.'

'Congratulations, Dundee,' Sandra chirped. 'I'll see you at the sales track launch.'

She was no sooner out of his office when she felt her legs buckle beneath her. She had never taken James completely seriously until now. She had not been able to see Nick as a murderer until Brett's death placed the irrefutable facts before her. Now she feared for her own life. James had obviously been right about everything and that thought terrified her. She could not afford to make even the slightest slip.

If I quit, she reasoned, Nick will suspect I know something and am running scared. There'll be no place safe to hide from him. She shuddered at the thought. Worst of all, that could lead Nick straight to James... it could mean death for both of them by some diabolical method Nick would invent. She struggled to remain conscious against the horror of her new reality. Her breath became rapid, short panting breaths. She clung on to the pockets of her suit as though this feeble action could somehow fortify her. The thought of Nick being a mass murderer was so unbelievable that it denied all power of speech.

She crossed herself instinctively, praying she would wake from this living nightmare to find it was all a dream. How could this abomination be human? He was so cool and so controlled that even in her terror Sandra found him strangely fascinating. A man at once hideously cruel and yet magnetically masterful. He could be so many things. A chameleon of passions.

*

James sat in his lounge, looking sadly over the article Sandra had given him.

'You wanted him to make a slip,' Sandra said.

'Another death...' James said blankly.

'And with Brett out of the way he can implement anything he wants to.'

'There must be some way to prove he did this.'

'You were the one who said he was a clever man, my love. My God, he's been so blatant. He must be bloody sure he's covered his tracks to have pulled it off this way.'

'Oh, he's sure. He's had a lot of practice.' James clenched his fists in rage. 'That murderous bastard. He has to be stopped, Sandra. Jesus Christ, he has to be stopped,' James cried, jumping up from his chair in anger.

'Well you're probably the only one who can do it,' Sandra said in an attempt to calm him down.

'I can't bear the thought of you being close to him – get out. I don't care what excuse you use, just get out.'

'James, I can't. We both know I can't. If I leave now I must just as well put the noose around my neck myself.'

'It's a nightmare. Why did I ever get you involved in this?'

'Well, I am involved, and I've passed the point of no return.'

'That's true, I suppose—'

He hadn't finished his sentence when the doorbell rang. James went to answer it.

'Sandra, this is Ray Cooper,' James announced, returning with the detective. 'He's in Sydney heading up the investigation into Brett's death. I made contact with him as soon as I heard the news.'

'Pleased to meet you,' she said automatically.

James turned to Sandra. 'This guy is the most tenacious person I have ever met. They've got the right man on the case to bring him down.'

'Thank you for the compliment,' Ray smiled.

'But all the tenacity in the world hasn't proven

successful before,' James added soulfully.

'Do you mind if I stay? I'd like to hear what you have to say,' Sandra asked.

'Not at all,' Ray answered.

'It's good to see you again, Ray. Have you unearthed anything since we last spoke?' James asked urgently.

'Well, I'm curious about one thing,' Ray began.

'Only one?' James quipped.

'One at a time, anyway. Didn't anyone check Nick's credentials before offering him this job?'

'Brett was too overwhelmed with his reputation,' Sandra answered. 'Do you check the credentials of God?'

'I see. Well, it doesn't look like we're going to get much assistance from Gus Fletcher. When I tried to talk to him, all he'd tell me about was the business with Winston Life.'

'Lily-livered coward,' James growled, without realising how much like Nick he sounded. 'He's too frightened of starting a scandal that will damage his pension. Any proof will have long since been destroyed, I'll bet.'

'There is a chance we can still flush out some witnesses.'

'Witnesses!' James exclaimed. 'There wouldn't be any witnesses.'

'Never assume anything in this line of work,' Ray answered coolly. 'Gus might not have been helpful, but the New York police confirmed your suspicions about Eddie's death. If you're right about all those policies, it may be possible to get one of the original clients to talk.'

'I doubt that,' James scoffed. 'Who is going to admit to murdering their own child for insurance money?'

There was a long cold silence. The truth about volumes of infant policies resulting in mass infanticide had not been articulated before. It was that true no one could actually blame the salesmen for the deaths, but then again they had deliberately targeted people they knew could not afford the policies. If premiums weren't kept up their commission would be written back... unless of course the policy wasn't terminated but finalised through pay-out. A pay-out which could financially change the lives of the parents and their other children for ever.

Desperate times, James thought. At least the law had been changed decades ago so this could never happen again, but the thought that everything his life represented had been built on the success of his father's business – and his father's business had been a success because of these sales – was almost more than he could bear.

'There's another thing,' Ray said. 'You know the cabin at Enoch's point, where Brett died?'

'Yes,' Sandra and James both answered.

'It happens to be owned by an old colleague of mine.'

'That's right,' Sandra piped up. 'Denis Granger, he's ex-vice squad, right?'

'Correct,' Ray verified.

'Jesus,' James muttered. 'He's got some nerve. Or do you think it was some sort of clever double bluff?'

'Difficult to say,' Ray admitted. 'Possibly a little of both.'

'Do you think Denis can help?' Sandra asked.

'I'm not sure.'

Ray didn't want to give too much away until he was sure about Sandra and James. It was still difficult for him to assess where loyalties lay, although so far their stories checked out.

'I think I must be overdue for a visit to Mildura,' Sandra said quietly.

*

Nick marched into Mark Fitzgerald's office unannounced and was pleased to see Sandra talking with him.

'You two together again. Admit it. You're foolin' around with her, aren't you, Fitzgerald?'

Fitzgerald just laughed.

'Sandra, I have a few matters to discuss with your friend here.'

She didn't need to be told twice.

'That's all right, Nick, I have to get back to my office anyway. I'll see you both later.'

Nick watched her leave the office and shut the door. He looked slowly towards Fitzgerald before taking a seat on the visitor's side of the desk.

'There's only a few more weeks to go,' Nick began, still looking into Fitzgerald's face to check his expression.

'I'm very well aware of that. Are you here to tell me that I've got a job?'

'What do you think?'

Fitzgerald reached for his cigarettes, offering one to Nick before taking his own. 'I think you're here to tell me I've got a job,' he said slowly.

'You're right.'

Fitzgerald closed his eyes in relief. He had been trying desperately to think about what he might do if Nick said the regional manager's role was to go to someone else. He couldn't have stayed on with Prime in a lesser role, his ego wouldn't have allowed it. He also doubted that he could have found a position anywhere else that would have paid as well as the regional manager's position. It was a warm feeling of relief that swept through Mark Fitzgerald.

'I'm making you the regional manager for Northern Sydney,' Nick continued, aware that the man he faced felt at ease for the first time in months. 'I want you to start looking for new premises right away. We don't have much time to set you up. I assume you'll be taking your secretary with you?'

'Naturally.'

'Good. Then what you need to find is an assistant to help you with agent support. Your territory covers a huge geographical area, you can't do it all alone.'

'I've been looking after the entire company for operations,' he said indignantly.

'I know. But all you had to do was kick a few managers in the butts. This is a much more complex position and you Aussies have to come to terms with the expansive areas you travel. I don't want you spending three-quarters of your time in the car travelling from place to place. You'll have to set up a system whereby a colleague, someone you get along with and trust, can be your eyes and ears. Effectively you need to be in more than one place at one time.'

'So whom do you suggest?'

'That's for you to decide. The region is yours to run as you see fit; I'm just here to keep an eye on you and the other RMs to make sure you don't go off the rails. I can't manage fifty sales managers all around Australia at the one time either. I'll have to concentrate on the twelve RMs.'

'And I thought you were Superman,' Mark quipped.

'I am. That's why I know my limitations, and you should too. Even Superman found there were things he couldn't do.'

Fitzgerald started putting a vision together in his mind of the person who might be able to assist him in his new role. They would have to know the business, have at least three or four years' experience. They would have to understand, and enjoy the company of sales people. They would have to be prepared to travel and work long hours, which required either a single person or one with a very understanding spouse. He couldn't think of anyone who fitted this description.

'It may take me some time to find this assistant. Is there anyone you could recommend?'

Nick frowned. It was the expression he chose to look

both thoughtful and disapproving. He walked across the office to avoid looking at Fitzgerald. It would give the man a chance to think about his words more carefully. Nick had observed that Fitzgerald often spoke without clearly thinking through the ramifications behind his statements.

'Why is it going to take you so long?' Nick finally asked.

'I've got three weeks and in that time I have to find an office, furniture, move all my files, and locate a potential genius.'

'Your secretary can do all the legwork with offices and furniture. All you have to do is give the final approval. Learn to delegate, my man.'

'Oh.' Fitzgerald was embarrassed. Nick had a talent of coming out with a one-liner that was obvious and simple and put Fitzgerald's complicated thoughts in check.

'Write down a job description and a salary package for the person you would want to employ.'

Mark wrote down his earlier thoughts and combined them with a few dollar figures. It was scrawly writing, not easy to read, but when finished Nick perused it carefully. There were no surprises.

'Doesn't this remind you of anyone?' Nick asked.

'I wish it did.'

'What about Sandra?'

'Sandra?' he yelled. 'But you've just made her director of sales and marketing.'

'I know, and I want her to get that product finished. But she's losing sight of the coalface being tied to her computer. I want her out where the action is to make sure this product she comes up with has real market appeal. Getting her involved as an assistant to an RM, with the prospect of becoming an RM herself in time, is the perfect choice.'

Fitzgerald thought for a moment. There had been several

occasions when Sandra had complained about losing touch with the agents. But working under Fitzgerald would less than enthral her; hell, it would infuriate her.

'She loves the agents, right?' Nick helped him out.

'Yes.'

'They enjoy working with, and respect her?'

'Yes.'

'She wants to create a great product and move on to greater things herself?'

'Yes.'

'Well the RMs are now the most powerful people in this company – after myself, of course. I have an idea. Invite her to the launch of my new sales track. Let her see the support we are giving the agents versus the sort of support she is able to offer them in her sales and marketing role. It could be just the right seed to start a little war going in her mind. The highest authority she can go to for advice is me and when she runs in all concerned, I'll make the suggestion out of the goodness of my heart.' He leered at Mark. Nick knew that the idea appealed to him. Nick hoped that by putting her back in the heart of the agents, she would be inspired to get her product out. It had been a source of continual frustration that it was taking her so long to finalise it.

'Right.' Nick's lips curled in a reassuring smile.

'Say,' blurted Mark, 'are you going to invite Ray Cooper to this sales launch too? I reckon he'd make a bloody good recruit.'

'Is he still snooping around?'

'I think he likes my aftershave,' Mark laughed.

Nick became uneasy at the mention of the detective's name.

'What's he been asking you now?'

'Oh, he's been asking me whether Brett approved of the forthcoming changes, and whether I think that certain people's positions would have been so secure under the reign of Brett McLeod. That sort of stuff.'

'And what have you told him?'

'That it was Brett McLeod who brought you out here for the express purpose of making these changes. I don't know who knocked the old bastard off, but this Ray Cooper is obviously barking up the wrong tree.'

Fitzgerald's words calmed Nick somewhat. Ray Cooper was clearly getting nowhere with his line of questioning. The people in Prime were loyal to Nick; there was absolutely nothing that Ray could do.

It was always difficult for Nick to sleep the night before a sales track launch. He repeatedly sat up in bed to write things down, whatever came into his head. He wrote down facts, conjectures, possibilities, even impossibilities. He had warned the agents, sales managers and regional managers to study their manuals well and come armed with questions or there would be hell to pay. With this threat in mind, he had to be sure he could answer whatever issue might be raised. Regardless of the complexities of growth, and the excess diversification of his sales team, the fundamental of life insurance remained the same. People insured their lives to protect the people they loved against financial hardship. It was this unwavering belief in the product that was more important than any given sales track, but it was a fundamental not easily instilled into some of his people. They required the security blanket of a well-oiled sales pitch and so that was what Nick had to supply.

*

At ten minutes to nine, Nick arrived in the main training hall of Sydney's head office. He went over his notes and stood by the podium with the predictable cup of coffee and a cigarette.

He stood on the platform to go through his opening remarks in his mind, aware that this position flatteringly accentuated his size.

'Happy New Year.'

Nick looked towards the voice to see the first of his guests arrive, Sandra Upton.

'G'day,' Nick replied in the broadest Australian accent he could manage. It made her laugh. 'Do you like that? I've learned to speak Australian.'

'Somehow I don't think you'll pass the test,' Sandra said as she took her seat near the front of the hall, hiding the intense fear that automatically manifested whenever she was in Nick's presence.

By five past nine the hall was nearly full.

'Good morning and Happy New Year to you all.' The microphone enhanced Nick's New York accent. 'I have brought you here today to go through the kits you were given at the annual conference. I take it by now you have all had a chance to look over them, so I expect there will be some questions. Would anyone like to raise any of these before I commence?'

An agent halfway down the room put up his hand.

'Ma*h*ony,' Nick pointed to the agent with twenty years' experience at Australian Life and now Prime.

'The name is Mahony,' he said indignantly, pronouncing his surname distinctly as 'Marny' not 'Ma*h*ony'.

'It's spelled with an h, right?' Nick asked.

'Yes,' Mahony admitted.

'Then it's Ma*h*ony.'

The agent hated Nick for ridiculing him this way but decided to ignore the wisecrack rather than inflame the situation.

'I don't understand about the calculation table that's referred to on page nine.'

'That's good, because I have the details here to go

210

through with you. At least it shows you've read your manual. Anyone else?'

It was a gruelling day for Nick, explaining the basics of sales techniques that this group should have already been familiar with. He wondered how they had managed to sell at all before Nick Abbott arrived in Australia and decided that it must have been attributed to pure Aussie naivety and a good deal of luck.

It was gratifying that the agents took to the concept so well. Now Nick had to convince George Hamilton and Ralph Black that they would be advocating Nick's methods through their training sessions as a back-up to the launch. They weren't going to like it, but that was their problem. He would make sure that they obeyed directives if they wanted to keep receiving their huge training salaries.

'Nick, can I have a word with you?'

Sandra was trying to push through the crowd of agents to reach Nick. He was surrounded by adoring agents who treated him like the Messiah who had just arrived.

'Sure, Sandra, what is it?'

She took him to one side. 'It's this sales track; I'd like to talk to you about how we will adapt it for the new product.' As she spoke the disgust she felt for Nick made her dizzy. She was using herself as live bait, deliberately trying to ruffle his feathers. It was the most terrifying experience she had ever known.

'Yes, that's concerning me too, but it's a painting by numbers process. This track can be used by a brand new agent as well as the veterans. If we start talking to rookies about the complexities of a new product they're going to get lost. The veteran agent, on the other hand, will be trained separately. I just don't see a way round it, unless you can come up with something better than I have?'

'I hardly think so,' she stammered. 'But it bothers me when you say that all agents are to use this track exactly as it is, no deviation.'

'I can see we need to talk about this in more detail. Are you going to be at Hamilton Black's Melbourne training session next week?'

'Be there? I'm one of the guest speakers,' she announced proudly.

'Oh, well pardon me. We'll arrange to meet afterwards and I'll explain a few things to you. I just haven't got time right now.'

'I'll look forward to it.'

That should give her just enough time to figure out how she needs to adapt her role, Nick thought smugly.

'I wouldn't advise it if I were you,' Sandra heard someone say as she walked back into the crowd.

'Are you talking to me?' she asked, noticing the statement came from George Hamilton.

'I know what you're up to,' George added in a whisper, most uncharacteristic for him.

'Do you now?' she said quizzically, as he ushered her into a corner of the hall.

'Could you be a little more specific, please?' she asked.

'Denis told me about your meeting with him in Mildura. Denis is an ex-copper, he's used to taking risks,' George said fatherly.

'Denis had no right to repeat that conversation to you,' she hissed angrily.

'Listen love, Denis knows he can trust me. We all know the truth; Denis, you and me. And we know it's not the first time.'

'So what do you suggest, George? Just let him get away with it?'

'What do you suggest, love? Provoke him into doing you, too? It's one hell of a way to get proof,' he murmured.

'I have no intention of becoming a sacrificial lamb. Ray explained to Denis that if we can destabilise him, he could slip into revealing something which may help nail him. Denis used to do it all the time. It's easy,' she explained in an undertone.

'If it's so easy, how come he's never been caught before?'

'Shh. He's coming this way...'

*

Sandra had the launch kit spread out over the lounge and was making notes. Nick had done an excellent job of putting his methods into a sales track. There was more material there than Sandra could have digested in a week. The basic need for the product of life insurance came through with fanatic compulsiveness. The fact that agents were seen as untrustworthy creatures, whom no one took seriously, was an issue this sales pitch was going to eliminate conclusively. The testimonials, the newspaper headlines: these were all slanted in such a way as to shame the intended client into buying the product.

James picked up a portion of the work and read the power phrases Nick had outlined:

1. If you can't afford the one hundred dollars per month premium now, how are your family supposed to find the one thousand dollars per month they will need without you and your income?
2. When you strip the emotions aside, what we are discussing is taking out a maintenance agreement on the machine that produces your income.
3. Do you want your widow to be in a position where she has to remarry just to survive?

James could visualise his father pronouncing with great intensity many of these phrases to promote sales. He thought of his own life insurance requirements and, while he realised these phrases were cleverly worded sales pitches, he saw the sense in them. He recalled the manipulations that Sandra had spoken of and knew she was dealing with an expert in the art of emotion control. He decided she had learned enough.

'It staggers your imagination, doesn't it?' said James, rising from his chair.

'What do you make of it?' Sandra asked him, without really looking for a response.

'Enough to frighten me.'

'What are you talking about?' Sandra was too deeply engrossed in her study to realise the power of James's statement.

'Just how do you plan to pull something this good to pieces?'

'I'm not sure yet,' she answered truthfully. 'All I've managed to say so far is that this mystical new product won't fit into it.'

'That should be sufficient, I would think.' James walked to the window. 'But one thing is clear: if you feel you're getting too close to the fire, you must get away before you get burned. Nick has a brilliant mind. You're going to be playing the master at his own game.'

'You may be right. I know I'm taking a huge risk, but Ray told Denis he doesn't seem to think he'll be able to get evidence of the act any other way.'

'Damned if you do, and damned if you don't,' James murmured.

Sandra didn't hear him. She was concentrating deeply. After several minutes she spoke to him across the room.

'There's a meeting next week at Hamilton Black. Nick said that he would discuss it with me there.'

James looked at the preoccupied, uncertain woman before him. For several seconds he said nothing, merely sucking breath through his teeth as if trying to formulate a reply.

'You're a brave, beautiful woman, Sandra Upton.'

'It's not what the one person is worth, James, it's how quickly one can manipulate events.' She stopped, thinking she was beginning to sound like Nick.

'I find it incredible that so few people are bothered by Nick taking over the company. There are only three or four people who seem to think that something fishy is going on.'

'Why should anybody care about Brett? He never empathised with the agents. Nick is offering them systems, products and sales tracks better than they've ever seen before.'

Sandra was exasperated. She clenched her hands and brought her clenched fingers to her chin. 'For a man whose intelligence exceeds his imagination, that comment doesn't surprise me.'

James fell silent for a moment and looked at the woman he loved.

'Have you considered for a moment that you could be destroyed by this battle, even if you win?'

'I have.'

'Do you really want to risk that?'

'Yes. I feel responsible.'

James felt tempted to pour himself a stiff drink.

'I think this whole business is going too far. Sandra, I love you, and I'm terrified for you.'

Sandra's weary eyes were closed.

'I think there's a little of Nick in each of us, James. It's all part of human nature, twisted human nature. I've fought to get where I am today, devoted my time into building my reputation. It's been a stimulating, all-consuming game and I've played it well. What I've learned from Nick Abbott, and what many observers fail to realise, is that it is not the acquisition of profit that matters, it is merely the by-product. It's the acquisition of power. I now know that is what I want and feel equipped for the responsibility. The more convinced I become the more obvious it is that others are not equipped. It becomes a personal crusade, I think.'

'I feel like you're slipping through my fingers and there's nothing I can do to bring you back.'

She picked up her notes and went into the bedroom, closing the door behind her leaving James in the large sitting room.

He thought for a moment that his woman was on the verge of tears. He had been dismissed. Sandra was becoming more and more detached. She often apologised for her behaviour, but in apologising, acknowledged it. He began to realise what was happening. He was coming in a poor second to the excitement and stimulation she received from trying to catch a killer. He understood completely what Sandra felt.

Would this be the end of Sandra? Could he ever be finished with her? He told himself no. He began to wonder if she was capable of the correct judgement. He had been idle in recognising the situation as it developed. What had he done? Could he undo it? He was living on the outskirts of a world he couldn't cope with. But she didn't belong to it either. She belonged to him. She had to.

*

Ray sat at his desk in the homicide department, flicking back and forth over all the notes he had taken about Brett's murder. He was trying desperately to seek out those who could be allies in his investigation. Even a passing comment about suspicion, resentment or fear would be enough. There appeared to be plenty to choose from. Apart from Sandra and James there were the interesting characters of George Hamilton and Ralph Black. George and Ralph had never trusted Nick and confirmed James's suspicions about Eddie's death, a death also linked to cocaine and rat poison. The New York police had confirmed a willingness to reopen the files on both Norma and Eddie if they could find sufficient evidence, but that was one thing Ray didn't have. He could find the means, the motive and the opportunity, but no court in the land would give a conviction on that without evidence of the act. Denis Granger was more than helpful. Coming from vice, he understood the procedures and was a useful source to spread disinformation and covertly direct internal inquiries.

As both an ex-colleague and old friend, Denis, Ray realised, could not feel more involved in this investigation.

George Hamilton, despite his apparent willingness to assist, was of little use. Nick already suspected his disloyalty.

Sandra, on the other hand, was perfect, if he could believe her intentions.

Catching Nick Abbott was quickly becoming a personal pursuit for Ray. Nick Abbott was a mass murderer. There were three deaths at least. If James was right, the big picture was even more horrendous. Damn, he thought, why are my superiors taking so bloody long to authorise one simple trip to New York? As his frustration intensified, he noticed his pencil had snapped between his fingers.

*

The Prime agents were all ready to hear of the latest developments in their ever-changing environment. They came from all directions to learn about the new concept which was to be launched. Some sat poised with notepads ready, others talked excitedly to one another about the prospects they planned to approach first. Six agents stood in a circle speculating about what Sandra was likely to say at this meeting, all wanting to ensure they would be positioned to take full advantage of whatever it was. They realised it was always tricky coming to terms with something new. They stood like hunters about to track some new prey.

The advance was on. This was the first of many new initiatives that Nick had promised them. Like soldiers waiting for a briefing, they buzzed about their good fortune at having such visionary leaders.

Slowly the hall filled. The hum of the overhead projector fell mute beneath the rumblings of chatter and faint screeching of chairs being moved. George sensed they were ready for the proceedings to begin.

'Welcome,' George Hamilton bellowed, 'to another Hamilton Black training session. It is my personal pleasure to introduce someone who needs no introduction. A person who has worked tirelessly to get this new concept packaged for you. Your own director of sales and marketing, Ms Sandra Upton.'

George led the applause. Sandra had become quite close to George. Sharing secrets they dared not repeat to anyone, except the wily ex-cop, Denis, created a sense of camaraderie between these common adversaries of Nick Abbott. A camaraderie they could not afford to let others become unduly aware of.

Sandra tingled with nervousness. Nick was in the audience to see her deliver the cross-selling launch; she had to make it good.

'Thank you. I'm here today to explain how we can use to our advantage the latest changes the Labor government has thrust upon us. At first glance they seem onerous and not easily interpreted. However, devoting a great deal of personal time and energy to the eighty-four pages of the statement, I am pleased to tell you that the prospects are good.'

'We don't need you to tell us about it,' interrupted Mahony. 'Just come out on the sales calls with us, that will sort it out.'

'Shut up, Mahony, and keep your comments to question time,' Nick said firmly, smiling at Sandra to indicate she was clear to continue. He wasn't going to let anyone interrupt this important speech.

Nick Abbott observed her carefully. He would wait until after the meeting and take her for a quiet drink at the Regent. It was more conducive to his strategy. He ignored the occasional suspicious glare that George threw in his direction. Whatever George might suspect, he was powerless in Nick's new world; this knowledge gave Nick immense satisfaction.

*

'Sandra,' Nick began, his expression sombre. 'What we discuss here tonight will go no further than this table. Is that understood?'

She nodded like an obedient lapdog.

'The reason, Sandra, that my sales track had no room for your new product is because I'm concerned with the amount of time it is taking to get it out.'

'I see,' Sandra answered with a cold dryness in her mouth.

'I know you've explained to me over and over that it has to be perfect, and I agree with you, but I'm afraid I am going to have to put some sort of deadline on you.'

'How long have I got?' she asked numbly. In an instant Nick had thwarted her plan to rile him. The tables seemed to have turned on her completely.

'A month,' he said firmly.

'A month?' she asked, the pressure upon her already more than she could bear.

'Why are you telling me all this?' she asked nervously.

'I know you're close to something.' Nick frowned. 'There is no one else who has both your capacity to understand legislation and your rapport with the agents, but you seem to be getting too caught up with the fine print and losing sight of the fact that our agents need this product now. I like you, you know that. And I respect you, and what's more the agents respect you.'

Her concentration deepened.

'What I want you to do is give me a detailed report of your current status so at least I have something to feed the agents. I want you to talk to the agents to assess their specific needs too. You might find you need a greater involvement with the RMs for this, so I will authorise you to act as agent support, whenever necessary. At least you will get back to the coal-face. I'm just concerned you could be losing your perspective. I don't want to see a promising career ruined.'

Her eyes widened. She had no choice. Sandra took out a pad and pen to make notes of some ideas that entered her mind. Even as she did so, she realised the futility of her actions.

*

Against her better judgement, Sandra sat down in her study with the door closed to formulate a strategy to cope with the challenge Nick Abbott had set for her. Her large grey desk was covered with paper. There were copious notes, crossed out and rewritten. The whole exercise made her quite uncomfortable but she had to make this look good.

'Sandra.' James tentatively tipped his head around the door.

'What is it? I said no interruptions,' she grumbled.

'I'm sorry. It's Ray Cooper. He says it's important.'

'All right.'

She put down her pen and rubbed her eyes. It was ten o'clock in the evening and she felt as though she had been drained entirely of her energy.

'Come in,' Sandra said, holding the handle to her office door and directing the detective towards a seat. 'Would you like some coffee?'

'No, thank you.'

His crisply ironed shirt and beige-coloured suit enhanced his cool, controlled appearance. James joined him in the study, listening intently to the conversation.

'You look troubled,' he said soothingly.

'I am.'

'I just called in to see how it went with Nick last night,' he said compassionately, although Sandra doubted there was an ounce of genuine compassion in his words.

'Terrible,' she answered nervously.

'Oh,' Ray answered.

'Before I had a chance to provoke him, he put the pressure on me to get this product fixed. I don't know what to do.'

'I see. Well, we have had some luck. We found the dealer that sold Brett his drugs. He swears the drugs he sold him were clean and, given his detailed statement, we believe him.'

'So?' She shifted in her seat to listen more carefully to the detective.

'At least we know it was laced after it was purchased.'

'Big deal, we both already knew that,' she answered with disgust.

'Knowing it and proving it are two different things. Believe me, this is progress.'

'Look,' Sandra said, adopting an assertive tone. 'If this is the best news you have, I think you should let me get back to work before you find yourself investigating my death. Trying to work on James's new brainchild and make Nick believe I am developing it for him is no easy matter.'

'I'm sure, and I'm sorry I can't be of any further help.'

It concerned Ray that Nick obviously placed a good deal of faith in this woman. Despite her protests about Nick, he obviously still trusted her. For this reason Ray refrained from giving her any information that she could not have acquired elsewhere about his investigation. He simply fed her sufficient to let her think he was confiding in her.

'I know this is very difficult for you,' he assured her. 'I do understand the pressure you are under. I'll give you both my pager number. You can reach me on this number any time of the day or night. If there's anything at all you need, just let me know.'

'Thank you,' she said quietly. 'I'll make sure I keep this handy.'

'Me too,' James murmured.

'I'm going to New York in a couple of days. Who knows what I may be able to unearth there.'

Ray left Sandra to her work, wishing for once he knew whom to trust. The only thing he knew for certain was Nick was guilty and somehow he was going to be the one to put the cuffs on him. No hotshot from New York was going to beat him to this prize.

*

The best of the ideas Sandra was able to come up with was to arrange a meeting between the new regional managers. Perhaps if she could get them to say that something was missing in her basic design, it would be sufficient to stall her progress a little longer. The thought of Nick making a fortune out of James's brainchild was too horrible to consider.

No time like the present, she decided, and proceeded to

put her plan to work.

She folded her papers neatly and put them in her top drawer for safe keeping. Taking a deep breath and straightening her suit, she walked towards Mark's office. It was full of packing containers as he prepared to move to his new regional headquarters.

She knocked gently, hearing that he was on the phone.

'Come in,' he called, barely interrupting his train of thought.

He acknowledged Sandra with a wave of his hand, inviting her to take a seat.

This man was only an arrogant fool. In Sandra's eyes, that made him far easier to deal with than the terrifying presence of Nick Abbott. She shut the door and sat down, patiently waiting for him to finish his call.

'Well now, Ms Upton, what is it I can do for you?' he asked with a complacent smile that annoyed her.

'I'm not quite sure how to say it.'

'Just out with it is usually best.'

'All right. I'm afraid I have to tell you that I don't feel my product is quite right. Something seems to be missing. I'd like the input of the RMs on this one and I wondered if you'd be able to call them to a meeting for me?'

He sat back in his chair smiling contentedly. Sandra's revelation was just what Nick had told him to expect.

'Sandra, I'll be happy to arrange the meeting.'

'You will?' she commented, a little surprised that he had agreed so easily.

'That's what I said.'

'Thank you. I'll prepare some discussion notes right away.'

She stood to leave and then remembered she hadn't shaken his hand, as was expected. She turned back towards him, smiled and offered her hand then ran up the fire escape stairs to Nick's office.

'What is it?' Nick asked, buried in his own mound of paperwork.

'I'm calling a meeting of the RMs to analyse the strengths and weaknesses of the new product. Things are proceeding on schedule at this time.'

'Excellent. I'm very pleased.'

'I'm going to start drafting an agenda and suggesting a few alternative dates. Can you give me a few dates that suit you, assuming you want to attend.'

Nick picked up his diary and scribbled a couple of dates on a piece of paper.

'There.' He handed Sandra the paper and watched her hurry back downstairs. He grinned to himself at her diligence.

'What was that about?' Nick's secretary asked.

'Sandra's got RMs to attend a meeting about this new product.' Nick shrugged. 'It's a step in the right direction.'

*

Nick's optimism was short-lived. 'Damn,' he cussed out loud. What was wrong with her? Nick understood coming to terms with something this radical wasn't easy, but he was impatient to see his plan get off the ground.

'Sandra, would you come into my office for a moment?' he growled over her intercom.

'I'll be right there.'

'Shut the door,' Nick ordered without looking up, when she arrived.

'What is it?' she asked, experiencing an uneasy feeling about this meeting.

'I was very unhappy about the way that meeting went.'

'I know,' she said anxiously.

'The RMs are not happy with what appear to be careless flaws; what's going on with you?'

'I overlooked a fundamental issue, I'm sorry. I'm working on fixing it right now.'

'Sandra, you've got a great future with this company, don't blow it by fucking this up.'

'But—' she protested.

'There are no buts – I want that product. You've got one week.'

'Only one?' She spat the words in disbelieving fear.

'For your own good, perhaps you'll work better under pressure.'

Nick's anger was evident; she knew she had the means to push him further but her courage fell limp. Although she knew she was letting her side down she just couldn't bring herself to tempt the wrath of this man.

'What can I say?' she asked.

'You can say, "Thanks, Nick. Thanks for giving me the chance to prove I can do it."'

'Thanks,' she said feebly.

Nick had used his last trump to get her to perform. Something was not right, why was she stalling him? Perhaps he had misjudged her after all?

She had to admit to herself that she had failed. It was a sickening admission. There was nothing left for it now but to consider alternative methods, and fast. She thought she was strong enough to act as bait, but when push came to shove she just couldn't do it. Her fear of Nick, she admitted, was even stronger than her love for James. Or perhaps it was simply the love of her own life that prevented her from provoking him. The only way to get the pressure off was to give Nick what he wanted or find some way of removing him from power, and that was ridiculous. But how could she hand over the one product which would give him what he wanted when that product belonged to James? It was a hopeless situation. She sat down with a cup of black coffee and considered her limited options.

Suddenly a light bulb flashed in her mind. She remembered the ISC warning about reserves and remuneration systems. If she could get evidence that the reserves were low, that would automatically halt any developments.

Within her mind, Sandra wrestled with her idea. She was aware her actions could cause serious disruption at Prime. She justified her actions by assuring herself that Prime was quite capable of getting back on its feet once Nick Abbott had been removed.

She called Edward Townsend.

*

Fortunately for Sandra, the ISC moved swiftly. Any word about a company playing Russian roulette with policyholders' money was quite sufficient to start a major investigation into reserves.

'Have you heard the news?' Mark blurted the words down his telephone to Nick Abbott.

'What now, Fitzgerald?' Nick had too many things on his mind to deal with Mark Fitzgerald at that moment.

'The ISC report, it says our reserves are getting perilously low. How can this have happened?'

'Relax, once sales of this new product hit our investment funds, everything will be back on track. It's all part of the overall plan. I have to pay for your huge commissions from somewhere. Volume sales are the answer.'

'But there's supposed to be a freeze on the new product until the reserves increase.'

'Stop panicking, man, I've got that issue under control.'

'Are you sure the product will be ready?' Mark urged.

'It *will* be ready, you can count on that.'

On the eve of the forthcoming Hamilton Black meeting, no work had been done at Prime. There had been much drinking and theorising, but no work. The drinking went on late into the night. When they finally settled their nerves it was already early morning. Some of the agents had come hundreds of miles for this meeting, others drove or walked from their homes scattered around Sydney. Many arrived with heavy heads and sore eyes. Others lurched along feeling no pain at all, except for a slight bursting of the bladder.

Nick Abbott had not received the ISC news well. He had dealt with crises before, plenty of them. Yet each time the rage he experienced flourished as if it were a new bud bursting into bloom. He had flown to Canberra immediately, but the ISC officials were unrelenting. They didn't care what his plans were, the facts were simple. Prime's reserves were dangerously low and he had to take action, or they would be forced to take action for him.

Nick had demanded to know why they had selected Prime to check on. Had someone tipped them off? Not surprisingly, they had declined to answer him. All reports received by the ISC, they explained, were accepted on a no-name basis. This situation required business cunning. For now Nick had to control the darker side of his anger and create a plan to get out of this mess.

'All right you lot, settle down,' George Hamilton said in his usual bellowing manner.

'Ding-ding-ding,' George called, trying to sound like a school bell.

George's efforts to quieten the crowd, however, proved unnecessary. Nick Abbott entered the hall and a hushed silence fell. Everyone watched Nick glare around the hall to get some idea of who had tipped the ISC off to investigate reserves.

If Sandra hadn't told him her product was all but finished he would have been certain it was her.

Aware of the situation she was in, Sandra moved towards Nick to offer any assistance she could in helping

Prime out of its current crisis.

'Thank you, Sandra,' he said quietly.

There was a low hum around the room.

'But your support will not be needed in this instance. There's some good news I wish to impart at this meeting,' Nick announced, throwing a cold stare around the room.

'Places everyone!' George yelled at the top of his lungs.

'I think we'd better sit down,' Sandra whispered to Mark.

Nick took his place at the podium.

'I know you're all concerned about the latest rumours from the ISC,' Nick began. 'As usual, these short-sighted boffins can't see further than their noses. Your new remuneration system is putting a strain on our reserves, but that was expected. Had our new product been launched the volume of sales would have counteracted this, but now we are told all new products are to be frozen until the reserves increase. With the share market running at the rate it is at the moment, there is a very easy way to fix the problem. We will transfer funds from our capital stable fund into equities, just a sufficient amount to boost the reserves by the high interest we will gain from this switch. Within a few weeks we will be back up to acceptable levels, the new product will be ready, and the funds can be transferred back. It's simple, effective and foolproof.'

The agents applauded earnestly. They knew they could count on Nick Abbott to come up with something brilliant. He hadn't let them down.

Sandra couldn't believe her ears. Nick had done it again.

*

Working late into the night, Sandra put the finishing touches to James's brainchild. Her eyes were blurred, her mouth dry and she desperately needed sleep, but she owed

James at least this much after her dismal failure with Nick. The city lights shimmered outside her window, dancing like fireflies trying to keep her awake. Eventually exhaustion got the better of her and Sandra collapsed over her computer, but not before the final touches were made.

'Can I come in?' a voice asked gently.

Sandra looked up, weary and not fully conscious.

'Of course,' she said automatically, without realising who was there.

'How are we going?' the voice asked.

The question sounded vague.

'Um, fine,' she said, wiping her eyes to clear her vision, realising the morning sun was just appearing.

A hand gently turned her computer screen away from her.

'You've finished it, haven't you? I knew you could do it.'

Now fully awake, Sandra realised Nick was viewing the complete prototype of James's product.

'It's brilliant,' he said proudly. 'I knew you could do it. But look at the state of you. You poor child, you've worked through the night to make sure it was ready on time. Well, you take the day off. I can get this going from here. Rest today and I'll take you out to dinner tonight – it will be a celebration dinner.'

Sandra's eyes were wide with fear and horror. What had she done?

'You look like an owl,' Nick laughed. 'A wise, beautiful owl who has just saved the company. I'm so proud of you. You'll be well looked after for this.'

'Thank you,' she answered, trembling with dread.

'Sandra, my dear girl, you need some rest,' he said with a note of genuine concern in his voice. 'You're shaking like a leaf. I can't have my star collapsing on me. I'll put you in a cab. Meet me tonight at the Regent. Seven thirty. Is that okay?'

'Fine,' she answered, still in a state of shock.

'Sandra,' Nick began. 'You've done well. Very bloody well.'

*

The first call came from Mark Fitzgerald. He was on the phone to Nick Abbott shortly after Sandra left the office, around nine thirty in the morning.

'Brace yourself, today is going to be like no other you have ever known. The finance market will remember today as the one where millions lost their fortunes,' Mark advised.

Prime's head man in the finance department of Sydney, Percy Meacen, was chain-smoking, wondering what on earth he could do to avert the catastrophe; knowing in his heart that it was already too late. Prime would be shot dead within a matter of months and there was not a thing he could do to stop it. He considered the greed and fervour that spread with the bull market was unparalleled since the rush in the late twenties. No one could see an end in sight to the huge returns being earned on the stock market. Nick had forced him to invest more and more into equities in an effort to raise Prime's income above the increase in commission payments going out, and now it was too late to switch it back.

The duty clerk at Prime Benefits Consulting passed by reception noticing that, even at that early hour of the day, the board was alight with incoming calls.

At that moment, Mark Fitzgerald walked by saying all hell had broken loose. The day hadn't started and panic was already stretched across the entire company, probably the nation. He kept getting garbled accounts of people ready to commit suicide or kill their investment advisers or withdraw all their funds. Five intercoms were buzzing around his office and he had to get out.

Just as he left, his new superannuation consultant said to him, 'It's official, you know. October's "Black Tuesday". The market has crashed and it's too late to switch funds.'

Mark walked back into his office, shutting the door behind him. It was like leaving a wasps' nest in your living room. The financial correspondent of the *Financial Review* had corrected his story from the previous day, admitting now that there was no doubt. The market had gone through the floor and this was likely to be the start of one of the deepest recessions in history. He had been spotted walking around his office prophesying that the fat cats of the eighties were about to become scrawny starving creatures whom no one would have any pity for.

In Hamilton Black's headquarters the telephone boards lit up. All of Prime's agents were asking questions about how to avert a massive client loss. They had seen recessions before. In 1982 the market had taken a downturn, but this was a far deeper collapse than the moderate falls of a few years ago. It was nearly ten o'clock when George Hamilton decided the situation warranted calling an emergency meeting to advise Prime's agents on how to handle the situation. He stood between Ralph Black and an office girl, standing in the way a policeman would stand, slightly backwards over a line of balance. He took his tie off and rolled his sleeves up. This was going to be one tough son-of-a-bitch day.

From his window George noticed an increase in traffic activity for a Tuesday morning. There was no good reason for it, he surmised, just the mass state of confusion that the country had suddenly toppled into. The commotion was stirring in his brain. He closed his eyes and visualised the bad B-movies that showed people throwing themselves off buildings at the start of the Great Depression in the Thirties;

he could see it happening again. Nick had run them straight into the ground.

'Now the first thing people do in a situation like this is panic,' George said, calling the meeting to order.

'Well, I'm glad I'm doing things in the right order,' Mahony piped up.

'Shut up, Mahony. This is serious. Now what you have to explain to your clients is that they haven't actually lost anything until – and unless – they withdraw their funds. Right now it's just a paper loss. If you've sold responsibly your clients should be able to afford to leave their money where it is until the market recovers, that way nobody loses. Economies are cyclical, this is just a phase and we will come out of it. The worst thing anyone can do is panic.'

Privately, however, George was panicking too. Clients were one small issue. Saving Prime, he realised, was going to be a much bigger job.

*

It was fortunate for Sandra that pandemonium broke out. Everything was forgotten. Nick, James and everyone in the industry were trying to figure out what to do in the wake of one of the largest stock market crashes in history.

At least it gives me the time to figure out how I am going to break the news to James, she thought.

During November and December there were frequent reports about a sign of recovery. There were numerous whispers around Prime: 'It's picking up, I can see the signs.'

Nick opened his daily paper to look for some sort of inspiration.

EASTBANK LIFE'S MR BIG ACHIEVES RECORD SALES

South-African born Tom Weinstein, the driving force behind

Australia's newest life insurance company, Eastbank Life, a wholly owned subsidiary of the banking giant, Eastbank, today revealed that the growth of new business sales has already reached levels far beyond their highest expectations. In answer to critics, who claim his success is solely due to the fact that he had a captive following in the bank's existing clients, Mr Weinstein has this to say:

'Naturally, part of our success has been due to the bank's existing clients. These people were obviously going to become the logical base for my new sales team. The real test, however, was attracting non-Eastbank clients who traditionally buy from life insurance companies to buy from us. This we have achieved with figures far better than I could have hoped for. This achievement is purely to do with having the right people at the coalface...'

God, you are looking after me today. Nick smiled. He stared at the report, scarcely believing his good fortune. He had shown good judgement in thinking Tom would be worth cultivating. Arranging Tom's residency in Australia was going to turn out to be a very intelligent move.

A meeting was arranged.

*

Tom Weinstein swore quietly, closed the file Nick had left with him and stared down at the street. The spring rain had stopped, but there was still a fierce wind. He could see tiny pedestrians thirty floors below with heads bent down as they hurried about their business.

Tom had understood that Nick would call on his favour to be reciprocated sooner or later. He had done his homework or, to be more specific, James had done it for him. James too had known of the favour and that it would be called in.

Tom knew everything about Nick's situation at Prime, and about his dealings with Winston Life. He knew James was right when he advised him to stay out of it for his own sake. Tom was not about to become another casualty of the Abbott war, no matter how big the favour had been. Tom had fought his way up, step by step, serving his industry faithfully and with honour. He had paid his dues. Like many traditionalists, he believed that hard toil and perseverance would create sustainable wealth, not the type that falls as quickly as it rises. He was utterly loyal to this business. Eastbank would not come to Nick's rescue.

Tom laid Nick's report on his table and walked across to a chart of life insurance companies which almost covered the wall opposite his window. He studied it carefully as the minutes ticked by. His eye fell on one particular company. Tom knew Champion would gobble up Prime when the time was right.

He sat in his high-back leather chair and reached for the phone to tell Nick that, while it was an interesting offer, it was not suitable for Eastbank at this time.

Chapter Eight

It was Christmas of 1987 when Nick realised he had some very serious decisions to make. He was only too aware that without certain levels of reserve money the insurance and superannuation commissioner could close Prime down. They were was getting perilously close to that level which required swift and drastic action if they were to stay in business. He went to the offices of the Life Insurance League and started thumbing through the *Who's Who* of Australian- and overseas-owned life insurance companies. He knew exactly what he was looking for. He would try making cutbacks to raise the reserves.

As long as I can get the ratios to a sufficient level to launch the new product, Nick considered, I can still pull it off. If that doesn't work, then I'll find a big brother.

He would be expected to make some sort of announcement at the annual conference in January; something that would set the agents' minds at rest and direct their energies back to selling instead of worrying. That was not going to be easy.

He practised his speech.

'I don't have to tell you that the last few months have been, shall we say, tough. I have had a good look at the profit and loss of every company in the Prime Group and I am going to have to make some difficult decisions.'

He could hear someone asking the question, 'Are we selling out?'

'At this stage,' he announced, walking around his office as he continued to rehearse, 'I will not rule anything out.

You must remember the golden rule... he who has the gold makes the rules. If the best alternative for Prime is to merge with another company, then that is what we will do. This, however, is not, I repeat not, an imminent possibility. With certain rationalisations, we should be able to keep the company afloat. I have determined that in many areas of our operation we have two people doing the job that one could do just as effectively. This is a luxury we can no longer afford.'

Nick sat down as he uttered those words. He knew he was going to have to axe a couple of hundred jobs if they stood a chance at survival; there was no easy way to deliver that message.

'I'm not just referring to clerical jobs either. There are plenty of examples of duplicate roles within the management of this company. Of course, I don't need to tell you that you have to have a chief executive.'

He wondered if that would create a ripple of laughter or deepen the wound he had just inflicted.

'The most important part of our operation is our agents. They are our very lifeblood. This year will be the year of the agent and by way of deciding who will stay and who will go I will be listening to agent feedback; through their sales managers, regional managers and ultimately Nick Abbott. Any person who does not treat the agents with the courtesy, respect and efficiency they deserve will be out of the door first.'

At least that should instil some incentive for staff to work harder and smarter, he thought. It could be that the cull would leave him with one slick, economical and efficient machine. Every cloud has its silver lining, he told himself. These cutbacks could be just sufficient to keep the reserves at a level where the product could be launched.

*

'Have I got everything ready?' Sandra asked herself aloud, hopping around like a cat on a hot tin roof.

'Stop worrying,' her secretary called back. She handed Sandra her reports, dated 1st February, 1988.

'You'll see,' Sandra began practising her speech, 'that despite the doom and gloom in the market we are in a position to launch the variable income policy, or VIP as I choose to call it. You all know about annuities: a product purchased with a lump sum to pay a regular income. Clients must decide at the outset how much they want to receive as income, and for how long. Once that decision is made they are locked in for at least ten years. Well, we have received legal opinion, and while the law defining an annuity does not say you *can* change your mind about your income levels, once the initial decision has been made, it does not say that you *cannot* either. As an annuity is taxable in the hands of the receiver, it could be a considerable advantage to clients who have changes in circumstances to alter their income level. They may want to receive less money, to negate a tax liability, or more money, because of an unforeseen emergency. With other annuities on the market, this is not possible. With Prime's VIP product, you can tell your clients with confidence that this can be done.'

Sandra took a deep breath to practise her big finish when Nick joined her and read from her final notes.

'Do you know how much money comes out of superannuation funds into annuities every year?' He smiled. 'Hundreds of millions of dollars. That is hundreds of millions of dollars you will now be able to pick up before any of your competition. Just think of it. A unique and revolutionary product. There is no one in the industry who can touch us now. Prime the innovator, Prime the way of the future. Prime to victory,' Nick said triumphantly.

Lowering his voice he turned to Sandra. 'And I owe it all to you.' He smiled charmingly at her.

Sandra stared anxiously at Nick, wondering what tricks he would be able to make her perform next. It had saddened her to watch the change that had occurred in her nature. She had become cold and hard. Nick had led her straight into his complicated, well-woven web.

She had noticed she was beginning to use Nick's mannerisms, Nick's gestures, Nick's methods. If she didn't know better she would have thought she was totally bewitched by this man.

Nick thumbed through the entire launch kit, gripping the file firmly, leaning against the wall as he read. His eyes were on the anticipated level of production of this new product. He remembered Gus Fletcher and thought of this triumph as a warning to all who tried to hinder him. Nick Abbott would not be stopped. It was a momentary diversion. His thoughts returned to the matter at hand. He smiled with vain pride.

'I'd like to see the training programme now,' he said happily.

'Certainly,' she answered obediently.

'Excellent,' he said, reviewing this new file's contents.

Sandra clasped her hands together, willing herself to wake up from this nightmare. She tried to force her strength into Nick's heart with a deadly blow, but he simply stood there glowing with delight.

'You're a star among stars, Sandra.'

A sigh left her lips.

'Have a seat,' Nick offered, as though the office was his, not Sandra's.

'No one could have done better.'

His charming smile spread into an uncontrollable grin.

She knew that was high praise indeed coming from Nick Abbott.

'Thank you,' she said politely.

'We will have dinner tonight, after the cocktail party for the launch. I think we need to start discussing a future career path for you.' He looked serious as he sat on her desk in front of her.

'Where do you see yourself going?' Nick asked her casually.

'How about first female regional manager?' she said flippantly.

'Excellent. One problem,' Nick retorted.

'What's that?'

'All my regional managers share rooms when they go to conferences. Who are you going to share with?'

'We'll just have to make sure that there are an odd number of people,' she answered, not taking the comment seriously.

'No. I'll have to make the sacrifice,' Nick said pensively. 'You'll have to share with me.'

Sandra tried to laugh.

'I think it's time we started grooming you for the next step. What do you think?'

'It sounds good to me, chief,' she said mechanically.

'Good. Well, it's settled then. We'll discuss the details over dinner.'

*

The cocktail party, in a private room at Sydney's Regent Hotel, seemed lavish beyond reason to Sandra. She guessed Nick's theory behind spending the money was to instil confidence back into the shattered shell of the Prime agents. The stock market collapse had taken its toll on sales as well as the agents' self-esteem. This was just the boost they needed to put them back on top of the world. The master had spun his fatal charm once more and the room buzzed with talk of success and fortunes to be made.

Nick was halfway through his cigarette. He inhaled deeply, with a degree of satisfaction, knowing that by morning he would have this woman he had toyed with for so long. She would be transformed forever from the purity of virtue. She would become another player in his scheme to dominate and rule.

Nick convincingly kept Sandra on the outer edges of the conversation during the party, entertaining his agents with stories of how he did this at East West Life and how he thought that could work well in Prime Financial Group. Agents stared at Nick as sixteen-year-old groupies might stare at a pop idol.

This infuriated and frustrated Sandra. She shifted from one side of the room to the other, praying for some escape, for the earth to open up and swallow her. Anything would be better than this. She wanted to tell the agents to change their awful, stupid expressions. If she could only hold a mirror in front of them, they would see how ridiculous they looked. Even the way some agents leaned their head to one side, as if they were about to take a deep love-struck sigh. It was a sickening display of hero-worship.

The more angry Sandra became, the more she fidgeted, trying desperately to stay alert and yet give the impression of being the confident and happy hostess.

When Nick told the story about his Salvation Army jacket, she had heard just about all she could cope with.

'Good grief, you can't expect Mark to do that,' she stated forcefully.

Nick turned slowly towards her, looking with a disapproving frown as though she had no right to speak until spoken to.

'Are you telling me that he can't do the job?' he asked.

'Of course not.'

'So what's your point?'

'I'm just saying that you have two different natures and two different personalities. Not everything that suits one is necessarily going to suit the other.'

'My dear girl,' he said, adopting his most patronising voice which incensed her further, 'if you are going to become a regional manager, I think there is something you better understand right now. There is only one way to do things while I'm in charge and that's my way.'

She said nothing, allowing him to return to his dissertation.

Nick was using expletives freely in front of her for the first time. She considered that this was probably his way of accepting her as 'one of the boys'.

It was ten thirty before the crowd dispersed. Sandra tried to glide out with the last agents but Nick effortlessly drew her back.

'I guess it's more time for a late snack, rather than dinner,' Nick commented to her, looking at his watch. He tipped his head towards one of the waiters.

'What's happening?' Sandra asked nervously.

'I didn't see the point in going out when we are already at one of the finest hotels in Sydney, So I've hired the room for another few hours and arranged a meal to be brought in here.'

Sandra watched as the waiters arranged a sofa in front of a table and proceeded to produce an array of sumptuous appetisers, fit for a king. Although, she reminded herself, she should expect nothing less, for Nick was the undisputed king of this business.

'I want you to put a business plan together,' he explained over their feast. 'We will go through it together and see if it meets with our standards. You are to include the number of recruits you think you can place in twelve months, what you think their earnings will be at the end of that period, and what you are going to need to spend to set up your agency. I will keep you on your current package for the duration of the twelve months by which time you will either be operating profitably in your own right, or—'

'Or be terminated.' She completed his sentence for him.

'Correct.'

'That sounds fair enough to me.' At last, she thought, he's giving me the way out. I just have to fail at recruiting and I can be peacefully fired without raising suspicions.

'You'll be my number one manager,' Nick announced. 'You mark my words.'

'They're marked, be sure of it,' Sandra assured him.

It was around twelve thirty when Sandra could stand no more. Her nerves were shattered. She began to rise out of her seat, hoping Nick would take the cue as he had always done in the past.

'Where do you think you're going? It's still early,' Nick said, ordering her back to her seat.

'I thought I might go home. It's late and I'm really quite tired.'

'No you're not. Sit down. I haven't finished with you yet.'

His voice was like ice. She obeyed without question as though self-will was a luxury she no longer possessed.

He ordered another round of drinks and dismissed the remaining waiters.

'What's happening at Prime Benefits?' she asked uncaringly. 'Are they still performing below your standards?'

'Ohow,' he drawled, a whining sort of sound. 'I don't want to talk about them.'

'What *do* you want to talk about?' she asked, taking one of his cigarettes.

He shrugged and remained silent, not casting a glance in her direction.

'How do you feel about having a female regional manager at last?'

He grinned to himself.

'It feels pretty good.' He shuffled in his seat, moving closer towards her.

'Mark's shaped up as a pretty good regional manager, hasn't he?'

She was struggling for topics of conversation now. Nick was being most unco-operative, inflaming her exasperation.

'He'll do.' He shuffled in his seat again.

'Tell me,' she paused, appraising the wisdom of her next question, 'what got you started in the industry?'

'It's a long story,' he said, rubbing his eyes. He looked up at her with tired eyes. 'My father was a clerk at East West Life. He worked there all his life. He gave the job everything and got nothing back. I was determined that this was not the life for me.'

At least that much was true, she knew. She could see in an instant the years of struggle and heartache. The attempts to claw out of an unrewarding and meagre existence. There was a rumbling of sincerity which made him somehow more approachable. As he continued to tell her about his life, she felt the charade become meaningless. Nick Abbott had been knocked right into hell and had come back fighting. In a way, she had to admire that.

'So you became all the things your father never was,' she said, evaluating this complicated man before her.

'That's right, and it's been a real bitch, I can tell you.'

With his tired eyes and soulful expression, he looked vulnerable and alone. He put his emptied glass on the table, this time moving as close as possible to Sandra.

'You must miss New York, do you ever think about going home?'

'My home is here now.' With those words he pulled her towards him. His kiss was long, hard and resolute.

Startled by his actions, she forgot for a moment who she was with. Even coming to realise what was happening, she found herself not wanting to fight him. Against her better judgement she returned the kiss; just politely, not in the manner of the one delivered to her. Knowing what she did of Nick Abbott, she felt showing fear or rejection would have been self-defeating acts at best. Nick Abbott would have fed on those emotions as surely as the hunter tracks the weakest in the pack to be his prey.

Gathering her senses, Sandra knew she could not succumb to the desires of this man. She was sickened by the curious temptation she experienced, picturing what he might be like as a lover. A flash of passion charged in her breast. It was wild, mad and impulsive.

This man is a murderer, she told herself. He killed his top agent and Brett McLeod and, if he hadn't lured Ted away from his safe job, he might still be alive today as well. Despite her reasoning there was still something fatally attractive about Nick. Something as potent as it was magnetic; as fascinating as it was threatening.

She must not encourage this, not even for an instant. A polite kiss and swift retraction was the most appropriate course of action she could think of in her intense, and accelerating bewilderment.

She freed herself and searched for some rational words. There were none.

He looked away, able to simulate a slight flush of embarrassment.

'I'm very flattered,' she said, dropping her voice to a whisper, 'but this is wrong. We can't mess up our working relationship like this.'

'Ohow,' he mumbled, turning away to fiddle with his cigarette packet.

'I'm not very good at this,' he eventually said as though it was an admission. He returned his gaze towards her.

She had to bite her lip not to allow a nervous laugh to escape. That line had to be one of the most polished of all time, she thought. Nick Abbott, the most recognised sales manager in all the world, was 'not very good at this'. The 'schoolboy lost' effigy in front of her was the most immense lie she had ever witnessed. She wished she could have told him so. She took a deep breath. To run out like a frightened animal would be tantamount to committing suicide. To offer him comfort in his moment of simulated humiliation would also be suicide.

'Nick, I...'

He pulled her towards him again. The kiss was harder than before. His arms enclosed her, holding her firmly in position. Her sense of bearing momentarily deserted her with a single shuddering breath. This time she struggled to break free. Reaching for something to give her leverage to escape, she planted her hand firmly on the only solid object within her reach: his leg.

'I knew you wanted me,' he said triumphantly, leering at her mistaken touch.

His pause was sufficient to enable her to pull free and gain a piece of clear ground on which to stand.

'Nick,' she spoke more forcefully this time, 'you are undoubtedly the most exciting man I have ever met. However, I think you've had too much to drink to know what you are doing.' She hoped he would take this cue to make an acceptable excuse for his behaviour.

He pouted and looked down. 'I have not had too much to drink.' He looked back at her and saw the determined expression on her face. Resigned and angry, he stood up.

The sight of him sent a quiver of fear through her bones.

'Are we still friends?' she asked obtusely.

'Yeah, I er, yes.' He readopted his embarrassed tone.

'I think it is best that we just forget this ever happened. All right?' she asked nervously.

Big sad eyes stared at her.

She gathered her belongings and headed for the door.

'Let me.' He headed her off to open the door like a gentleman. She turned towards him and gave him a peck on the cheek. This time the touch of his flesh made her skin crawl. She felt the need to justify her rejection of him in a more tangible manner. Their eyes locked for endless seconds.

'Nick,' she stammered.

He said nothing.

'I'm afraid.'

This was something Nick could understand, even feel proud about.

'Of what?' he asked.

'There's still a murderer out there somewhere.' Whether this was a very clever or very stupid thing to say, she wasn't sure, but it seemed to work.

Nick put his hands on her shoulders.

'I've been very insensitive, haven't I?' He looked her dead in the eye. 'You're tired, exhilarated, frightened and all I can do is make a pass at you.'

'I'm glad you understand,' she responded, trying to look longingly back at him.

'It's going to be a long night,' he said sadly as she stepped into the freedom of the cold night air.

With the door closing behind her she felt her legs go weak. Hurrying to her car for fear she might not make it walking slowly, she fumbled with the keys and did not breathe evenly again until she was safely inside. It was madness to drive in her state of intoxication but it was immeasurably more dangerous to wait around for Nick Abbott to come back for more.

She started the engine and raced towards James with no regard for speed limits or other laws. She was free. James was moments away and she had to get to him quickly. She wanted to feel his arms around her; comforting, caring and warm. She didn't feel it prudent to confide in James – he was liable to kill Nick with his bare hands if he knew what had happened. The events had stimulated her sexual appetite. She imagined all the different ways in which she could awaken James on her return. It would be one o'clock in the morning by the time she reached him. He would surely be asleep, although she knew that was madness. James had probably already alerted the police to start looking for her.

Her passionate cravings escalated. Her suit was suffocating her. Her foot crushed the accelerator to the floor as she charged towards Vaucluse with intoxicated recklessness.

Sweating feverishly she put on some blaring rock and roll music to exorcise her demons.

*

Over the next two months Sandra collected and rationalised her thoughts. In the cold light of day, and with a clear head, the intended seduction by Nick Abbott became unimportant. Why should he be any different from a dozen other men who would try the same thing? You can't blame someone for trying, after all, she reasoned.

'Good morning,' Nick cheered in a jovial manner, entering her office. 'And how was your weekend?'

'Well, not as good as yours I'd say, judging by your mood.'

'Yes,' he reflected. 'I'm in an excellent mood today.'

'I'm pleased to hear it,' she answered, watching him sit down in her visitors' chair. 'Do you feel like sharing the reason for your good spirits with me?'

'Your product is selling madly. I've never seen anything like it.'

She felt a lump lodge in her throat.

'You are undoubtedly my prime asset in Prime.'

'That's wonderful,' she answered respectfully.

'You're the only one who's got it right. Well done.'

Sandra didn't know what Nick was up to but she was sure she wasn't going to like it.

'I'm organising a big Easter conference-cum-party for my star people. It will be at Cape Schanck Country Club in Victoria. You'll be there of course.'

'Of course,' she answered, knowing full well that was an order, not an invitation.

'Good. You'll receive an official invitation later today.'

The thought of three days and two nights at the same country club resort as Nick Abbott was disturbing to say the least. Sandra was determined not to allow a repeat performance of the product launch and knew just how to obstruct it.

Sandra called Nick's secretary into her office after he left.

'Jill, can I have a word with you about the sleeping arrangements for the conference?'

'Of course. Is something wrong?'

Jill was a sweet, unquestioning girl and loyal to Nick beyond reproach. Her peaceful brown eyes and simple straight brown hair created an impression of imperviousness to the chaos that often surrounded her. Her skin glowed with a natural healthy look, probably from her happy-go-lucky nature, Sandra guessed. Jill collected the file marked 'Conference' and took it into Sandra's office.

Sandra studied the plans carefully. There was a list of names against condominium numbers and a map of the resort showing where they were situated. The country club had four sets of four condominiums. Three sets were located close to one another; the fourth was at the far end of the complex.

'How many females are attending the conference, Jill?'

'Six, including you and me.'

'And how many of the delegates would you put in the

"rowdy" category?'

'About fifteen out of seventy.' She leaned forward to establish what it was that Sandra was staring at so intently.

'Wouldn't you say that it made sense to put the rowdy ones in these far condos – they would take up three of the group of four – and put the girls in the fourth one. We all like to party, don't we?'

'That's no problem to organise,' Jill agreed.

'Good. We can make our condo the party condo. What do you say?'

'Sounds great to me.'

'That way we won't risk annoying any guests of the resort who may be staying up here.' Sandra pointed to the spot on the map that might have other guests. 'And we can put our quieter people near to the actual conference hall. I'm sure Nick Abbott will expect to be located as near as possible: he can't be expected to walk all that way now, can he?'

Jill laughed. 'I have to agree with you there.'

'Good. Then all the speakers can stay there and we'll just take the cars down to our condos so we can drive back and forth to the talks.'

'I'll organise it.' Jill made some notes, assembled the papers, and went to institute Sandra's guidelines.

It was a weight off Sandra's mind. Nick Abbott would not only be incapable of physically getting to Sandra's bedroom on foot but, should he find some other method of transport, he would find a raging party going on. There would be no chance of a discreet seduction under those circumstances.

At that moment it occurred to her that someone from Hamilton Black should be invited as a guest speaker too. That would really throw a spanner in Abbott's works. She could feel relatively safe knowing George or Ralph was there.

'Nick?' she called on her intercom.

'Yes.'

'Is the agenda finalised for the conference?'

'Not yet, why?'

'Would you like me to ask a representative from Hamilton Black to speak there?'

'What on earth for?'

'Well, it could be a good opportunity to help promote their training programme to the RMs. They are using all of our material now, you know.'

'I see your point. It's a good idea. Set it up, will you?'

'With pleasure.'

*

'Okay boys, I'm here now. Everybody take five.' Sandra felt like she had walked back in time when she visited Hamilton Black. They seemed so untouched by the dealings around them.

'Cheeky bitch,' George retorted, appearing from his office holding a mug of coffee. 'It's good to see you never change.'

'Any particular reason for the visit, or just passing through?' Ralph asked.

'I'm allowed to share a cup of coffee with my mates, aren't I?'

'Oh, I don't know. Ralph, what do you think?' George grinned.

'I think we can afford to give her a cup of coffee,' Ralph added.

'Na,' said George. 'I reckon she's come here to ask for a favour or some advice. Ms Director of Sales and Marketing, soon to be regional manager, never comes to see us just to say hello any more.'

'George, that's not fair,' she protested. 'Actually,' she

admitted, 'I am here to ask a favour.'

'I knew it,' shouted George. 'I told you. Bloody women, only want to know you when they want something.'

'Actually, George, the favour is not for me, it's for Nick.'

'What does the Yank prick want now?'

'A guest speaker for an Easter conference, at Cape Schanck.'

'Ralph, that's your department,' George bellowed. 'Ralph's got a farm down that way, it will suit him perfectly. Anyway, I've done enough guest speaking arrangements lately. My poor little larynx needs a rest.'

'Listen to you,' Ralph laughed. 'It looks like it's up to me. Will I do?'

'You'll do very nicely. I thought you could give the Hamilton Black programme a plug.'

'At least if he wants us at this conference it means we won't be axed as part of his ongoing rationalisation programme.'

'Little prick,' George muttered.

'That's all right,' Ralph continued. 'They need us more than we need them. We could always solve all of their problems in one hit and defect to Federal Mutual. Ha ha.'

Sandra shook her head. 'Where's it all going to end?'

In one big shit heap if they're not careful, George thought to himself.

*

Sandra took a long deep breath. The air was filled with the sweet fragrance of freshly cut grass and the warbling song of the dusk chorus. Inhaling deeply she held the sweetness in her lungs, squinting against the flat glare of the rising moon as darkness began to fall. The shadows were clearcut now; shadows of trees and rocks and bushes. Very sharp, very black shadows.

From her position she could see the country club's entrance drive. Cars were continually arriving, heading to reception and then back to the condos.

She pulled her blue suede jacket closer around her as the night chill settled in, touching every blade of grass and swaying tree. It seemed a shame to Sandra that such a tranquil setting was about to be the venue for a sales conference. Savouring her time alone before her colleagues arrived, she thought about part of the Hamilton Black training. If you don't set aside time for yourself and your family, they would say, to do the things that you want to do, you will burn out before you get a chance to enjoy your hard-earned money. All those in high-pressure sales preached that line. With Nick Abbott it was 'Time to smell the roses'; with Mark Fitzgerald it was 'Quiet time'. The message was always clear and the same.

Squinting again she could see one of the cars heading in her direction. It was Jill.

'Everything under control down there?' Sandra asked.

'It looks that way. Happy hour has started. Why aren't you down there with them?'

'I'm in no rush. I'll go down with you when you're ready.'

'That's not like you. Where's your party spirit? I thought you were the one planning an all-out rage for tonight?'

'I'm indulging in a little peace and quiet before the massing throngs get going. That's all.'

Jill accepted her explanation and quickly took her cases inside.

Sandra psyched herself up, deciding to bowl into the bar as though nothing had ever happened. It was the best way.

'Ready?' called Jill.

'You were quick.'

'You might not be in a hurry to get down there, but I'm thirsty.'

'Let's go, but don't forget we have to at least be semi-conscious for the speakers tomorrow.'

The bar buzzed with excitement. The agents were all in their casual clothes, not one without a drink in hand. Sandra checked off the important people in her mind. They were all there: Ralph Black, Mark Fitzgerald and Nick Abbott.

Most of the agents were wearing pullovers of some description. Nick, however, had opted for a white Oke shirt which he had left casually undone to his chest. Sandra presumed that to be part of his casual look.

'G'day,' Nick said when he spotted Sandra.

'G'day,' she returned.

'That's bloody good,' laughed Ralph. 'A Yank saying "G'day". What's the country coming to?'

'Drinks are on me,' called Nick.

There was a charge to the bar as though no one had consumed a drink all year, despite the fact that many still had full glasses in their hands.

Predictably Ralph and Nick found a corner in which to exchange a few words.

'Can I guess what you're talking about tomorrow?' Nick asked sarcastically.

'I suppose you could. The Hamilton Black programme.'

'Oh. That will be interesting.'

'And what are you talking on? The agent in the eighties? That will be bloody interesting too.'

'Watch yourself, my man. Don't forget who runs Hamilton Black now.'

'I give you six months. You won't be able to manage us.' Ralph smiled confidently and took another swig of his beer.

'Is that right? Perhaps I'll give you three months,' Nick responded pointedly.

Ralph towered over Nick. Nick's threats meant nothing to him. He already had all the money he could ever want and didn't share Nick's lust for power. The worst thing that could happen to Ralph Black was that he would take an early retirement to his farm and play golf all day. The little Yank prick has chosen the wrong mark with me, he mused.

'Time for dinner,' the maître d' announced, rounding up the assorted group to enter the main dining area.

'Saved by the bell, Black,' Nick hissed.

Seven tables were set up with no particular plans for who sat where. It was first come, first served. The ambience of the conference was designed to relax, as well as motivate. They could then return with fresh minds to sell enough life insurance to blow the J-curve off the graph.

Ralph joined Sandra on a table with eight delegates. Nick sat on the next table with a few of the guest speakers.

'He is quite a character,' Ralph said looking towards Nick and directing the comment at no one in particular.

'I'm glad you're here,' Sandra confided in Ralph.

'You're a bloody character too,' he said, turning his full attention back towards Sandra.

'Not the same type, I hope?'

'Definitely not.'

Sandra's normally ravenous appetite had disappeared completely. She just played with her food, thinking all the time of the intended seduction last month and wishing that James was there with her.

'Are you in love, or sick?' Ralph asked, looking at her untouched meal.

'Just not hungry,' she answered feebly.

'No, I reckon you're in love.'

'Really, who with?' she asked. No one knew about James, not even George or Denis. Ralph's comment concerned her deeply.

'You've been seeing quite a lot of that cop from what I

hear.'

'Oh,' she laughed. 'You mean Ray Cooper?'

'That's him.'

'I hear from him now and again. Do you have a theory on Brett's death?'

'I do.'

'Would you care to share it?'

'I wouldn't.' He threw his serviette on the table to indicate the subject was closed. Sitting up and stretching out his arms, Ralph looked around the room to assess whom he should make polite conversation with. 'Jesus, what's that?' Ralph noticed four men bringing in large black boxes and placing them behind the area used as a dance floor. 'Abbott's organised a band.' He quickly cast his eye round the room to estimate the ratio of females to males. 'You're going to have your work cut out for you,' he informed Sandra. 'It's roughly ten to one in here.'

She sunk her head into her palms. Nick had all the subtlety of a rampaging bull at times.

'I hope you like to dance, kid.' Ralph laughed.

'Shut up, Ralph.'

'Oo. Pardon me.'

'I'll just dance with you all night. We can start the rumour mongers gossiping.' Her eyes were almost pleading as she made the suggestion to Ralph.

'Oh no, you don't. I have enough to contend with, without you starting rumours for me.'

'Thanks for the support. I thought you were my friend.'

'Oh, don't whine. Say you've got a headache or something.'

Nick Abbott paced the floor towards the band leader. Sandra saw them talking and then Nick disappeared. When he reappeared it was behind her chair.

'Care to dance? Now don't say no.'

Nick had already pulled the chair away from under her.

She understood she had no choice.

'Have fun, you two.' Ralph winked at Sandra.

Nick ignored his presence.

The band played 'Help Me Make it Through the Night'. Nick held her as close as was physically possible, singing the words softly in her ear as he swayed around the dance floor. Instead of holding her right hand in the traditional manner, he somehow twisted it around so their fingers were entwined and touching the upper parts of their chests. Occasionally he would stroke the tips of her fingers with his forefinger. It was her second, and last, chance to succumb. She should consider herself lucky, he thought; it was not often that Nick Abbott gave his victims a second chance.

As the next song started Sandra tried to leave the dance floor. With only twelve people dancing she felt uncomfortably conspicuous.

'One more dance, then I'll let you dance with someone else,' Nick insisted.

She was heated with fear and loathing. Although she tried to stop it, her body trembled slightly.

Nick sensed her every thought. She was perfectly primed to be his. She wouldn't escape a second time.

'Who organised the sleeping arrangements?' he asked quietly.

'Jill did.'

'With anyone's help?'

'I made a few suggestions.'

'I thought so.'

'Aren't you happy?' She pulled back to look at him as she asked the question. 'I put you in the very best location. You're in walking distance of the main facilities.'

'That was very thoughtful.'

'You wouldn't want to be where we are, you would have to drive back and forth all the time.'

'That was also very thoughtful.'

They were both keenly aware of the intent of the other.

Sandra feared that the eyes of every person in the room were upon her. She swivelled her gaze left and right and was consoled to see she was quite wrong.

He pressed close to her again. Their cheeks touched and she felt his warm breath on her neck.

'I think we need to talk. Will you come and see me later tonight?'

'I can't. I've already arranged to host a party in my condo. We can talk tomorrow.'

'We will *talk* before I leave?'

He stopped dancing for a moment, just holding her still in his arms.

'Yes. I promise. We'll talk,' she stammered, trembling as she spoke.

At last he released her.

'Okay boys.' She turned to the band leader. 'Let's rock till we drop.'

This was the type of music Sandra loved to dance to. Good old rock and roll. As she moved around the floor she made sure everyone knew the party started in the girls' condo as soon as the band finished.

*

'Oh, no. Are those my eyes? They won't open past halfway,' Sandra groaned as she stared into the mirror the next morning.

The pain of the hangover covered Sandra's entire body. A burning thirst felt like sandpaper in her throat. Her eyes were two red bulges, her stomach felt like a Ferris wheel and her head was only steady in a horizontal position. 'What have I done to myself?'

'Sandra?' Jill called on hearing movement in Sandra's

bedroom.

'Jill, is that you?'

Sandra ventured outside and saw Jill looking worse than Sandra's reflection, if that were possible.

'Was Mahony really trying to play Frankenfurter from the *Rocky Horror Show* last night?'

A vision flashed through Sandra's mind. A beer belly hanging over the descending waistline of a pair of trousers, with a pair of some female's suspenders on top of them, and Mahony trying to wiggle like a woman.

'Yes, I think so. Try not to think about it, you look sick enough. I think we better get a gallon of water, some aspirin and some vitamin B down us.' Trying to stand upright, Jill offered the advice with as much concern for her own well-being as Sandra's.

'Good idea,' Sandra conceded.

'Oh. Who had too much to drink last night then?' Ralph laughed as Sandra joined the conference.

'Have some respect for the dead, Ralph.' Sandra looked up at him, shading her eyes as she did so.

'Huh. The demon drink. It will get you every time.'

'Thanks for the warning.'

At least she had an excuse to sit at the back of the room in silence for the day. Alcohol was fast becoming Sandra's only means of numbing herself against the harsh realities she was ceasing to cope with.

Nick searched high and low for Sandra that evening with no success. She told Ralph to pass on a message that she was still feeling unwell and had to go to bed.

Secretly she took the car and spent a good deal of the night watching the waves crash in at a local beach. No one would find her there, they could speculate all they wanted as to her whereabouts, which didn't matter. It was her time.

'Where did you get to last night?' Nick asked her at the final breakfast.

'I went for a drive to clear the cobwebs away and then to bed.'

'You missed a big party back here.'

'So I heard. You all managed to enjoy it without me though.'

Fully recovered, she was enjoying a large breakfast while others suffered the hangover symptoms she had experienced a long twenty-four hours ago.

'You better watch how much you drink in future, young lady,' Nick advised.

She nodded and went back to eating.

'Would you do me a favour?' Nick asked casually.

What now? she wondered.

'I hear there are some spectacular beaches around here. I wondered if you would take me on a tour before we leave. You don't mind, do you?'

'No, I, er, no...' Damn, she thought.

One thought and one thought only went through Sandra's mind. This is how he's going to do it. He's going to throw me off the edge of a cliff and say it was an accident. Her appetite suddenly left her. She looked around for some avenue of escape, some excuse she could use.

'Well, it looks as though you don't want any more breakfast. No time like the present, I guess,' Nick said with determination, taking hold of her hand as he did so.

Sandra seethed at the ease in which Nick could manipulate events. Her fear quickly turned to anger. Let Nick try his worst; she would be ready.

The coastline stretched as far as Sandra could see, sheltered by a great grey buttress of solid rock, scarred by deep fissures and trenches, smothered with dark green growth. Sandra had not remembered it looking so grand yesterday evening when shadowing images had teased the perspective of the vast expanse. The picture filled the horizon rising up to the heavens, covered by a deep blue sky with only a smattering of small white clouds. Rolling endlessly across their vision the fluffy white, billowing vapours seemed to clip the wings of passing seagulls then vanish miraculously as though they had been sucked into nothingness. Each detail of the rock was finely etched, pure golden sand lapping at its feet, as startling gold as the shining wattle that glistened nearby.

Nick stood by Sandra in silence, observing the grandeur of his surroundings with a measure of respect. He moved slowly towards the edge of a natural balcony overlooking the entire panorama, holding a man-made railing which had apparently been fixed to prevent enthusiastic sightseers falling to their deaths.

Warm breezes danced through the air. Sandra turned her head to face the current so as not to allow her loosely brushed hair to be obscure her sight.

'It's magnificent, isn't it?' she commented from a safe distance.

He nodded.

'In a place like this I can almost forget our business world exists,' he commented quietly.

Nick turned to face her. He could see the fear, sense her tension. She had given him everything he wanted professionally; there was only one threshold left to cross.

Nick sauntered towards her, giving her a long searching gaze that made Sandra feel he could see all the way to her soul. To her vast relief, Nick appeared not to notice the effect he had on her. She expected him to say something, anything. She wondered if he was waiting for her to make the first move. Was she expected to say she'd been a fool and that she wanted him desperately? The silence immersed her. She yearned for him to speak, but the man of a thousand words remained silent.

'Would you like to move along and see the other beaches?' she asked.

'No. Let's stay here a while,' he answered simply, placing a cigarette between his lips. He held the cigarette skilfully at the edge of his mouth while he searched his pockets.

'Do you have a light?' he asked.

Sandra produced a lighter and offered it to Nick. He held her hand gently as she performed the task for him, releasing her only after lifting his gaze to meet her eyes. A sense of awareness pierced an invisible barrier between them.

Suddenly Sandra's whole life seemed to her to have been the long preparation for the moment that would pose her highest challenge. So many obstacles had been overcome, obstacles made mountainous by the fact that she was a woman. She studied Nick carefully, perhaps for the first time. He had the presence of a man she could admire or despise. He was a hard professional soldier, tempered by constant skirmishes on the border of control. She guessed there had sometimes been cruel encounters and that he always distinguished himself. His rapid promotion had been proof of that. Could this man who helped her at Prime, when he had no real reason to do so, really be the cold calculating murderer she knew him to be? It seemed impossible. His presence closed around her, like a cocoon surrounding a fragile embryo from which a beautiful butterfly would emerge. A delicate sensitive outer case which if exposed too early would cause instant death.

Nick looked out to sea as he spoke. 'Last time we were together you said you were afraid.' Now he looked towards her. Their eyes met. 'I don't want you to be afraid.' With that statement he produced from the back of his waistband the old German Luger.

Sandra's eyes widened. She gasped in terror. My God, he's going to shoot me, she thought.

Without warning he turned the gun around and handed it to Sandra. She looked at him in total bewilderment.

'What? Why?' she asked, staring at the cold instrument of death.

'This belonged to my father. It's precious to me. You are precious to me. I want you to have it to feel safe. I want you to have it to realise how much you mean to me.'

Sandra was frozen to the spot. What was she supposed to say? Nick offered his palm in an outward motion suggesting she took the gun. 'Please,' he urged.

Slowly Sandra's hand found its way around the Luger, closing on the cold metal.

Nick smiled. He'd take the Luger back in time – when he took her. For now it was just a ploy to gain her trust and lower her defences.

'Does it still work? It looks so old,' she observed.

'Oh, it works, we don't have to be young to still function,' he leered.

Sandra found herself looking at the floor before Nick's forefinger found her jaw and raised her head. As those murderous eyes met hers her grip fastened around the Luger. This could be her chance. It could look like an accident. She straightened the gun and pointed it at Nick.

'It's decision time,' he announced, his eyes fixed in the beady stare of a great white shark in search of food.

She nodded in acknowledgement of his intent. 'But not here.' Her words were unsteady, her hand with the Luger fell limp by her side. Nick may be a murderer but she would not stoop to join those ranks just to feel safe.

'So long as we understand each other.'

He smiled an evil smile. He knew she intended to resist him and knew she would not be able to. His eyes mocked her innocence. She had rejected him twice, that was more than any person could dare expect to get away with. He took one last sweeping glance over wind-driven lines of foam upon the ocean, cementing the decision in his mind. Looking at her now, he visualised her pretty face hardened with the pressures he would inflict upon her. His mood became expansive, his vision clearly piqued. She was finished. The time, the place and the method had all been carefully selected. The unholy splendour of it all was this childlike businesswoman still didn't have a clue. The gift would make her trust him. It was all so pathetically simple.

She walked stiffly back to her car, shoulders squared, trying to maintain an aloof dignity. Nick was a dangerous, clever man, but she firmly believed that if she could become an RM, fail in recruiting and be safely fired, she'd be out of his sights. It's a cinch, she convinced herself. There was no time for elaborate designing; her business plan had to be on Nick's desk within a week. She considered this carefully on the way back to Cape Schanck by way of occupying her mind against the silence.

'Until we meet again,' Nick said harmlessly, closing the car door.

Chapter Nine

Ray felt jet-lagged and frustrated after his trip to New York. He sketched out the information he had acquired on a huge whiteboard, trying to make some sense of it all.

Nick had taught Eddie how to sell record numbers of policies by using the most vile means conceivable: the infant policies. Eddie and Nick had become world record-breakers as a result. Eddie apparently turned to cocaine to blank out the guilt of what he had done. Eventually Eddie couldn't stomach the situation any longer and planned to come clean. At that point Nick murdered him, making it look like a suicide. The New York police, Gus Fletcher and Ray Cooper all knew that to be true, but had no evidence of the act.

His big break had come when one of the original policy-holders had called the New York police on hearing about the investigation. The man had become a respected citizen over the years, who had lived with the guilt of having once committed murder. Now he was dying of cancer and wanted to absolve his sins by confessing before he died. But it still didn't link Nick directly to any crime.

At least, Ray thought, I have enough evidence to install listening devices. Perhaps that will give me the break I need to get an arrest. Whatever it takes, he told himself, I *will* get this bastard.

*

'Nick, are you happy with my work?' Sandra asked,

marching into Nick's office with her new business plan in hand.

'That's got to be the dumbest question you've ever asked.' He looked up from a pile of papers on his desk. His eyes were blurred from scrutinising figures. 'What's on your mind?'

She sat in his visitors' chair, settling herself comfortably in its ridges.

'I would like to go through my business plan with you,' she urged.

He took the spiral-bound folder with eagerness, reading each page carefully.

'So you plan to recruit eight sales managers over the next twelve months, retain six of them and have those six recruiting ten agents per annum. That's a bit ambitious, don't you think?'

'Perhaps, but none of us are in the business for our modesty now, are we?'

'True.' He was pleased with the speed at which she understood the values that were important. 'Let's see, you plan to find potential recruits. Um, through advertising, mail-out campaigns and referrals from business contacts. It all looks fine to me.'

'There's nothing you think I should alter?'

She could tell Nick's preoccupation with other matters made him careless in his study of her document.

'Why should I alter what's already perfect? I wish you all the best luck with it.'

'Thank you, but there's one more thing.'

'What's that?'

'I have had my lawyers draw up a contract between you and me, stipulating the changes that have occurred in my employment. My original contract doesn't apply any longer.'

'Don't you trust me?'

Nick seemed angry at her suggestion that such close allies needed to put things in writing.

'Of course, I trust you, Nick, it's just good business practice to put any agreements in writing,' she explained.

'I'll look over it,' Nick said, taking the document.

This agreement is made on this 19th day of April, 1988, between Nick Abbott of Prime Financial Group and Sandra Upton.
1. While Sandra Upton will remain in the employ of Prime Financial Group for twelve months, and will also remain under the existing remuneration package as detailed in the agreement called 'director sales and marketing', dated 1st March, 1987, between Sandra Upton and Prime Financial Group, the duties and role of Sandra Upton will be altered as per the details in this agreement.
2. Sandra Upton will, from the 1st day of June, 1988, recruit, interview, select and train sales managers for the central Sydney region.
3. Sandra Upton will complete all necessary record-keeping paperwork as stipulated under the Nick Abbott guidelines for sales managers.
4. Sandra Upton will report to Nick Abbott on a monthly basis. The reports will be forwarded to Nick Abbott to monitor success and therefore acceptability into the role of regional manager in twelve months' time.
5. Employment with Prime Financial Group will terminate on the 31st May, 1989. At this time Sandra Upton will be confirmed as a full-time regional manager of Prime, functioning profitably within her own right. If she is not able to function profitably within her own right, all employment agreements will be terminated.
6. Nick Abbott agrees to the terms set out in Sandra Upton's business plan, submitted on this 19th day of April, 1988.

'It seems simple enough,' Nick commented, glancing over it casually. 'I'll get it back to you as soon as our legal people have looked over it.'

'That's wonderful,' she remarked, feeling somewhat relieved.

'Now, what about your budget?' Nick added.

Ah, she thought. Here it comes.

'The expenditure necessary to get my agency going will leave me without a cent, apart from my salary. I'll even have to find the money to buy a new car within twelve months. It's a big step, you know.'

'I know, I know. But you're more than capable. Let's see your expenditure plan.'

She pushed the file on Nick's desk towards him.

'Um, yes. Um, yes,' Nick muttered as he flicked through the pages methodically, repeating the exercise several times before speaking.

'Is there anything there you think I could take out?' she asked impatiently.

'I don't think so. Let's go through it item by item.

'Number one. You plan to buy a new computer and a printer for two reasons. Firstly, you need to have my record-keeping computerised if you are going to keep up with the other regional managers. Second, you are going to need to have access to a computer for mail-out campaigns, and so on. Your existing computer will be taken over by the product development department, so you will need access to your own machine to take with you when you eventually set up your own office.'

'That's going to cost me ten thousand dollars just for some decent equipment,' Sandra commented. She shuddered at the thought of this expense but knew Nick would not sign the contract. And how could she start spending money until a contract was signed? she thought smugly.

'What about this?' he asked, moving to the next item under 'Expenditure'. 'Advertising. I suppose that's essential. Stationery, letterhead, business cards. I agree you have to have all these things, but what about your allowance for lunches and gifts to people who refer recruits to you? You don't want to go overboard on that.'

'I know. I'm going to be careful, but I have to look after the people who look after me or they'll turn into cold contacts,' she said, standing to move around the desk behind Nick.

'Mail-out campaigns, um,' he continued. 'Australia Post never makes a loss, does it? You seem to be on target with all this. It's a lot of money, isn't it?' he asked reflectively.

'Nobody said running a business was cheap.'

'Tell me about it,' he sighed. 'This time next year you'll be laughing. You'll have your six recruits and your own office. You'll probably be earning more than me.'

'I doubt that, Nick. But I'll give it a damn good try.'

'You've done well as usual,' Nick smiled.

'Thank you,' Sandra said, returning to her office plagued with uncertainty, worry and menacing conflict.

Perfect, Nick smiled. I'll wait till she's spent all her money and she has no choice but to take me or lose everything.

*

Things rolled along smoothly until a memo dated, 23rd May, 1988, tipped Sandra off to the fact that Nick was not in a good mood and was about to make an inspection.

'Sandra,' Nick growled over his intercom, 'I want to see you.'

Sandra was deep in discussions with a potential recruit when Nick called. She had been trying to explain about the ten-year tax ruling of investment products and was not managing to get the message through with her usual ease. Through her window she could see that Nick did not look happy, not happy at all.

'Steve,' she said to the recruit, 'let's take a coffee break. I'll meet you back in here in ten minutes.'

The recruit stretched and yawned and slowly made his way to the kitchen to get some coffee.

'Hi, Nick. How are you this fine day?' Sandra asked casually, walking into his office.

'I'm not good,' he answered.

'What's wrong?' she asked innocently.

'I see you haven't made a start on establishing your region over the last three weeks. Why not?'

'But I have,' she protested. 'I'm talking to a potential recruit right now.'

'And how did you find him?'

'Through a referral,' she answered calmly.

'And how many others have you spoken to?' he demanded.

'Well, er...'

'None, right? And you've spent nothing on getting your systems and advertising established.'

'But Nick, you haven't signed my contract yet. How could I?'

He looked up at her and scowled. 'My other RMs didn't wait for their contracts to be signed. You know how long legal people can take. You can't stop progress. I want you out there getting your system together now, or you're likely to lose everything. Do you understand me?'

'Perfectly,' she answered bitterly, walking out of his office and shutting the door. She was no sooner through his door when a grin spread across her relieved face. Once Nick had fired her, he could feel he'd won. Freedom was close.

She noticed Steve was still drinking his coffee as she

returned to her office. She could hear her phone was ringing and she answered it while still standing in front of her desk.

'Sandra Upton speaking.'

'Hello, lover,' the voice answered.

'James,' she whispered, pushing the door closed and taking a seat. 'What on earth are you doing calling me here?'

'I couldn't wait. Things are almost ready.'

'Why? What's happened?' she asked urgently.

'I can't talk now. Meet me for lunch. You know the place. I'll fill you in then.'

What now? she thought. She put the phone down quivering at the realisation that Nick could soon be out of her life. He was a monster. Damn him, damn him to hell! Her breath was short as though she had been running fast.

'Steve,' she called.

'Yes.'

'Something's come up. Do you mind if we take a rain check on this meeting?'

'Not at all,' he answered in a relaxed manner.

'I'm telling you your ratios are too high,' Sandra could hear Nick saying to someone as she passed by his office on the way out. 'You have to isolate what is costing you the most. If that cost item is not producing an income for you, get rid of it. Let me see your ledgers.'

Sandra was exhilarated but still horribly afraid. So many things could still go wrong, she thought as she entered the elevator. She thought she might drown in her own fear. She needed comfort and searched her mind to find it. She tried to exorcise her fear by yelling into the empty elevator, but the yell was just a whimper in her throat. She was unprepared for this feeling of misgiving. It seemed as though the devil in the office upstairs was about to suck out her very soul. A tiny voice within tried to calm Sandra but it was so far away, and so small, that she disregarded it. Her suffering felt endless. She tried to alleviate it with her utter stillness, freezing the moment in time. Suddenly she could breath again. She took in air with a great rushing gulp and immediately her anxiety changed shape.

Sandra thought over and over about what James might have to tell her. Arriving at their usual rendezvous, Sandra spotted James already waiting. There were only ten people in the small, tucked-away restaurant that Sandra could count. All strange faces, she was relieved to notice.

'So stranger, you want to buy a poor girl a bite of lunch?' Sandra asked without saying hello.

'You look troubled, kiddo. What's the matter?'

James was controlled and charming as always. He could see Sandra was deeply disturbed; her skin had paled and her eyes were red.

'I have good news,' he said happily. 'Sit down.'

Sandra obeyed, alive with curiosity.

'So tell me, I can't stand the suspense,' she demanded.

With satiny professionalism, James took his lover by the arm and looked deeply into her eyes.

Sandra didn't notice the bare brick walls or dark wooden chairs of the restaurant around her. All she was aware of was her wonderful man.

'So?' asked Sandra. 'What is it?'

'It's the ISC. They're ready to move.'

'Huh,' she cried out loud, immediately covering her mouth for fear her indiscreet outburst might arouse suspicion. 'That's wonderful.'

James explained the plan in full detail.

'Are you absolutely sure?' she asked, looking into James's spellbinding eyes.

'Absolutely sure,' he stated firmly.

Sandra found herself suddenly sucking air through her teeth.

'Tell me it's true,' she whispered.

'Oh, it's true. I have friends in the right places, my dear,' he said confidentially.

'He was going to wait for me to spend every cent I had, you know.'

'That's his way. Wait till you are most vulnerable and strike hardest. At least he didn't consider you worth murdering. Lecherous bastard, I knew he'd make a move on you sooner or later. I can't believe he gave you the Luger. That actually did mean something to him you know. I've never seen him quite this intent on getting a woman.'

'Well, you have it now, as it should be. A family heirloom.'

'Some heirloom.'

'It will soon be over,' Sandra cheered.

'By the time he figures it all out, it will be my blood he's after, not yours. Then we've got him.'

Sandra endeavoured to stop her eyes filling with tears. The sight of James made Sandra weak.

'Oh, darling, you're wonderful,' she murmured. 'Take me home now. No one will miss us for a couple of hours.'

The feel of his body next to her, so warm and loving, allowed her to forget the events of the day. It was as though it had happened to someone else in another lifetime. She began to undress him, kissing every part of his exposed body.

'You're frisky,' he remarked with a smile.

'Am I? Maybe it's the reaction of the condemned woman,' she joked.

'I wish I could be there to see the look on his face when he reads the paper tomorrow,' he said stoically, pushing her away as he thought over what was about to happen.

She pouted at his rejection.

'I wish I wasn't going to be there,' she replied.

'You'll call me as soon as it hits the fan, won't you?'

'Of course.'

'Leave the office as soon as possible and tell me everything.'

'This is really the beginning of the end, isn't it, James?'

'The end for him, and the beginning for us.'

Sandra had never seen James this way before. She fell in love with him all over again. He was inspirational.

'We've got him boxed into a corner. He can't escape this time,' James said proudly, polishing his fingernails on his shirt. 'Have you got all that?'

She nodded obediently.

'Good.'

Satisfied with his work, he dropped his professional posture and looked at Sandra with a lover's gaze. 'Come over here,' he said gently.

*

Mark drove to Prime's head office with a copy of the daily paper on his passenger seat. He was grinding his teeth in anger. He seemed to notice every derelict in the street and picture his own face on them. Everything looked shabby today. Damn, he thought, another red light.

The wisdom of hindsight is a wonderful thing, he mused. How could Prime's disgrace be displayed so publicly? There is no justice in this world.

He grabbed the paper, having screeched to a halt in Prime's underground car park, and raced up to Nick's office.

'You should have listened to me a year ago. I told you that you were backing the wrong horse,' Mark said, pacing in front of Nick and flashing his copy of the *Financial Review*. He was as angry with Sandra as he was with Nick Abbott.

'I don't believe this,' Nick roared. 'There has to be some

mistake. I saw the legal interpretations. She worked on that product for months. I know it's foolproof.'

'Well, tell that to the ISC,' Mark spat back at him. 'We're ruined. How do you plan to dig us out of this one?' he asked furiously.

'By not panicking for a start. That's a recipe for sure disaster. Let's think about this logically for a moment.'

Mark sat in Nick's visitors' chair, waiting for some words of consolation from his leader.

'Damn,' he raged. 'Damn! That bitch nearly brought down this entire company!'

'That's right,' Mark scowled. 'The first thing you have to do is fire her, you know that, don't you?'

'Don't tell me what I know,' Nick snapped back. He thought back to Sandra's diligence and couldn't believe this mess was possible.

'With our reserves back to the level they were before VIP, we'll have no option but to merge with another company, will we?' Mark asked.

'You're wrong,' Nick answered. 'The reserves are not back to where they were before.'

'Really?'

'No. They're lower.'

'What?'

'Well, they will be if the ramifications of this are carried through. First our reserves were drained through the new system of higher commissions. To fix that problem we switched large investment funds into equities to raise capital quickly. I'm sure I don't need to remind you that the stock market crashed a few weeks later. Despite all my rationalisation of staff and companies, we still only managed to maintain bare minimum reserve levels after that. The VIP injected vast wealth back into the company but a good degree of that has gone in agents' commissions and management fees. If we have to refund all the money, it will just about break us.'

'Shit,' Mark said bitterly.

'Yes, shit is right. I have to find out what is behind this. I'll challenge the ruling in the High Court if I have to, I know the product is good.'

'Or is it that you just don't want to fire that piece of skirt?' Mark demanded.

'Don't be stupid, man. She means nothing to me,' Nick spat, storming around his office. 'As a matter of fact, I had just about finished wasting my time with her anyway. I don't need her to fix this.'

'I'm relieved to hear that at any rate,' Mark commented.

'What's the matter, couldn't you cope with the competition?' Nick asked, glaring at Mark as some symbol at which to vent his rage. 'Get out of my office and let me think clearly.'

'You were stupid for listening to her,' Mark said in an unprecedented moment of boldness.

'And what makes you think the ISC are right? They do make mistakes, you know. The ISC have me to contend with now. Tell her I want to see her, will you? And tell her I mean *now*!'

'It will be a pleasure,' Mark responded with a smile, throwing his copy of the paper on Nick's desk.

Nick read it over and over again, hoping that somehow the words would change.

VIP A SHAM!

Champion Life is to launch a challenge against the legitimacy of Prime's latest brainchild through the ISC. All future sales are to be frozen pending an investigation and Prime is likely to be forced to refund all monies invested into this product, unless its definition of annuity products is upheld in court.

'You wanted to see me?' Sandra said, entering Nick's office and standing to attention to brace herself for the onslaught.

'Yes,' Nick hissed. 'I thought we should have a little talk about this.' He threw the paper down in front of her.

'Yes,' she agreed. 'I've seen the papers. It's horrible.'

'What do you have to say for yourself?' Nick demanded.

'Well,' she began. 'We know Champion Life are trying to race us for the number one position. I would say that they have been trying to get a copycat product out and want us out of the way while they're doing it.'

'So you're convinced this claim has no foundation?' he asked more optimistically.

'Quite convinced. I think it's a smokescreen to buy them time and stop us stealing market share.'

'I see,' Nick said thoughtfully. 'Sit down.'

Sandra obediently took a seat opposite this deadly foe.

'What do you suggest we do about it?' Nick asked in a more controlled manner.

'Unfortunately there's very little we can do, apart from defend our viewpoint in court. If Champion Life are set on taking this course, we will have to accept the ISC's ruling to freeze sales until after the hearing,' she explained, looking Nick straight in the eye.

'But that could take years,' he shouted.

'I'm aware of that, but I don't know what other options we have.'

'And what about this threat to force us to refund all monies already invested?'

Sandra picked up the paper and read the article for the nineteenth time, as if trying to find an answer to Nick's question.

'I guess,' she stammered, 'your best bet is to request that

existing policies be honoured if you make a commitment to freeze future sales.'

'Do you think the ISC will go for that?'

'I assume you want an honest answer?' she queried.

'That would be helpful,' Nick answered sarcastically.

'The honest answer is no. I don't believe they will go for it.'

'You know what that means, don't you?' Nick asked.

'I do. You'll be forced into a merger to stay alive.'

Nick sighed deeply and sat back in his chair.

'Sandra,' he said with mock melancholy, 'you've done everything that I've asked of you and more. Much more. But the fact of the matter is that I can't afford to keep you on while this investigation is under way. The first head the ISC will demand is the head of the designer.'

She glanced at Nick's out-tray. There was an order form already completed for Sandra's severance pay. The ebb and flow of doubts about her situation ceased instantly. She was free. If she could just contain her excitement a little longer.

'I don't want to lose you though,' Nick added quickly. 'You're everything I could want in a woman, professionally and personally.'

'You mean if I sleep with you I can salvage some sort of job with this company, is that what you're saying?'

'That is not what I said,' he answered ambiguously.

A momentary surge of optimism flickered and died in Sandra's heart. My God, she thought. Doesn't he ever give up? He's facing the worst professional crisis of his career and all he can think of are his overactive glands. Or maybe he thinks he needs me to help him out of this mess.

'Nick, I can't stay on under these circumstances,' she said unsteadily. She wasn't sure whether it was best to sound insulted or defeated, and hoped her answer contained a little of both.

'No? Well, what will you do?'

'I'm not sure what options I have,' she answered despondently.

'You can become an agent,' Nick offered in feigned optimism.

Sandra found her voice rising. 'That's ridiculous.'

'Nonsense, for someone with your skills it'll be easy,' he scoffed.

'Really?' she answered bitterly.

Although Nick tried to look confident and unashamed, he knew the facade failed abysmally. He had the satisfaction of breaking her career but his own was hanging on a cliff edge.

'What do you want from me?' he asked.

'Exactly what I expect to receive. Nothing,' Sandra felt nothing but disgust for this man who controlled the lives of so many. She had to make her display of martyrdom sound convincing.

'You've flipped, love. Why would I want to get rid of you when I've told you you're the best thing that ever happened to this company?'

'Pride. Vain, masculine, pride.'

'You've gone mad.'

'Have I? Unlike the others around you, I don't jump through hoops and sit up like a trained circus dog.'

'Sandra, you have a month to work out your notice.'

Nick took up his pen and started to write a memo advising the accounts department of his decision.

'And what am I supposed to do in that time? Bring in more recruits for you?'

'I do still pay your salary, you know.'

She stormed out of his office, looking inflamed with betrayal.

Returning to her own office, she slammed the door shut and called James. 'It worked.' Her words were cold and determined. 'I'm free.'

'And the best is yet to come,' James added. 'Once the ISC force Prime to refund all the VIP money, Nick won't have enough left to sustain a long-term legal challenge. He'll have to merge... and I'll be waiting.'

'And VIP will be waiting too,' she laughed. 'We both know the product is good. So what if we have to wait a while before we can sell it? We can afford the time and can demonstrate the ambiguity of the law is sufficient to prove it *is* legitimate.'

'My dear,' said James, 'you are absolutely correct.'

James put the phone down and looked out of his window. He could feel the thrill of success. James hadn't fully believed, until that moment, that his plan would actually work, although he realised this was only phase one.

He set about the task of formulating a merger offer. It gave him a sense of power. His single regret was that he had to go to such lengths to bring Nick back on to his turf for a final showdown. This manipulation could hurt hundreds of careers, he considered. I must make sure the damage control strategy will work. There were times, he realised with dread, when he was too much like his father. He was shaken by his own insight. He sighed deeply. Yes, this will be the final showdown, and I have to win.

*

Sandra went back to her office the next day to clear out a few things.

'I'm sorry I yelled yesterday,' Nick said, walking into what was once Sandra's private office.

She looked away from him. If he wanted absolution from her, he would be waiting a long time, she thought stubbornly.

'By the way,' he added. 'I've been rereading the latest contract you signed... the one detailing your position as director of sales and marketing.'

She gritted her teeth and shut her eyes to stop from striking out at him with all her pent-up rage.

'And what exactly have you been doing that for?' she asked pointedly.

'Well, I wanted to check something. You see it says here' – Nick pointed to the relevant paragraph – 'that if you leave Prime you are not able to get another job with a competitor company in the same industry for two years.' He smiled disarmingly at her. 'Are you sure you won't reconsider my offer?'

She banged her fist on the table. 'Damn you to hell, Nick Abbott. How dare you threaten me after firing me?' She was shocked at the strength and determination in her words. She had forgotten, for a moment, who she was facing.

'I'm just thinking of your best interests,' he assured her.

'Well, thank you very much for your consideration, but no thanks.' You bastard, she thought. I'll see you in court and in hell before I'm through with you.

'Oh,' he said, as though the rejection was no surprise. 'I'll have Mark drop by and check that nothing is leaving the office that shouldn't be before you go.'

She watched him leave and for long minutes she sat in her office doing nothing, her head in her hands in a state of prolonged shock. At least she had the foresight to remove the vital documents before her meeting with Nick. And at least James had worked out the way to turn adversity into advantage.

With a few meagre packing boxes full, Sandra called a taxi and left the head office of Prime forever.

George and Ralph amazed her. It didn't matter what chaos occurred in the world, they continued in their own way, untouched by everything around them. That was the surprising truth of it. Despite their huge success they remained the pure country boys who made good; unpolluted by the filth and treachery around them.

The reception desk at Hamilton Black was deserted but Sandra could hear movement coming from the boardroom. Strange, she thought, there's no training meeting today.

'Where is everyone?' she called.

A scurrying, shuffling sound echoed within.

'Shit! It's a Prime spy. Turn the TV off,' she heard Ralph say. Sandra followed the noise to see the Hamilton Black staff surrounded by Chinese takeaway containers and a few bottles of wine.

'That's no spy,' yelled George. 'It's Ms Director of Sales and Marketing.'

'Hello, George. What are you all up to?'

'We are watching the Hamilton Black bloopers,' George explained to a ripple of laughter from the surrounding staff.

'The what?' Sandra asked.

'Turn it back on,' Ralph ordered with a wave of his hand. 'Have a drink and some Chinky grub,' he offered.

She gladly accepted the food and wine and sat down bursting with curiosity about the 'Hamilton Black bloopers'.

It only took a few frames for her to realise what they were. Hamilton Black had made a promotional video. Sandra had heard it was used as a recruiting aid for new agents. The object of the exercise was to show the background and experience of George and Ralph. It told people who George and Ralph were at work, as well as at play, introducing the staff and the training programme which would be offered if they joined Prime. The video had taken a week to put together, mainly because so much of it had to be re-shot. The bloopers, Sandra thought, would probably have made a better recruiting aid than the finished product.

'Oh, no,' Ralph said. 'Not the putt. I must have missed that shot a hundred times. I think I should buy myself a new golf club to practise.'

'You mean a putter?' Sandra asked.

'No, stupid. I mean a club. You know, a country club.'

'Oh. I should have known.' She looked back to the TV monitor.

'Now I've fucking told you – oops – wipe that.'

'Good old George,' Sandra commented, giggling as she watched his faux pas.

'What is this?' one of the office girls asked.

George was holding a golf club and dancing around his office.

'You didn't know I used to star on Broadway, did you?' George asked.

'That's the broad way,' another girl piped up, gesturing with her hands that she thought George was wide in the beam.

'Cheeky bitch,' said George, 'you'll keep.'

The next scene was George pulling a silly face with his eyes shut and a row of glossy teeth shining out. Behind him was Ralph making the victory sign.

Everyone in the room roared with laughter. One girl nearly fell off her chair altogether with tears rolling down her cheeks.

'Would you like to hear another funny story?' asked Sandra when the video finished.

'What's that?' asked Ralph, wiping a tear from his eye.

'Oh, you'll love this one,' she said, looking directly into Ralph's eyes. 'But I think it's better told in private.'

The room fell silent, waiting to hear the order to leave.

'Better come with me,' Ralph said, taking Sandra by the arm.

Ralph took Sandra into his office, closely followed by George who shut the door.

'Well, the first piece of good news is,' she began, 'I've been fired.'

'Because of VIP?' Ralph asked.

'Because of a VIP is more like it,' Sandra answered.

'Huh, that would be right,' George laughed. 'I'm sorry to hear that,' he added quickly.

'Don't be,' she smiled. 'I'm not.'

A minute's silence passed before George commented, in his usual frank manner. 'Fucking shit! He put the hard word on you, didn't he?'

Sandra lowered her head to laugh, thinking she should have felt embarrassed, but instead enjoying the flippant way in which George trivialised things.

'Do I assume he's not having a good strike rate?' Ralph grinned.

When the laughter died down, George spoke thoughtfully. 'You're not here to tell us about that, are you?'

'No, George, I'm not.'

'So, if that was the good news, what's the bad?' Ralph asked.

'You know Prime is going to have to merge now, don't you?' she asked.

'That's seems pretty obvious,' George agreed. 'What of it?'

'I just want you guys to hang in there. You just never know when a call may come out of the blue at a time like this.'

'If you mean an offer from another company to buy our services, we get those all the time,' Ralph said, admiring the trophies in his office. 'We don't need the work, you know that. To tell you the truth, we've been thinking of quitting the business altogether.'

'I know that, guys. But I'm asking you, as a personal favour, to hang in there a little while longer... until the issue of mergers is well and truly resolved.'

They looked at one another curiously.

'I don't know what kind of crackpot scheme you're

cooking up, my girl,' George said, 'but put it this way, what have we got to lose?'

'You're always so logical, George,' she beamed.

'Yeah, love. Always logical, that's me. I'm curious about something though,' he added.

'Oh?' Sandra enquired. 'What's that?'

'How did he do it?'

'Do what?' Sandra asked.

'I mean, what did he do? Did he say, "I wanna fuck", or what?'

She flushed at his insolence. 'Well, in my case, he simply pulled me towards him and kissed me on the lips.'

A gasp of air was taken by both George and Ralph. Ralph held his laughter in with his hand while George's eyes nearly popped right out of his head.

'You're joking,' George exclaimed.

Sandra shook her head solemnly.

'Silly bitch,' George said affectionately. 'Serves you right for being a bloody attractive woman.'

'Thank you, George. I really needed those endearing words of encouragement.' She smiled.

'Listen love. I wish there was something else I could do, but if you want us to sit tight for a while, no worries. That's what we'll do.'

'Excellent. I knew I could count on you two.'

'He's a clever man,' George warned. 'You're not the first to be conned by him and you won't be the last. Maybe you should think carefully about your alternatives.'

'Don't worry, George, I already have.'

Chapter Ten

On the forty-fourth floor of the Champion Life building, outside the national agency manager's office, Sandra waited as any other client might, flicking through copies of the latest *Country Life* magazine. The girl at reception was too busy answering phone calls to start a pleasant discourse with Sandra so she let her eyes wander the expansive area until she noticed their latest annual report. Nestled into the large tan leather couches she received a twinge of pleasure seeing her lover's name listed as the second most important man in the company.

Either side of her were meeting rooms. Clients were never taken into their agent's office, James had explained to her. For one thing they were too untidy, and most did not have the impressive view that was enjoyed on the south side of the building. For another, it was too risky to allow a client the chance of seeing the confidential documents that inevitably lay all over a working office.

Sandra meandered across to one of the open doors; she could see the meeting table was inlaid with grey marble and surrounded by black padded leather chairs. There was a troll on the cabinet to one side of the room and a painting of modern art, which Sandra could not appreciate, on the other. She growled inwardly as a rabid beast might have done. This time, she promised herself, I won't be waiting for years to avenge myself in a dream. This time I want to shed real blood, and shed it quickly. She could taste vengeance and it tasted sweet. She craved for it; lusted after it. It would be hers.

She pictured Nick Abbott in jail, reduced to the status of a common criminal having had every cent and privilege mercilessly stripped away from him, rejected by his peers as the failure he was. Only a failure could allow himself to be manipulated so completely, she thought sanctimoniously. Inside that thought, however, was the realisation that she had let herself become as trapped as Nick.

'Hello, my lovely,' James called.

As he burst into the room with a bunch of red roses, it seemed to Sandra as though he breathed freshness and promise into her. Shutting the door behind him, he rushed to give Sandra a warm, lingering embrace. Her nerve endings tingled with delight and excitement at her lover's touch.

'Hello, gorgeous,' she murmured, holding him as tight as she could manage. 'What sort of offer have we made?'

'A bloody generous one under the circumstances. Nick already has the offer from Russell Miller, our chief executive. As soon as the ISC rule that the VIP funds have to be refunded he'll have no option but to accept.'

'Well, that brings him on to your turf, but then what happens?'

'As I see it,' he said, taking a seat, 'and I should know because I wrote the contract' – he winked at her and grinned – 'the board of the merged group will demand a field test. Our system and method of operation is totally different to Prime's, which will create a major destabilising effect on all agents; Prime's and ours. Only one system can be finally adopted so Nick and I will have to fight for the collective support of both groups of agents. He can't oust the CEO of the merging company; he's in no position to do so. He goes back to being national agency manager. With James Cartwright as the existing national agency manager, the agents must decide which of us stays and the board will decide which of the systems stays. It will be a fight to the death, culminating in a board meeting after a suitable test period.'

'But what if he wins?' she asked.

'With Phil Langdon-Smythe on our side, hardly likely,' he said confidently.

'And how do you plan to keep out of his way until the board meeting? He's going to want to meet his major adversary.'

'I'll have to be interstate keeping my troops on my side. Nick will expect that, he'll probably be doing the same thing. It's quite conceivable that James Cartwright will remain just an annoying name until the board meeting.'

'You're certain there's no chance of him finding out earlier?' Sandra asked.

'I am absolutely certain.'

Sandra couldn't possibly see how James hoped to lead Nick's flock away from him, there were too many unanswered questions in her mind.

'We have another little problem,' Sandra added with a sigh.

'Really?' James asked as though it couldn't possibly be important.

'My contract with Prime says I can't work for a competitor in the same industry for two years.'

'That's not a problem,' James laughed. 'You won't be with a competitor. As soon as the merger is announced, Prime and Champion Life become one and the same. Besides, I won't give you the position officially until after the battle. My father will smell a rat from ten miles away if he hears your name mentioned. You'll have to work covertly, but I would say you are becoming a veteran at that by now.' He smiled his father's smile at her.

'Devious Abbotts,' she giggled, and moved forward on both elbows, folding her arms in front of her.

'That's what we get paid the big money for,' he said confidently.

'I love it when you talk business, James,' she whispered, stroking his arm gently.

He fought to keep his thoughts on business as she teased him.

'I love you,' she added, walking behind him, putting her arms around his neck and kissing him gently on his cheek.

'Thank you. I know,' he answered, submitting to her caress.

'What can I make you for dinner tonight?' she asked, pulling out his chair and sitting on his lap.

'Really, this is most irregular,' he commented as she settled herself upon his lap.

'I should hope so,' she retorted, smiling sweetly.

'Hum. Dinner?' James thought out loud while she ran her fingers through his hair. 'I think we should book a room at the Hyatt and order room service. What do you think?'

'I think I'll head down there right away and wait for you.'

'It's only one o'clock.'

'I'll try to find something to do to amuse myself. I'll get a nice bubbly spa going, and a bottle of champagne.'

'You wretch. Stop it or I'll never make it back to my office.'

'That is the general idea, my love,' she uttered the words so softly they were like a breeze filtering through his senses. Her lips pulled gently at his, her tongue teasing its way inside his mouth.

'Get off me, you wicked woman,' James managed to utter, slapping her gently on her behind. 'I have work to do. I'll put this together right now. We will deliver an offer to Abbott as soon as the refund of monies has been demanded.'

'The fight becomes fierce from here on in.'

'We're in this together now,' he assured her. 'You and I against the world.'

'In that case, they don't stand a chance.'

She examined him closely, noticing the strong, stubborn lines of his jaw and the devil-may-care lift to the corners of his lips. He possessed courage, integrity and compassion.

When this was over, he decided, she would be his forever.

Before leaving the office, Sandra straightened her hair and repaired her make-up in the mirrors of the elevator walls.

'Sandra?'

She spun around in the street to see where the voice was coming from.

'Sandra,' she heard again. This time she saw a man running towards her and waving his hand.

'George! You're about the last person in the world I expected to see today. How are you?'

'A good deal better than Prime. It's been confirmed that all VIP monies will have to be refunded. Nick received notice of it an hour ago.'

'Good news travels fast.'

'I don't know what you're up to, my girl, but I hope you've been bloody careful in planning it.'

'I have received the help of an expert, George. If I told you who it was, you would never believe me.'

'You'd need a bloody clone of Nick to be able to outsmart the old bastard,' George muttered.

'Spot on,' she agreed.

'What are you going to do?'

'I can't tell you just yet. What has Nick said he's going to do about refunding the monies?'

'He has no choice. A merger is definitely on, we just don't know who it's going to be with yet.'

'I see,' she said, hardly able to contain her excitement. 'I wonder if I could make a guess?' she teased George.

'Something tells me you'd be able to make a pretty bloody accurate guess if you ask me,' he observed.

'Wise men tell no tales, George. You'll have to be patient and play dumb.'

'Well, I'm pretty good at playing dumb anyway,' he said, grinning stupidly.

'Good,' she announced. 'Well, just sit tight a little longer. I have been assured that there will be a very important role for you in the scheme of things – and pretty soon.'

'I love it,' George answered, grinning widely.

'What are you looking so smug about? You don't know what it is yet.'

'Ah,' he answered, 'but the old adage is true, isn't it?' he sniggered.

'What's that?'

'Be nice to everyone on the way up, because you don't know who you're going to meet on the way down.'

'George, you have never spoken a truer word.'

She took her new business cards out of her pocket and read the title again and again: 'Assistant Agency Manager'. She smiled to herself as George disappeared into another building.

'I look forward to telling you what is going on George,' she said out loud. 'More than you could possibly imagine.'

George was waiting at an elevator, which as usual seemed to be taking forever, thinking about all the things Sandra could be working on. He knew if this situation was managed correctly she could be the answer to his prayers – to everybody's prayers. Immensely satisfied with himself for having the foresight to befriend her when they first met, he considered the new level of her potential. The twist of recent events could have made her one of the most powerful players in the game. He wasn't sure of that yet, but he would take great pleasure in helping her in any plan that meant the downfall of the murderous Nick Abbott.

Sandra watched assorted shapes of men disappearing into buildings crowded with dozens of other men in dark blue and grey business suits. Thinking about her brief conversation with George, she began to puzzle over the facts. How *was* James going to use George against Nick? How could he be so sure the agents would follow him over the man they saw as the Messiah? Why was James so determined to drive his father into a death-defying rage?

She was driving towards the Hyatt Hotel when it eventually hit her. When James talked about a fight to the death, he wasn't speaking metaphorically. Ray Cooper had said Nick would have to be provoked into making a mistake, and James was going to risk his life to do it. How else *could* he do it? It all started to slot into place with frightening accuracy. James had told her that he intended to set things straight, no matter what the cost. She should have realised when James spoke about his father being too clever to be caught that simply discrediting him wasn't going to be enough. She prayed she was wrong, but knew she wasn't. How on earth could she avert this potential tragedy? she asked herself. She wanted to shout from the rooftops for him not to be so foolish, but realised the futility of trying to stop him.

Driving aimlessly down Sydney's streets, she thought over all the lies she had been told. Lies by Nick Abbott. How he respected her and liked her. These were unimportant lies. There were also the big lies, however. James and Nick had both manipulated her with equal ease. A festering anger slowly emerged; a small black hole in her mind which swirled and magnified. Her sense of reason had been buried by the excitement of events around her. At last she plucked it from a silent zone inside her mind, a zone muffled by the stimulus of rapidly occurring events. The forward area of her mind had told her that she had made her own decisions, and made them correctly with the information at hand. Now she realised for the first time when the deception had begun. Who could create a man like Nick Abbott? What other lies had he told, what other damage had he done? Going through her mind she listed the possibilities. As she did so her eyes widened, her anger turning to sickening abhorrence. Instead of going to the Hyatt, she abruptly changed direction to Kingsford Smith Airport. This was too important to discuss over the phone. If she made the two thirty flight to Melbourne she could still be back at the Hyatt by seven that evening. It would be close but she could do it.

*

'St Kilda Road Police Station, please,' she said to a taxi driver at Tullamarine, with a determined flick of her hair.

The biggest problem was the complexity of the issue. It took big, sophisticated minds to understand. No newcomer would understand what she knew about the Abbotts. You had to have a track record. Gingerly, stealthily, she walked into the police station, trepidation running through her bones. There were only four people who were likely to understand the wisdom of her new-found knowledge. Of these, Ray Cooper had been the most logical to approach.

She felt a peculiar misgiving inside the station. There had been murderers and rapists walking about in the very building she now stood in. Perhaps there was one there now. She shuddered and turned to leave. She didn't want any part of this ugly scene, but a small voice inside her stopped her. Turn around, you must have the courage of your convictions or you are no better than the man you are trying to bring to justice. She obeyed reluctantly, praying that Ray would be able to come up with a suggestion to solve her dilemma.

She walked back towards reception, not noticing the spiral decor on the lofty ceilings and rear wall. She didn't even notice the myriad of people buzzing in and out. She was focused on one name.

'I'd like to speak to Ray Cooper, please.' She spoke through a hole in what she presumed to be bulletproof glass.

A young uniformed policeman with dark hair and a scar under his right eye answered without emotion, 'Where does he work?'

'Homicide.'

The young policeman looked at her suspiciously and checked for the number.

'Your name?' he asked.

'Sandra Upton.'

'Just a moment.'

Turning away from her, the officer dialled the number and muttered something that was inaudible to Sandra. Replacing the receiver he turned his face back towards the hole in the glass.

'Wait over there.' He pointed curtly to a cheap-looking set of fabric armchairs.

Sandra looked towards them and thought she would rather occupy herself looking around the reception area than risk changing her mind. She wandered over to a glass cabinet filled with all types of police paraphernalia. There were ties, glasses, paperweights. They all had the same slogan on them: 'Victoria Police – we care and uphold the right'.

'Just passing by?'

Sandra recognised his voice without turning around. Did she want to go through with this? She turned slowly. He had no jacket on, just the usual crisply ironed shirt. She envied his ability to maintain a controlled calm expression.

'There are a couple of things I would like to discuss with you,' she answered abruptly, ignoring his quip.

'Can I get you a cup of coffee?'

'Thank you.'

He signed her in and led her towards the elevator. She followed him silently to a sparse interview room.

'How is your job going at Prime?' he asked politely, as though he didn't know.

She permitted a small laugh to leave her lips before answering. 'Not so good.'

'Oh? Anything you want to tell me about?'

'It's a long story,' she began.

He patiently listened without probing for details to start with. She went through all the conversations she had held with James about his plan to take over Prime and force Nick into a showdown. It took Ray a great deal of self-control not to reveal the fact that he already knew everything she was telling him as a result of installing listening devices in both offices, but experience had taught him that you never knew where one vital clue might be hiding.

'He plans to stay invisible until the board meeting,' Sandra explained.

'Are you sure he has no idea that VIP was a clever scam?'

'I'm quite sure of that.'

'I don't understand,' Ray admitted. 'What are you trying to tell me?'

'If I'm right, James will make his appearance at the board meeting. Even if he wins the corporate battle for control of the agents, that still leaves Nick on the loose, agreed?'

'Agreed.'

'We all want to see Nick in jail, agreed?'

'Agreed.'

'And so far we still have no evidence that he actually committed any murders, agreed?'

'Agreed,' Ray said reluctantly.

'Even with the testimony from Nick's old client in New York, Nick can't be jailed for a murder committed by someone else. Even if we could get some sort of conviction based on his policy sales, it would be minimal at best—'

'What's all this leading to?' Ray asked, getting a little tired of this line of conversation.

'I believe it is James's intention to provoke Nick into trying to kill him, and Nick is likely to do just that.'

'I see,' Ray said thoughtfully. 'You could be right.'

'I'm sure I'm right. You were the one who put the idea in his head,' she shouted.

'Me?' He cried. 'How do you figure that?'

'You kept saying the only way to get him was to provoke him into making a mistake, well, that's exactly what James is going to do.'

Ray sighed deeply. Why couldn't these meddling civilians leave these things to the professionals?

'Does James know you're here telling me all this?' He sounded like a disapproving or suspicious parent.

'Of course not. If he had wanted me to know he'd have told me himself. He's not going to admit it.'

'Let me think about this for a moment,' Ray said, buying time to assimilate this new situation into the ever more complicated plan.

Sandra wanted to help him. She struggled to find additional information that might be useful.

'What about arresting Nick for those policy sales?' Sandra asked. 'Could we do that?'

'Doubtful,' Ray answered, growing ever more concerned that this situation was getting out of hand. When Ray arrested Nick, he wanted to be sure it was for Brett's murder, not for some crime committed in New York years ago. Nick was his, and if Sandra was right, Nick might just say something which would give him the last elusive key to unlock this complicated jigsaw puzzle. If James could provoke Nick to say, 'You know what I did to Brett, I am going to do the same to you for disgracing me this way', it would be enough. A confession through a threat, Ray thought, that's all I need to finish him.

'Jesus,' Sandra mumbled, 'all those deaths and nothing to hang the bastard with.'

'I have an idea,' Ray announced. 'Are you absolutely certain James will stay out of Nick's way until the board meeting?'

'Yes, absolutely.'

'Okay, so he's safe at least until then, right?'

'Right,' she confirmed.

'Then this is what we'll do.'

Sandra listened eagerly to his plan. It sounded both simple and effective. If she was right, Nick would go to jail and James could live his life knowing his father couldn't hurt anyone again. If she was wrong, they would be no worse off than they were right now.

'It's a bit of a long shot,' she said when Ray finished explaining. 'Do you think it will work?' she asked him imploringly.

*

In a warm towelling bathrobe with 'Hyatt' sewn on it, Sandra settled on the fluffy pillows of the king-size bed waiting for James. Her heart skipped when she heard the key in the door.

'Hello, darling. Hard day at the office?' she asked, getting up to greet him.

'Hard? You wouldn't credit it. Some mad woman came rushing in wanting to take over her ex-boss's company. She was absolutely hysterical.' He removed his Christian Dior tie as he spoke, throwing it on the floor.

'Really?' Sandra pushed his jacket casually off his shoulders. 'And what do you plan to do with her?'

She saw his mouth open without words as he lowered his head towards her. His mouth tasted sweet, even perfumed, as it was, with the scent of coffee. His tongue explored her gently. Her fingers caressed his face while he smoothed her hair back from her temples, lightly touching her closed eyelids. She trembled at the gentleness of his touch.

As he slowly removed her bathrobe she felt the strength go out of her body and she leaned against her lover for support.

He removed his mouth from hers, leaving a cold empty feeling. She slowly opened her eyes to see him bowing his head to her breast. She touched his thick black hair, encouraging his advances.

His own clothing seemed to fall away like used wrapping paper. She had never seen anything so exquisite.

Her head was flung back and her eyes filled with tears of joy. She clung to him and arched her back. She could feel his body tense and firm as he cradled her in his arms.

'I've been dreaming of you,' she admitted breathlessly, twining her fingers in his black hair. 'Wild, wicked, wonderful dreams.'

It was all he had been waiting to hear. With a muffled groan, he lowered his lips to her throat. Her scent was as potent as his passion, her taste as warm as his blood. Picking her up in his arms, he carried her the few feet to the bed.

Sandra clung to him, her head spinning with the familiar hunger that only he could create.

She looked so fragile and so beautiful. His teeth closed around the rosy tip of her breast, creating a flash of heat that spiralled to her very core. His mouth was everywhere, tasting, tempting, racing on a crazed journey from her lips to her toes. His hands slid unerringly down her body, discovering secret hidden flash-points of pleasure.

With a sense of greedy wonder she responded, running her hands over James's body, delighted with the way his muscles rippled and clenched beneath her palms.

Her scent surrounded him in a sultry hypnotic cloud. His body throbbed, his blood swimming with a red-hot desire he wished would never fade.

A heat flared inside her with the slow movement of her hips, breaking free from earthly restrictions into divine deliverance.

He dominated her in a way she would worship and cherish forever. His heat seemed to fill her until she could not bear it any longer. She thought she might die of it; it burst within her and she felt herself falling, tumbling like a feather down a mountainous crevice.

When she finally opened her eyes she saw that his face was spotted with little beads of perspiration. He appeared to glow like a golden icon.

*

The wait for news of the announced merger seemed to be taking forever. Sandra kept finding new ways to amuse herself until the time arrived when she could take up her new position with the merged group. James fussed round her like a mother hen during those endless weeks. He was so warm and loving, she couldn't bear to think of him planning to tempt fate in the way in which she had told Ray.

One morning when she woke, James was gone. She buried her head in the dent of his pillow to savour his fragrance which lingered like a hazy mist. She could hear strange noises coming from the kitchen.

'I thought you might like a champagne breakfast,' James announced, carrying a tray with a dozen red roses on it. He was dressed in his stunning silk smoking jacket.

'Sounds wonderful.' She smiled and stretched her arms as far as they could reach, the sensations from last night still gracefully gliding through her body. 'I don't have to go to work today after all.'

'Well, here we have eggs Benedict and bubbly for two,' he announced.

'James, you were sent from heaven. Do you know that?'

'I do.'

'What's this?' Sandra took a baton-shaped object from the tray. 'How quaint,' she observed. 'You've wrapped the daily paper up in a silver serviette ring. Shall we see what is in the day's news?'

She unravelled it while James organised their meal.

'My God,' Sandra exclaimed, sitting upright in bed. The headline read: 'PRIME FINANCIAL GROUP TO BE MERGED WITH CHAMPION LIFE AUSTRALIA'.

'James. Look at this.'

'I don't need to.' He smiled.

She read the article.

The final obstacle to the merger between Champion Life Australia and Prime Financial Group was overcome yesterday when the Federal Court approved the proposition.

The merged group is now the third largest life office in Australia with assets of more than ten billion dollars.

The merger became effective from yesterday as Prime policyholders became Champion Life policyholders.

The chairman of Champion Life, Mr Fred Chambers, said yesterday that the merged group has reserves of 1.4 billion dollars, putting its reserve ratio at twenty per cent, which is more than 900 million dollars. This is far more than the solvency margin required by the insurance and superannuation commissioner...

'And that's no merger,' James commented smugly. 'It's a takeover. And it's Champion Life who has taken over Prime. Look, it says here that Prime policyholders have become Champion Life policyholders,' he said proudly.

'Well, you can confidently say that Champion Life is not a low-profile organisation any more.'

'Nick played right into our hands, just like I said he would. What do you have to say about your lover now?'

Sandra considered the possibilities. 'You're a genius. I always said you were a genius. But this could still see Nick leading the merged group if he get the agents to stick with him. Are you ready to tell me how we are going to tackle that little issue?'

'Almost ready, I would like to read this article a couple more times first.' James relished the words slowly, a contented smile spreading across his face.

'Enough,' Sandra shouted, grabbing the paper from him.

He grinned at her, feeling a wave of contentment.

'Don't get overconfident, my love. Nick Abbott isn't going to roll over and die so easily.'

'And I thought you had blind faith in me,' he quipped.

'You may have changed your name, but you're still an Abbott. And I've vowed never to have blind faith in anyone again.'

'That was uncalled for,' James responded, looking deeply wounded.

'What are you going to do?' she insisted, realising she'd made a hurtful remark. 'I can't stand not knowing a moment longer.'

'Well, we'd better get dressed and go to the office, then I can show you.'

She considered telling James about her meeting with Ray Cooper, to warn him not to go too far.

'And it starts all over again?' she asked despondently.

'Sandra, let's not argue. Be patient, it will all be over soon, I know it.'

James had newspaper reports all over his desk; clippings of rumoured mergers and the final announcement that it had taken place. He had spent a good deal of time liasing between East west and the New York police to get the information he needed, but it had come together just beautifully on schedule. Now James knew he stood only a short distance from revenge.

He checked the documents again, ensuring they had all the messages in them that Sandra would need to see. The legal agreements were there too. All drawn up and ready for the Prime agents to sign – to sign over their allegiance to James Cartwright. His excitement almost caused him to palpitate. Ideas were tumbling one over another in his mind. He assumed, because he wanted to assume, that Nick's days were numbered.

'Mr Cartwright, you've done very well for yourself,' Sandra commented, admiring his plans.

'Thank you. It's not bad, it is?' he said, with a degree of self-admiration. 'And look, this is where the assistant agency manager, that's you, my love, will fit into the plan after this is all over.'

They both looked through his plans in great detail. It was a complicated network of intricate ploys and counter-ploys which stretched Sandra's capacity of comprehension to the limit.

'What am I supposed to make of this?' Sandra asked, pointing to the section titled 'Agent Loyalty'.

'There is one almighty power struggle going on. Every-thing about the two companies pulls in opposite directions. One has an agency structure where the agents receive high commissions and pay costs; the other pays lower commissions and pays all running costs. One markets to the high net-worth business arena; one markets to blue-collar workers. The ethos of Prime is opposed to that of Champion Life. Both teams of agents will be scrutinising both systems and both managers. All they want to know is what's in it for them and who's going to look after their interests the best.'

Sandra looked at the articles to try to find some explanation within their words.

'What does it mean to the Prime people?'

'Simple. They are all owned by Champion Life; an organisation which is profit driven and ruthless. Prime has fewer agents but those agents sell larger policies. They will want to go on working under Nick's system, no question. But who's to say they need Nick to do it? If I can illustrate a structure which effectively combines the systems, so as it is profitable for both company and agent, I am sure the board will accept it. Then it's just a matter of deciding who heads this new hybrid system. That will be a matter for the agents to vote on.'

She mulled over his words. 'Correct me if I am wrong, but what you are saying is it all comes down to who the agents decide to follow?'

'Correct.'

'James, darling, I love you. You know that. But—'

'Stop worrying. Once Phil, Tom and Eastbank are added to the menu there is no choice to make. I really should thank my father for helping them get into Australia, don't you think?'

'And how do you propose to communicate that?' Her voice trembled as she spoke.

'I told you, I have a plan.' He smiled confidently. 'Your friends at Hamilton Black have the trust of the agents, even if Nick is the man they look up to.'

'You're talking in riddles,' she protested.

James moved towards the more informal meeting area of his office, where a pot of brewed coffee awaited. They sat on opposite leather couches, either side of a large glass coffee table.

'James, your top lip has disappeared, I know that means you are being very devious. What exactly is your plan?'

'First I will show – correction, you will show – the Prime agents my prototype of the new system. They must have doubts in their mind about Nick's system surviving. Despite his protests, the fact is, Prime went broke because of his commission rates.'

'That's not entirely true, James. The agents aren't fools. They know that other factors were involved, even if they are not aware of the full extent. I still say they are going to want to work under his system, with him.'

'So, we prove to them that his system is doomed, mine will be just as lucrative and that Nick has no chance of leading them in this or any other company.'

'It's a pretty picture but how do you propose achieving this complicated scheme when they still worship the ground he walks on?'

'We use an Abbott technique. We play on their fear and greed. Nick will be doing everything within his power to assure them he planned this whole merger to give them access to larger funds, a larger company, bigger reserves, and so on. But they can't be certain of that, no matter what he says. It's a two-horse race and each man has to decide who the winning horse is likely to be. If we can show them that the best horse is me, it would be insanity for them not to support our side.'

'How can we convince them of that? I don't understand.'

'Maybe this will help.' James passed her a letter.

To whom it may concern

It is my unfortunate duty to advise you that the myth behind the legend you all aspire to was based on one of the worst types of fraud of our time. Under the express direction of Nick Abbott, Eddie Schwartz sold record numbers of policies by returning to his impoverished childhood neighbourhood to market to the blue-collar and unemployed population who desperately needed money. Over one hundred million dollars' worth of cover was sold by Eddie...

Sandra didn't need to read the rest of the article, she just looked for the author.

Gus Fletcher, Chief Executive Officer, East West

'How did you ever get him to write this?' she asked numbly.

'Actually, it is thanks to our friend, Ray Cooper. His snooping has unearthed a witness to testify that this actually took place. It may not be enough to arrest Nick, but it's sure as hell enough to make sure he's out of the industry for good. Gus has no choice but to admit this took place, not now there is someone to point the finger at. Without this statement Gus would look as guilty as Nick.'

'So why don't you just use it? Give it to the board right now,' she insisted.

'Oh, no. I've put too much into this. I want to see him squirm before I put in the knife. I want my father to know I've beaten him at his own game.'

'So we use this letter to give them the option to change camps quietly, without publicly disgracing anyone, and then use it anyway. Is that what you're saying?'

'Basically, yes.'

She scratched her left temple in confusion.

'How do you propose we go about this?' she asked, with puzzlement written all over her face.

'This is where your friends George and Ralph come in. They have a good feel for who is on whose side. It will only take one or two well-placed ringleaders to get the flock to follow.'

James explained in detail what Sandra needed to tell her friends George and Ralph.

'It's brilliant,' she cried. 'You're inspired. Nothing can stop us now.' Sandra let herself be carried away in a wave of triumph.

'It's not going to be as easy as it seems,' James explained. 'Granted, once the agents see this they will leave Nick in droves, but first we have to get to them all.'

She sat back in her chair, disheartened at the huge task that lay before them.

'You can't possibly expect me to get to all the Prime agents of Australia within two months.'

'I don't. That's the whole point, George and Ralph can do it for you. What I want you to do is explain all this to them. If they can convince the ringleaders, the others will follow like sheep.'

'Great. You want them to go to Mark Fitzgerald, the man who has become Nick's closest ally, and ask him to lead the defection?'

'I didn't say it was going to be easy. Mark may be Nick's longest-standing ally, but he's a soldier; we all are. He will recognise when withdrawal is better than defeat. Nobody wants to see their own blood spilled, no matter how veteran a fighter they are.'

'I can't do it,' she said coldly. 'I can't get George and Ralph to risk their positions to go to someone like Mark with this.'

'Then Nick has already won,' James answered, already having anticipated her reservations.

James sat quietly, letting the plan sink into Sandra's brain. It was an intricate, delicate plan, fraught with danger;

but he knew his woman was strong and shrewd enough to make it work. Soon she would decide that for herself.

'If I fail, we could both be finished,' she remarked.

'Irrevocably,' he agreed.

Sandra looked at James in an unusual manner. She looked as though she were a worried mother praying for the life of her child, a life which was hanging precariously in the balance.

'I have no arguments left to give you,' he said.

'You're asking an awful lot.'

'Not when you think of it. If you can get those in power to listen to you by my calculations we could have this thing sewn up within six weeks. Do you agree?'

Sandra felt frightened thinking of the prestige she could achieve or the complete devastation. For no reason other than to give herself space and the time to think, she walked to the centre of the room.

'Damn it! I don't know what I agree with any more.'

'You owe it to both of us to give this a chance. You're the only one who can do it. You know that.'

'Can you put some sort of package together for me to show them?'

'I've already done it.'

'I should have known.' She smiled, still feeling numb.

She sighed to think of the war ahead. 'They won't move before the conference in Singapore, you know that, don't you?'

'So let him say his piece, it won't make any difference.'

'We'll have to find an out-of-the-way place for this meeting,' she stated.

'What about Mildura?' James asked.

'Of course,' she said. 'Denis is bound to be more than sympathetic to the cause.'

Chapter Eleven

Sandra read in her 'in-flight' magazine that Mildura was known for its wine-growing regions and festive atmosphere. Located on a three-way border between Victoria, New South Wales and South Australia, it was the perfect location to hold a covert meeting: conveniently central for most sales people and sufficiently out of the way that there was no chance of being overheard by a Nick Abbott spy.

Sandra looked upon Denis Granger as a wily old man. He had told her that his life as an undercover vice cop nearly caused the break-up of his marriage and his morals. He left the force to find peace and quiet in the country but soon discovered that he couldn't cope without having a purpose to his life. Denis gave the impression of being the fatherly type; the sort of person anyone could confide in. Behind the facade of the drawling voice and slow manner, however, was one of the sharpest minds that had worked in vice. He had come across the insurance industry quite by accident. An agent, who tried to sell Denis life insurance when he first moved to Mildura told him that his sales manager was a moron. The news about the sales manager aroused Denis's interest. When he learned that a man called Nick Abbott was coming to Mildura to fire the manager, he made it his business to meet this American.

Nick had told Denis, she recalled, that he had some

doubts about employing him as the new manager. At the age of forty-five Denis could have been too set in his ways to start learning the procedure, Nick explained, so he decided to try him out as a sales agent first. As both sales agent and sales manager Denis had excelled, earning the recognition and respect of the national sales team.

Denis had always been fond of Sandra. He noticed she could switch from city slicker to country girl with surprising ease. When she visited him in Mildura to assist him with his superannuation prospects, he admired her knowledge too; superannuation was something he had never fully understood. When she briefly told him the news about her departure from Prime his first reaction was disappointment, then anger. This was swiftly followed by a determination to help both Sandra and himself out of the unholy mess that had been created. He had been an ardent admirer of Nick's in the beginning. Lending Nick his cabin at Enoch's Point had seemed a simple enough gesture to Denis until he learned of Brett's death. Despite his disbelief that Nick could have been involved, Denis gave Ray all the assistance he needed, ultimately admitting to himself that Nick was guilty beyond question. He had to find a way to prove it, to avenge the disgrace that Denis now felt associated with.

The plane jolted to a standstill in Mildura. Sandra sat in her seat and looked out of the window at brilliant sunshine, trying to see Denis's face in the group that had gathered to meet colleagues at the small airport. Mildura had a scrubbed look about it, pristine and new. It was a good disguise for the dirt which was about to be discussed with the heavies of the life insurance community. A discussion which would serve to intensify the conflict which was brewing.

She stepped down the metal stairway, looking anxiously for her one piece of luggage. She eyed the luggage trolley as it left the cargo hold, searching for a large black briefcase; a case she needed to hold with both hands because of the sheer weight of it. The briefcase was jammed with papers containing reports, contracts and market assessments. It was a total battery of weapons. The data included the net worth of each individual at the meeting; every resource she possessed was in that bag. It was, to her, a doomsday machine. What made the contents deadly was her secret weapon, the letter James had ardently sought to attain from Gus Fletcher. With this artillery, and the absolute certainty of success, she felt absolved from all feelings of doubt.

She noticed that Denis had lost a little weight since she had seen him last, in fact he did not look well. His dark hair was showing signs of greying and had receded a full inch. His eyes were black and intense. His height seemed less imposing because of a slight stoop he had developed trying to look people in the eye.

'It's good to see you, Denis.' She stretched out a hand to offer a firm handshake, but it wasn't sufficient. Instead she hugged him like a daughter would hug her father. 'How many have we managed to gather for the meeting?' she asked anxiously.

'All the regional managers except Fitzgerald. The eleven RMs who are here were told there was a problem with Fitzgerald and no one questioned it. This is about self-preservation, no price is too great for that.'

He took the heavy black bag from Sandra and headed towards his Mercedes. Undoubtedly the only Mercedes in existence that had a bull-bar on the front of it, Sandra thought. Only drivers in outback Australia would require the assistance of such a device to ward off stray animals crossing the path of unexpected traffic.

'Are George and Ralph here?' she asked, trying not to grin.

Denis nodded.

As an ex-cop, Denis was used to reading people's expressions and he spotted the satisfaction in her face.

'I thought that would make you happy. Careful now, I may get jealous,' he beamed.

'Who else is here?'

'We have twenty people here in all. That includes two of the top ten agents and a few sales managers apart from myself. We also have a few phone link-ups. As a matter of fact, one of Fitzgerald's sales managers rang me. He said he knew that something was cooking and he wouldn't ask me questions. But, he added, whatever it was we could count him in. "I know," he said, "that I don't have a very marketable regional manager."'

'I can guess who that was,' she laughed, picturing the words coming from one of her former colleagues.

'I'm sure. We are all very keen to hear what you have to tell us. Nick Abbott's counterpart at Champion Life is, as far as we can tell, a man as ruthless and determined as Nick. To tell you the truth, there are serious doubts about Nick surviving this one.'

'That's good,' she said with complete confidence. 'You've done a good job, Denis.'

'It's as much in my interest as yours, I can assure you. I've hired a room at the Grand Hotel. We'll be away from any possible interruptions there.'

The entrance to the Grand Hotel, Sandra observed, was indeed grand. It shone out as the jewel in the crown of Mildura. The front doors were ornate with handles and edges painted gold. The word 'Grand', together with the hotel's symbol, was also painted in gold on the thick glass doors. Forty feet beyond the entrance was a large hall. It was five minutes to twelve when Sandra entered the fray.

Denis and Sandra walked together into the hall where a massive table had been formed by linking several smaller ones together. It must have been twenty feet from end to end and seven feet wide. Seated around the table were twenty men with worried faces. They ranged in age from thirty to forty-nine and were all dressed in expensive suits, all looking towards Sandra Upton.

Sandra approached the table with confidence.

Denis held a chair out for her to sit down.

'Thank you,' Sandra said calmly, examining the notepads, pens and phones in front of each man. Every sales team member had brought with them a colleague by phone, making the total assembly forty in all. The forty most influential of Prime's sales core, she judged with immense satisfaction. She acknowledged George and Ralph with a tilt of her head to which they responded graciously.

The power she held in her briefcase charged her with an almost corrupt vibrancy. She couldn't remember when she had felt so alive.

'Good afternoon, gentlemen. Most of us have met before, the rest of you I know by reputation.'

The room fell silent. Some men managed slight smiles.

'We have a very interesting group here today.' Sandra spoke clearly, in a supervisory manner. She paused to place her briefcase on the table directly in front of her. The men around the table were aroused, apprehensive.

'We are all aware of the reasons for your presence, and the risk we are, each of us, taking in being here. For my own part, let us say it is sufficient for you to know that I am acting for the agency department of Champion Life, but without the knowledge of the board.'

The men murmured as they considered the risk the man in agency must be taking. He was obviously as clever and determined as their own Nick Abbott, they decided. Sandra had proved her loyalty to these agents time and again; none of them were happy when she left over the VIP issue. They all knew she had originally come from Champion Life, so it was no great surprise to them that she would go back there, especially if the rumours had been true about Champion Life using VIP as a means to force Prime into this situation. It made sense that they would want the person who designed it. The big question, which no one dared ask, was what would Nick Abbott do if he found out they were in that room.

'Certain fundamental issues involving the survival of your sales system have not been clearly resolved since Champion Life took over Prime. Does anyone object to my calling it a takeover?'

There was silence. The men were immobile like corpses, only their minds were functioning.

'If your system is not proved the more profitable, you will be left with two options. Stay at Champion Life or follow Nick to a new company where he can build your system up again. That is assuming another company will take him on after he bankrupted a company. Does anyone question the accuracy of my analysis?'

'Listen, love,' said George in his broad, gruff accent, 'we already know all this. Tell us something we don't know.'

'Before I do, I would like to hear from you how you feel Nick is looking after you.'

This time it was Denis who spoke up.

'It is no secret that I was an admirer of Nick Abbott. But the truth of the matter is that our futures are hanging in the balance here. We know we have some serious decisions to make and no bastard is giving us all the facts to make them with. Nick has argued, and I believe correctly, that the damage to reserves was done despite him, not because of him, but he is in no position to dictate to us at this time.'

'Is that the feeling held by the rest of you?' she asked.

They murmured and nodded as if in one body.

'I see. Well this is what I am in a position to offer you.'

She withdrew a pile of spiral-bound folders from her briefcase and handed them around the room. The front of each folder had a white laminated cover with the Champion Life logo on it.

'As you will see, Champion Life are prepared to make a very generous offer to the group as a whole. They have extracted the best features of both systems and plan to offer a new hybrid system for all the agents to operate under.

'Firstly, Champion Life agree to take over any outstanding loans you have for cars, mortgages and the like. They have further offered to reduce your already concessional rate of interest by a quarter of a per cent. For some of you that will make a substantial saving.

'Secondly, Champion Life will allow you to remain in your existing offices, using all the facilities you now have available, where possible.

'Thirdly, Champion Life will automatically grant offshore conference qualification to all sales managers, regional managers and all agents whose earnings were in excess of sixty thousand dollars in the last twelve-month period. For anyone who is interested, the conference will start in Greece, then go to Venice and the Bahamas.'

There was a murmur of contentment before she continued.

'The commission and overrider rates you are receiving now will be equalled once volume bonuses are taken into consideration. If you turn to the comparison chart on page six' – there was a rustle of paper as each person quickly turned the pages of the folder to the one marked 'six' – 'I have drawn up a comparison chart with an average agent, his sales manager and his regional manager. I have them selling the same number of policies for the same amount of life cover in a twelve-month period. The initial commissions are lower at Champion Life but you can see where the volume bonus begins to cut in. It indicates clearly your earnings will increase above those you are currently receiving.'

'It's a very generous offer,' Denis said.

Arthur Denton, Queensland's regional manager, whose imagination could not stop conjuring pictures of disgrace in defecting from his base at Prime, asked quickly, 'Why would Champion Life take such action? What is in it for them?'

'Good question,' Sandra replied and withdrew a document that had a legal appearance about it. 'Apart from the obvious attraction of increasing the existing sales force by forty per cent overnight, it is in the interest of Champion Life to bring you under their wing rather than see you try to follow a man who, in all likelihood, will not get another position in the industry. What I hold in my hand' – she waved the legal document in the air authoritatively – 'is an evaluation of the current market trends. It shows quite clearly that to bring across the Prime agency force at this point in time would increase Champion Life's market share to a level rivalling the number one company.'

A murmur grew into a heated discussion. They were all in this together, if one welshed, it was curtains for the rest of them. They talked amongst themselves, and to their colleagues on the phones, discussing the risks, the benefits and the opportunity. Sandra could see that they were almost convinced.

'Sandra.' This time Geoff Masterman, regional manager for Western Australia, spoke. 'I am a little overwhelmed by all this. I don't know about my esteemed colleagues here but I would appreciate it if you would explain why you think Nick will not get another position in the industry. You are asking us all to make an immensely important decision and asking us to make it quickly. This undertaking should protect us all collectively, or not at all, wouldn't you agree?'

'I would most certainly agree with you, Mr Masterman. I shall be happy to explain the logic behind our reasoning.'

She reached for the letter in her briefcase.

'There are no copies of this letter apart from the one I hold in my hand, and the one held by East West Life in New York. East West have asked that we do not make this public if at all possible, but when you read the contents you will see why the industry will not want to re-employ Nick Abbott. You will also understand why East West would prefer it to be kept silent.'

She handed the letter to Denis Granger and asked him to pass it around the room.

'I am sure you will find the contents as damning and horrific as they are unbelievable, but we can prove that they are true.'

The group scrambled to read the letter as fast as possible. Each man stood behind another to get a glimpse of it before it was passed to him in turn.

'I shall leave you to absorb this information and make your decision. Gentlemen, I will return at one thirty. Until then...'

She saw a flurry of calculators pulled from jacket pockets as she left. The men inside were frantically pushing buttons trying to work out if the comparative data was correct before discussing the issues of ethics and risk.

*

Five hundred miles away Sandra could envision the man called Abbott reacting to the unfolding circumstances in the Grand Hotel at Mildura. She could imagine all the awful things he'd say.

'Stop! Stop! You damn fools. You're demented. Listen to me. I know this shrew. She'll promise you the world and deliver nothing. Don't trust her, stay with me,' he would yell, enraged, flushed and banging his fists with all his might upon his table. The vision caused a sneer to creep across her face. The organisation it had taken him years to build would be wiped out in an instant. One long game that Nick's entire life had been spent on.

'Wait a minute,' he would cry when it was too late. 'If you do this, if you walk, you're dead. All of you, dead. You lily-livered cowards. Take everything I have and then desert. All right, well, I don't need you anyway. You're so afraid for your pathetic little careers. I'll cut you up and feed you to the sharks. Frightened little worms,' she could hear him saying. He would flash the inhuman, brutal eyes of a killer, for Nick Abbott was a killer, she reminded herself.

She didn't knock before re-entering the hall at the Grand Hotel. She felt too full of importance to have to ask permission.

'Have I given you enough time, gentlemen?' she asked.

'You have,' said Denis Granger sternly.

'I take then that you have reached a decision?' Her body quivered with anticipation.

'As duly appointed spokesperson for the group,' George Hamilton began, standing to deliver a message of such importance, 'I hereby inform you that our decision is…'

*

There were fifty separate reactions to the news that James Cartwright had the agents' support, each with a single common factor. Fear. A factor that, in its purest form, had been quite foreign to Nick Abbott until now. There were fifty separate ways in which Nick could dispose of this new rival, who was too afraid of Nick even to meet him face to face. His latest threat to dominate the insurance world, James Cartwright, national agency manager for Champion

Life, was fighting for his professional life against the world champion and Nick would stop at nothing to oust him.

'I won't have it. He can't have the agents' support. My agents outsell his, two to one. He can't possibly hope to hide that truth from the board.' Nick shouted his anger openly to his secretary, Jill. He was crimson with rage. 'That damned piece of slime spends every hour of his waking day trying to find ways of proving my system doesn't work. Imbecile. East West Life has run on the system successfully for decades. Let him try to tell the board that the number one company in the world doesn't know what it's doing. I have to prove that Prime's predicament was brought about by other factors not related to my increased commission payments. Jill, bring me the files on all expenditure items prior to my arrival in Australia and during my first year here.'

She had been standing silently taking the abuse. She shared Nick's sentiments for James Cartwright; the man was a weasel, there was no mistaking that. A shoe-licking, favour-seeking weasel and she abhorred the thought that he could take over from Nick Abbott. She left Nick's presence without speaking to get the files he wanted.

Nick continued his vigil over his agents with a renewed prudence. He hadn't come so far to lose everything to a little creature without substance. His priorities were clear: find a justifiable cause for the demise of Prime; settle the fears that he knew were in the minds of his agents; and discredit Cartwright in any way he could. He would find positions for Cartwright's better agents once he had won. There was no point in losing good sales agents because they had a weasel for a leader.

You little prick, he said to himself. I should break your goddam neck. I've known men like you before. Come riding in on the crest of a wave and expect to pick up the glory of another man's work. How dare he presume to challenge the might of Nick Abbott? Cartwright was not to be trusted, not even for an instant. Any sign of camaraderie would be treated with the utmost suspicion. His position would soon be obsolete. Cartwright is a misfit to be snuffed out as simply as one of my cigarettes. Nick scowled. I'll unite both companies' agents through a well-planned speech in Singapore then confront Cartwright at the board meeting back in Sydney.

Jill returned with a pile of files.

'Thanks.'

Nick barely acknowledged her, voraciously diving into the file on top of the pile. The crystal tab read 'Name Change'. There were piles of quotes and handwritten notes. Quickly he found the page he was looking for.

Blueprint

1. Discuss possible options for Australian Life's new name. Requires outside consultants, Australian Life staff time; as they will have to be taken off existing duties to assist. Replacement temporary staff will be required.

Budget: $500,000

2. Market research the public acceptance of a short list of new names. Select a cross-section of society – people who buy from us now and people we wish to target in the future. Research to be conducted in each state. Requires market research groups, clipboard questionnaires in the streets and meetings with chief executives of companies on their premises.

Budget: $1,000,000

3. Reprinting of stationery, business cards, letterheads, with compliment slips, computer paper, brochures, notepads, etc.

Budget: $1,000,000

4. A mail-out campaign to all customers of Australian Life to advise them that the change in name is not a takeover but a new image. Paper, envelopes, time and postage.

Budget: $1,000,000

5. Design an advertising campaign the like of which has never been seen in Australia before. Something that will put the name 'Prime' on everybody's lips. Electronic media, print media, flyers, brochures and mail drops.

Budget: $5,000,000

6. Design and produce promotional items with Prime's name on. Pens, watches, tracksuits, jumpers, umbrellas, ties, scarves, paperweights, pen holders, golf balls, golf tees, golf umbrellas, headbands, jogging suits, wallets, key cases and coasters.

Budget: $1,000,000

7. A cocktail party to launch the new name. Invite as many prominent individuals as possible. Politicians, celebrities, the media. Full silver service, a band, indoor fireworks, catering staff.

Budget: $1,500,000

Nick mulled over the figures in his mind. Ten million bucks, he calculated. Ten million bucks to change the name of a company. Not a bad waste of money, he smiled. Nick moved on to the next file: 'Building Renovations'. The costs were staggering. Nick doubted if McLeod had shopped around for the best deal. It looked as though the first quote had been accepted; probably somebody's brother, Nick suspected. McLeod had even allowed three hundred thousand dollars to be spent on a Persian rug to be placed in the entrance lobby in Perth; a rug designed to stop people slipping on the excessively shiny floor and which was now used to extinguish cigarettes.

Prime Benefits had cost another small fortune to establish as a subsidiary company. The waste of company money was in almost criminal proportions. The Hamilton Black file was equally helpful. McLeod had spared no expense to get his vision off the ground. It would not be difficult to prove that the rot had set in before Nick Abbott ever came to town.

The thought of controlling an agency force under Champion made Nick's mouth water. If I was forced into a situation where I had to merge, Nick concluded, I have certainly picked the right company to merge with. I now have a parent that owns property all over the world, including some properties that East West Life occupied. Nick couldn't believe his luck. Once he distinguished himself at Champion Life it would be easy to infiltrate the parent company. This whole unfortunate situation merely served to escalate his master plan.

Satisfied that he had the justification for Prime's downturn in reserves, he set about preparing a speech for Singapore: one that would ensure his agents would never leave him. Nick smiled. It was very thoughtful of the CEO of Champion Life, Russell Miller, to bring all the agents together before the final decision was made. The conference would give him the perfect opportunity not only to reinforce the loyalty of his own agents, but Cartwright's as well.

Chapter Twelve

Situated in the heart of Singapore, the Shangri-La Hotel stood out as an example of opulent elegance. Its fifteen acres of landscaped gardens, perfectly manicured, graced the aspect of most of the hotel's six hundred rooms. Traditional decor in red and gold gave an oriental flavour inside. The lobby was a throng of activity when the Prime and Champion Life delegates arrived. With a glimpse of his attention, Nick could see people checking in, booking tours at the activity desk and shopping in the many boutiques the lobby offered.

Nick had been booked into the newer tower of the hotel with a suitably magnificent view of the gardens.

He unpacked slowly, considering the events of his life that had taken him to this moment in time. A gaunt, unathletic, poor child from German migrant parentage was about to address a delegation of five hundred top agents in a glitzy hotel in the Far East. It had to be an address that would set the hall on fire.

For a brief moment he saw visions of his mother. He hadn't known her well, she died when he was just a boy. They were misty, warm, fond memories. She had loved him truly. He could feel the deep affection and loyalty he'd known when his mother gave him warm milk and cookies at three o'clock every afternoon. It was this same feeling he needed to create in the hearts of his agents; they had to love him like a mother, worship him like the Messiah and follow him to victory. He could feel a pendulum swinging above his head, the ticking clock of destiny which was etching out his fate. He had twenty-four hours to equip himself for the delivery of a lifetime. In that same space of time he also had to mingle with as many of both sales teams as possible. He had to know who was loyal and who could be offered up as a sacrificial lamb.

The first person Nick saw at the bar was Mahony.

'Mahony, how are you, my man?' Nick slapped him on the back in a friendly gesture.

'Pretty good. You must be sick though, you just pronounced my name properly.'

Nick shrugged. 'What's in a name?'

The effervescent George Hamilton joined them. Nick grabbed him by both shoulders. It was almost a hug. 'It's good to see you,' he said with profound sincerity.

'This is going to be some meeting for you,' George commented.

'Yeah. It's a real meeting of the minds.'

'Or a clash of the titans?'

'You're very astute.'

'I don't need to be astute to see what's going on here. A fight to the death between you and Cartwright.'

'So do you think I should start packing?'

Nick looked closely at George's expression. He would know if the answer was truthful.

'Let me buy you a drink,' George responded.

'That's not an answer,' Nick growled.

George swerved his attention towards the bar to place an order.

'Hitting the turps already?'

Nick knew that voice. That most hated of all loathsome voices. Just the sight of Russell Miller repulsed Nick. A small withered man with glasses. No leadership qualities at all. His lips were thin, frigid lips; his skin leathery from living most of his life in the Queensland sun. There was a pit in his facial flesh from a removed melanoma – a common problem for the inhabitants of Queensland, Nick had been told. Miller's appearance was completed by deep-set eyes which made him look like a tanned-out crocodile hide to Nick.

James Cartwright had been suddenly admitted to hospital prior to the Singapore trip. Probably a nervous breakdown, Nick decided with satisfaction. Russell Miller, this weak-statured CEO, was to make James's speech for him.

It proves James is not much of an agency manager if he can buckle so easily. He won't be much of a challenge at all, Nick considered.

'Hello, Miller,' he hissed. 'What's the matter, don't you drink?'

'Not when I have to keep my wits about me. I'd rather watch over my flock to make sure they don't get into trouble.'

'Why don't you join us?' asked George.

'No thanks. I have to have a word with my boys. I'll see you later.'

Nick watched his swaggering walk and called after him.

'Hey, Miller.'

Miller turned around.

'They're not your flock yet.'

'That's right... not yet.'

'Settle down, you're going to give yourself a heart attack,' Mahony urged, tapping Nick on his shoulder. 'I don't know why you want all of this, to tell you the truth. You're a wealthy man, why don't you retire?'

Nick looked slowly up at Mahony.

'That would kill me as surely as a bullet. This business is my life, everything about it. Tell me,' Nick asked bitingly, 'what are the offers like in the market?'

Nick was well aware that there would be offers. A merger always created uncertainty and therefore opportunities for those alert enough to find them.

Mahony dropped his head in shame.

'They're very good,' he admitted.

'I'll bet. You're the best group of agents in Australia. Not like this heap of garbage. Do you think I'll lose many of my men?'

Mahony shrugged. 'You must admit that you have been pretty quiet about the way things are going behind the scenes. The team does need some encouragement.'

'Don't worry. They're going to get it, tomorrow.'

'Oh, no,' George exclaimed, turning his attention away from Nick and Mahony towards the other side of the bar where a fight had broken out. On one side was a Champion Life agent; on the other one of Prime's.

'I suppose I'd better try and break it up,' said George, striding in a forceful manner to take charge of the situation.

'You motherfucking son of a bitch,' the smaller agent yelled.

'Oh, big words coming from a little man.' The big man wielded a punch with lusty glee, making up for the insult that the Prime agent had inflicted.

The Prime agent was pleased, wanting an excuse to use his combat skills.

George knew he would have to stop it soon or someone might get killed, but he had to admit the Champion Life agent did richly deserve the punishment after such a vicious blow.

The Prime agent scrambled to his knees and inflicted a full arm's blow to the back of the big man's knees, causing him to buckle and drop on all fours. When the big man sprang up again, the Prime agent floored him with a quick left-handed punch to the side of the head.

'All right, break it up,' George called, holding the Prime agent under his armpits. 'What's this all about?'

'That creep of yours accused me of only selling to little

old ladies and people who can't read English,' the large agent said.

The large crowd that had gathered laughed at his indignation. It seemed to most of the observers that this could well be true.

'Did you say that, Steve?' George asked, releasing his grip and trying not to grin.

'I might have made a comment about his natural market place. You can't expect super slob here to be selling in our league, now, can you?'

The big agent lunged forward again. Steve nimbly jumped out of his way causing the agent to fall on his face and get a bloody nose.

'Now look what you've done,' the slob agent grumbled.

'You did it to yourself,' George corrected him.

'Don't you start with me, Mr Bloody Big Shot,' the agent responded, rising to his feet. 'You're one of them. Reckon you're too high and mighty to mix with us. Just remember, your little band of kingpins would be in deep shit right now if it wasn't for us.'

'Your language matches the crudity of your work, Mr Jackson,' George answered, sounding indignant. He turned to the corner of the room where the Prime agents had gathered and gestured that they should disperse with a wave of his hand.

George returned to Nick at the bar. 'I'm afraid there's going to be quite a bit of this until we straighten out who is going to lead who.'

Nick nodded in agreement.

*

At last, Nick thought, three thirty. Time for my speech. He needed to hear the applause, to feel his agents' undying loyalty in their reverberating ovation.

The agents in turn sat longingly, wondering what Nick could possibly say that would make them believe their situations were secure.

Nick walked jauntily to the podium, full of confidence and self-esteem. He leaned on it casually, waiting for the room to fall silent. Only when he had the undivided attention of everyone would he begin.

His voice was strong, resonant and purposeful.

'As an archetypal entrepreneur, driven by economic realism via contingency planning, I have created here a most viable entity. I have provided us with a cost-effective, profit-driven motivated entry into new markets. The focus of the merged group will have a broader spectrum of stakeholders. That is to say, we will all become shareholders in the new organisation: staff, sales people and customers alike. My decision to merge our companies followed an in-depth analysis of company operations which determined where future viability was most at risk. It is you, now, who will chart the course for recovery planning. Your attitude as producing agents will reflect the new entity that emerges... assuredly one very different from the two firms that merged.

'Many years ago I was brought face to face with the very disturbing realisation that I was trying to supervise and direct the futures of a large number of people who were trying to achieve success, without knowing myself what the secret to success really was. And that, naturally, brought me face to face with the further realisation that regardless of what other knowledge I might have brought to the job with me, I was definitely lacking the most important knowledge of all.

'And so I set out to discover the secret which carried me through biographies and autobiographies and all sorts of dissertations on success and the lives of successful people, until I finally reached a point at which I realised that the secret I was trying to discover lay not in what people did, but in what made them do it. The common denominator of success – the secret of success, of every person who has ever been successful – lies in the fact that he formed the habit of doing things that failures don't like to do.

'It is just as true as it sounds and it is just as simple as it seems. You can hold it up to the light, you can put it to the acid test, and you can kick it around until it's worn out, but when you are all through with it, it will still be the common denominator of success.'

Nick worked himself slowly into a frenzy, the way a Sunday evangelist might have done.

'It will explain why people have come into this business of ours with every apparent qualification for success and given us our most disappointing failures, while others have come in and achieved outstanding success in spite of many obvious and discouraging handicaps. And since it will also explain our future, it would seem a damn good idea for us to use it in determining just what sort of future we are going to have. In other words, let's take this big, all-embracing secret, and boil it down to fit the individual – you.

'If the secret of success lies in forming the habit of doing the things that failures don't like to do, let's start the boiling-down process by determining what are the things that failures don't like to do. The things that failures don't like to do are the very same things that you and I and other human beings don't like to do. In other words, we've got to realise right from the start that success is something which is achieved by the minority and is therefore unnatural and not achieved by following our natural likes and dislikes, nor by being guided by our natural preferences and prejudices.

'The things that failures don't like to do, in general, are too many and too obvious to discuss here. So let's look at a common dislike peculiar to our type of selling. We don't like to call upon people who don't want to see us and talk to them about something they don't want to talk about.'

Nick could envision this part of his speech being used in many recruiting interviews. He had to excite and stimulate his audience, take the agents so high that they were going to have to look down to see heaven.

'Do you know what is behind this peculiar lack of welcome on the part of our prospective buyers? Isn't it due to the fact that they are human too? And isn't it true that the average human being is not big enough to buy life insurance of his own accord and is therefore prone to escape our efforts to make him a bigger person or persuade him to do something he doesn't want to do?

'Successful agents are influenced by the desire for pleasing results; less successful agents by the desire for pleasing methods. The latter group is inclined to be satisfied with such results as can be obtained by doing the things they like. Why are successful agents able to do things they don't like to do while failures are not? Because successful people have a purpose strong enough to make them form the habit of doing things they don't like to do in order to accomplish the purpose they want to achieve.

'Many people with whom I have discussed this common denominator will say at this point "But I have a family to support and I have to make a living for my family and myself. Isn't that enough purpose?"

'No.' He pounded his hand on the podium, shocking several of the audience. 'No, it is not. It is not a sufficiently strong purpose to make you form the habits of doing the things you don't like to do for the very simple reason that it is easier to adjust ourselves to the hardship of a poor living standard than it is to adjust ourselves to the hardship of making a better one. If you doubt me, just think of all the things you are willing to do without in order to avoid doing the things you don't like to do. All of which seems to prove that the strength which holds you to your purpose is not your own strength but the strength of the purpose itself.

'Here is the answer. Any resolution or decision you make is simply a promise to yourself which isn't worth a damn until you have formed the habit of making it and keeping it. And you will not form the habit of making it and keeping it unless right at the start you link it with a definite purpose that can be accomplished by keeping it. In other words, any resolution or decision you make today has to be made again tomorrow and the next day and the next.

'In the last analysis your future is not going to depend on economic conditions or outside influences over which you have no control. Your future is going to depend on your purpose in life. So let's look at what it is you have to sell.

'The miracle of paper and a little drop of ink.' Nick held up a life insurance proposal in his hand. 'Let's look again at a life insurance policy... a piece of paper and a drop of ink. I hold in my hand a piece of paper which guarantees that when my earning days are done, I shall have the right to live without working... a miracle which guarantees that my spouse and I may face our declining years without fear, serene in the knowledge that when I can no longer earn, or no longer want to, we shall have an income as long as we both shall live, and as the survivor lives thereafter.

'But that's not all.' He paused to look around the room. He had deliberately chosen to discuss a permanent life insurance policy rather than a term policy as the permanent policy had an investment competent which allowed totally flexible use. He also knew it was the more expensive of the two policies, but Nick's theory on that was, would you rather buy a Rolls-Royce or a Mini?

'I hold in my hand a piece of paper which guarantees that if my earning days are cut off by premature death, my spouse will know comfort and security as long as she shall live, and that alone is a miracle which will give me peace of mind beyond description.

'But that's not all. I hold in my hand a savings account which gives me a title to a share of the world's wealth – a cross-section of the finest bonds and mortgages and bank accounts – a piece of property which I can buy on instalments, which I can meet, and which is the safest financial plan ever conceived by the mind of a man.

'But that's not all. This savings plan is not only secure, it is creative. Creative because it wraps up in a single package my savings account, my guarantee for the future security of my spouse and my children and my hopes of financial success, and it is out of the reach of both creditors and petty temptation, yet it is instantly available in the time of an emergency.

'But that's not all. I hold in my hand a piece of paper which is perhaps the most remarkable contract ever held up by the laws of a civilised land. For this is unilateral – one in which the obligations are all on one side. By this contract great financial institutions bind themselves irrevocably to the certain future performance of these benefits which I have named. An obligation the insurance and superannuation commissioner ensures will be met. Yet I assume no obligation but merely the responsibility of saving money on a regular basis. At all times the right to terminate the agreement is mine, but never can the other party withdraw without my consent.

'A piece of paper and a little drop of ink?' he quietly asked his audience. 'No! The miracle of life insurance and the work that you men do.'

Although his finale was yet to come, he allowed the applause to fill the room. Agents cheered and clapped until their hands turned red.

'In closing, let me leave you with one further thought. Most of what I really need to know about how to live my life, what to do and how to be, I learned as a little boy. Kindergarten taught me that wisdom was not at the top of the university school mountain, but there in the sandpit of my nursery school. These are the things I learned.'

Nick allowed himself a glance towards Russell Miller. He could tell Miller was writhing in his seat. He could never deliver a message with such panache and power, Nick thought confidently.

'Share everything. Play fair. Don't hit people. Put things back where you found them. Clean up your own mess. Don't take things that aren't yours. Say you're sorry when you hurt somebody. Wash your hands before you eat. Warm milk and cookies are good for you. Live a balanced life. Learn and think and draw and paint and sing and dance and play and work every day. Take a nap every afternoon. When you go out into the world, watch for traffic, hold hands and stick together.

'Think of what a better world it would be if we all – the whole world – had milk and cookies at three o'clock every afternoon then lay down with blankets for a nap. Or if we had a basic policy in our life always to put things back where we found them' – he made an obvious motion to wipe a crocodile tear from his eye – 'and clean up our own mess, instead of running away and letting others clean up after us.' He glanced back in Miller's direction. 'And it is still true, no matter how old you are, that when you go into the world it is best to hold hands and stick together. Let us stick together from this day forward. Thank you.'

The audience stood and applauded as they had never applauded before. Even Russell Miller was visibly moved by the speech. The hall belonged to Nick Abbott. He felt positive that the men, and the company, were his from that moment on. Climbing down from the stage, Nick moved through the audience, shaking hands with everyone as though he was a presidential candidate. He knew he *was* their mother, the Messiah and their leader into victory; there could be no doubt of that.

*

With Singapore behind him, Nick's next priority was to discredit James Cartwright. He only had two days to prepare for the board meeting and still Nick had no ammunition. He could hear strong footsteps heading towards his office. Recognising them as Mark Fitzgerald's, Nick wondered what new revelations might be headed his way now.

'Good morning,' said Mark. 'That was quite a performance in Singapore, my friend.'

'Thank you.'

Nick put his pen down and stood to pace the floor.

'I hope you have something just as impressive for the board,' Mark said in a fatherly tone.

'I'm working on it.'

'Well, whatever you're doing, you better do it quickly. The tip is still that James Cartwright's got the numbers stacked in his favour.'

'Bastard, weasel. He can't have. It's just not possible.'

'And that's not all you have to worry about.'

Mark took a seat to deliver his latest piece of covert information.

'What now?'

Nick followed Mark's lead and sat down to listen.

'There are rumours around that some dark skeleton has been dug up to use against you.'

'What are you talking about?'

'I'm not sure. All I've heard are whispers, but I think your friend Sandra Upton is involved somehow.'

'Sandra? She's got nothing on me. She's probably trying to trump up some sexual harassment charge or something. Huh, you're overreacting as usual.'

'I hope you're right, but it sounds to me as though it's something bigger than that.'

Nick was silent. He couldn't cope with more than one catastrophe at once. He could feel the compounding build-up of pressure as though it was an iron bar tightening around his chest.

'She used to work for this company, you know. I realise that her contract said she couldn't work for another company for another two years, but now Champion Life and Prime are one, there's nothing to stop her getting some sort of position here, is there?'

'Yes there is...'

'What's that?' Mark asked simply.

Nick was silent for a moment. 'Me,' he said confidently. 'She was a little girl with a big title. My men are still loyal to me. We have nothing to worry about from Sandra.'

'Good. Well, you can get back to the matter at hand then.' Mark stood to leave but as he reached the office door he turned around.

'There is one other thing.'

'Yes?' Nick lifted his head to the statement.

'Does Sandra have any sort of claim against you?'

'Does it matter?'

'It might.'

'She's a fool. She let herself get trapped, if she tries to pull anything I'll be ready. She's the least of my worries right now.'

'How could this be happening?' Mark mused.

'Fitzgerald, you're a whelp. I'm running this ship and I'll continue to do so.'

'Well, it looks like this ship has been steered straight into a bloody iceberg. I'll see you at the board meeting.'

'Right.'

Nick put his head in his hands to consider this latest fly in his ointment. The motion of resting his head acted as a sedative, enabling him to think without anger, although the irritation of Sandra was ever present. Some time in the future he would deal with her. She was provoking his wrath for the last time, he decided. But there were more important issues to be considered. He couldn't allow a simple creature to interfere with his concentration. She was a freak, caught up in a world in which she did not belong. The board meeting would be the culmination of months of work, years of work, from his first decision to master the industry when he was barely more than a boy. He alone possessed the knowledge and skill to lead the company; this the board would have to acknowledge. He would isolate Sandra from the industry later, or perhaps he would administer the *coup de grâce*. Stupid freak, she deserved to die.

Nick was so deep in concentration that he didn't hear a timid knock at the door. His secretary, Jill, let herself in.

'Excuse me, Mr Abbott. I don't mean to intrude,' she said as quietly as a mouse.

'What is it?' he hissed.

'I thought a little company gossip might lift your spirits.'

'Jill, you're very sweet, but this is hardly the time for gossip.' He waved her out, but she stood firm.

'This is James Cartwright gossip, sir.'

He put his pen down and looked up. 'You'd better shut the door and have a seat.'

Eagerly she pushed the door closed until she heard a click. She sat in Nick's visitors' chair on the very edge, her hands twisting in knots.

'I had lunch with James Cartwright's secretary when you were all in Singapore. She can't stand him, you know. It seems that James has been working on a prototype system. He's trying to convince both groups it would be better to work under him and this new system. He's saying that it has board approval, when in fact it does not.'

'Jill, are you sure?' Nick's eyes lit up like light bulbs. He knew this was just what he'd been looking for.

'His secretary, Sharon, says he's been paranoid ever since he first heard the mention of your name. His behaviour has become quite irrational.'

Nick stood up and walked around to Jill, cupping her face in his hands and kissing her firmly on the forehead.

'Jill, my dear, I love you.'

She blushed and looked away.

'Can you get any sort of evidence? Copies of the new system he's been flashing around?'

'Sharon could.'

'Great. Ask her out to lunch. You are sure that she has no loyalty to him?'

'Absolutely none at all... well, actually she's in love with him but he's not interested in her. She told me she tried everything but Mr Cartwright ignored her. It's a simple case of the woman scorned.'

Thank God, Nick thought, I've always looked after my secretaries. 'Here.' Nick gave Jill a couple of hundred dollars. 'The two of you go out for a nice lunch and tell her that you will both be well looked after if she can get those figures to me.'

'It will be a pleasure, Mr Abbott.'

'And Jill.'

'Yes,' she said half standing and half sitting.

'Get me a copy of the Champion Life employment contract. I'll bet there's a clause in there about instant dismissal for this sort of thing if I can find it.'

'Right away, Mr Abbott.'

Cartwright, you bastard, I've got you, he thought. Hoist with your own petard.

Jill produced copies of the required information, duplicated and bound for each member of the board. She had handed them to Nick with a good luck card.

She's a good girl, Nick thought. I'll look after her.

Chapter Thirteen

The members of the board gathered silently in the main boardroom of Prime's old head office. The Champion Life staff had all but moved into Prime's old premises all around Australia, retrenching a large portion of Prime's staff to do so. The old Champion Life buildings were drab in comparison to the newly renovated buildings of Prime, so naturally Champion Life employees selected the most luxurious positions for themselves. From the forty-third level, Prime's boardroom had a spectacular panoramic view of Sydney Harbour. The renovations had replaced the old-style windows with floor to ceiling glass. They gave a bright pristine air to the room where decisions affecting hundreds of lives were about to be made.

Men in dark suits with grey hair and stern expressions assembled around the glowing board table. They each had a holier-than-thou look about them. Twelve stony faces that looked as though they should be gardening, not dictating Nick's future to him. At the head of the board sat Fred Chambers, the chairman. A tall sturdy man with a full nose, drooping jowls and thick lips. The sixteenth chair remained empty. Nick knew whom it was for. His rival, James Cartwright. Why was he taking so damn long? Nick wondered.

The door opened slowly. Nick stared keenly towards it, waiting to catch a first glimpse of this man who would try to undo him. He felt his mouth fall open as he saw the face which reflected a youthful appearance of his own.

'James,' Nick cried. His first sentiments were of joy to

see his son again, momentarily not making the connection that James Cartwright was actually James Abbott.

'Hello, Father,' James said in a cold but controlled fashion.

'Father?' Fred Chambers questioned.

'Yes, sir,' James said firmly.

'Why didn't you tell us this before?'

'If you will allow me a few minutes' indulgence, Mr Chairman, I shall explain.'

Suddenly the unholy truth hit Nick. His son had masterminded this whole operation. From challenging his product and forcing him into a merger to changing the system so he could beat his father in a showdown. He felt both anger and pride that his son could be so callous and manipulative in his dealings. Part of Nick wanted to race and hug his long-lost son; part of him wanted to end his life right there.

'As you have just heard, I am Nick Abbott's son,' James began. 'You no doubt have a thousand questions running through your minds as a result of that revelation, so allow me to answer them for you...'

In a room one floor below the boardroom, and directly underneath it, Sandra and Ray Cooper listened anxiously to the meeting progress through a listening device Ray had installed earlier. Two plain-clothes detectives on the boardroom floor tried to blend in with the staff as they waited for the word from Ray through their ear pieces that the time to move in had arrived.

'I left New York and dropped my father's name for reasons which are unimportant to this meeting. The reason I continued to keep my identity secret is simple. I knew my father had secured a position at Prime under false pretences. I tried to tell Brett McLeod. Unfortunately for Brett, he interpreted my warning as jealousy. Once Brett found out the truth, Nick murdered him—'

'How dare you make such an accusation,' Nick screamed. 'No one has been able to link me to Brett's death. I had no idea the man was even using drugs, let alone that someone had laced them. You have no right to stand here and make unsubstantiated accusations against me.' Nick was on his feet and red in the face as he responded to James's claims.

'Really, Mr Cartwright,' the chairman said, 'that is quite a statement, considering the police haven't arrested your father.'

'I'm aware of what I am saying, I can assure you, Mr Chairman. There's more, if I could beg your indulgence a little further.'

'I won't stand for this,' Nick shouted, banging his fist on the table. 'How can you sit there and listen to the demented ravings of a jealous son.'

'Jealous, Mr Abbott?' the chairman asked. 'How do you reach that conclusion?'

'He could never be half the man I am. That's why he left and changed his name. He couldn't live with the shame of not meeting my expectations,' Nick explained.

'You're right about that,' James agreed. 'I couldn't live with the lies and the destruction you perpetrated as though they meant nothing.'

'Lies,' Nick spat back, 'lies? You talk about lies. This, I believe, is a copy of your employment contract, Mr Chairman.' Nick held up a few photocopied pages and handed them over to the chair.

'It is,' Fred Chambers confirmed.

'And clause 7a(i) of that contract states, and I quote, "Any employee found wilfully misrepresenting themselves to Champion Life, or clients of Champion Life, shall be terminated without notice." Is that correct?'

'What's your point to all this, Mr Abbott?' Fred Chambers was annoyed by the introduction of such a trivial matter in light of such earth-shattering accusations.

James sat down patiently, allowing his father to become lulled into a false sense of security before he played his final trump card.

'My point, Mr Chairman,' Nick continued, 'is that I regret to inform you that I have evidence that James Cartwright here has been wilfully misrepresenting himself to you, and apparently in more ways than one.'

Nick had the undivided attention of the room. Fred Chambers raised his bushy eyebrows and listened to Nick's counter-attack.

'James Cartwright,' Nick proclaimed, pointing to his son and handing a further set of documents around the room, 'has been offering all the agents the chance to swear loyalty to him, promising that in return he will give them a new hybrid system to operate under. A system which does not have the sanction of this board.'

Nick allowed everyone time to peruse his evidence.

'I am not trying to tell you one system is better than the other, that is not my choice. All I am saying is that I presume you will want an honest man running the agents, no matter which system is adopted.'

'Cartwright,' the chairman said stoically, 'do you have anything to say in response to these allegations?'

'Mr Chairman, I cannot deny that I have been working on this new system, nor that I have been speaking to the agents, but my intentions were for the good of the company.'

'Really, Cartwright? And how do you suppose offering non-ratified remuneration systems is good for the company?' The chairman's nostrils flared with rage at the thought of one of his own people being publicly disgraced.

'Whilst I do not believe the system is the issue of contention here, if you look clearly at those forms,' James explained, 'you will see that they state the offers are subject to ratification by the board and subject to the agents choosing me as their leader. I have not given any guarantees, just an example of what I propose to do for them if they follow me. Surely none of you can want a man leading the agents who has already led one company into bankruptcy?' James pointed a finger at his father.

Nick said nothing. He played with the papers in front of him; further artillery for the showdown with his son.

'Very well,' the chairman said, sounding relieved. 'That seems fair enough.' He turned to Nick. 'We would all be interested to hear your explanation of Prime's poor financial demise, Mr Abbott. Would you care to respond?'

'Thank you, Mr Chairman.'

Nick passed over another set of documents to the board. They contained figures that Nick had gone through thoroughly the day before.

Nick was now standing in a dignified manner, confident he was going to win. 'These are some expenditure items that were incurred before I joined Prime. As you will see, the expenditure level on impractical components of Brett McLeod's master vision was excessive to say the least. The reserve levels were already depleted beyond recovery when I took over the organisation. This, compounded with the fact that I admit we were overexposed to the share market when it crashed, caused a situation where I had to find a partner or see Prime collapse within a period of three years.'

'A partner, Mr Abbott?' the chairman spoke condescendingly.

'All right, a parent,' Nick conceded. 'The point is that the depletion of Prime's reserves was clearly evident before my structure was put in place.'

'Well, it seems the issue of systems remains an open one,' the chairman said. 'Mr Cartwright, I cannot consider your allegations of murder seriously. Your father has not been charged with any such crime and is, after all, one of the most respected names in our industry. We have a representative from both groups of agents ready to address this board, so at this time, I would like to bring in the representative from Prime.'

As the chairman spoke, Nick sat down, looking towards James with an expression that told him that Nick Abbott still held the aces.

Fred Chambers lifted the boardroom telephone and dialled reception. 'You can tell him to come in now,' he said simply and returned the receiver.

The door handle turned slowly. All eyes pivoted in the direction of the opening door. Nick was visibly shocked when Denis Granger walked into the room.

James acknowledged Nick's concern with delight.

Denis took the head of the table, adopting his policeman's stance, a grim expression of acquiescence on his face.

'It is with a great degree of personal anguish that I am here today,' Denis began. 'Before I tell you the reasons for my presence I should like to tell you that I admired Nick Abbott above all other men in our industry. His achievements were legendary; his reputation beyond reproach. Eddie Schwartz, Nick's star agent, was a remarkable man whose achievements each of us in the sales force aspires to equal. He was the finest man I have ever read about. His skills and knowledge in the field outshone the brightest star. His work at East West Life proved that to me beyond doubt. Eddie built, with his bare hands, an image the like of which has not been seen, before or since. He was an asset any company should be proud to have.

'As for Nick Abbott's agency system,' Denis continued, 'it is with confidence that I say the system is the most lucrative I have ever seen. We have a fine sales team collected at Prime, I doubt anyone will dispute that. None of us want to consider going back to the dark ages of salaries and cars now we have seen what can be achieved. The system Nick Abbott introduced inspired each of us to strive for greatness, instead of reconciling ourselves to mediocrity. This can only benefit the companies who adopt it, or a similar, system.'

Nick and James glanced at each other with cold, determined eyes.

'Having said all this, I have one further comment.' Denis sighed deeply. 'It is a comment I make with immeasurable sorrow. I have with me the signed intentions of ninety per cent of Prime's sales team to join James Cartwright's system.'

Nick's tongue became a soggy lump in his throat, blackness swimming over him in waves.

'What?' Nick yelled, jumping to his feet again. 'Have you taken leave of your senses? You just said my system was the best in the world.'

'Yes,' Denis admitted. 'Your system, your reputation, your records. All the best—'

'And all a lie,' James interrupted. 'The police may not have been able to get any evidence convicting Nick for Brett's murder,' James continued, 'but during the course of their investigation, they uncovered a much darker secret which I think you will all be interested to hear. I am going to read you a letter which has been kept silent to protect East West's good name and avoid a collapse in consumer confidence generally.

To whom it may concern

It is my unfortunate duty to advise you that the myth behind the legend you all aspire to was based on one of the worst types of fraud of our time. Under the express direction of Nick Abbott, Eddie Schwartz sold record numbers of policies by returning to his impoverished childhood neighbourhood to market to the blue-collar and unemployed population who desperately needed money. Over one hundred million dollars' worth of cover was sold by Eddie. Nearly half of that was claimed within the ten-year period over which it was sold. Any underwriting statistic in the world will tell you that is an extraordinarily high mortality rate. There have always been people who tried to use life insurance policies as a means to get out of a financially difficult situation. The jails are full of people who have committed premeditated murder to claim on a policy sold in good faith by the company.

Many of the policies Eddie sold, which were claimed on during this period, were not paid out as a result of police and insurance company investigations. It was discovered many had, in fact, committed premeditated murder to collect on their policies. But worst of all, these were all insurance policies taken out on the lives of children by their parents!

As chief executive of the company, it was not my position to question the integrity of my number one agent or sales manager. If their clients were abusing their policies to achieve financial gain, neither Eddie Schwartz nor Nick Abbott could be held responsible. Our only protection was to lobby Congress to tighten the laws governing insurable interest. As you all know, it is no longer possible to take out a life insurance policy on the life of a child which will pay a death claim, unless the child is over ten years of age.

We never suspected a spectre to raise its head from the past and explain how our faith in these two men had been misplaced.

I regret to say, a witness has now come forward to advise us otherwise. The late Arthur Gibson, a respected New York businessman who passed away last week, made this testimony on his deathbed:

'It appears that I am not the only person living with

these terrible sensations of guilt. The insurance pay-out on my baby son's life set me up in a business which is now a multinational concern. My other children have had decent educations and I've lived a good life. They have had a chance at a lifestyle I could never have given them without the insurance money. Yet every day I see my baby's face in their reflections. I live with the knowledge that whilst my son's death gave them these opportunities, we are each undeserving of enjoying the benefits of our lives. I murdered my baby for that money, and it was Nick's agent who showed me how easy it was to do. All I had to do was buy a policy, wait for a reasonable period of time, and create some sort of accident. He joked about how easy it was. As long as the policy was on a wife, a child, an employee or someone in whom I had an interest, that was enough. It was easy to make an infant death look like misadventure. It was said as a joke but what it was, was a seed. He knew we couldn't afford the premiums. We were desperate people living in desperate times. This was a way out of the darkness. Well, I received my pay-out, but I have lived with the fear of retribution all my life. A fear which I now take with me in terror to my grave.

'*I understand Eddie did not really believe people would commit these crimes. He used the method almost in jest to explain what life insurance could be used for if the life insured did meet an untimely end.*

'*When so many of these children met with fatal accidents, Eddie could not deal with the truth. He turned to drugs and ultimately wanted to expose how Nick Abbott had exploited this loophole in the law. Unfortunately he was never able to do so.*

'*This is my dying confession and I swear it to be true and correct.*'

This has been sufficient for the New York police to open up an investigation, but no other clients are willing to come *forward to point the finger directly at Nick Abbott. Arthur Gibson never heard Nick Abbott give him this advice directly, so Nick Abbott is still a free man.*

I caution any person who reads this letter to be wary of this man, Abbott. I pray that for the good of the industry and the public at large, you will never allow him to be in a position of power again.

Gus Fletcher, Chief Executive Officer, East West

'You can't believe this,' Nick declared, shaking with horror and disbelief.

James looked towards Nick and said simply, 'It's over, old man.'

'Fletcher!' yelled Nick. 'Fletcher cooked this up to get back at me for leaving East West. I'll sue him for slander. Sue the bastard,' Nick ordered Fred Chambers.

'Really, Mr Abbott. This is a pretty damning letter. It won't take much to check the records and the authenticity of the testimonial. Do we really need to do that?' the chairman asked, feeling sick that anyone could have perpetrated such an act.

James couldn't help smiling to himself at Nick's imminent defeat.

'It seems, gentlemen,' Fred Chambers said, without waiting for Nick to answer and directing himself to the members of his board, 'that these proceedings are concluded. Mr Cartwright?'

'Yes, Mr Chairman,' James answered.

'Under the circumstances I shall overlook your imprudence but, mark my words, I want to see an *independent* analysis of both systems on my desk within a month. I hereby entrust you with the duty of amalgamating both agency forces under your control. Congratulations.'

'Mr Cartwright,' the chairman continued, 'I salute your courage in bringing these matters to our attention. I know how hard this must have been for you. Gentlemen, this meeting is adjourned.'

'Wait a minute,' Nick yelled after them. 'You can't—'

'It's too late, Father,' James snarled.

As the last board member left, James shut and locked the door behind them.

Underneath the boardroom, Sandra and Detective Ray Cooper looked at one another with broad smiles. They shared the surge of triumph that James had just experienced but each knew that the final conflict was only just beginning.

'Now we'll find out if you were right,' Ray commented.

'I just pray that James will get him to make a confession. That will be enough for you to get an arrest, won't it?'

'I should say so,' Ray answered, checking the recording equipment was working properly.

'At least we know Nick isn't stupid,' she said. 'He won't, he can't try to kill James in the middle of a busy office, can he?' Can he? she wondered anxiously.

'You piece of useless garbage,' Nick spat. 'How could you do this to your own father?'

'You disgust me,' James said, standing to face his father head on.

Nick Abbott closed his hands around his face. The realism had not properly sunk in. His empire once again had been mercilessly stripped from him. It was horrible. He felt paralysed. His face was covered with red splotches as his blood pressure rose to a dangerous level. He had a feeling of belonging nowhere. The battle had been fought and lost, he admitted despondently.

Nick started to shake from both anger and anxiety. He yearned for a clear space, as though he needed it to breathe more freely.

'Someone had to clean up the legacy you left.' James

uttered the words without emotion. The act of confronting his father filled him such violent rage that if he let his emotions start tumbling out, he would surely throttle Nick with his bare hands.

'Oh?' said Nick, with an uneasy feeling growing in his stomach.

'I've dealt you a lethal blow in the only place possible to hurt a man like you,' James explained. 'You've been stripped of everything; publicly disgraced.'

Nick remained silent for a moment, absorbing the magnitude of his son's statement.

'Why?' Nick asked, genuinely puzzled. 'Why am I the object of so much hatred in you, son?'

'You really don't know, do you?' James answered. 'It sickens me to think your blood runs in my veins.' With that he produced the Luger from the back of his waistband. James had meant to show Nick that Sandra was never on his side, even there, son had beaten father. Nick glared at the Luger, realisation suddenly hitting him.

'But you are very much my son, James,' Nick said feeling a sense of admiration for the man who had defeated him. 'I'm proud of you. Who else could have masterminded such a brilliantly conceived plan? You used your best friend's widow to get to me, didn't you? You planted her in Prime knowing I would use that product and knowing the law was ambiguous enough to challenge it. You manipulated Champion Life, the ISC and Sandra to force me into a merger.'

'That's right,' James admitted.

Ray looked towards Sandra. He knew it had been her idea to check up on James, and that James was unaware of the listening devices, but he wondered if she was ready to cope with the revelations which were about to unfold.

'It's all right,' Sandra said. 'I willingly helped James once I learned the truth. Nick had this coming and we both used what we had to make sure he couldn't get away with it again,' she assured Ray.

Ray returned his attention to the listening device.

'It's not too late to make things right between us, is it, son?' Nick asked, as if he was almost pleading.

'Too late? You are a murderer,' James shouted, as if reminding himself as well as his father.

'You can't really believe I am responsible for all those deaths?' Nick asked in his most fatherly manner.

'You know, Father, I don't even care.'

Nick looked into his son's eyes, curious and silent.

'What you have done repulses the entire industry, but it's not why I am here.'

This time Sandra looked at Ray.

'What on earth is he up to?' she asked.

'I'm not sure,' Ray admitted.

'I wanted to ruin your life,' James said bitterly, his gaze becoming filled with poison. 'I wanted to make you suffer the way I have suffered all my life. It was just never enough for you, was it?'

'Why, you little…' Nick took a swing at his son.

James nimbly jumped out of the way and pointed the Luger at Nick.

'What are you doing?' Nick asked nervously, momentarily frozen to the spot in shock. 'Have you taken leave of your senses?'

'All those deaths. All those lives destroyed… but I am here for just one.'

Nick looked confused.

'You still don't get it, do you?' James didn't let his gaze leave Nick's for an instant.

'You murdered my mother.'

At last Nick realised that James had confronted him with the one dark fact from his past which Nick had no argument to justify.

'I watched her die in agony, begging for mercy. Begging for help. I watched her' – James fought for the strength to continue – 'writhe in torment as she drowned in her own vomit. There has not been a single day I haven't seen that vision. When Ted died I heard the agents talking about other "suicides", about Eddie's... about how he did it and then I realised. Two deaths, two suicides, the same method. How the hell did you get away with it?'

Nick was silent.

'Since then I've thought of nothing except making you pay.'

In a state of panic Nick made a grab for the gun.

'Yes, that's it, old man,' James said, struggling with his father, 'give me an excuse.'

The gun went off, shattering the boardroom window with a deafening explosion.

'What the...' Ray had no way of knowing until that moment that there was a gun in the room. 'That's it, I'm going in,' Ray announced, radioing to the detectives upstairs to move in. He drew his own revolver and ran for the fire escape stairs, Sandra close on his heels.

James grimaced with a grave and attentive expression, like a mathematician considering a complex problem.

Nick struck him a swift blow to the stomach, almost bringing James down. He lunged to catch his balance, but, as he did so, dropped the gun which slid across the highly polished floor, out of reach.

Nick grabbed a letter-opener from the boardroom cabinet and stabbed James in the left shoulder with the long bright blade.

James spun away from the sting of the steel with scarlet spreading wetly down his shirt front. He was forced to fall back, clutching his wound, struggling to clear his vision and recapture his revolver.

Skilfully Nick herded him towards the broken window.

James felt the jagged glass cut into his flesh, realising he was trapped.

Nick pounced at him, his lips drawn back, baring nicotine-stained teeth.

James snatched Nick's arm, circumventing the intended blow and in the process throwing Nick off balance. Nick hurtled through the window, snatching hold of James's arm with his right hand.

The two men glared with hatred into one another's eyes as they strained together with the weight of Nick's swaying body. The pressure brought a fresh burst of blood from James's wound.

James's face darkened, his teeth grinding in rage and despair.

Nick's eyes widened as he saw the hatred in his son's face.

'Your mother was going to destroy everything I built for our future, son,' Nick gasped, pleading for his life. '*Your* future, James. Look at what I've given you. Everything you have, I gave you. You're my son, for God's sake. I love you.'

For a moment longer James resisted him. He reflected over Nick's logic, and how close he had become to being his father's image. He had manipulated everyone around him to achieve his goal, he must not complete the circle by becoming a murderer as well.

'James,' Sandra cried at the boardroom door, 'open this door.' She struggled with it, shaking and turning the handle. Before she could speak again, Ray thrust her to one side, firing at the lock.

James used every ounce of strength to retrieve his father, dragging him back to safety. In doing so he was admitting that Nick was an albatross around his neck.

Nick sneered with a glow of triumph as he climbed back through the jagged glass. He stood in front of the opening, wild winds whisking around him. Nick looked coldly into the eyes of his son.

'Anyway,' Nick growled with the force of an erupting volcano, 'it was your mother's life insurance which paid for the final years of your bloody expensive education.'

James's mouth opened in a crawling burst of despair. 'Nooo!' he yelled.

James clenched his fist and swung at Nick's jaw to purge himself of the abomination before him. The force was sufficient to send Nick flying through the window again.

Sandra and Ray burst through the door in time to see the terror in Nick's widened eyes.

A sharp pain struck Nick's soul as he fell like a rock through the atmosphere. A pain which swept through him, becoming horror as he realised that his son had finally released him to his fate. The pain seemed to crush down upon him, suffocating him; the sheer weight of it took possession of him. He closed his eyes for an instant. He thought he could see the deformed faces of Norma, Eddie, Brett and Ted waiting for him. He opened his eyes to escape their venomous glare. He saw wild hallucinations of a swooping, taloned creature poised to grab him. For long precious seconds he gasped as a suppressed scream choked in his throat. Suddenly, with repulsive reptilian swiftness, an unwelcome unfamiliar darkness closed around him as he hit the cold sidewalk with a sharp thump. A darkness from which there was no escape.

'It's over,' James murmured, turning to Sandra, who rushed forward to embrace him as his legs seemed to buckle underneath him. All that Ray Cooper and his detectives could do was look on. Years of experience told Ray that James had just exorcised his ghosts.

A crowd of curious eyes gathered at the ruined boardroom door. James looked back to the window. A piece of

Nick's torn jacket still hung there blowing in the wind.

*

It was a beautiful spring morning. Flowers were blooming, birds were chirping. James and Sandra approached a solitary grave at the edge of a graveyard. The grave lay in disrepair.

    The tombstone read:
Nick Abbott
Except ye be converted, and become as little children,
ye shall not enter into the kingdom of heaven.
Matthew 18:3

Author's Note

There are hundreds of cases which have been documented internationally of parents murdering their own children to receive the life insurance money.

This is not fiction; it is fact.

Child abuse (which is hard enough for the civilised world to understand) has not been confined to acts of mindless violence... it has been perpetrated in a premeditated manner for financial gain. This is probably the darkest secret of all life insurance industry secrets, but one the industry itself cannot be held accountable for. Life insurance regulatory bodies have legislated to ensure that this can never happen again – at least in terms of not being able to take out a risk-only policy on a child under ten years of age. In 1994, however, a grandmother was convicted of murdering her twenty-five-year-old stepson in Melbourne for the insurance money, $180,000. Even more unbelievable was *how* she killed him. She killed him slowly over a month by mixing weed killer into his favourite drink.

*

In early 1986, Capita Financial Group launched a new and revolutionary product called the Variable Income Annuity. It was structured as a result of the 1985 budget in which Treasurer Keating announced incentives for people who rolled their superannuation money into income-producing products rather than splurging the money and relying on welfare. The product had advantages for clients who were not sure about future income needs and did not want to be locked into a specific income stream for the rest of their lives.

The product was a major success for Capita, selling for eighteen months until competitors in the industry challenged the legitimacy of the product by receiving rulings from the taxation department which declared that the Variable Income Annuity was not a true annuity because of its flexible structure. This meant that Capita's annuity would lose its concessional tax treatment and severely disadvantage clients.

While the legal battle ensued, Capita was put into a situation where it had to refund all monies to Variable Income Annuity clients, or convert them into traditional annuities. It took until March 1992 for the taxation department to finally recognise the variable annuity as a true annuity – by which time Capita had ceased to exist and competitor companies had their versions of the variable annuity ready to sell in the new market place. This is not fiction; this is documented fact.

OTHER TITLES BY LYNN SANTER
ALL AVAILABLE FROM THIS WEBSITE:
www.ghostandscreenwriting.com

Sins of Life – Lynn Santer's debut novel turned best-seller
Into the Fire – Sins of Life Part Two
Evil By Design – Sins of Life The Final Chapter
Land of Free novel
Land of Free DVD – non-fiction
The Magical Scarecrows Book One
The Magical Scarecrows Book Two
The Magical Scarecrows Garden with Catherine Chapman
The Magical Scarecrows Games & Colouring Book
The Magical Scarecrows First Story Book
The Israeli Magical Scarecrow's Chanukah Adventure
The Israeli Magical Scarecrow's Purim Adventure
Beyond World Safari –Alby Mangels authorized biography
Brother Doctor (ghosted)
Waiting for Spirit to Tell Me (ghosted)
Whirly Girl # 530 (ghosted)
Rolaboi Renegade Skater (ghosted)
Professor Midnight – story by Peter Andrew Wright
Celebrity DVD Readings Of Magical Scarecrows Stories
www.themagicalscarecrows.com
Scared in the Bush read by Tippi Hedren
Scaredy Cat read by Oberon Zell-Ravenheart
Scared Little Joey read by Nikki Webster
The Scary Tower read by Barry Crocker
Scared of a Bully read by the Passion for Peace team
The Scary Pantomine read by Auntie Lynn
ROSY APPLE read by Dr Who girl Katy Manning
COOL POTATO read by Australian Idol's Cosima De Vito
Coming soon -*Santa's Scary Christmas* read by Leo Sayer
Currently unavailable: *Farewell Brave Babylon* and *Beyond the Darkness.*